THE RUNAWAYS OF
Phayendar

THE RUNAWAYS OF
Phayendar

Carol Strote

ISBN 978-1-957582-60-3 (paperback)
ISBN 978-1-957582-61-0 (eBook)

Printed in the United States of America

CONTENTS

PROLOGUE

The Almighty God, eternally existing as Father, Son, and Holy Spirit, had created planet Earth to bear a unique importance. But the first humans on Earth had fallen into disobedience; and as they had been created to be important to all of the material creation, so their fall set all of that creation groaning, waiting for its redemption.

God then made other worlds with life, but placed them so far away from the world of Adam and Eve that the original human race would have no knowledge of them until the universe was redeemed. Since death had already entered the cosmos through sin, these additional worlds could not be altogether free from the curse; but God would ensure that inhabitants of these worlds could learn enough about his nature and His work of grace that they also could be saved through faith.

One of the first new worlds he made, called Breidoblik, received a special outpouring of his grace, for He would create on this planet a race which was as close to being sinless as the defiling of the universe would permit. He made Elves, tall, slender, graceful and lovely to behold, having a language that was pleasing to the ear and mysterious to all but themselves. They were truthful, kind, and lived on Breidoblik with the fairies. The creator gave them power to receive visions from Him, to heal, to protect themselves, and to use discernment of good and evil. He gave them wisdom and long life and a desire to help others. They would have a chance to do so on Phayendar.

The Creator made Phayendar, a planet much like earth, with land masses divided by water. There was abundant foliage, and the

Creator also made animals and people, the most ancient of which was the dwarves. He made them strong. They were hard workers and serious, but had the capacity for great compassion and joy. They delighted in the things they found in the ground. In those days there were gems in rocks on top of the ground and just beneath the surface. The Creator was well pleased with His dwarves. They didn't forget Him. They took time to communicate with Him. Farindom, the city of the dwarves, was located in the center of the major land mass and consisted of huts of various sizes. The huts were sufficient to their needs and they were happy there for a very long time. In the north of this land mass wass amountain range they called the Aikasse Mountans. It extended from the Lake Perilough in the east around to Lake Inari in the west.

But there was also a darkness in the land, full of evil with malevolent intent. Out of that darkness came ugly creatures with great ability to do harm. The darkness was a spiritual darkness with the ability to influence or to hinder God's creations.Out of that darkness walked giants, strong and full of anger and conceit. Giants brought with them large wolves. Large lizards called grustobists, and deadly snakes roamed the water's edge and stinging insects and poisonous lizards roamed the land. The age of the giants was upon them. The giants inhabited the land, making huge buildings. They weren't interested in creating beauty like gardens or fountains. When they made desolate one area, they moved on to the next. Eventually they learned to build boats and moved to a beautiful, lush island. The volcano in the middle of this island erupted and it sank into the sea.

The dwarves retreated north to the Aikasse Mountains where they dug tunnels into the mountains for hiding and for mining. There they lived happily and peacefully for many generations.

Finally, the Creator, being disappointed in the development of Phayendar, made humans. Humans were intelligent and creative and were endowed with compassion, love, and kindness, but also had the capacity for negative qualities like greed, cruelty, and hate. Creator God also gave them the knowledge of right and wrong and a strong desire to be right. He gave them the ability to contact Him and gave them His Spirit to live in them if they asked for it.

Humans would create out of their imaginations. They would add much beauty to the world. They populated the main continent and helped to restore the foliage and bred animals for their farms. The called their land Aksanda, Orendia and Gullandia. Some humans traveled by boat to other lands on smaller land masses. Out of their negative qualities came corruption, the accumulation of wealth and men seeking power over others. Eventually, this led to war between neighboring countries.

Father God decided to transport many Elves to Earth to help humans by ministering to them. Here the Elves were to be mentors to their shorter lived kin. He made it known to them that He had made Phayendar's moon able to support life; but this moon was to be of no concern to Elves or to Phayendar's natives for ages to come.

Through the ages, there were wars to decide borders between countries, wars to settle disputes, and wars over riches. When the Elves arrived, they tried to work with the humans to create lasting peace, but peace was short lived. Some humans tried to use the casting of spells using a dark spiritual power, and when the spells worked a contingent of elves decided that they should have those powers too. These elves were bitter against Father God for not giving them these powers, so they sought out those powers on their own. They truly became dark and bitter in their souls and thus were called Bitter Elves. They sought to destroy humans through theft, murder, and pollution of spirit. They gathered as many as they could for a war against the Bright Elves. This was called "The War of the Elves".

The next age was the Age of Reason when there was mostly peace. Beautiful buildings were created and paintings and fountains. The countries each had a library of writings in the castles of the kings. Healing arts were practiced. Farmers were able to grow enough food to feed the country. Small towns grew up along the waterways. Commerce was conducted peaceably. However, The Bitter Elves, being jealous of this prosperity, grew in strength and numbers, and again sought the happiness that they thought arose from this prosperity. They again stole riches and even children to sell to men from foreign countries. The slave trade was born. It is during this time that our story commences.

THE RUNAWAYS OF PHAYENDAR

by

Carol Strote

A seventeen year old maiden walked along the path through a fearsome woods holding her head high and trying to look as strong and as bold as she wanted to be. She had to appear totally in control and capable to inspire the confidence of her companions. Liadra used a walking stick that she had chosen for its strength and durability. It could double for a club if need be. The woods were cool and damp, and she led her companions on a path to avoid being seen by anyone traveling on the road. She led two girls and one boy, her friends from farms near Talath. She had shoulder length brown hair and brown eyes that were very observant, constantly looking for danger like the presence of Bitter Elves.

The runaways had walked for days to get to Malwood forest and had entered it with no small amount of fear. Stories about this forest were in abundance. There were robberies, murders, abductions, not to mention wild animals. However, Liadra was confident that, if they were careful, she could lead them through it. Her problems were just beginning. Melody loved animals, so when she saw a cat, she chased it, not looking where she was going. "No, Melody!" screamed Liadra. "Stop!" Liadra ran after her and just barely caught her before she ran into a razor tree. She would have been sliced up badly had she landed against that tree. Its bark has ridges that are very sharp running up and down the tree.

It was turning dark and cold and the path was so rough that Melody had fallen and muddied her knees. The cold, wet feeling was making her miserable. Somebody had stolen their extra clothing the night before as they dried on some bushes. At least the teens had thought of bringing some extra clothes. Running away was proving to be more difficult than they had imagined.

They each had grievances in their respective homes that they thought could be solved if they were on their own. Liadra was the first born of five children and was expected to watch her four brothers, making them behave and do their chores. They resented her bossiness and rebelled against her as if it was their sworn duty to do so. She was capable and strong willed and wanted to get away from these angry boys who treated her badly. Melody was the spoiled baby of her family, crying to get her way. She thought she could do whatever she wanted if she were on her own. Amidra wanted love and romance, but there were no young men in her area who were at all appealing to her. She thought that she could find more young men elsewhere. Trag felt that he deserved more respect. Sure, he made mistakes a lot, but at least he tried, and his aunt didn't properly appreciate him. Because she knew how to, Liadra led the group.

"Liadra, I really need my warm pants. I wonder if anyone in these woods might know who has them," Melody whined tearfully.

"Let's ask," replied Liadra. "It's worth a chance, anyway, but we must be cautious. Anyone we might chance to meet may be Avidora's spies." Avidora was a witch they had heard about around the fireplace at home. Uncle Cadril had told them some hair-raising stories about Avidora and how mean she was to children – just for the fun of it. They thought that Uncle Cadril was exaggerating just to scare them, but the disappearance of children did continue to happen with no explanation.

"Oh, it's getting cold and these pants aren't warm like my thick fuzzy ones that were stolen," whined Melody.

"Hullo!" said a stranger stepping out from behind a large boulder beside the path. He handed them a message scrawled on tree bark. Liadra read, "If you want your clothes back, we'll sell them to you for three silver pieces."

"Silver pieces!" yelled Liadra. "How dare you ask her to buy back what is already hers!? We won't do that!"

"Wait a minute," Melody said, pulling her aside. "It would be better to buy them back than to not get them at all, and I have the silver that we earned cleaning the Lakewood Inn."

An angry and frustrated Liadra turned back to the stranger and said, "Oh, I don't believe that you are honorable at all, but if you will take us to our clothes, we will buy them back. Where are you located? Is it very far?"

"Not far," he replied. The stranger stood up to his full height. He was tall with blonde, tousled hair and a kind, manly face, a strong jaw and a dimpled chin. His brown leather cloak blew back revealing large, muscular arms and a massive chest. Yet his manner was that of a person who was unaware of his own potential and, so, was easily led.

Liadra, in her take-charge manner, gathered their provisions into a pack and strapped them to her back, wishing all the time that Trag had not left them. He could have been a big help right now carrying their blanket rolls, but he had wandered off trying to get to a campfire that he saw out in the woods and had not returned. These woods were dangerous, and the little troop had just wanted to get to the other side where there was a small town with some new people to meet and lots of fun places to visit.

AVIDORA

Meanwhile, at Avidora's castle, a rather small castle set on a hill, with a moat around it filled with large fish with teeth, the little, gnarled, old witch was fervently pacing back and forth, hurriedly making plans to leave and shrieking commands to her servant Trag, a very harried young man who pretended to be interested and jumped at her command. All the while, he was making some last minute changes of his own. He must escape and meet his friends in the woods, but his meeting was planned for tomorrow. He thought, "Oh, why can't Avidora delay for just one day?" But there is no reasoning with a witch who's in a dither and in a hurry. He would have to make do with this opportunity for escape and hope that the little cave was still unoccupied. "These gems could be useful," he thought grabbing fistfuls of green stones and filling his pockets.

"What's that you have?" asked the witch, suddenly turning on him.

Trag shrugged his shoulders and, putting the stones into his pockets, answered, "You might need these, Maam."

"Yes," sneered the witch. "I just might at that." Her eyes narrowed for a moment, and her nose twitched as if smelling a good buy at the slave market in Malwood. She returned to her pacing and giving orders. He would have to choose his time well. "Hurry up, knave," said the witch. "If we miss the slave auction, you'll pay with your skin!" Trag was loaded down with charms, amulets, potions, and talismans to be traded for unfortunates who had been caught by mercenary agents, beat into submission, and marched from place to place until they could be sold or killed. Trag pushed his blonde hair out of his eyes and cast a baleful look at the stack of objects to be carried down fifty steps to the cart. This was his sixth trip down the stairs. His heart was beating too hard and his breath came in short, quick gasps. Avidora, for all her wickedness, had fed him well, knowing that a fat servant is slow to run away.

Loading his arms for the final time, he padded his way down the steps behind the zealous Avidora, who was still muttering to herself as the wind snatched at her patched black skirts, fluttered her threadbare, black cloak, and scattered her short, grey, wiry hair. "Ho, beasts!" she hailed. Two bushy-bears snarled up at her from the cart harness. "Ready to earn your keep, you slug-a-beds?!" she said, climbing into the driver's seat. Trag sighed in relief. He was terrified of the beasts, who hated him as much as they feared Avidora. She knew this and regularly threatened to feed him to the bushy-bears to keep him in line.

Trag rode in the back of the cart as it bumped along the path, fairly shaking him to bits. Various objects sharply poked his soft flesh as he was tossed to and fro among the wicked merchandise. Avidora cursed the beasts for every bump in the path and whipped them furiously as they passed from grassland into Malwood. The huge trees groaned and creaked as the odd little group passed under their crooked, outstretched limbs. Trag shuddered. This was his second time to be in the ill used forest. On his first trip, he was fettered and blindfolded, and was led stumbling and footsore in a slave drive to Malwood Market. He wished he had never left the girls to go looking for a campfire he saw in the forest. It was a childish move. He was caught by the slavers and bought by Avidora.

Deeper into Malwood the cart sped carrying its ominous cargo and one very frightened, bruised young man. The air grew heavy, carrying with it the odor of rotting vegetation. They passed small groups of people wearing many types of costumes indicating varied degrees of position and wealth. One of these groups surely must have been an envoy from royalty. Traveling on horseback, richly clad in velvets, polished high boots and plumed hats, five men rode single file. Looks of surprise at the bear- drawn cart quickly changed to disdain at the sight of the muttering, cursing old woman. Numerous traveling individuals and groups increased with each hour that passed. Few people traveled singly in Malwood. Those who did were subject to possible robbery, enslavement or murder – except those, of course, who were engaged in such activities.

Trag had heard rumors about the horrors of Malwood Forest while working in Avidora's kitchen. He knew that his friends were in danger if they had entered Malwood in search for him, and this caused him great agitation. Melody, Liadra and Amidra knew nothing of these woods having recently fled the safety of their homes.....Home....with Aunt Manda showering affection and scolding him for his bungling ways seemed like heaven to him now. He longed to feel the safety of her arms around him and wondered why he had felt so stifled and indignant about her care before. He had felt so self righteous, defiant, and strong when he left home. Tears trickled down his cheeks and the ache in his chest would not go away. He had heard tales of great dangers and brave deeds when he was a child. Witches were not real then, but were characters in fairytales, and here he was, riding very uncomfortably in the back of a witch's cart.

What's this? The cart slowing down and voices chattering interrupted Trag's rumination. The cart jolted to a halt in front of a long, low building made of long planks with a wooden shaked roof, which was the center of much activity. People were bustling to and fro carrying interesting packages and animal skins for trade. The air was so heavy and still that the smells of spicy foods and animal dung stifled Trag, aggravating his stomach, which was already upset from his long, bumpy ride. It was midday and soon this festive group would be bidding against each other and making threats. Some, not wanting to disappoint their masters, would even kill to get the best flesh on the block. Malwood was well known among merchants as the most dangerous and profitable of markets.

Avidora was greedily licking her lips in expectation of today's catch. She was certain, in her pride, that no one would best her in this game. She hopped down muttering to herself, "I'll have what I want alright. The best and the freshest of slaves will be mine – young and fresh and not too strong. Won't have no struggles on MY hands! Someone easy to dominate. Yes. Someone to scream at and make cower in the corner. Yes, that would do. Not some sickly piece, either. No. Very healthy and young, maybe. Yes, young and pretty. Make them work hard and pinch them and hit them sometimes. What fun! Oh yes, yes." Avidora was working herself into a frensy. She tied the bushy-bears to a tree. "Stay there, you fat, bungling fool!" she screamed at Trag. "The bushies will get you if you move!" She scurried away, howling in laughter. Trag was really too ill to move, and the buzzing of flies in the hot, dank air made him so sleepy that he was soon dreaming of Aunt Manda's cool hand on his forehead and his very own bed.

HOME FIRE

Amidra, Melody and Liadra had spent the night tucked away snug in their warm blanket rolls near a merry, crackling fire. The robber's messenger proved to be a good provider. He had gathered dry wood and had hastily built the fire after stomping down the undergrowth, creating a small clearing beneath several , very tall trees. He then produced a sack of small, dried roots which he ground into powder on a flat rock, mixed it with water and baked it by setting the rock near the fire. The cake had a slightly sweet, yellow vegetable flavor and was very filling. So, having satisfied their hunger and having sipped some berry wine which the stranger kept in his wineskin, the girls felt much more contented. The tall stranger hadn't said a word since he met them. He had pointed the way and had grunted in answer to their questions, but, after several cups of berry wine, he felt more relaxed.

"What's your name?" asked Melody. "I mean, if we're going to spend some time with you, we should know your name, shouldn't we?"

"Steben," he replied quietly.

"What?" asked Melody.

"Steben," he said more loudly and looked directly at her.

"Well, how long have you been here, and how did you get to know those robbers? I mean, you don't seem like a bad man. You've been so kind to us and made us food, so why do you know robbers? I mean, it doesn't make sense," chattered Melody, her red curls bobbing around her freckled face and getting stuck in her spectacles. All these questions at once were too much for Steben, so he just stared at the fire blankly as if he hadn't heard a thing.

Amidra had been listening intently to this conversation as she sat with her head bowed, her long, blonde hair partially obscuring her lovely face. She marveled at how handsome he was and strong, yet helpful and kind…and working for robbers? She gently asked, "How old are you, Steben?" He shrugged. "Does your mother live here?" He shook his head. "Where does she live?"

"Yardrel," said Steben, his face clouded with worry.

"How long ago did you leave home?" asked Amidra.

"Didn't," replied Steben.

Puzzled, Amidra asked, "Did someone bring you here?" Steben winced as if someone were striking him.

"Bad men. Pushed Mama. Fire! Tied me," he fretted, rubbing his wrists as if they still hurt. Silent tears rolled down his face, gathered in his dimpled chin, and dripped onto his big hands.

Amidra's big, blue eyes softened and filled with compassion as she asked, "Were you a little boy when this happened?"

"My 13th birthday. My cake smashed. Mama screamed! Mean men! Hate them! Hurt Mama!" Steben said loudly.

"Steben," said Amidra, "You look about nineteen years old NOW. That means, giving a year for travel, you've been here for five years." She noticed that his clothing, obviously sewn from fine leathers, was in good condition. His sandals laced up around his calves to his pantaloons. His waist was girded with a string of round, polished copper pieces of good workmanship. He wore a leather vest laced up the front, but his arms were covered only by blonde, curly hair. His cloak was long, extending to the middle of his calf and was made of unshorn leather with fur on the inside. Great care had been taken to ensure his comfort both during hot days and cold nights. "This doesn't seem the work of slavers. Who would steal a child and burn his mother's house?" thought Amidra."Where are those men now, Steben?"

"Dead," said Steben.

"Dead!?" cried Melody in alarm, her green eyes widening in fear. "Did you kill them?" she asked, moving away from him.

"No," said Steben. "Rando killed. Cut 'em. Big knife. Killed 'em. Took me. Home Fire. Took Vela, too," His face softened. And a smile slowly crept across his face.

"Now we're getting somewhere," thought Amidra. She didn't quite know how to approach the subject of his speech impediment, not wanting to offend him. Hesitantly she asked, "Steben....did you ever hurt your head?"

"Mean men. Hit me. Big stick. Hurt so bad. Got so sick. Couldn't see good. Long time," said Steben.

"I'm sorry, Steben. How does your head feel now?" asked Amidra.

"Feel fine. Well now." He put his fingertips to his lips and said, "Talk funny," and he threw his head back laughing as if he had told a good joke.

"You talk just fine," Amidra said. "And you're very nice. I like you. But I'm getting sleepy. Let's go to bed." At that the girls suddenly became aware of the forest around them and of the strange animal sounds and bright little eyes peering at them from nearby brush and trees. Melody put her blanket next to Steben between him and Liadra, while Amidra cuddled up next to him resting her hand on his warm chest. Steben smiled contentedly and fell asleep.

Morning brought the sun, and even though the trees blocked most of the light, the air warmed almost immediately. The girls rose to a new fire and the smell of salt pork sizzling. Steben had lovingly fixed the best breakfast food that he could with his limited supply. He had soaked thin strips of dried meat, had warmed them, and had fixed more of the cakes. He had even gathered some berries for desert. Liadra, Melody and Amidra enjoyed this food and really appreciated it; their own supplies had dwindled and they had been on short rations for days now. Amidra kept watching Steben. He amazed her. He was so handsome and capable and he genuinely liked the girls. How could he have been through such a traumatic experience and still be such a kind, loving person? She thought, "Thank you, God, for sending me this wonderful man."

After striking camp, Steben donned the pack of provisions and led them slowly down the path. They were walking up and down a hilly path in gradual descent toward their unknown enemies. Steben seemed particularly happy this morning, humming to himself and smiling as he helped the girls over an old tree that had fallen across the path. Melody found the going rough. "I'm hot. I wish we could take a bath. Isn't there a river or a pond around here? I feel like a perfect bumbkin. My clothes are dirty too. I could swim with my clothes on and wash them at the same time. Smell your clothes, Liadra. Mine smell like smoke, don't yours?"

"Oh, Melody," said Liadra impatiently. "Don't be such a crybaby. We'll be all right until we reach Steben's Home Fire. I'm sure those people must bathe somehow. Steben, where do you bathe?"

"Perilough," said Steben. "Lake, suntime, not moontime. Long Neck. Big teeth. Bite, tear, crunch."

"Are you sure it's safe during suntime?" asked Amidra.

"Sure. Long Neck hate sun," replied Gus, trying to reassure the girls.

"I want to go home," whined Melody.

"We can't go home and leave Trag here all alone, can we?" asked Liadra.

"No, I guess not, but what if he can't get away? What if that elf was lying?' asked Melody.

"Elves don't lie." said Liadra. "Don't you remember the stories of the Bright Elves?"

"What if this one isn't a Bright Elf?" asked Melody.

"Well, at least he knew about Trag, and he had nothing to gain by lying, and he did give us Trag's ring as a token. So, let's give it a try," said Liadra.

Steben had been listening intently to this conversation. "Trag?" he asked.

Melody replied without thinking, "He's our friend. Avidora's got him and he's going to escape and meet us at the…"

"Shhh! That's our secret!" whispered Liadra.

"OK. Steben help. Avidora bad. Mean witch. Steben help girls. Steben friend."

"Oh, Steben, if only you could help us. We don't know where the cave is exactly. That's where we have to meet Trag. After we get our clothes, could you help us to find it?" asked Amidra , who would love to have an excuse to keep Steben with them longer.

"What cave?" asked Steben.

"It's on the edge of the wood, by a river, next to a waterfall," said Liadra, "and there is writing above the entrance."

"Steben know. Steben help. Get clothes. Find cave," replied Steben.

"Then we'll all go back home! I know," said Melody."We can help Steben go home, too. Would you like that, Steben? I'll bet your Mama would like to see you."

Steben stopped and turned around so suddenly that Melody bumped into him. "Home?" Steben said eagerly. "Yardrel. North."

"Yes, Steben," said Liadra. "It's the least we can do to repay your kindness. We know part of the way and I'm sure that we can find others to help us the rest of the way."

"Home? See Mama? Yes. Good. We go. Take Vela, too," said Steben.

"Steben," said Liadra rather tenuously, "Do you realize that these are robbers that you're living with, and that it seems like they have made a servant out of you? Steben, do you help them to hurt people?"

"No. Steben good man."

"What about Vela? What does Vela do?" asked Liadra.

"Vela make clothes. Vela make food. Vela like Mama," replied Steben.

"Whew!" sighed Liadra in relief.

"Ho! Steben!" hailed a voice from down the path.

"Rando!" called Steben.

Melody shuddered remembering the story about Rando murdering the slavers. "I'm afraid," she whined.

"Hush. We'll just pretend to not know anything about them. We'll do our business and get out of here," said Liadra.

"Yes," said Steben. "We leave. Moontime. Take Vela. Very quiet. Walk soft. You see."

"What took you so long?" asked Rando scowling.

"Girls tired. Cold. Need rest," answered Steben.

Liadra said indignantly, "If this is the only welcome you can manage, perhaps we should turn around and go about our business."

Rando, taking a different tack, said, "You're close to our Home Fire now. You can bathe and have some soup. Follow me." Now a bath and some soup sounded good to Melody, but she still said nothing and hung back behind Steben. She had the distinct feeling that they were being led into great danger and she wanted to turn and run.

The final descent was very steep down a natural, winding staircase formed by chunks of rock upended in various positions, polished flat to form each stair and cemented together to prevent a landslide. There were conifers growing severally between rocks on the various levels. The lake below was clearly visible. Sunlight gleamed on the surface and a tiny boat about the size of a leaf could be seen. Amidra slipped, scraping her hand, so Steben held her arm, carefully guiding her steps. By the time they reached level ground, the girls' muscles were trembling and they flopped down to rest. "I hope we never have to climb up it!" said Melody.

Rando stood by impatiently, scowling at the girls. He was dressed in the same manner as Steben, but wore a sword sheathed at his side and a knife with a jeweled handle tucked into his belt. Winding around his arms he wore silver and gold bracelets shaped like snakes and winding about his head, a scarlet cloth held his straight, black hair out of his face. His nose was thin and pointed. His small, dark brown eyes shifted from one thing to another quickly. His ample lips were generally set in a smirk with both corners pointed down. His high forehead would have lent him a noble look had his demeanor been less cruel. He nervously clenched and unclenched his fists.

As Steben walked over to Rando, Amidra noticed that Steben was taller by about a foot. She reflected, "How strange it is…. this gentle, kind young man in the service of such an obviously wicked person. How easy it is for a truly kind person to overlook the faults of others. What did Mother call it? Spirit flowers? Like kindness, forgiveness, and patience and here he is, abiding in complete safety among a group of robbers in Malwood." Warmth flooded Amidra as she watched, her eyes beaming love and understanding to the young man who knew so little and so much.

"Enough rest! Move these girls out. I'm hungry," said Rando, stalking off down a path to the right. Steben helped the girls to their feet and followed, supporting one on each arm. The path gradually sloped down, veering to the left through slender trees with rustling, heart shaped leaves. The air grew cooler and fragrant as they approached Home Fire. There was a wall of vertical logs lashed together with a large open gate. The wall surrounded Rando's camp. He said, "The wall is for protection from animals and men. We post sentries outside of the wall to warn of any approaching dangers. We are located on just enough of a hill so that the lake never floods our camp."

'Oh, look!" cried Melody. Her attention focused on a clearing inside the wall with many tents surrounding a large, crackling fire. Children were huddled in a small group eating from gourds, and adults were seated on logs around the fire eating meat and drinking from jeweled chalices. There were several dogs walking about looking for handouts. The men were armed with bows and arrows. Most of the people looked to be in their twenties and thirties.

The exhausted girls were led past a structure that was used for food preparation. Fur pelts were stretched out to dry on this small log building and thin strips of meat were drying on a large rock in front of the door. Aromas of cooking, herbs, spices, and meats reminded the girls of lunch and the hollow spots in their stomachs began really hurting. The guest shelter was located near the log building. It was built of small logs fastened together with twine and leaning up against a stone wall. One end was open and the other was covered with a thickly laced flowering vine. The girls flopped down on the freshly prepared mats of fern covered with a thick, woven material.

A medium sized woman in her thirties with a kindly face and her hair pulled back into a bun came in and introduced herself. She said that she would be looking after them. Vela brought them a bowl of cooked roots and meat and a skin of light, fragrant, berry wine. Vela's kindness soothed fears and encouraged the tired, wary girls. She looked on them as darling children in need of a mother. She treated them as she had treated Steben all these years – as she would have treated her own dear children if the slavers hadn't stolen her from her field. Her son and daughter had been staying in the village with her mother when the slavers surprised her in the field as she pulled weeds. She had grieved for years over the loss of her children, but caring for Steben had helped to fill the emptiness in her heart and lessened her grief.

After the girls had eaten, Vela brought a comb and carefully worked the tangles out of Melody's long, red curls. The teeth of the comb were real, about two inches long, and set in a jawbone. "Vela, what animal did that come from?" asked Liadra.

"Girl, you're such a baby. Where have you been all your life? This comes from a terrible animal. It lives at the water's edge lurking about for its prey, slithering in and out of the water, hiding in the tall weeds there. Its hard, spiny body makes it very hard to kill. Its silence makes it dangerous to hunt. More than one young hunter has been torn apart by the grustabist's teeth such as these. Melody shuddered and shrank back from the comb.

"Did these teeth eat anybody?" asked an alarmed Melody.

"No, child, not these teeth," Vela answered. "This was taken from a young Grustabist that strayed too far from its mother. One of the camp guards spotted it and killed it last spring." Melody relaxed a bit and allowed Vela to finish her combing.

"Is the grustabist like the long neck that Steben spoke of?" asked Melody.

Vela answered, "No, the long neck lives further out in the water and is much larger. The grustabist is only about twelve feet long and stays near the water's edge in the weeds. I'll bet you would like to bathe and change your clothes. You have to pay Rando. I'm sorry, but that's just the way it is here." Melody gave her the silver pieces. Vela led the girls down a path to a secluded spot next to the lake where they could bathe. She gave them some of her scented cakes of soap to use. Vela used the usual recipe for soap except to add extra fat and flower petals. The water was cool, but felt good on their sore muscles.

"How lovely!" exclaimed Amidra. "This is wonderful." It felt so good to be clean after a week without bathing and walking such a long way. As the girls were dressing, Amidra asked, "Vela, how did you meet Rando?"

Vela replied, "Slavers took me from my home and were going to sell me at the auction in Malwood. Rando and some of his men were hunting and saw them almost dragging me along. I was so tired and sore that I could hardly stand up. Steben ran toward me to rescue me and the rest followed to help Steben. I am so grateful to them. How horrible it would be to be stripped down and sold at auction! I've heard stories of women being passed from one man to another at that auction, and some of those women are no older than you. Please be so careful out there. Anyway, Rando asked me to join the group to cook and sew clothing. I jumped at the chance to be safe. I miss my children, but there is no way I could get back by myself, and I'm sure my mother is taking good care of them."

"What about your husband?" asked Amidra.

"He was taken to serve in King Aryante's army, leaving us to fend for ourselves. I don't know what happened to him," she said tearfully.

"It's not fair!" said Amidra. "A person should be able to live a normal life without other people wrecking it. This world is horrible."

"I agree in part," said Vela, "but through all of the bad things that happen, Father God above lets us know that there is also good – like sending Steben to help. Father God can also use people like Rando. He is a thief, but he helped most of the people here and he protects us.. Of course, he thinks he's smart having us work for him, but we all work together to live. Come on. Let's go back to Home Fire."

The girls didn't have to be asked twice. They were eager to get some rest on those mats, which they did, falling asleep for a while. They awakened to the smell of food and the sound of singing. A group of about twenty people were sitting in a circle around the fire. Several children were running about playing. Melody thought that this didn't seem too scary. They got some food and joined the group around the fire. Amidra spotted Steben and sat down next to him. "I feel better," she said. "How are you?"

"Steben fine." He looked at her, smiling, and said, "Happy." Amidra smiled back hugging him.

After dinner, the group went back to their shelter and Steben told them to get ready to leave. They would have to leave as soon as the others had fallen asleep. Steben knew a way to slip past the guards unseen. He had spoken to Vela, and she had decided to go with them. She had packed enough dried meats and roots for a short journey for all of them. Soon they were headed for the cave to meet Trag.

AUCTION

Back at the slave market, Trag awakened from his nap to a torrent of activity. The place was crowded with merchants setting up booths to market their wares and slaves being herded like animals into a large pen. The pen was constructed of many small logs lashed together with a heavy twine. Avidora had tied Trag to one of the side slats of the wagon. With one of his green stones, he bribed a young servant to bring him food. Avidora was busy scoping out the place for a good spot to set up her own little business. She wanted a spot close to the auction block so that she could bid and still keep an eye on her wares. She also didn't want to be close to the foreigners who looked and acted dangerous. They were dressed in silken clothing and wore turbans and beards. They spoke a different language and always gave her dirty looks. People said that they came from other lands across the sea and that they would kill if they didn't get what they wanted. Others were there from Orendia, a country west of Aksanda.

Suddenly there were cheers from the crowd as a young maid was led onto the auction block where they removed her velvet robe to reveal a beautiful girl with wavy, black hair flowing down her back to her waist. Tears were flowing from her big, brown eyes falling onto her perfectly formed breasts. Bidding was fierce, and she fetched a high price from an obviously wealthy gentleman. Trag thought, "That scoundrel. If he wanted a pretty girl, why didn't he just marry one?" Next, a young, strong man, restrained by two guards, was led onto the block. He struggled until a third guard gave him several stripes with a whip.

Trag realized that he had to escape to warn his friends, but he couldn't untie the rope that bound him to the wagon. He asked God to send him the Bright Elf who had taken his message to the girls. The elf had seen this in a vision and was already on his way. He arrived before the auction ended. He had traveled on foot for hours following little known deer paths to the auction site and had sneaked quietly passed the guards to find Trag's cart. The elf untied Trag who grabbed two blankets and a bag of food before being led away. There was a shriek from the auction as Avidora realized that her slave was missing. She walked into the woods, burned a mixture of herbs, and spoke the words of the location spell, which the Bright Elf countered with a shield. She would have to conduct her business the hard way – by herself.

Trag was thanking the elf profusely for setting him free and asked if he would guide him to the cave, offering him a green stone as recompense. The elf told him that he would, but that no payment was necessary. He hinted that Trag would have need of his stones on his journey. After walking for several miles, the elf decided to make camp in a very small clearing beneath some trees with bushes around to provide some privacy. Finally, having a chance for some conversation, Trag proceeded to satisfy his curiosity. "What is your name?"

"In Elven it is Tunda Fanyare. It means Tall Sky," said the elf. Tunda Fanyare was six feet tall with blonde, silken hair to the middle of his back, fair skin, pale blue eyes and fine features. He was dressed in fringed, soft leather and sandals lacing up to his knees.

"Why do they call you Bright Elves?" asked Trag.

"At times we can appear to be very bright to frighten the enemy." replied Tall Sky.

"I've heard stories about bad elves called Bitter Elves, but that's confusing," said Trag.

"Bitter Elves have different powers than we do. We have apacina where we can see visions, heal, tell if a man is good or evil and resist attacks. The bitter elves were not content with our God given powers, but wanted power to strike, to destroy, to control men, and to gather wealth. They were bitter against God for keeping these powers from them, so they sought out knowledge of warfare and of dark wisdom, some of which Avidora uses.

"Can you just decide to see something, like where my friends are?" asked Trag. "I'm really worried about them. I'm afraid that they will get caught by slavers or be attacked or something."

"No, but I can ask God to give me a vision or a word of knowledge about them," replied Tall Sky. "I will speak to God about it while you sleep." He made a small fire and heated some berry wine for warmth. After eating bread and cheese and drinking some warm berry wine, Trag rolled up in his blanket near the fire and went to sleep. Tall Sky, wrapped in his blanket, sat guarding and praying. The next morning he told Trag that he had seen the girls walking with a tall, blonde man and a woman, and that they appeared to be well. After breakfast they continued their journey to find the cave and their friends.

Steben knew that any main paths would be full of danger because of the activity of travelers going toward the auction, so he chose to follow deer paths toward the waterfall. It would take most of the day to reach the cave, so they continued at a steady pace stopping only briefly for rest and refreshment. They had high hopes that Trag would manage to escape Avidora and find them. Vela had prayed that the Bright Elf to whom the girls had spoken would help Trag. The girls were sure that he would. Just as the sun was reaching a low point in the west, they heard the waterfall.

Steben told the girls to stay behind while he checked the area for any possible dangers. He was relieved to see only two people sitting at the pool's edge – Tall Sky and Trag.

"Tall Sky!" hailed Steben.

"Steben!" replied Tall Sky.

They ran to each other and embraced, patting each other on the back and laughing. "It's so good to see you. Girls! Come on down here. They're here!" called Tall Sky. The girls came running to meet them.

Melody hugged Trag crying. "I'm so glad you're well. Did the witch hurt you? What was it like in the witch's castle? Was the auction terrible? Is Avidora chasing you? Did you get enough to eat? Where did you sleep? How did you get away?" Melody couldn't contain herself. She was full of questions and all of her pent up worry and emotions came pouring out at once.

"Melody, give him a chance to breathe! Let's sit over on these rocks and have a bite to eat. Then we can have a nice talk and catch up. OK?" suggested Liadra.

"Sounds great," said Trag," I've got some pretty good food from Avidora's kitchen. I helped make it myself." They all sat down to a good meal, passing around bread, cheese, meat and wine. "Who is the new lady?"

Amidra smiled and said, "Trag, meet Vela. She is the lady who took care of us at the robbers' camp called Home Fire. She was saved from the slavers by Steben and Rando's men and they took her to Home Fire and gave her a job. This is Steben. He knew where this place was and brought us here." She then gave Steben a kiss on the cheek which made him blush.

"I see how it is," said Trag, and everybody laughed. It was a wonderful evening that would not be forgotten. They shared stories and information about the bright elves and the bitter elves, how the Bitter Elves were greedy and wanted what humans have to the point of killing them and enslaving them. The Bitter Elves were angry with God for not giving them these things and for not giving them magical powers, so they studied dark magic. Bright Elves followed God's directions and loved God and helped others. Trag told them about the slave market and how young people were beaten and stripped down and sold like animals and of a particular girl who stood there crying. He told them about being chained to the wall at night and about Avidora's practice of beating her slaves and feeding a bad one to the bushy-bears. Trag had the worst stories to tell. The girls had two protectors to help them at the robbers' camp.

"Liadra asked, "Do you know what the writing says above the cave?"

"Yes," said Tall Sky, "It is a message in runes. It says, 'Safe Haven for the Weary'. We could stay there tonight without fear of attack from man or beast. My people made this during the Elven wars. We needed a safe place to rest just as you do now."

Melody asked, "What are the Elven Wars? Were the elves fighting each other?"

"Yes, they were," said Tall Sky. "This was many years ago. The elves had split into two factions. One called themselves Bitter elves, because they rebelled against Father God and hated anything that was good and true. They wanted power and wealth and would do anything to get it. They stole and sold harmful herbs to people and killed anyone who got in their way. The other elf faction called themselves Bright Elves and they resisted the Bitter Elves with force. Good cannot afford evil to continue to have its way. This Malwood Auction is part of that problem. You can forgive the evil doer, but that does not mean that you allow him to continue to do evil things to others."

"It would be great not to have to be afraid and worry all night," said Melody.

"Yes, Culina," said Tunda Fanyare fondly. "I shall call you Culina for your pretty, red curls." Melody blushed. "Now, let's go into the cave and get a good night's sleep." Culina decided to sleep next to her new friend and Amidra cuddled up next to Steben. Liadra slept between Melody and Amidra. Melody awoke with nightmares about being chased through the woods by slavers. She cried out in her sleep, waking Tall Sky, who held her as she wept. He enfolded her in his strong arms and quietly sang an Elven lullaby.

Soft winds are sighing,

Bird songs are lilting,

Hushabye baby,

Butterflies are kissing you,

Sweet baby, sweet.

When you wake

In the morning,

You will kiss the sun,

And wave goodbye to the moon.

Melody felt calmer now. With her head on his chest, the fear drained out of her, and she felt content and safe again. Tall Sky felt attracted to Melody which he never expected. He thought, "How am I going to handle this? I really like this girl, but if anything develops here, she would grow old and I would not during our time together. I have to give serious thought to this. It feels so right being close to her like this." Their little fire kept them warm and cozy until the morning.

For breakfast they had dried meat strips, little cakes with honey, and an apple.

"We should pray before we get started," said Tall Sky. "Creator of all, Giver of life, we thank you for all of your kindness, for food, for the sun's warmth, for the joy that you bring us, and for our friendship. We ask for your guidance and protection from those who do harm."

Tall Sky started to get up, but Liadra said,"Tell us about God."

He answered,"God is for everyone, not just for elves. He created all and He loves us. That is why He has great patience with us. God has three parts: God the Creator, God the Intercessor, and God the Restorer. All three parts are God. God the Creator is the maker of all. God the Intercessor talks to the Creator about us and about things happening here. God the Restorer will help people when they have done wrong and want to change. God wants us to have good lives, so he gives us gifts like healing, love, joy, and discernment – that's where you can tell good from evil. It helps to keep us safe. God's Spirit can live in you, giving you an advantage in talking to Him. What God have you worshiped before?" They told him that their parents prayed to God, but the children didn't really know God.

"I want God's Spirit," said Melody.

"Is there something you would like to tell God about?" asked Tall sky.

"I have been very selfish, demanding my own way, and throwing temper tantrums and crying to get my own way. I told Mama that I hated her. I'm so sorry now." She cried, and through her tears, asked

God to forgive her. "Would you please live in me? I promise to do better." She looked at Tall Sky and asked, "Is that alright?"

"Little Culina, God loves you and I love you too." Melody hugged him and kissed him on the cheek.

"Here we go again," thought Trag.

"I want God's Spirit too," said Liadra. "My brothers were so mean to me that I told them I hated them and wished they would all get sick and die," she said, tears rolling down her cheeks. I don't really want them to die. Would God forgive me for that and help to take care of them while I'm away? Please forgive me, God, and live in me too."

"I'm sure that God forgave you and is with you already," said Tall Sky. "Liadra, you need to forgive your brothers."

"I do forgive them," said Liadra.

"There is rebellion here. Someone has been disobedient and gave the parents great pain," said Tall Sky.

"That would be me," said Amidra. "I wouldn't stay until my parents found a suitable mate for me, so I ran away without telling them. They must be hurt and so worried. I feel guilty about that."

"God will help you with that," said Tall Sky. "Just ask Him to forgive you."

"Oh, I do ask Him to forgive me for being so cruel. And, God, please live in my heart, too," said Amidra.

"Steben want God, too," said Steben.

"Do you want to tell God about something, Steben?" asked Tall Sky.

"Steben sorry. Hate bad men. God forgive. God live here," said Steben, patting his chest.

"Steben, do you forgive those bad men?" asked Tall Sky.

"Steben forgive. No more hate," said Steben

"I want you to understand something about the forgiveness of others. You can forgive them and not feel hate any more. That is what God wants, because hate will only hurt you. But it doesn't mean that you won't defend yourself from this person. It doesn't mean that you approve of him. It just means that you let go of the feeling of hate. Mercy is another thing. It is important to show mercy whenever you can do so without putting others in danger."

Melody said, "Trag, you should do it, too. You really need protection from Avidora."

Trag flinched as if being struck by an unknown assailant. "Yes, I do want God to live in me. I want him to protect me and I'm sorry that I Ieft Aunt Manda. She was good to me and she took care of me when I was sick and I told her that I hated her when she said I did something wrong. He looked down and said, "I don't hate her." Will God forgive me for that?"

"God forgives the ungrateful," said Tall Sky.

"Then, please, God, forgive me and come to live in me," said Trag.

"I'm sure He will, Trag, and He will protect you from Avidora," said Tall Sky.

Vela had been silently praying through this. She said, "Where are we going from here?"

"That's a good question", said Tall Sky. "Steben comes from Yardrel." He started drawing a map on the ground. "Here is the forest. Here we are on the west side of the forest. Yardrel is on the other side where Lake Perilough is. Vela, where do you come from?' asked Tall Sky.

"I lived on a farm outside of the village called Talami." replied Vela. "It's near the mountains."

"Where did the rest of you live?" asked Tall Sky.

Liadra replied that they had all come from farms near Talath.

"I know it well. Nice people live in that area. Many times they have shown me hospitality when I was in need of food and a place to stay," said Tall Sky. "Visiting four separate areas will take much travel and currency of some type. Trag, do you still have Avidora's gems?" asked Tall Sky.

"Avidoras' gems?!" cried everyone.

"Where did you get the courage to do something like that?" asked Melody. "Weren't you afraid? She might chase us to get them back. Will she, Tall Sky?"

"She will want them back, alright, but we have power that she doesn't have. You'll see," said Tall Sky. "We need to exchange the gems for small pieces of silver to pay for food and other things on our way. There is only one place where people have that much silver, the Malwood Market."

"Nonononono," said Melody. "Trag said that Malwood was BAD."

"Culina," Tall Sky cooed, putting his arm around her."I will protect my little one." Her big green eyes looked at him adoringly.

"We will enter the forest here, riding horseback, so as not to be conspicuous. No one will know who we are. Avidora will not see you, Trag. I will shield you. On the edge of the forest is a farm with horses. I know the owner. He is a shrewd trader, but a good man. You will stay there while I bargain for clothing at the edge of the forest where merchants enter the forest on the road. We should leave the farm tomorrow morning as the sun rises, "said Tall Sky.

The group took that as a cue and packed their things. Tall Sky led them down a path next to the stream. It was just a deer path, but it was clear of undergrowth. They walked silently for hours thinking about all that had transpired and wondering what the Market would be like. Melody was walking close to Tall Sky, holding his hand. When the sun reached its zenith, the group saw the farm and the horses. The farmer walked toward them to greet them. "Tall Sky, so good to see you. It's been a long time. Who do have with you?"

"Lars Horsefriend, it is good to see you. These are friends I helped who were lost and need to be reunited with their families. Lars, I wonder if we could buy a few horses and perhaps stay with you for a night. We could stay in the barn on some hay. We have our own blankets."

"I will make a good cushion of hay for you and you will sleep like babies," said Lars. "Also I have horses and ponies. The girls may like the ponies. I recommend horses for the men and for the woman."

"That should do nicely. Thank you," said Tall Sky.

"Come along. You must be hungry and thirsty," said Lars. "I will have Ella to bring us bread and cheese and wine. Then you can rest."

"That's fine, but I have to leave to purchase some clothing for us," said Tall sky.

Tall Sky left the group and headed to the entrance to Malwood Forest. As he suspected, the closer he came to the entrance, the more travelers he saw. The entrance to Malwood was a broad opening on the edge of dense forest. It was the start of the Malwood Road which was about five riders wide.

It didn't take him long to encounter a merchant with a good amount of wares and was able to buy the clothing and a tent. He loaded these things on an extra horse and rode back to the horse farm arriving just in time for dinner. Ella had fixed a thick, rich stew and freshly baked bread, some wine, and a berry pie for dessert. The girls had helped with dinner and with cleaning up afterward.

"Now," said Tall Sky, "You each have new clothes to try on in the barn." Excitement ran high. The girls ran to the barn to see these new wonders. There were gowns and velvet capes for the girls and leather clothing and velvet capes for the men. He had also purchased a tall, round tent for them with satin pillows for the girls.

"Did you buy all of this with Trag's stones?" asked Liadra.

"No, I used my own," said Tall Sky. "I always carry stones or silver with me. I get them from trading with the dwarves in the Aikasse mountains. I trade with them for things they can't get while working in the mountains – like certain foods and cloth."

"Thank you," said Melody, and kissed him on the cheek. Tall Sky wondered if Melody was also feeling an attraction to him or was it just gratefulness.

Everyone settled in for the night. They all slept comfortably and happily until the morning when they were awakened by a familiar sound–a rooster crowing.

Lars called to them saying that breakfast was ready, and everybody hurriedly donned their new clothes and went to the house for breakfast. They had little sausages, eggs, honey cakes and hot tea.

"Lars and Ella, I want to thank you for all of this food and for the comfortable bedding. It has been great to see you again." After paying his friend, the group went to their horses and ponies. Having lived in the country all of their lives, everyone knew how to ride, which was a blessing.

After an hour of riding, they were at the entrance to Malwood Forest where they joined the groups riding toward Malwood Market. They rode behind a group of well dressed men who were obviously there to buy. Behind them were carts filled with bundles to sell and several people walking beside the carts in plain work clothes. Several men in armor rode by them. The girls felt like princesses, while Trag felt terrified. He remembered the horrific sights at the slave auction and how he had felt as a captive slave tied in Avidora's cart. He was glad to have God's and Tall Sky's protection.

Arriving at the market, Trag noticed that the smells were still disgusting, and there was talking in several languages. People were busy at the brightly colored booths. There was no auction at this time. He was glad of that. Tall Sky located a bare spot of ground to erect the tent and tied the horses on nearby trees.

The girls waited with Steben in the tent while he and Trag looked for a vendor in jewels. Tall Sky found one with whom he had traded before and received a fair price for Trag's gemstones. Trag was amazed at the amount of silver pieces that they received in the trade. They bought some meat pies and wine and returned to their tent to eat in peace. They would leave before the slave auction would begin. It was something that Tall Sky did not want the girls to experience. Trag heartily agreed to this. They broke camp, packing away their things in their blanket rolls and saddle bags and rode away on the road to the west.

After riding for several hours and almost at the edge of Malwood, they stopped to relieve themselves. Melody found a blue egg about double the size of a chicken egg. She put it in her pocket and returned to the group to drink some wine and have a piece of dried meat and bread. She could hardly wait for it to hatch, which it did, in her pocket. What emerged was a little lizard with green eyes like hers. She was delighted and immediately fed it some cheese and gave it some water in her hand. The lizard climbed up to her bosom and curled up for a nap against her warm skin, softly purring. "Tall

Sky, see what I found?" she said excitedly. Tall Sky examined the creature and proclaimed it a miniature dragon.

"You realize that this little dragon thinks that you are her best friend for life. Dragons bond with the first human they see. You really should ask me before picking up things in these woods," said Tall Sky.

Melody looked balefully up at him with her big, green, heavily lashed eyes and asked, "Are you mad at me?"

"No, Culina, if you want her you can have her. I just want you to be more careful," said Tall Sky.

"OK," she said cheerfully and got back on her pony.

Tall Sky knew of a fishing village called Loadrel which would be a good place to spend some time. It is located near Lake Perilough south of Home Fire. Many good, hard working people live there. They fish, raise some animals, and garden. There are also a few small businesses like a bakery, a grocery, a glass blower, and a furniture maker. As usual, there was an upsurge of business activity due to the Malwood Market Auction. There would be unsavory characters who could put them in danger. There were four pretty women and a goodly amount of silver in his charge, so Tall Sky wanted to avoid the main street of the town. He instead stopped at a home to see about a possible lodging arrangement. The woman who answered the door was thin and careworn, unusual for this village. Two poorly dressed children held onto her skirt.

"Hello. My name is Tall Sky and these are my friends. We have been traveling for some time and we're looking for a place to stay away from the business of the village."

"I am Moira. You are welcome to come in and rest for a while, but we have nothing to eat but a few potatoes from the garden," she replied.

"Where is your husband?" asked Tall Sky.

She looked down and said, "He is at the tavern where he is every night. He drinks and gambles with his friends. If my husband wins tonight, we might buy some food tomorrow. One day my boys will be able to fish and bring us food."

"We will rest here for a while and I will buy food for us and bring it back," said Tall Sky.

Moira's face brightened up and she said, "Bring in your friends. They are welcome." Steben and Tall Sky went shopping, while the girls and Trag stayed with Moira.

At the Laborer's Reward, Beldock Fairman was serving ale and mutton stew. Several of Beldock's good friends were there. "How was fishing today, Kroom?" asked Beldock. "Great!" replied Kroom. Kroom and his partner Jaston had brought in a record number of fish that day. They were tired and wanting a mug of ale and some food before going home. They had no desire to be near the gambling table and listen to a bunch of jibber jabber from the foreigners, so they sat back by the kitchen where they could relax. The place was filled with wayfarers from different places wanting food, drink and entertainment. The only entertainment available was gambling. Moira's husband kept losing his silver, so Beldock drew him aside for a talk. "Jafer, what are you doing? These people are from other lands and they're good at what they do. If you keep losing at the games, you won't be able to feed your family," said Beldock.

"What do I care? They can go without or beg!" said Jafer.

Beldock asked Kroom to watch the place for a while. He grabbed Jafer by the neck, dragged him outside and marched him down the street yelling at him about duty and compassion. Jafer struggled some, but he knew Beldock was an army man who was twice his size and ten times as strong. When they arrived at Jafer's house, Beldock was surprised to see Jafer's family and guests sitting down to a meal. "Tall Sky my friend! Never have I been so happy to see someone!" Beldock exclaimed. "And who are these lovely creatures?"

"These are my friends who were lost in Malwood and needed a little guidance," replied Tall Sky ."Who is this man you brought here?"

"This is the worthless man of the house. The worm was squandering his earnings instead of feeding his family. Where did this food come from?" asked Beldock

"We brought it," said Tall Sky. "We need a place to stay away from ruffians and evil men."

"My inn is full, but I have a friend who would be happy for some company. He lost his dear wife and has been despondent ever since. His name is Laskron Truehand, a glassblower by trade. A better man you will never meet. He saved my life once. He dragged me out of a fire at the inn and helped me repair it, too. And, Tall Sky, there is one of yours, a Bright Elf named Quickturn. Turning to Jafer, he said, "Now for you, you squandering piece of dung, if I ever catch you neglecting your family again, I'll beat you within an inch of your life! And you know I can do it! Moira, I will send food for your family tomorrow and we will keep in touch. See you at the inn, Elf." Scowling at Jafer one more time, Beldock left.

"Wow," said Liadra, "Where do they make men like that?"

"We will be staying with another good man," said Tall Sky. Having finished their meal, they thanked Moira and hugged her. Melody gave her some silver and told her to hide it. Spirit flowers were already blooming in Melody's heart. The group donned their capes and left. They rode to the inn and tied their horses. Beldock had his friend Laskron there to meet them. They chose a table near the kitchen, next to the wall, somewhat apart from the others.

Laskron was dark haired, medium height and strong. His brown eyes widened when he saw the pretty girls. "I did not know that you brought princesses to meet me. I am honored." Laskron's hand went to the scar on his face – a scar inflicted by fire when he saved his friend. It didn't hurt, but he was self conscious of it. His beard covered most of it, but some still showed on his left cheek. Beldock tells me that you need a safe place to stay. You are welcome in my home. I have plenty of room, since my wife and I planned for children. As it is, we only had time for one. Elise, come here, baby. Elise came forward shyly, saw Liadra, and extended her hand to her. Liadra took it and said, "I hear you're a very special little girl." Elise smiled and went to stand by her daddy. Liadra beamed a warm smile to Laskron who returned the same warm smile.

Trag thought, "Three down and one to go."

Beldock called his wife over."Mina, Tall Sky brought some friends with him. Would you please bring them some wine?" Beldock excused himself saying that he must help Mina with clean up and end of the day chores. He said, "Stop by the kitchen on your way out and I will send some food with you."

An amazed and somewhat perplexed Laskron asked Tall Sky how he met the group. While Tall Sky explained, little Elise sat on Liadra's lap. Elise had long, dark hair and the cutest little baby face with brown eyes and long lashes. Liadra was a goner. She had only rambunctious boys in her family. Holding this little girl was an astounding miracle to her. She was so delicate with tiny fingers and fragile features and, "She likes me," thought Liadra. This was a rare treat.

Tall Sky excused himself to go across the room to visit with Quickturn. "Quickturn, my friend, what brings you to this part of the world? Are you and your friends chasing some new enemies?" Tall Sky said in jest.

Quickturn replied, "As a matter of fact, we are. We've been following a group of Bitters who are communicating with other groups. There is something big going on and, with them, it could mean a lot of killing and destruction. They have a leader you probably know of named Tupragult the Reprobate – killed his family a while back and causes no end of trouble everywhere he goes. He is almost impossible to kill, or we would have done so already. He took a potion he got from Avidora that made him almost indestructible. It is said that his skin is almost as tough as that of the Grustabist."

"I have heard of him. Is he near here? Are any of them near here?" asked Tall Sky.

"They are days away to the southeast, but each group travels at its own speed. They're a nasty lot. Stay vigilant. We have come ahead of them to warn others. And Tall Sky, they have something to do with the slave trade," said Quickturn. "I want to talk to Beldock as well." Tall Sky motioned for Beldock to come over. "Beldock, I want you to know that there is some serious movement of Bitters heading your way. They are only several days away and they are causing great trouble on their way. You need to set sentries and be vigilant and ready to fight. I've been meaning to ask you about that weapon you're carrying. Would you show it to me?"

"Sure," said Beldock. "This is a hooked sword that is good for catching a sword, sliding down the handle, and inflicting injury or reaching it around a man's neck from behind and pulling it toward you almost severing his head from his shoulders. This is a punch dagger that you wear on your hand. It's very good for close combat."

"Thanks for showing me," said Quickturn

Just then, Melody's dragon Daisy woke and made a mewing sound. She looked at the bread and cheese on the table, crawled down and had dinner. Again, Melody gave the little dragon some water in a saucer. Elise thought this was great fun and put her face right up to it. The dragon responded by rubbing its face on Elise's cheek. Then it crawled back up Melody and took its perch on her shoulder.

"Let's head on over to my place," Laskron said. He carried Elise and they left through the kitchen to pick up the food. "We live very close to here." Laskron led his guests next door where there was a house with a block building out back. The interior of the house was spacious. He showed them two rooms they could sleep in and told them to deposit their things and come back to the sitting room where they could visit. In the meantime, Laskron put Elise to bed. She wanted Liadra to say goodnight, so Liadra came to her and told her of a butterfly that sat on a little girl's finger talking to her about blue skies and flowers. At night the butterfly slept on the girl's pillow to keep her company. Elise said, "Like Daisy." Elise turned over and fell asleep.

Laskron said, "You are good with her. She really likes you."

"Yes, and I love her. I wish she were my daughter," said Liadra without thinking.

Laskron said, "That is a wonderful compliment. She is very special to me."

Laskron showed them some items that he made in his shop. "People like to buy glass bottles to put liquids in and colored vases for flowers. Here are some drinking glasses that I made. You see, there are pretty glass balls that you can use to keep paper from blowing away. Sometimes I take colors and swirl them together like this one. It is very hot work, but I really like it. Sometimes a customer will want a window of glass so that they can have outside light without rain coming in. I will show you my shop tomorrow."

"Laskron, has there been any bad activity or trouble from the foreign visitors here?" asked Tall Sky.

"Just the usual spats among the locals, but everyone is on edge and suspicious because of the strangers in town. Beldock and I listen to their conversations to detect any plots or underhanded dealings, but they mainly talk about their families back home, or about their politics. They also discuss what is being sold at auction and at Malwood Market. I find it difficult to listen to talk about the selling of people. It makes me want to punch them, but I have my little girl to worry about. She needs me to stay safe to take care of her. Still, I wish there was something that could be done about it," said Laskron.

"Has Beldock talked to the army about it?" asked Tall Sky.

"He has, but the army has been busy with border skirmishes between Gullandia and Aksanda. They want our land for grazing for their reindeer and they attack our farmers south of the mountains, so the army hasn't been in this area," said Laskron. "I've heard about the disappearances of children in other areas, and I've wondered about a connection to the auction." He looked at his own little girl and thought that if the slavers ever took her, he would tear them apart with his bare hands. "It is time to get together a local militia and ride to the auction and free whatever slaves are there. I'll ask Beldock if he knows some military men like himself who would be willing to do that."

"Good idea," said Tall Sky, "and I will be happy to go with the militia and help with that."

Everyone said that it was time for bed and went to their respective rooms. When the girls had settled down in their room, they just had to talk before going to sleep. "So much happened today," said Liadra. "I just love Elise, and isn't her father dreamy? He's so nice and handsome. It's too bad about his wife dying. A little girl should have a mother."

"And you would like to be her mother, wouldn't you?" teased Melody.

"I don't know….maybe," said Liadra. "So what if I do? She's a perfectly behaved, adorable little girl and she likes me."

"She's not a pet like my dragon, you know. She's a person who needs a lot of care, and teaching, and love. Well, I guess you know about that because of taking care of your brothers." said Melody.

"That's right, except this child is so different from them. I want her alright," said Liadra.

"But what if he goes to fight with the militia? He sounded pretty interested in that," said Ella. "My husband went with the army and didn't come back."

"But this isn't the army. It's just a local militia, and he should only be gone overnight," argued Liadra.

"Are you willing to take on the responsibility of Elise no matter what?" asked Ella.

"Yes. Definitely," said Liadra..

Melody put Daisy on her pillow next to her and everybody went to sleep, thinking of their favorite men.

The next morning they were awakened by an excited Elise announcing that it was time for breakfast and pulling covers off of them. She had never had visitors before, so this was like a party. The girls put on their regular clothes and headed for the kitchen. Ella made eggs, ham and sliced bread with jam. The men smelled aromas of food and hurriedly got dressed and joined the girls at the table. "This looks good. It's nice to have women in the house," Laskron said, smiling at Liadra. She thought, "I love you," and smiled back.

Tall Sky and Melody were feeding her dragonette, "Isn't she cute? Look at how she gulps down the little pieces of ham. She likes the bread and jam, too. What a little darling," said Melody.

"You're the little darling," said Tall Sky, "And the dragon, too."

"When are you going to free the slaves? Will you have many men with you? Will you all be riding horses? Will you have spears and stuff? Is it going to be dangerous? Are you going?" asked Melody in her flustered way.

"We have to get the men together first. We may leave tonight, armed and riding horses," replied Tall Sky. "Laskron, after breakfast let's go to the inn and speak to Beldock." Trag remembered the auction. He hated how they treated young people like animals and auctioned them off. He remembered the beautiful girl with tears running down her sweet face and he got mad. Something like iron was forming in him. He was determined to go with them.

"Steben go too," Steben said standing up. The four men left the table to go to the inn next door.

At the inn, the five men devised a plan and made a list of men who were good fighters. Although Trag had no knowledge of fighting, he could sneak around taking one horse at a time into the woods and tie them there. Trag was also strong, having worked on his Aunt's farm all his life. Hopefully the men would be drunk making it easy to confuse them and to fight them. Tall Sky and Steben would visit Rando at Home fire and entice him to join their militia for a raid on the Malwood Market. With a large group and much loot to be had, Rando would be hard pressed to say no. He and his men would meet their needs for a long time with a take like that. They were free men and they hated the slavers, so this would be a chance to do what they do best. The slaves in the caged area would be easy to release with Tall Sky's help. The ones who had already been purchased would have to be taken from their owners' tents. Trag hoped that the girl he saw being auctioned off would still be there unharmed. He said a silent prayer for her.

Beldock sent away his boarders saying that his wife Mina wasn't feeling well. He closed the inn and was off to round up the militia. Tall Sky and Steben took off on horseback toward Home Fire. Liadra stayed at Laskron's to watch Elise. Mina, Amidra and Vela set about preparing food for the entire group. Trag carried beer and wine and potatoes up from the cellar. He also moved the tables into a circle and set the tables with plates and silverware. Laskron gathered weapons and set them in a corner of the inn. The plan was in motion.

So much depended on getting Rando's help. The extra men and their expertise in fighting the slavers would be invaluable. Within the hour, they met two of Rando's men out hunting. The men recognized Tall Sky and Steben and accompanied them to Home Fire. Rando immediately saw the advantages of this plan and wanted in. He would have exclusive rights to the loot and would be able to kill slavers with the help of more men. This was a good plan. Rando left the common traveler alone, but he had no qualms about killing slavers and robbing them. That's how he had acquired Vela and Steben. He was now very glad that he had saved Steben from the slavers long ago. He looked at Steben with the pride of a father, and he said, "Well done, Steben. You have grown into a man." He gave Steben a sword and gathered his men to tell them of their good fortune. "There is a battle to be won and treasures to be had! To your horses! We ride for Loadrel!" cried Rando.

At the inn preparations were almost ready. One by one the men had come in bearing a variety of weapons. They all had children and had wanted to clean up the auction to keep the slavers from threatening their own children. Stopping it at its source was their idea. All of the men on the list had responded favorably. With Rando,'s group, the place was filled. Mina and the girls brought out bowls of stew, bread, cheese, and mugs of ale. Jelsareeb, the baker, brought out sweet pastries and told them some sordid stories about beatings and rapes that she had overheard from the foreigners. She had learned enough of their languages to understand what they said. She was very happy that they were going to take out the slavers and their customers. She said that she was proud of them and wished them God speed. After the militia and Rando's men had their fill, Beldock laid out the plan for them. Late afternoon the brave hearted men rode toward Malwood.

THE PURGE OF MALWOOD

The group rode quietly, single file on a deer trail known to Tall Sky. They arrived at a thicket near the Malwood Market and tied their horses. From there, they walked up close to the market and sat down watching. People were drinking, laughing and talking about their purchases. There were many tents and booths scattered, but most of the tents were placed on the edge of the clearing. The militia waited until the fires were low and the men had gone to bed. It was time to strike. Trag followed Beldock and Tall Sky to the slave cage. Beldock sneaked up on the guard, and using his hooked sword from behind, he pulled it toward himself almost severing the guard's head. Tall sky entered the cage and told the slaves they were being rescued and to be silent. Tall Sky shielded them and led them to the thicket where they were told to wait for the rest.

Trag decided to check some of the tents. He went to a round tall tent and peaked under it. There was the lovely girl he had seen on the auction block. He grabbed a heavy stick, walked to the front of the tent and swung that club with all his might splitting open the head of the guard. He then untied the girl. They crawled under the back of the tent and he led her to the thicket. Tears were again streaming down her face. She hugged him and thanked him for saving her. "That's alright," he said. "I was Avidora's slave when I saw you auctioned off and taken to that tent. I got so mad at that I just had to do something about it. I want you to stay here while I bring more horses."

Rando himself killed Avidora. He lopped off her head with one swing of his sword and put it on a stake as a gruesome reminder. The real battle had begun. The guards were mainly mercenaries, hardened, trained, fighting men. They were well armed with swords and relished the idea of a good fight, but they were drunk. Rando's men were also good fighters and were well armed. They were fierce and conditioned to kill slavers. The militia was made up of farmers and fishermen, but they could fight and had the incentive of protecting their children. This made them a formidable group. Tall Sky helped by shining bright light into the guards' eyes especially when they were fighting fishermen. Beldock and Laskron fought next to each other so they could come to each other's aid if need be. Kroom and his friend Jaston fought near each other. Many of the militia fought in pairs.

There was a din of battle with swords clashing, and men yelling. Kroom threw a net over a guard and swung his gaff to puncture the guard's throat. He then helped Jaston with a particularly tough swordsman by throwing a net over the man. Kroom then plunged his sword through the man's side, piercing his heart.

The dandies who had come to the auction to abuse women were slain outright by Rando's men. Their satin clothing was now drenched in blood. Rando was matching blow for blow with one of the guards when another guard came up behind him ready to plunge his sword into Rando's back. Seeing this, one of Rando's men threw his spear through the guard's back and he went down yowling.

Laskron was attacked by a guard wielding a sword and he parried blow after blow until he was slashed on the left shoulder. As the guard pulled his sword back, Laskron lunged, burying his sword in the guard's abdomen. Another guard noticed that Laskron was wounded and moved in to finish the job. Beldock turned just in time and caught the guard's sword with his hooked blade, deflecting the direction of the guard's thrust, sliding his blade down the sword to cut off the man's hand. He then used his punch knife to pierce the guard's chest. Beldock helped Laskron back to the thicket where one of Rando's men bandaged his arm to stop the flow of blood.

Prelick Holdfast, a weaver without much experience in fighting, had chosen his targets well, but the heat of the battle overcame him and he turned to parry a guard's thrust. Prelick's sword flew through the air as the guard's sword punctured his heart. The tailor, who had been fighting alongside Prelick, swung his sword at the guard's back killing him instantly. The guard fell at Prelick's feet. Several of the freed male slaves grabbed swords and killed their owners. Then they continued killing slavers and their customers.

Trag continued leading horses out, while Rando's men were filling bags with loot. As the battle wound down, the militia searched every tent for bound slaves and freed them. Most of them were girls, who were frightened and confused. Trag and Steben rounded up the slave girls and led them to the thicket. The girls didn't need to stay there and watch the carnage. There were pools of blood, arms, legs, and heads all over the ground. The militia checked the dead for any of their own. They identified three men and loaded them onto a cart.

There were carts full of goods, food, and bags of silver, gold, and gems. There was too much for one group, so Rando's men took what they wanted and gave much to the militia and to the slaves. Determined to completely obliterate the market, they tore down the tents and the booths and tossed them into a big pile. They tore down the large cage which was made of wooden stakes tied together with twine and threw it onto the pile. Then they gathered the bodies and body parts, threw them on top of it and set fire to it. They even set fire to the cook's building. There were many injuries, and five men had fallen in the battle, but it was a total victory. They had slain every one of the slavers and their customers. The men were tired, but in good spirits. They sat down on some logs drinking wine and watching the fire burn. The slaves came back to join the group. They were relieved to be free and unafraid for the first time in weeks.

"This battle will hence be known as the Purge of Malwood!" cried Beldock. At that the group assembled horse drawn carts and slaves on horseback. They all rode single file toward the east. As they approached Loadrel, Rando turned his group to the north toward Home Fire.

LOADREL

If they weren't so tired, they would have felt happy or exultant, but they were all exhausted and just wanted to be home. When they arrived at the Laborer's Reward, they found all the lights on and a group of worried women ready to clean them, bandage them, and meet the slaves. Liadra, Amidra, and Melody had readied the rooms in the inn to accommodate the freed slave girls.

There was water in each room and fresh linens on the beds. First the girls sat down for refreshments. They had a snack of bread, cheese and apple slices with some ale. After this they were ushered up to their rooms. Some of the townswomen had donated nightgowns for the girls. They slept two per room. The boys went home with some of the militia. Not many questions were asked because of the late hour. Liadra was still up waiting for the men to come home. She was appalled at Laskron's condition and immediately set about getting together clean rags, soap and bandage material. She had bandaged her brothers' injuries many times and was familiar with what to do. Tall Sky and Trag helped him change clothes and get him into bed. Liadra cleaned his wound and bandaged it. She slept beside his bed in a chair all night.

Elise awoke first and looked into the girls' room for Liadra. She pounced on Melody and asked, "Where is Liadra?" The dragon woke and climbed up to the little girl purring and rubbing her face against Elise's face. Elise laughed and Melody awoke. They went looking for Liadra by Laskron's room. There was Liadra sound asleep in the chair beside Laskron's bed. He was awake and letting her sleep. "Daddy, your arm," said Elise. "Does it hurt?"

"Yes, it hurts, but it will get better. Do you want to help? Bring me some water," said Laskron. Melody poured a glass of water and gave it to him. Liadra woke up and went to his side to check his bandage. It was still bleeding some, so she washed it, put some ointment on it and bandaged it again. She then went to the kitchen and asked Vela for a plate of food for him. Vela was already up and cooking, so she made up a plate of breakfast food for him. Laskron was famished and ate every bit. "I would have been alright, you know…without you sleeping in the chair."

"I didn't know that. I thought you might develop a fever or wake up alone and in pain. I just wanted to make sure," said Liadra. "Come on, Elise. Let's go get some breakfast for you. I'll send Trag in to help you dress." After breakfast, they sipped tea and discussed last night's adventure. Melody and Trag took Elise next door to meet the new girls, so that Liadra and Laskron could talk.

Liadra said, "Can you talk about last night yet?"

Laskron said, "It was horrible. I'm so glad you were not there. The place was full of vile characters who really deserved death, but it was so awful to dispense that type of justice. We knew that we couldn't leave even one of them alive, so we kept fighting and killing them. It was inhuman and I can't even conceive of such a thing, but there I was in the middle of it. And it was so noisy with screaming and shouting and swords clashing. I hated it and there was no way out. Then I got wounded and thought I would surely be killed, but Beldock came to my defense. He killed the guard who was trying to kill me. There was blood everywhere. Beldock helped me back to the group of slaves in the woods where one of Rando's men bandaged me and I passed out for while. When I came to, they were throwing bodies on top of a pile of stuff and then they set fire to it. We were all so tired from it that we sat down on some logs, drank some wine and rested. We brought home a lot of goods to be shared. I dare say that you girls will be busy making clothes from all the material that we brought home. You will all have some jewelry and silver pieces. Later we will divide it among everyone."

Liadra said, "Thank you for helping to keep all of us safe. I really appreciate it. I'm sorry that you were wounded and I will do what I can to help you with that. You should probably get some sleep now."

Laskron went into his room and sat down. He really liked Liadra, but felt sad about his first wife. It had been years since her passing, but he had not tried to move on with his life. He spoke to her saying that he would always love her, but for his sake and for Elise's sake, he needed to move on. He told her about Liadra and how much she cared for their daughter. She would make a good mother for Elise. "Would it be alright if I moved on with her?" he asked. Just then he heard the beautiful tahilu bird sing and he felt that it was his wife letting him know that it was alright.

At the inn, everyone was sitting down to breakfast. There were happy voices and good aromas of food and aromatic tea. The girls could hardly believe their good fortune. Arinya, the girl that Trag had freed, was sitting with him and Elise sipping tea. Arinya was slight of build with dark eyes and hair. She had a fragile look about her as did Elise. Trag told her about his experience with Avidora and how Tall Sky had helped him to escape. She told him that the man who bought her was working for another man who wanted a virgin of her description. That is what saved her from being brutalized. All the girls wanted to see Melody's dragon, but the dragon wanted to remain on her shoulder and had a bunch of her red curls wound about with its tail holding on for dear life.

"Come, Culina, let's get some rest. There will be a dividing of the goods this afternoon before dinner. Then tonight there will be a party for the girls and the militia. They went to Laskron's house to take a nap, and found that Laskron and Liadra had the same idea. They were fully clothed, and sound asleep on Laskron's bed. Amidra and Steben were asleep in Steben's room, so they took the bed in the girls' room. Trag and Arinya put Elise down for a nap and decided to remain in the sitting room to get to know each other, but they too fell asleep.

They were awakened by a bell ringing at the Vision Hall down the street. Townspeople were gathering to say their farewells to the fallen militia men. Everyone went down to the Vision Hall to join the people there. Laskron would be saying the words of farewell. When everyone was seated, Laskron, his bandaged arm in a sling, walked to the front with Tall Sky to steady him. He said, "My brothers and sisters, we are here to say farewell to members of our town who gave their lives to keep our children safe. They were good men. They were brave men. They did well in battle killing many of the evil ones who sought to do harm to children. We are proud of them and we honor them. These we will see on the other side where we will all meet again. Creator of all, we ask that you will receive unto you these three men. We ask that their loved ones will be comforted and taken care of. We thank you for our lives, for our children, and for the provisions that you have given us. We thank you for your love and for your forgiveness. Amen." Tall Sky said, "The carts are lined up outside. They are loaded with goods taken from the Market. We will all meet back here for division of these goods. The widows will receive their husbands' shares. Now we will carry these three to their resting place." Everyone filed out of the building and walked to the cemetery. At the cemetery they sang the song of parting and put a small remembrance in the coffins. Then everyone returned to the Vision Hall.

At the Vision Hall, bags were opened and the goods were divided among the militia men, their widows, and the freed slaves. This was done quickly, quietly, and respectfully. They had learned that what truly matters in life are not things, but your loved ones, your family, and your friends.

Liadra, Amidra, Melody, and Vela waited at the inn, taking care of Elise and helping Mina with preparations for the party that night. Vela helped Mina with the cooking and Liadra played with Elise.

Melody and Amidra readied the dining area, setting the tables. Melody made a banner that said WELCOME HOME SOLDIERS and they hanged it above the kitchen door. They put a vase of flowers on every table, and put some colored cloth streamers hanging in every corner. When Beldock walked in, he was surprised and very pleased.

Some of the freed slave girls sat at the tables talking. Some of them stayed in their rooms to process what had happened to them. There was one girl who sat staring into space. She would say nothing. Melody led her upstairs to a room and brushed her hair. "I know what happened to you was very bad, but you will be alright. She took up a mirror and held it in front of the girl. You see that pretty face and that pretty hair? That's you and that girl went through a lot to be here. Many people died for you to be here. All the bad men are dead. They will never hurt you again. Do you have any injuries?" asked Melody.

"Feet," said the girl.

Melody looked at her feet. They were bruised and had cuts on them. Melody said that she would be back in a minute and brought Liadra to bandage them. Liadra helped to clean and bandage the girl's feet and told her to lie down for a while. She then checked the feet of the other girls and bandaged them when necessary. Then she told Mina that some of the girls were injured and Mina sent for a midwife to check them for more of the unseen types of injuries. The midwife checked them and found most of them to be unharmed, but several of them needed stitches. "Whoever marries these girls will have to be very gentle with them. They will be afraid of men for a while," the midwife said.

The girls were given soft socks to wear for the evening. Their spirits all lifted when the guests arrived and the food was served. Mina had hired extra help for the evening so that she and Beldock could enjoy the festivities. She wanted Elise to have a babysitter, but Liadra wouldn't hear of it.

Liadra and Laskron were sitting against the wall next to the fireplace. Liadra said, "I missed you when you were gone and I was worried. I kept praying for you to be safe. I didn't think that God would take you from your little girl. I told Him that if anything did happen to you, I would take care of her for you."

He put his arm around her and said, " I'm so glad you came into my life. You have already made me feel whole again. You make me happy just being with you."

"Laskron, I am so proud of you for talking at the Vision Hall today. You could have stayed home. Nobody would have blamed you," said Liadra.

"I wanted to get you something special to wear tonight," said Laskron. He pulled out a box with a lovely, multi-colored necklace in it and fastened it around her neck. I wanted to thank you for helping to take care of me and Elise. We three need more time to get to know each other better before making any type of plans, but I hope that you won't be leaving any time soon. With that they kissed and those watching applauded. This evening was getting off to a great beginning. Elise was delighted and wanted to sit on Liadra's lap.

Soon everyone was eating sumptuous stew and drinking ale. Jelsareeb brought cakes and pastries for dessert. She brought a wall hanging that Prelick had made and showed it to the group. They applauded. Everyone had liked Prelick and they were wearing clothing made from his materials.

Beldock stood and said, "Yesterday's deeds were brave and true. The battle was won. The slaves were freed. These young people were torn from their homes to serve the purposes of evil men who hurt them for no good reason. The battle was a horror to the good men of our militia and I am proud to call them friends. You fought as well as the soldiers I fought with in the army. None could have done better. Now, let's to the merriment!

"I know some lazy soldier jokes," said Minson who was always at the ready with something cheerful.

"I know some of those," said Bondrel, who had also been in the army.

Beldock said, "We will have a contest, and the last man with a joke will win free dinner tomorrow! The two of you sit up here. Minson, you begin."

"I know a soldier who was so lazy that after he ate, he expected someone else to do his defecating for him!" said Minson.

"I knew a soldier who was so lazy that when he raised his spear at the ready, he expected someone else to push the point of the spear into the enemy," countered Bondrel.

"I knew a soldier who was so lazy that we gave up trying to wake him in the morning, so we carried his bed roll over to the parade field to stand inspection for him," said Minson.

"I knew a soldier who was so lazy that when he was wounded, his blood refused to come out!" said Bondrel.

"I knew a soldier who was so lazy that he dropped his knife down the cliff hoping the rocks would sharpen it," said Minson.

"I knew a soldier who was so lazy that he would laugh hard on the first day of each month and make that count for every joke he would hear until month's end," said Bondrel.

"You think you know lazy soldiers? I knew a soldier so lazy that by the time he fastened his cloak. It was spring again!" said Minson.

"I knew a soldier so lazy that, when he yawned, the wind changed direction," said Bondrel.

"That's nothing! I knew a soldier so lazy that he wouldn't even grow older on schedule and the Bright Elves mistook him for one of theirs!" said Minson.

"The winner is Minson!" yelled Beldock. Everyone applauded.

At that, Sention pulled out his flute and played a happy tune.

Melody and Tall Sky were cuddling in a corner with Daisy curled up on her bosom taking a nap. "I'm so happy," said Melody. "But I can't help thinking that those girls are going to need to talk to someone about what happened to them. One of the girls couldn't even talk. She just kept staring at nothing. They need to know that they will be alright and that they are really safe now."

"I know," said Tall Sky. "We will take them to the Vision Hall tomorrow for a talk. I will ask Laskron and Vela to help." Melody and Tall Sky decided to leave and go next door to talk more about the matter. In fact all of the men were tired and they thanked their host and left. Just before leaving, Tall Sky spoke to Beldock to let him know about his plans for tomorrow.

Back at Laskron's, Tall Sky told Vela and Laskron what he planned to do at Vision Hall tomorrow. They thought it was a good idea to counsel with the girls before they built up feelings of hate and self loathing. So far the girls had been busy getting to know each other and just trying to get from one day to the next. But when the reality of what they went through really sets in, there could be a variety of unpleasant repercussions. Melody already tried talking to one girl with minimal results. Trag made friends with Arinya, and she seemed very happy with him. She responded well to his kindness and caring and he would never forget her tears. He wanted so to make her feel safe and loved.

With everybody home at Laskron's and the group tired from the day's activities, they all went to bed for a well deserved rest. The girls just had to chat a bit before dropping off to sleep. "Liadra, you got such a pretty necklace from Laskron."

"Yes, it is. He just wanted to thank me for helping with Elise," said Liadra. She smiled and said, "Then he kissed me."

Melody said,"That's good. Amidra, how are you and Steben getting along?"

"Just fine," said Amidra. "I love for him to hold me. He wants to build me a house. He says we will have horses and chickens and babies. We will grow food in a big garden. I think that we should try to find his mother first. That way he can stop worrying about her."

"Good idea," said Melody. "Tall Sky and I will help. Trag could help, too, but he is kind of involved with Arinya right now. Of course, we wouldn't leave right away. We are going to have some talks with the girls who the militia rescued and make sure they're alright before we go anywhere."

"Don't forget me," said Vela. "Beldock is going to talk to the army about my husband to find out where he is and see if he could come home. If he is already home, I could go home to be with him and the children. Now we should all get some sleep. Tomorrow I will see what clothes can be made of the material s that the militia brought home."

Daisy was already curled up on some of Melody's red curls softly purring.

Morning came early with Elise pulling off Liadra's covers and petting the baby dragon on Melody's pillow. She then sat in the middle of the floor telling everyone what a sunny day it was and how much fun they could have. "Okay, we're awake," said Melody sleepily. They went to the kitchen and had tea and pastries for breakfast. "Jelsareeb sure makes good rolls." They all agreed.

The men were not so easily pleased. Laskron said, "Let's go over to the inn and see what Mina is cooking. Besides, we have to talk to them about the Vision Hall meeting."

"Great idea," said Trag. The three men showed up for breakfast at the inn. "Now this is more like it, a hearty breakfast for men."

Beldock thought that Mina should explain the meeting to the girls. She would tell them that they were to discuss their future and their feelings about what happened to them. The girls would be able to ride to the Hall in a wagon because of their sore feet. Mina had no trouble in convincing them to go to the meeting. Tall Sky, Laskron, Melody, Jelsareeb and Vela went over to the Vision Hall first to get the chairs in place. They were arranged in groups of four to encourage close conversation.

First, Tall Sky addressed the group. "I'm pleased to see you today. This is an important time in your lives. It is a time for you to reflect on your experiences and to form an idea of what you would like for your lives to be like in the future. Sounds easy enough, doesn't it? Well, it isn't. My girl Melody is here because she chose to run away. You did not choose to be here. You were stolen from your homes and forced to walk to Malwood Market where you were or were about to be sold to the highest bidder. You did not know what was going to happen to you. You were afraid. Some of you were beaten, and some of you were raped, which is a violent crime. I want you to know that none of this is your fault. If a flower is stepped on, is it the flower's fault? No, it is not the flower's fault. It is the fault of the man who did not appreciate the loveliness of the flower as it was. There are many bad men in this world, but there are many more good men who marry, work hard, and raise children. You must not even think that all men are like the ones who stole you. They are not."

"I want you to consider, there were a great many evil men at the Malwood Market that day, but a greater number of good men cared about you enough to fight for you and some died for you in order to free you from the men who harmed you. Children mean a lot to good men. Freedom means a lot to good men. Nobody I know blames you for what happened to you. We just want you to be happy and cared for and safe. Now, we will talk in small groups so that each of you has the opportunity to be heard and to ask questions. Vela, Jelsareeb, Laskron and I with Melody will be seated among you to answer any questions and to help you to sort out your feelings." The girls paired up and sat with the various adults. There was talking and crying and hugging. Most of the girls wanted to go back to their families, but some wanted to stay in Loadrel.

On the way back to the inn, Tall Sky and Melody heard a commotion in front of the Laborer's Reward. A grustabist had come out of the water after what it thought would be easy prey. A three year old had gotten away from his mother Alma and was headed for the lake. Alma was calling to him, but the little boy did not see the danger. Melody remembered the comb that Vela used on her hair. It had come from a baby grustabist. Now she knew what a full grown one looked like. They were close to the water's edge at this point and, without thinking, Melody ran full speed toward it. Tall Sky shielded her as she swooped up the child and kept on running, Daisy holding on for dear life and screeching all the way. The little boy was fine, but Alma, threw up. Daisy hid under Melanie's hair peeking out to make sure the grustabist was nowhere near.

Beldock and some men at the Laborer's Reward heard the commotion and came running out armed with spears that Beldock kept behind the bar. Five men including Beldock fought the beast with spears. They couldn't get too near it. Swords would just bounce off the plated armor that was its skin. Laskron was the best marksman of the group. Even with an injured arm, he could throw a spear. Tall Sky went bright and the beast stood there with his eyes staring. Lascron aimed for the creature's eye and threw the spear with all his might. The spear flew true and hit its mark. It pierced the eye and the brain. The creature yowled and went down with a great thud. The men cleaned their prize. They built a fire with a spit mounted over it and roasted the meat. The women cooked vegetables, baked breads and pies and got ready for a picnic. They boiled the jawbones clean and hung them on the outside wall of the inn. They would make armored vests out of the plated skin of the grustabist.

Mina was kept busy that evening with customers drinking ale and talking about the day's activities. Several young men stopped by to inquire about the girls, and a few of the girls did want to meet them, so Beldock asked them upstairs to a room where they could meet and talk. Beldock told them to be very respectful and that he was acting like their father in this. They agreed. Beldock introduced them. Chan, Belrad, Pantor, these young ladies are Lindrel, Cally, and Lotus. They are here as my guests. Leave the door open. Vela will be seated right outside the door. Chan began by asking them about their homes. "Did you live on farms or in towns?" he asked.

Lindrel said, "We lived on farms with our families. We raised crops, and chickens. We had goats. I had a dog. I'm so glad she was in the house when the slavers came. I'm sure they would have killed her."

Cally said, "They took my horse too, but I got her back thanks to the brave men in your town. I am so impressed. I never knew there were men like you."

Lotus looked at Pantor and asked him if he was wounded in the fight. He said that he was, but it was just a cut. She touched his bandage and said, "I'm so sorry. I wish I could make it better." He blushed.

Pantor said, "I heard that you girls had cuts on your feet that had to be bandaged. Are you alright now?"

"We are getting better every day, and it helps to have pretty materials to make clothes from. It keeps us busy and gives us hope," said Lindrel.

Chan said, "You should have hope. You are young and there is a bright future ahead for you .... starting tonight."

"Are you planning on staying here, or will you be going back home?" asked Pantor. "Lotus, I sure would like for you to stay. I would like to take you on walks, and eat here at the inn. I would like to get to know you better. Would you come to my house tonight? My mother would like to meet you."

"I would like to meet your mother and thank her for raising such a brave man," said Lotus.

"Lindrel, I would like you to meet my family. Would come to my house tonight?" asked Chan.

Lindrel said that she would. Belrad asked Cally and she said that she would be happy to.

The couples left for their respective houses after telling Vela that they would be back after dinner.

The grustabist feast was getting underway with what seemed to be the whole town there setting up tables, blankets and lots of food. They had it set up on the lawn in front of the inn. It was a grand celebration. Beldock had told some of them to have one of the girls to join their family group. So when the girls came out, one by one they were led to a family to have dinner and fellowship. Beldock thought this would make them feel more at home and welcome.

Tall Sky was proud of and angry with his little Culina, who charged the Grustabist and saved the little boy. Tall Sky said, "How could you do this? You could have been killed. You promised to be more careful. And your little Daisy was so terrified, I'm surprised that she didn't jump down and run away."

"I did my best. I couldn't just leave that little boy to be eaten by the Grustabist! It seemed like the only thing to do at the time. I've always been a fast runner. I can outrun a cat," Melody said.

Tall Sky touched her hair and said, "This is my little Culina who was afraid of a bad dream in the cave. This is my little heroine who runs at a beast to save a child. God's Spirit has made you bold and strong, Culina. I love you."

Melody smiled and said,"I love you, too." "Melody, have you thought about the fact that you and I will not age at the same rate? If we stay together, you will eventually grow old and I will not. Will this bother you? Your aging will not make me love you any less, but will you keep on believing that I will always love you even as you grow older?"

Melody said, "I will try to keep on believing you. Tall Sky, you are so truthful, of course I would believe you." They kissed and held each other until the fear in them subsided and happiness reigned once more.

"Look, Melody! Vela helped me to make my very first dress. Isn't it pretty?" Amidra said, twirling around. "Vela's showing all of us how to sew. You should come tomorrow and learn how to sew. It's really fun to see a dress come together after you imagine what it should look like." Amidra's dress had a full, gathered skirt, a laced bodice, and puffy sleeves. It was made of a blue, silken material.

"It's beautiful," said Melody. "Sure, I'll give it a try, but I want green material to match my eyes and Daisy's eyes."

Two of the young men who were liberated by the militia sought out Beldock to speak with him about marriage. "Beldock, we understand that you are the acting father for these girls. We would like to marry and stay here in Loadrel. We got to know several of the slave girls and want to marry them. I would like to buy Prelick Holdfast's home and operate his business. Nina says that she will help and that she knows how to alter clothing, too," said Garoc.

"I would like to be a fisherman, and my girl Celia says that we can hire someone to help us build a nice little house right here in town. What do you say to that, Beldock?" asked Torry.

"I think that it's a fine idea. When do you want to get married?" asked Beldock.

"The girls just finished making pretty dresses, and they want to be married soon. We all really like it here," said Torry.

"I'll talk to Laskron about it. He may be able to marry you at the Vision Hall tonight after the picnic," said Beldock. He went looking for Laskron and found him with Liadra and Elise. Laskron was pleased with getting four of the rescued youngsters settled down and agreed to do the ceremony after the picnic. Other men at the picnic had spoken with him about seriously courting the girls. All in all, Beldock was pleased and proud of his town.

There was a particularly young girl, only twelve years of age, named Lystra who was supping with the Brindels. They asked her to come to their house for a while. They took her to their home and showed her a nice room all decorated for a girl. "We lost our child and we would love to have you come to stay with us and be our little girl," said Mrs. Brindel. "I know that you lost your parents, and we thought you would rather have a home than to be working for others as you were doing. We like you and think that you are fine young lady."

Lystra cried and said she would love to be their daughter. "This is the greatest day of my life," Lystra said. They all went to tell Beldock the good news and to get Lystra's things.

Beldock announced to the crowd the weddings and the adoption to be held at Vision Hall after the picnic. There was a loud applause. Nina and Celia went back to the inn to get ready for their weddings.

After cleaning up after the picnic, many of the people went home to get ready to attend the weddings and the adoption. They all brought gifts for the couples. There were household things and some used clothing that their own children had outgrown, including coats and scarves for the winter.

The weddings were lovely with Laskron presiding. "Marriage is a serious thing to be entered into solemnly. It entails love and work. You must be patient with each other and kind to each other. When hard times come, as they must, turn to God for guidance. I will be here for you or another like me will. Garoc, would you please place a ring on Nina's finger, and Torry, would you please place a ring on Celia's finger? Nina, are you sure this is what you want to do?" She nodded yes. "Celia, are you sure this is what you want to do?" She nodded yes. "Garoc, you may speak to your bride."

Garoc said, "Nina, when I first saw your blue eyes, I almost fainted, and when I saw one of the guards hit you, I wanted to pick you up and rush you out of there. I am so happy that we are safe and that I can marry you and keep you safe and happy."

Nina said, "Garoc, I will love you and respect you and help to take care of you all my life."

"Torry, you may speak to your bride," said Laskron.

Torry said, "Celia, I give you my heart. I will always love you and defend you from evil."

Celia said, "I will honor you and be kind to you and help you in any way that I can. I love you."

Laskron said, "Behold your husband and behold your wife. You may sit down. Will Lystra and the Brindels please come up here? We have another happy occasion this evening. The Brindels are adopting Lystra. All we have to do is sign the papers and here they are. In these papers you promise to love her and take care of her giving her proper guidance and bringing her to Vision Hall for worship." The Brindels signed the papers. "There are gifts on the tables in the back. Congratulations to all." After the gifts were opened and thanks given, the couples went back to the inn. All of the girls helped carry the gifts for the happy couples.

Melody kept looking at Tall Sky wishing they could be sleeping together tonight. They went back to Laskron's with Trag and Arinya, and Amidra and Steben. Liadra and Laskron went to the inn to toast the happy couples. Then they headed for home.

Everybody was tired. It had been a long day full of special events. Liadra and Laskron put Elise to bed and then they joined the others in their rooms. As usual, the girls had to chat a bit before going to sleep. "Wasn't the wedding great?" said Melody. "It made me think about saying those things to Tall Sky."

"I know, I kept looking at Steben and wondering what it would be like being married," said Amidra.

Liadra sighed. "I know that Laskron and I will be married, but I don't want to wait very long. We talked about going to my parents' home to get married, but that is a long trip for Elise, and there could be dangers. I don't want to leave her behind, because if something happened to us, she would be all alone in the world. I just think it would be better to send a messenger to my parents inviting them to come here for the wedding. At least they would know that everything is okay."

Vela said, "You know that I am a mother. If it was explained to me that way, I could accept it, and I would probably attend the wedding here. It is not unheard of. Many people travel to attend weddings. It's like a vacation."

"That's what I'm going to do," said Liadra. "I'm going to go tell Laskron."

"Don't be gone too long," said Melody. Everyone laughed.

Laskron was still awake. "Laskron, I've been talking it over with the girls, and I think that I want to get married right here at Vision Hall. We will send a messenger with a letter to my parents and ask them if they can come here for the wedding. They need a vacation anyway, and my aunt can watch the boys. My uncle is strict and that would be good for the boys. Oh, please say yes. I don't want to leave Elise here. She's too young and she would be afraid. She is too little to make the trip with us, so it just makes sense to stay here with her and have my parents come to see us. What do you think?"

Laskron replied, "I think that I'm engaged to a very smart woman. It's a wonderful idea. I love it, and I love you. He pulled her down to him and kissed her a long, soft kiss and said, "Now off with you before your friends wonder what we're up to." She went happily off to bed.

"Well, what did he say?" asked Melody.

"He said it was a wonderful idea and that I'm smart," said Liadra. "Now let's get some sleep."

Daisy curled up on the pillow putting her head on Melody's red curls and purred softly as Melody went to sleep.

The next morning a messenger arrived with news about Vela's husband. The messenger had crossed the King's River and had ridden sixteen hours to Loadrel. He said that Vela's husband Rusken had been located with the army near the Aikasse Mountains to the north. He had completed his tour of duty and could be discharged when he wanted. Vela was overjoyed. "I can see him again! When can we go? I can hardly wait. I hope he's okay," said Vela.

Tall Sky said, "We planned to go with you. Let's talk to the others. Amidra and Steben are next door having breakfast. Melody, let's go have breakfast at the inn."

Amidra and Steben were seated with Beldock at a corner table next to the fireplace. "Great news, Beldock," said Tall Sky. "Did the messenger say how Rusken is?"

Beldock replied, "Rusken is healthy, but tired of the army and wants to go home. He doesn't want to miss Vela, so he will wait there for her. He knows that she will not be traveling alone. He thanked us in advance for bringing her. I would like to accompany you. I can get Kroom to watch the inn for a week or so. It would give me a chance to see some of my old friends, and I think an extra man might come in handy if there was any trouble."

"When do we start?" asked Vela.

"Well, first we need to talk to the girls and see if any of them live north of here and want to go with us to their homes," said Beldock.

"Not all of them want to stay here and get married. Some of them have boyfriends back home."

"Yes, and some of them are too young for marriage and need their families," said Vela.

"We also have to pack supplies and clothing – enough for about two weeks," said Tall Sky. "Trag, will Arinya want to come with us or stay here?"

"I don't know. She might not feel comfortable leaving here so soon after traveling so much already. I'll go ask her," said Trag. Arinya came down the stairs and waved to the group. "Arinya, we have a question for you. We are all going on a journey to the Aikasse Mountains to take Vela to meet her husband. He has been in the army for years and is ready to go home. How do you feel about going with us? It may take two weeks of riding horseback and camping out most of that time. Or you could stay here at the inn and wait for us to come back."

"Two weeks is a long time to be alone here. I would rather go with you, Trag," said Arinya.

"Okay, let's get packed," said Beldock. "We leave as soon as everyone is ready. Mina will get our food ready and I will saddle the horses and talk to Croom about managing the inn. Arinya, would you talk to the girls and find out how many live north of here and want to go home?"

"Sure, I'll do that right now and I'll get packed," said Arinya.

By lunchtime all preparations were done and farewells were in order. Four of the former slaves, two girls and two boys, were going with them. Word had gotten around town about the adventure, and two more military men wanted to join Beldock for protection and to meet with their former comrades in arms who were fighting near the Aikasses. The party of fourteen rode out of town after lunch taking the road north toward Home Fire.

Since she was practically born on horseback, Daisy was perfectly contented to sit on Melody's shoulder purring and chirring in her ear. Melody was delighted to be on another adventure with Tall Sky. For her part, Arinya would have liked to be riding in Trag's vest pocket, but she settled to ride her horse next to Trag's. Vela was so excited that she rode up front with Beldock. Amidra and Steben rode next to each other talking and laughing. The former slaves rode behind them and Beldock's friends brought up the rear as a guard.

The sun was low in the sky when they reached Home Fire. Rando met them and welcomed them to his fire. "What brings you here, my friends?" asked Rando.

Beldock said, "We are headed to the Aikasse Mountains to deliver Vela to her husband and to return these abductees to their homes. We have a gift for you, Rando. Steben, get that slab of meat off the horse."

Steben brought a large slab of meat, gave it to Rando, and said, "Grustabist meat for you."

"Ho!" said Rando. "Did you kill this, Steben?"

"No. Lascron kill. Threw spear. Right in the eye," said Steben laughing.

"We also brought you a keg of ale," said Beldock.

The group sat around the fire with Rando's people and had dinner. "Beldock, tell me what happened with this grustabist killing," said Rando.

"Tall Sky, you tell it. You were part of it," said Beldock.

Tall Sky stood up to tell his story. "We had just had a wedding at the Vision Hall where two rescued slave couples were married and we were walking back to the inn when we heard a lot of screaming. A large grustabist had come onto shore after a three year old boy. Melody saw this and ran toward the grustabist as fast as she could. I immediately shielded her so that the beast could not see her, and I followed her. If it wasn't so dangerous, it would have been funny. Picture this. Melody running toward the beast, her red curls bouncing in the wind, and on her shoulder, Daisy with her head up screeching in terror. She grabs the boy and runs off with him. I became bright, stunning the monster long enough for Laskron to throw a spear into its eye and brain. There was all this meat to dispose of, so we had a picnic right there. You can see the jawbone of the beast hanging on the wall of the inn right under the Laborer's Reward sign."

Tall Sky sat down to a din of applause and shouts. "'Tis a brave tale indeed and we thank you for the meat and for ridding our waters of a murderous grustabist," said Rando.

Melody said worriedly, "Tall Sky, was I really funny?"

Tall Sky replied, "Culina, you truly delighted me with what you did, and yes, it was funny for a moment, but when it set in just how much danger you were in, I could have cried. I love you so much." Tall Sky kissed her tenderly, and there was yet another applause. Then all the couples kissed and hugged and drank more ale. It was a great celebration.

After a while, everyone went to their tents. Vela slept in her own tent with the two former slave girls. The boys slept in the hospitality shelter that the girls used on their first visit to Home Fire. Steben and Amidra slept in their blanket rolls close to the remains of the fire. Melody cuddled up to Tall Sky with Daisy on her pillow.

Trag and Arinya slept next to each other for the first time. "Trag, I'm so glad I came with you. It feels so good to be cuddled up next to you."

Trag kissed her and caressed her hair and said, "I love you, Arinya. Would you marry me when we get back? We could go to live near my aunt's house, or we could stay here in Loadrel if you like."

"Trag, I would love to marry you, and either place is fine with me as long as I'm with you," Arinya said.

Trag thought, "And that makes four."

A very happy group of campers slept peacefully until the morning. Vela rose early to help make breakfast. There were more people than usual, so several of Rando's group also helped. They made eggs, honey cakes, and smoked meat. It was a good hearty breakfast that would keep them going for a long ride north. "Rando, this was really a good time," said Beldock. "I look forward to seeing you again."

"Home Fire will always welcome you. We are friends. Take good care of Steben for me," Rando said, patting Steben on the back. "Vela, I hope all goes well with you and your husband. We will miss your cooking and your sewing. Maybe you will find your children, too."

The group mounted their horses and rode north in the following line up, two by two: Beldock and Vela, Tall Sky and Melody, Steben and Amidra, Trag and Arinya, the four abductees, and Beldock's friends. They also had several pack horses and several extra horses. It was a good sized group. The girls were dressed like men to lessen any curiosity from other travelers. The condition of the road wasn't bad, but it was just a dirt road with trees growing along each side of it with intermittent breaks of grassland.

They had been riding for about three hours when they noticed a suspicious little group over to the left, keeping off the main road. Beldock and his two friends Salek and Parin rode over to check it out. "Hello fellow travelers," said Beldock. "What do we have here?" Two men had three young girls tied together and being led on a tether. One of the rough looking characters said, "Taking 'em to the slave market, we are. We'll let you have 'em for twenty pieces of silver each right now, save us the trouble and we can find some more." That was the last thing the slavers ever said.

Beldock took the slavers' silver and gave it to the girls. "We're taking you home," Beldock said. He led the girls up to the horses. "Can you ride?" Beldock asked. Two of the girls said they could ride, but one who was only about six years old said that she couldn't. "That's okay, you can ride with Amidra." Amidra put her arms around the child and said, "Are you okay?"

The little girl looked at Amidra, smiled and said, "I'm okay now."

They came to a stream flowing out from the mountains with cold, clear water and Beldock called out, "We take a rest here!" Everyone dismounted, watered the horses, and took out some of the provisions like bread, cheese and apples. The new girls were famished, not having eaten since yesterday when they were captured. They thanked Beldock and kissed him on the cheek. He blushed and said that he was happy to be of service. Amidra said, "So, little one, what is your name?"

"My name is Emmy," she said. "I am an orphan. I stay in the barn and work in the house for my food. Sometimes, when I am done with my work, I go out in the field and think about what I want to do when I grow up and pick flowers. That's how those mean men got me. They pretended to ask directions to the nearest village and then they grabbed me and tied my wrists and led me away. I screamed, but nobody heard me. I'm so glad that you found me. I could hardly walk another step." Amidra studied her. She had blonde hair down to her shoulders, a little rounded nose with freckles sprinkled across her nose and cheeks. Her eyes were olive green with flecks of gold.

Amidra said, "Come here." She hugged Emmy and wiped her face clean with a hankerchief. Steben was watching this and said, "Our child. We keep her." Amidra's eyes widened, and she smiled happily.

"You're going to keep me? Oh boy! They're going to keep me! I'm going to have a home and parents and everything!" Emmy jumped up and down and hugged Amidra and Steben. Just like that, a new family was born.

The other two girls said that they came from families just about an hour's ride away. They were also grateful for being rescued from the slavers.

Beldock said, "Time to go. Let's get these two girls back to their families." With that, they all mounted up and rode on until the girls pointed out a farm that was theirs. They rode up and Beldock walked the girls up to the door and explained to their parents just what had happened. They were happy and relieved to have their children back. The father wanted to ride out and kill the slavers, but Beldock told him that his men already killed them. He also told him that the slave auction had been destroyed in Malwood.

"Would you like to bed down in the barn tonight?" asked the father. "It looks like it might rain."

"Now that you mention it, the clouds have been rolling in for a while now. What do you think, Tall Sky?" asked Beldock.

"Great idea," said Tall Sky winking at Melody. "I sure don't want to be out in the rain tonight with all these girls getting wet. We thank you, kind sir, for your hospitality."

The group dismounted, put their horses in the corral, fed them and rubbed them down. They made mats of hay and put their blanket rolls on them. The mother of the girls said she would make a pot of stew, and Beldock gave her a big chunk of grustabist to add to it. She also baked bread and pies. Beldock's group rested in the barn with their new little girl. She cuddled up to Amidra and fell asleep for a nap. So did Daisy who was quite done in by all this activity. "What an astonishing day," said Melody.

"I'm so happy," said Amidra. Steben kissed her. At dinner time they brought their bowls up to the house to get their food. They all sat around on the floor eating grustabist stew and bread and pie.

One of the girls said, "Tall Sky, the slavers told me that there was an elf who told him how to find us. You don't do that do you?"

"No, child. You must do what we call testing the spirits. Ask the elf to pray for you to be healed. A bitter elf will not be able to do it. He will probably make fun of the idea. You see, there are bitter elves who hate Father God and want to do harm to those who belong to Him. Children are one of their chief targets for this sort of thing. I am a Bright Elf who loves and serves God."

When the thunder started, they thanked the parents and ran for the barn. It was good that they stayed the night, for there was thunder and lightning and hard rain. The group was warm and cozy all cuddled up in the hay and their blankets. There was much hugging and kissing going on among the couples. As usual, Daisy cuddled up to Melody purring. They all went to sleep, warm and happy and full of good food.

By the next morning, the rain had stopped. Everyone got up and readied themselves for another ride. Emmy could hardly believe her good fortune. What the Bitter Elves meant for evil, Father God turned to good. They bid farewell to the farmers and their children and got an early start munching on bread and cheese on the way. Everyone was in good spirits and the sun warmed them on their way. The road was muddy, so they chose to ride in grassy areas as much as was possible.

Melody asked, "Tall Sky, is there an inn anywhere between us and the Aikasse Mountains where we might bathe?"

"Getting a bath for fifteen people at an inn might be difficult. This area has small villages and, now and then, a tavern with a few rooms. We might be better off bathing in the river even if it's cold. Do you think you could stand it, Culina?" asked Tall Sky.

"I bathed in Lake Perilough, and it was pretty cold. You kind of get used to the cold as you're bathing. How far is the river?" asked Melody.

"We could take lunch there and bathe. It won't be too long now. The water is clean and there are no animals in it. You know, I've been meaning to talk with you about Daisy. Her skin will suffer if you don't oil it, especially as she grows. She is a very special animal. I wouldn't recommend bathing her in cold water, though. We can wait until we can warm some water for her. I do have some fine oil that will work for her, so when we stop for lunch I want you to oil her," said Tall Sky.

"Sure I will," said Melody. "I will take care of my baby, won't I little sweetheart." Daisy rubbed her head against Melody's cheek chirring. Melody looked at Tall Sky and said, "It's true love."

Tall Sky said smiling, "It sure is, Culina, it sure is."

"How is my new little daughter doing?" asked Amidra. "Are you getting hungry yet?"

"No, Mama, I'm fine. It's fun to ride on the horse. It's so high up," Emmy replied.

"I'm so glad we have you. Now we're a real family. You can call Steben Papa now. I think he would like that. When we get to a place where we can buy clothes, we are going to buy some nice new clothes for you to wear. Maybe the next village will have some," said Amidra.

"New clothes? I've never had new clothes. I can hardly wait," said Emmy.

Trag and Arinya were talking about their wedding. Neither one of them wanted to wait a long time. Both of them wanted to stay in Loadrel. "I really like the people in Loadrel, and I like being in the town instead of out on a farm," said Arinya. "That way I can make friends, go shopping, walk near the water, have fresh fish to cook, and go to meetings at the Spirit Hall."

"Then that's what we will do. We will build a house, maybe raise some chickens, and I will open a store. I am not really the farmer type. I am happier working indoors," said Trag. "We will get married at Spirit Hall. We can ask your parents to come to the wedding. Do you want to get the house built first or get married and stay at the inn for a while?"

"I think that we should stay at the inn while we get the house built," replied Arinya. "I do need time to make some clothes. Of course, I could have that nice tailor to help me with that. We can have a big party at the Laborer's Reward."

The land was getting hilly with more of the evergreen trees and some pretty little flowers. The road had become more of a wide path now and was more rocky. They could hear the river flowing nearby and decided to stop for lunch and a bath. There was more foliage growing near the water's edge.

Bushes and tall reeds were there affording privacy for the girls. The girls got their cakes of soap and towels and proceeded to bathe. Tall Sky held Daisy for a while and fed her until she was contented to take a nap on his shoulder. There was much giggling coming from the water as the girls happily bathed in the cold water. The men bathed in another area also sheltered by bushes and reeds. Tall Sky waited until Melody was done and gave her some oil and the dragon. While he bathed, Melody oiled her little dragon. Daisy chirred, really enjoying this.

Lunch consisted of some berry wine and sandwiches of meat and cheese. It wasn't hot, but it tasted really good after riding all morning. Trag shared his news about getting married in Spirit Hall and staying in Loadrel. The soldiers were anxious to get to the battle front to see their friends. Beldock said, "We should be there by tomorrow afternoon barring any mishaps. You never know out here. This area is full of unseen dangers, especially as we approach the mountains. We should be going. Let's mount up."

Later that afternoon the group was riding up a rocky incline with a tree covered hill to the right and a steep drop-off to the left. Tall Sky sensed danger and told Beldock, who slowed the group to a standstill. He told Tall Sky and Trag to stay and guard the girls. The rear guard and Beldock rode around the hill and sure enough there were five bandits waiting with knives drawn ready to jump on the horseback riders. Beldock and the soldiers drew their swords and rode toward them shouting, "Death to the robbers!" The bandits, seeing soldiers with swords on horseback, ran toward their horses, but were too late. The soldiers slew them as they ran. Then they confiscated five horses and rode back to the group. In their saddlebags were bags of silver and gold pieces and blanket rolls with more food. All was distributed equally among the group members. Even Emmy was given her first pocket of silver.

The rest of the afternoon was uneventful as they rode up and down rolling hills toward their next campsite. "Over there would make a good campsite. It's off the path and high enough that we have a good view of the surrounding area. We'll make a campfire and have a hot meal for a change." There were some trees nearby with a cliff behind them. "We'll make a fire here. Men, let's gather wood for the fire." While the men gathered wood, the women readied blanket rolls, got out the cooking utensils, and fed the horses. They took out food for the meal and combined roots, smoked meat, and spices in a cooking pot. When the men returned, they made a fire. They drank some ale and waited for the stew to cook. Soon it was boiling and Vela put some flour in it to thicken it and also placed some flour balls in it to make dumplings. By the time it was ready, everybody was so hungry that they claimed it was the best stew they had ever eaten. Vela was a good cook with lots of practice, having cooked for Rando's group for ten years. Daisy had been dancing around on Melody's shoulder in excitement, so Melody put a little stew in a bowl and blew on it. The little dragon ravenously ate the stew and settled down on Melody's lap to take a nap.

The sun slipped down behind a hill giving a beautiful, rosy sunset stretching from the north to the south. Five elves rode up to the campfire. "May we share your fire and rest a while?" asked an elf. "We are tired and have been riding all day. Who is this little girl you have with you? She looks familiar." Steben stood up, arms akimbo, and said, "My daughter. You touch her, I tear you apart!" The elves stood back a few paces.

"Why do you ride to the Aikasse Mountains?" asked Beldock. "There are border skirmishes there."

"We are going to the dwarves to conduct some trading," said the elf.

"If that is so, where are your goods for trading?" asked Beldock.

"We don't need goods to trade with those filthy little beasts. We take what we want," said the elf.

Tall Sky stood up and said, "My brothers, come, sit down, and pray with us. Pray to Father God that we don't slit your throats!"

"Father God will not help us," they sneered. "We have all the power we need."

"I know He will not help you, evil ones," said Tall Sky, "but He will help us. Begone, you workers of iniquity!" Tall Sky grew very bright and walked toward them. They ran to their horses and galloped off.

"That was scary enough," said Arinya. "Is he always like that?"

"Pretty much," said Trag. "In the battle he used that brightness to blind the enemy so that inexperienced soldiers could be successful. It saved a lot of the militia men."

Beldock posted a guard to be replaced every three hours until dawn. Everyone slept near the fire for warmth. Melody cuddled up to Tall Sky and said, "I am so proud of you. You saved us. You are my hero." Daisy crawled up on Tall Sky and licked his cheek and settled down on his chest.

"And I am proud of you, Culina, for being so brave and quiet during that. I could feel you getting angry, but you held it in and did not attack them like you wanted to," said Tall sky. "You have grown, Culina. You are quite a woman." Melody felt all warm and happy inside and fell asleep in his arms. As she slept, Tall Sky took off her spectacles, and, covering her eyes with his hand, he prayed for healing. His hand glowed bright and the light awakened Melody.

"What are you doing? Everything got so bright." said Melody. "Where are my spectacles?"

"I think you will find that you don't need them anymore," said Tall Sky.

"You're right! I can see just fine!" exclaimed Melody. "Oh, thank you."

The morning brought a flurry of activity. They all knew that they would arrive at the base camp by afternoon. Vela was excited and hurriedly got out some breakfast food. They all agreed to eat on the hoof, so to speak. Within minutes they were ready and mounted. "Forward!" cried Beldock. Fourteen people and nine extra horses traveled single file toward the mountain range which they could see in the distance. Beldock rode around in a circle and stopped. He said, "I was wondering how you would feel about stopping at farms to see if we could purchase some supplies to take to the camp and to get Vela and her husband started when they get home. I know that a soldiers' camp is always in need of supplies, and we do have the money we collected from the slavers and the bandits. Everybody said, "Yes."

Tall Sky said, "This is a great idea. We will all need a good meal tonight and Melody and I plan to minister to the wounded. They will need prayer and healing. I know that it is important for Vela and her husband to have supplies right away when they reach their home. Maybe we could buy a wagon to put the supplies in and a cart for the happy couple. I also need to buy some supplies to trade with the dwarves. I know of several places we could stop, and, Steben, one of the farmers has several daughters. They may have some clothing we could buy for your daughter."

"Sounds like a good plan," said Beldock. "Let's go."

Beldock and Tall Sky led the group because they knew where every farm and settlement was. The farmers in the area were in need of cash to buy lumber and other things to make repairs, so they were happy to sell some of their grain, fruit, vegetables, cheese, and smoked meat. They bought a wagon at a blacksmith's business, and some clothes for Emmy. They were also able to get some chickens, goats, and pigs. Stopping at these places took some extra time, and they were traveling a bit slower, so they didn't arrive at the camp until late afternoon. They were met by a sentry who led them into the camp.

"Jaylek, my friend," said Beldock. "I've brought you some supplies. I'm sure that you can use some fresh food and seven horses." He showed Jaylek the supplies. Jaylek was amazed.

"We are almost out of food and you know how worn out horses get after awhile in the army," said Jaylek. He ordered some men to get the supplies and take care of the horses. He then showed the group to a place where they could sit near the fire and rest, and he went to get Vela's husband Rusken. Vela paced back and forth waiting. When Rusken walked up to the group, Vela threw her arms around him and kissed him. They sat down on a log by the fire and talked.

"Are the children okay?" Vela asked.

"The children are with your mother and they are fine. I didn't know where you were or even if you were alive or dead. How did you survive?" asked Rusken.

"I was taken by some slavers, but then Steben and Rando's men rescued me and gave me a job at their place called Home Fire. It's by Lake Perilough north of Loadrel where Beldock has an inn. I cooked and made clothing for them until three girls came to the camp and said that Steben and I could go with them to go home. Steben led us to this cave where we met up with Tall Sky and Trag. Trag had a bunch of gems that he had taken from Avidora, the witch, so we took them to the Malwod Market to sell them for silver pieces. Then we went to Loadrel and Beldock got in touch with Jaylek to see if you could come home."

Rusken sat there with his mouth open. "You knew Avidora? You went to Malwood Market? You have been busy lately and in danger!"

"Yes, I have, and that is not all. The Loadrel militia, led by Beldock, marched to Malwood Market, releasing the slaves and killing the slavers and their customers. Then they set fire to everything there. And there's more. They killed a grustabist."

"We've seen our share of action right here in the mountains. I'm really tired of it. I've wanted to go home for a long time now. What is Avidora like?" asked Rusken.

"I really don't know. You'll have to ask Trag. He was her slave for a while." said Vela.

"Trag, what was Avidora like?" asked Rusken.

"She was the meanest, nastiest female I ever saw. She muttered to herself all the time about what she was going to do to everybody.

Once a slave aggravated her and she had the guards feed him to the bushy bears. The poor guy shrieked as they tore him apart. I had to sleep chained to a wall in the kitchen. She made me work all the time, and she would punch you, kick you, pinch and slap you, and when she was really mad, she would whip you. I was so glad when Tall Sky rescued me," said Trag.

"So where is she now?" asked Rusken.

"Rando killed her. The only thing left standing in Malwood Market is Avidora's head mounted on a stake," said Trag. At that the dinner bell rang and everybody formed a line to get some food. They had stew and bread and ale. There was enough for everybody to have their fill.

Tall Sky looked at Jaylek and said, "The wounded. Where are they?"

"They are in that tent," he said, pointing to a large tent about twenty feet away. "It's just far away enough to stay safe from the fire, but also to stay warm."

"Melody, the wounded will have had their dinner by now, so let's go see them," said Tall Sky. "Remember, compassion is not just feeling sorry for them. It is also listening to their story and seeing what deeper problem may be hiding there. It is showing love to them by offering forgiveness and hope. A wounded soldier needs something new to think about, like what type of home he might like to build after the war, or what woman he might like to marry. He might make some comments about your physical beauty.... Remember, they don't know that you're a heroine," he said smiling.

"Melody, get Amidra and tell her to bring water, ointment and fresh bandages." The tent smelled of bodies that had not been washed for a week. He then asked Beldock for fresh clothing for the soldiers. Beldock said that they didn't have any, so Tall Sky went to Beldock and his men for clean clothing that they might have. He brought the clothing into the tent and said, "Men, you are brave fighting men, but I ask you now to be courteous and patient. There are three beautiful women who are going to wash you, change your bandages, and change your clothes. These women are familiar with wounds and are ladies, not camp followers. You will treat them with the same respect as you would give to your mothers." When the girls came into the tent, the men were in awe. One said, "They are like angels, so beautiful." Tall Sky asked Amidra to care for the worst of the wounded first. She cleaned and rebandaged the wound. Then Vela removed the soldier's clothing and washed him. Melody clung to Tall Sky and would not look.

Tall Sky reassured her, "It's all right, Culina. We do for him what he cannot do for himself. Just think of them as your brothers. Now our work begins. "Soldier, what is your name and where do you come from?" The soldier said that he came from a farm west of there and that his name was Selton. "Selton, how did you come to be wounded?"

The soldier replied, "I was fighting on an incline and I slipped and fell. The man who wounded me would have killed me if my friend had not pushed him. My friend then killed him. They brought me back here and did their best, but it hurt so bad I just wanted to die. I didn't want to be in the army in the first place. They took me from my home and taught me to fight. I hate the army for doing this to me."

"I understand," said Tall Sky. "Have you prayed to Father God to help you?"

"I don't know how to pray or even if Father God wants to help soldiers. We fight and die and there doesn't seem to be an end in sight. It's digusting. Does God really care?" asked Selton.

"Be assured. God cares very much. He loves his children and is very concerned with their well being, but he will not force them to love him back. If you ask Him, He will forgive you for any wrong doing or wrong thinking and will send His Spirit to live inside of you, giving you strength and healing."

"Would you help me to pray to Him?" asked Selton.

"Yes. Tell Him what you told me and ask Him to forgive your hate. Then ask Him to live in you."

The soldier did this and Tall Sky asked Melody to put her hand on the soldier's bandage as he did. Tall Sky asked Father God to heal the man. Melody's and Tall Sky's hands glowed. The soldier said, "The pain is gone! It just disappeared. You healed me!"

"God healed you," said Tall Sky. "We just let God's Spirit flow through us. Thank God for this." The soldier got up and walked out of the tent and told the soldiers what God had done for him.

One of the soldiers asked, "If God cares so much for us, why doesn't He just stop the enemy from trying to take our land and kill our families?"

"God will sometimes interfere with the affairs of men, but He is mostly concerned with the hearts of men, with their ability to love and to live honorable lives. You see, this life is short, but after this life, you will have eternal lives in Heaven. It is important that you are ready for this, so God uses difficult situations to build into your character strength, compassion, patience and love. These are the characteristics that you will need to have in Heaven, for these are God's characteristics."

Tall Sky and Melody continued to minister to the wounded well into the night and exhausted, cuddled up near the fire to sleep. Daisy was so tired that she had already been napping on Melody's shoulder.

The morning brought a feeling of relief and merriment to the soldiers. Tall Sky asked Rusken about the border problem. "Why do people attack you here on the border? What is it that these people need?"

Rusken answered, "Grassland is not plentiful on the other side of the Aikasse Mountain Range. Those living on the other side have herds of deer that suffer during the winter. They want to use our land for pasture. This is good grazing land, but it is also good farm land, and it is part of Aksanda. Some of the youngsters get tired of the cold there, and they cross the border to try to live here. It's really sad. They're nice kids, but they have no way of earning a living here and no place to stay. Some of them die on the mountains. If the dwarves catch them, they feed the kids and send them on their way. If the slavers catch them, they get sold into slavery."

"There has to be some kind of compromise that could be reached. Do you have any prisoners here?" asked Tall Sky.

"We have one, but he's not very talkative," said Rusken. "I'll take you to him." He was sitting in a tent, tied. Tall Sky sat down and gave him some berry wine from his wineskin. The two of them sat drinking berry wine without saying anything. Finally, the prisoner said, "What is your name, elf?"

"My name is Tunda Fanyare or Tall Sky. What is your name?" asked Tall Sky.

"My name is Varaak," he said. "I got wounded."

"Let me see," said Tall Sky. Varaak showed him a wound on his chest. It needed a new bandage. "I'll get something for that. Varaak, have you asked Father God to heal this?"

Varaak answered, "Father God has much to do. He can't be bothered with the wound of a soldier."

"Of course he can. He sent me here and He has healed many soldiers here. Did you know that God's Spirit can live inside you, giving you strength, healing, wisdom, and many other good things?"

"No," said Varaak. "How can I have that?'

"Are you willing to forgive these people and try to work with them on finding a solution to the grassland problem?" asked Tall Sky.

"Yes, I am," answered Varaak.

"Then you must tell Father God this and ask Him to live inside you," said Tall Sky. "He will forgive you."

"Father God, please forgive me and live in me," prayed Varaak. Tall Sky laid his hand on the soldier's wound and he was healed.

"Varaak, I will talk to your leader and our King and see if we can reach an agreement. What can your people offer in return for the use of our land?" asked Tall Sky.

"All we have is the herd of deer. We could give the farmers deer meat and hides for the use of their land for the winter," said Varaak. "I could talk to them about it if Rusken would let me."

"Try to get them to stop attacking long enough for me to talk to the farmers and for Rusken to talk with the king," said Tall Sky. I will arrange your release with Rusken.

"I will talk to the Gullandia Chief," said Varaak.

They all wanted Tall Sky to stay, but Tall Sky said that he had to help the girls back to their families and accompany Vela and Rusken back to their home. After breakfast, they packed the horses and the wagon and left the camp, traveling west along the mountain range. It wasn't long until they found an injured elf lying beside the road. He appeared to be near death. Tall Sky knew in his spirit that this elf was one of the bitter elves, but he couldn't just leave him there to die. "Where are your companions?" asked Tall Sky.

"Those worthless bums left me here in the dirt to die," said the elf. He had a deep gash in his side. Tall Sky asked Beldock if they would take Melody and wait for a while just a short way from them. He asked this for privacy and for their own protection. A miserable bitter elf may be dangerous to others. They had dark powers, the ability to strike out, and a lack of self control. "Melody, I want you to take Daisy over to the group and wait for me there." He didn't want to take any chances with his little Culina. With just the two of them there, Tall Sky proceeded to talk with the Bitter Elf. "What is your name and what happened to you?" he asked.

The elf replied, "My name is Dondro and we were fighting with the dwarves over some gems that we had taken from them, and one of them just threw an axe at me. My friends grabbed my pouch of gems and ran away. Are you going to kill me now, Tunda Fanyare? I don't want to die. Help me."

"Only Father God has the power to heal. You should know that. Tell me, who brought this trouble on you? When you really think about it, wasn't it stealing that caused the dwarves to pursue you? And when did you decide that stealing was alright?" asked Tall Sky.

The Bitter Elf frowned and said, "My friends told me it was okay when I joined the group. It's their fault. I was just going along with them. I wanted everything that people had, and I wanted to be the ruler of a great city. Now I'm going to die and God won't even help me."

"I'm going to say this just once," said Tall Sky. "God does want to help you, but first you must see that it was you who walked away from Him. It was you who rejected Him and went along your own selfish way! Who created you and gave you food and clothes and guidance through your parents? Were your parents Bright Elves or Bitter Elves?"

"They were Bright Elves. They said that God created me," said Dondro.

"That makes sense," said Tall Sky. "You know, if you gave God a chance, He would make you a strong and probably a great Bright Elf who would be respected by all and whose needs would be met. There is a lot to be said for happiness."

The bitter elf's eyes widened and he said, "You mean God would take me back and heal me?"

"Sure He would. You only have to ask and mean it. Ask Him to forgive you for your evil ways and ask Him for the power to change. Ask Him to send His spirit to live inside you. Do you want to do this?" asked Tall Sky.

"Yes. I would. My old life was crappy anyway. So what do I do?" asked Dondro.

"Talk to God like you are talking to me. Ask Him to forgive you for your selfishness and your pride. Ask Him to forgive the wrong things you have done like stealing and for your rebellion against your parents. Then ask Him to live in your heart and to heal you both spiritually and physically," said Tall Sky.

Dondro asked God to forgive him and to heal him. He asked God to live in his heart. Tall Sky put his hand on the elf's wound and prayed for God to heal him. Minutes later Dondro felt much better and asked Tall Sky if he could ride in the wagon. "If you come with me, you must submit yourself to my guidance. You have much to learn about the Spirit controlled life. From now on you will be called Aleph. The name has a deep meaning, which you have no way of knowing unless I tell you. Aleph, are you listening to me? There is another world far away, a world much like Phayendar, with people similar to you, and it was to those humans that the Creator first revealed Himself in the material universe. None of us will ever visit that world in bodily existence, for that world has no need of us to help with God's purposes there. But in that world, there is a language which was spoken by many great servants of God. In the writing of that language, the first letter is called Aleph; and being the first letter, it symbolizes new beginnings." It seemed as if Tall Sky had a new trainee.

The group continued their journey with a new soul in their wagon. Tall Sky asked Beldock to be patient with the new elf. Aleph needed to learn elf control and many other things that take time and experience. "We don't have to take him back to his parents do we?" asked Beldock.

"No, he's not ready for that yet. He's like a brand new baby who just got his diaper changed, but isn't potty trained yet. The Lord tells me that he will become a great Bright Elf….but, I think, I've got my work cut out for me with this one," said Tall Sky.

"I suppose he will be staying at the inn, but I don't know what my customers will think of that. I discourage elves because of the bitter ones. Of course, if he is with you, they will probably accept him. You say his name is Dondro? Was that the name his parents gave him?" asked Beldock.

"I think so. I gave him a new name. It is now Aleph meaning new beginning. He said that his parents were Bright Elves, but he wanted everything and he wasn't willing to wait, so he joined this group of bitter elves who convinced him that all they had to do was to take what they wanted. At least he had some decent parents who loved him. That's something to build on," said Tall Sky.

"How far do we travel to Talami?" asked Beldock

"It's at least a day's journey, maybe more," answered Tall Sky." We will drop off the two girls on the way. Their farms are somewhere between here and Talami."

"Tall Sky, would you ride back here with me for a while? I miss you," said Melody.

"Culina, my darling, it has been a long journey and you are getting tired. We will stop soon at a farm and have some lunch and return one of the girls to her parents. That will make all of this worthwhile, yes?" said Tall Sky.

She looked adoringly at Tall Sky and said, "I love you." Daisy looked at Tall Sky and chirred.

"Daisy has been already picking up on your moods. When dragons bond with a person, they learn to sense what their person is thinking and feeling. It is quite a unique relationship. You may be able to hide your dislike for a person, but Daisy will know and will hiss at that person. I once knew a dragon who would fly up to the rafters of a building and would not come down until the disliked person left the building. She will keep you honest, that's for sure," said Tall Sky. He flashed a smile at her that made her blush.

The group was able to travel two by two now because the grasslands were coming up. The road was still pretty rocky and there were foothills to the left leading up to the mountain range. The sky was clear and a deep shade of blue and the sun warmed them. It was a great day for travel.

"You okay, Emmy?" asked Steben. Emmy was riding with Amidra, her new mommy.

"I'm doing fine, and I like my new clothes. They are pretty and warm enough. I am getting hungry, though," said Emmy.

"Well, that's good. We stop soon. Have lunch," said Steben.

"I think Miril is the next girl to be returned. She lives fairly close to here. Beldock has her up front so that she can lead us to her home," said Amidra. "I can hardly wait to start our own home. Emmy will have her own room with her clothes and her toys in it."

"I will have toys?" asked Emmy. "Can I have a cat?"

"Of course you will have toys and a cat," said Amidra.

Arinya said to Trag, "I would like to have a cat, too. I love them. They're so soft and cuddly and they purr like Daisy does." She looked at him with a hopeful smile.

"You can have anything you want," declared Trag.

"In that case, I want a front porch on our house so that I can sit there and rock a baby," Arinya said.

"Babies, I hadn't thought of that, but I suppose there will be children," Trag said in a worried voice.

Vela said, "Don't worry about children. When you have them, you will love them and they will add so much joy to your home. I can hardly wait to get home to ours."

Beldock veered off the road to the left riding towards a farm.

The parents were so happy to have their girl back that they prevailed upon the group to stay for lunch. They all dismounted and spread blankets on the ground to sit on. The happy parents brought out some wine, cheese and bread. They were delighted with Daisy and brought her a saucer of milk. They wanted to hear all about their daughter's rescue, so Beldock gave them a brief description of that, leaving out any gruesome details of the battle. The parents knew the second girl and said that they would be happy to return her so that the whole group would not have to travel out of their way. Miril's parents were worried about children who sometimes come by wanting food. They were running away from Gullandia, but really have no place to go to for a home. They fed them and then the children would continue south.

Tall Sky told Miril's parents about the proposed solution to the border problem. "You know, these people are good people who just need to graze their deer in the winter. Gullandia has too much snow in the winter for the herd to survive. They would be willing to give the farmers deer meat and hides in exchange for the use of the land. And, if you think about it, the herds would leave good fertilizer behind to help with the growing of crops. They only need to graze them here for a few months during the heaviest snowfall." Miril's parents agreed to this idea and would pass the word on to other farmers in the area. It was a successful stop, but it was time to go.

Beldock led his group on toward Talami, which was now within less than a day's ride. Tall Sky still had goods to trade with the dwarves. "Beldock, we will have to turn north soon for me to trade with the dwarves. We will probably have to spend the night near the mountains," said Tall Sky.

"I was just thinking about that. There is a large cave that will suit our purposes. It will give us shelter in case of rain, and it is always cooler near those mountains. I remember it well from my army days," said Beldock. "We could pull in there and help you carry your goods into the mountain."

"Sounds good. We will leave Trag and Rusken to help guard the women," said Tall Sky. "I would like to introduce Melody to them and take Aleph to make restitution to the dwarves. They need to know that he is changed in case of any future contacts."

Soon they were pulling up to the cave. They unloaded supplies and tied the horses in the cave. They built a small fire and began preparations for the evening meal. Beldock, Tall Sky, the two abductees, and Beldock's two friends carried supplies into the mountain tunnel to trade with the dwarves. They were met by a guard who ushered them into a room with places to sit.

Tall Sky said, "Khaan khuzd shekheh al dekhel."

The guard answered, "Gromdar Durak haar kurs gunud." The guard turned and went down a tunnel.

Tall Sky said, "He is going to get the dwarf who tried to kill Aleph." Aleph stood there in shock, not knowing what was going to happen to him. When this dwarf comes to meet you, hand him this bag of gems and say, "Skilag no tohsti Vaarak."

The guard came back with Gromdar. Tall Sky said, "Ghul glus. Vass bi leibz tnam?"

"Miz tnam bi Gromdar Durak," he said.

Aleph gave the dwarf the pouch of gems and said, "Skilag no tohsti. Vaarak likkag Tunda Fanyare.

Gromdar's frown turned to a smile as he realized this elf was trying to make a sincere apology, even if his dwarvish wasn't that good.

Tall Sky proceeded to complete his trade of supplies for gems and was pleased with the results.

When they got back to the cave, Tall Sky said, "Aleph did well. He stood there in front of the dwarf who wounded him and gave that dwarf a bag of gems and an apology. The dwarf smiled and proceeded to trade with me. I did learn that there have been pretty regular problems between dwarves and bitter elves. It could easily escalate into a war."

"I'm tired of war," remarked Rusken.

"Is dinner ready? I'm hungry enough to eat a grustabist," said Beldock.

"You ate one back in Loadrel," said Vela. "Come over here and sit down. I will serve you," said Vela.

After dinner, they cleaned up and made their beds close to the fire. It was warm and cozy in the cave. It had been a successful day and a tiring one. Before long they dropped off to sleep. Daisy looked around and then cuddled up on Melody's pillow purring in her ear.

They woke up to the smell of food. Vela had cooked a good breakfast of eggs, honey cakes and strips of bacon. They grabbed their bowls and filled them with yummy food. Daisy had her own little bowl of food and a saucer of milk from Vela's cow. After that breakfast Vela and Rusken were ready for the last leg of their journey. They were going home at last. "When will we be there?" Vela asked.

Rusken answered, "We will be there today. It's been so long; we probably won't recognize the children. Kids grow fast. They are teenagers now and Silmo could be taller than I am. Mila could be almost as tall as you are."

"We've missed so much of their lives," she said, tears running down her face.

"Now, we'll have none of that. They are well and we have the rest of our lives to love them and there will be grandchildren someday." Rusken said, stroking her hair.

"Beldock, are we expecting any trouble between here and my home?" asked Rusken. "We had small problems with the elves at base camp, and there were rumors of Bitter Elf gatherings, but nothing specific, no battle plans. They would strike from too far away to catch them."

"We will keep a close watch, but we will be traveling away from the mountains. The livestock and the wagon slow us down some, but we should be in Talami before sunset," said Beldock. Even so, we must be vigilant. The bitter elves are obviously very interested in the dwarves' riches. Aleph! Come here for a minute. I want to talk to you. Tell me what you know about any organized attacks against the dwarves, and do you think that we are in danger traveling south from here?"

"I traveled with four other elves. They didn't seem to be thinking about anything but gathering personal wealth, and they didn't care how they got it. I heard about other gangs of elves traveling north toward the mountains and they were always talking about the dwarves' gemstones and gold. I think they're planning something and it wouldn't be wise to be in their way," said Aleph. "Tall Sky should be able to sense any trouble from them and he can ask God for a vision and for guidance. If he tells you to do something, do it. It could save our lives."

Everybody packed up and mounted up. Aleph still rode in the wagon and Daisy was sitting on Melody's shoulder. Tall Sky rode up front with Beldock for lookout purposes. He asked Aleph to join him.

They traveled quietly and steadily. There were small groups of travelers staying off the main road, but not many on the road. Tall Sky and Aleph prayed for guidance and vision. They arrived at Talami without incidence. Because of the upcoming battle, they decided that the women should stay in the town of Talami instead of on the more isolated farm.

They pulled up to Vela's mother's house and dismounted. Vela and Rusken ran up to the house and knocked on the door. Vela's mother opened the door and said, "Vela, my darling." She hugged her and cried. Rusken embraced his two children and said, "Some friends brought us and we owe our lives to them. You must welcome them. I have important news to tell you. We could all be in danger."

Everyone gathered in the sitting room to listen to Rusken. "This is Tall Sky. He is a Bright Elf who healed many of our wounded at Base Camp. He and his party brought us here after trading with the dwarves. There are many bitter elves who won't trade with the dwarves. They want to kill all of the dwarves and steal their riches. These bitter elves travel in small bands, but are traveling north to the Aikasses. They plan to attend a gathering not far from here where they will devise their battle plan. That is why you must stay here in town for a while. One of us must ride back to base camp with this news. They must be warned and asked to help defend the dwarves and the people living in this area. Also, there is a Bright Elf battalion in the area that has been tracking the movements of the groups of Bitters."

"Yes," said Tall Sky. "Quickturn is the Bright Elf who leads that battalion. He informed me of the Bitter Elf gathering and said there would probably be a battle. Aleph and I will go to warn the dwarves and help them to get ready for battle. There is much for them to do. Rusken, I want you to stay here and ready the townspeople for possible attacks. Beldock, I want you to take Melody, Trag, Arinya, Steben and Amidra back to the inn. Stop at Yardrel, warn them, and see if you can locate Steben's mother. Your two friends Salek and Parin should ride with you. You should stop at Home Fire and warn Rando. Tell him that the bitters are involved with slavers. They may want to join the fight or help to defend Loadrel. I would ask our two young men who we freed to stay here, if they would, to help guard this house. We have supplies out in a wagon that must be brought in. There are also some animals that need to be penned. Vela, you must bury your gems and silver. It will not be safe to leave them about the house."

The men brought in supplies and sleeping rolls and the women worked in the kitchen to get dinner ready. Everyone rolled out their sleeping rolls and sat on them to eat dinner. There were fresh vegetables and fruits, stew, and bread. It was a great dinner, and everyone was ready to sleep after it.

Melody looked sadly at Tall Sky and pleaded, "Please don't send me away from you. I couldn't stand it. You know how much I love you. What if you were hurt and needed me?" Daisy whimpered.

"You're upsetting the dragon," said Tall Sky. "I need you to be away from this action, or I will not be able to concentrate on my duty here. If you are on your way with Beldock and two soldiers, I would know that you are safe. Besides, Trag and Steben will also be with you. I think that it is a safe enough group for you to travel with. Wasn't it you who promised Steben that you would help him to find his mother? You should fulfill that promise. We haven't been apart since I met you and you have become a very brave person. You will be alright. What if I promised you that we could be engaged when I get back?"

"You mean it?" said Melody. "You want to marry me? I want to marry you too. How long do you think this battle is going to take?"

Tall Sky laughed. "I don't know, but if things play out like I hope they will, we should have those Bitter Elves defeated and on the run in a few days. The preparations will also take a few days. You can't rush these things and battles have a way of surprising you at every turn."

Melody cuddled up to Tall Sky with visions of a happy wedding day playing in her head. On the other hand, Tall Sky prayed for guidance and a vision.

The next morning brought a flurry of activity. They decided to snack on the way to save time, so they packed the horses and were on their way. Salek decided to ride to the Base Camp and tell the soldiers of the upcoming battle and ask for their aid. Having had a taste of battle, the two abductees went with Salek to join the army. The rest of the adventurers were ready to travel shortly after daybreak. Their kingdom Aksanda had become a rather unsafe land.

Melody kissed Tall Sky goodbye. "I love you my darling and you come back to me safe and sound and that's an order," she said smiling.

"Culina, you will be my Culina forever and ever. I will come back to you as soon as I can. Be safe. "said Tall Sky. They rode their separate directions on the same road.

Melody rode up front with Beldock. "How long will it take to get to Yardrel?" asked Melody.

"We should be there for lunch," said Beldock.

"You know, Tall Sky said that when he gets back we are going to be engaged. It won't take too long will it? You've seen battles before. Do they take very long?" asked Melody.

"Well, it really depends on what's involved, but this one is mainly about jewels and gold. For the Bitters it is not about God and country here," replied Beldock.

The ride from Talami to Yardrel was over a fairly smooth road with few travelers. The land became a bit flatter and grassier as they progressed. Steben rode up to Beldock and said, "I know this place. Close. We are close." Steben came from a farm, so it was probably this side of Yardrel. The other side of Yardrel is Lake Perilough. Of a sudden, Steben galloped off to the right. The group followed him to a burned out building. Steben stopped the horse and cried.

Amidra dismounted and held him. In looking about the place Melody noticed a carved toy horse. "Steben, look what I found. It's a wooden horse and it hasn't been burned. It's clean. It's like someone just put it here."

"My horse," Steben said. He looked around and said, "Mama." He smiled. "We go." At that he mounted and rode off with everybody trying to keep up.

The town of Yardrel was close by. When they arrived, Steben was already in a café asking about his mother. All these years he thought his mother could be dead, but she was alive and living in Yardrel with his Dad. His parents lived on the edge of town. Steben left the café very excited and said loudly, "Mama's OK! Let's go!" They rode through town and dismounted in front of a house with flowers growing in front of it. Steben opened the door and called out, "Mama! I'm home! "

His mother came into the room and said, "My boy! I just knew you were alive. Let me look at you. You're all grown up and so handsome." His father came into the room. "Look, Papa, it's Steben come home to us!" He hugged his son and Steben gave him a ruby. His father looked at him with wide eyes.

Steben said, "For horse." Steben knew that his father had carved this one just as he had carved Steben a toy horse, years ago. Steben took Amidra by the hand and said, "Amidra, my fiancé. Then he took Emmy by the hand and led her to his mother, and said with pride, "Our daughter Emmy." His mother's eyes widened and she looked from Emmy to Steben and to Amidra. Amidra hurriedly told them that they had rescued her from slavers, that she was an orphan and that they are adopting her when they get married. "Emmy, I'm your Grandmama and this is your Grandpapa." She sat down and held Emmy on her lap." Steben's father bade everybody welcome and to come in and sit down. They all brought in their blanket rolls and some food and sat down to lunch.

"So, Steben, where have you been all of these years?" asked Papa. "How did you survive the attack on the house?"

Steben answered, "Rando took me, and Vela got me well. Lived at Home Fire. Vela like Mama. Made clothes and cooked food."

"How did you meet Amidra?" asked Mama.

Steben smiled and said, "Amidra, Melody, Liadra in Malwood. Steben help them to Home Fire."

Amidra explained that Rando's men were bandits who hated slavers and stole from them. She told them that she and three others were runaways looking for adventure and new places. Then they met up with Tall Sky who had rescued one of their friends named Trag who had been caught by Avidora.

"Avidora the witch?!" exclaimed Papa.

"Yes," said Amidra, "And that's how we got gems like the one that Steben gave you. Anyway, we all met up with Tall Sky. He's a Bright Elf who helped us exchange the gems for silver pieces at the Malwood Market. Then we went to Loadrel and stayed there for a while at Laskron's house."

Beldock intervened at this point, "Laskron Truehand is one of our town's leading businessmen, and my trusted friend. He had rooms available in his house when I had no unused space in my inn. He graciously agreed to let them stay in house with him and his daughter. The people in Loadrel had put up with the foreigners coming into town because of the Malwood slave auction. They were sure that their own children were in danger, so they decided to ride to the auction and free the slaves and kill the slavers and their customers. So we did. You can stop worrying about that witch. Rando killed Avidora . That witch was a nasty murderer."

Melody said, "Steben is a good man. He helped us and fed us and kept us safe in those woods, and when Tall Sky told us about God and God's spirit, we all asked God for forgiveness and asked God to live in our hearts."

Steben slapped his chest and said, "God here."

His Mama laughed and said, "I'm so glad. You know, there is a small farm nearby. It is owned by an older couple who want to move into Yardrel. You could buy that one and be close to us. You could be married right here in this house."

Steben said, "Mama, no. We marry in Loadrel. Live here." He looked at Amidra and said, "OK?"

Amidra smiled and said, "Perfect. You see, Laskron conducts marriages and adoptions at Spirit Hall in Loadrel. Beldock, could we see the farm before we go?"

"Sure, we have a little time." said Beldock.

"First you must see my workshop," said Papa. "I make furniture now and I have a big bed, a small bed, and a rocking chair for a child." Papa stood up. He was a tall man with white hair and a short cropped beard. His face was suntanned with crinkles at his eyes. "Come, let me show you."

The group went out to a separate building and saw his wood working shop. There were the finished beds, a table and chairs, and a small rocker with a beautiful doll sitting in it. Emmy ran to the rocker and sat in it holding the doll. "I wondered what child I made this for. It was just something I knew that I had to do. I felt that God wanted me to make these. Now I know why. There was a special little girl He knew who would need these."

Emmy ran to her Grandpapa and hugged him saying, "I love you, Grandpapa."

"And I love you too," said Grandpapa. "Now let's go get that farm!"

The farm was just about fifteen minutes away. It consisted of a house, a barn, and a corral. There was a wagon out front. The owners were an older couple who were very happy to sell the farm to Steben and Amidra. After moving their belongings to town, they would also sell their wagon and team of horses to Steben. The friends decided they would stay and help accomplish this move. By the end of the afternoon, the older couple was in their home in town and the furniture from Grandpapa's workshop was in Steben's new home on their farm. The group decided to spend the night there and head for Loadrel in the morning. His parents decided to ride with them so that they could also see Home Fire.

Steben's parents slept in the big bed, and Emmy slept in her new bed. Everyone else bedded down in the barn on mats of hay as they had done before. Melody was so lonesome for Tall Sky that she shed a few tears while Daisy chirred in her ear trying to comfort her.

Grandmama prepared a big breakfast for everybody, so that when they arrived at the house, it would be ready for them. They had potatoes fried with ham, eggs, fresh fruit, and bread with jam. It was delicious and the group left satisfied and in great spirits. Melody and Amidra helped clean up the dishes while the men fed the horses and put the bedrolls on them. All was going as planned. The group left Yardrel and headed south toward Home Fire. Grandpapa and Grandmama were happy to be traveling with their son and excited to see the place where their son had grown up. "Beldock, when will we get to Home Fire?" asked Melody.

Beldock answered, "We will eat lunch there. Home Fire is not far, but I'll bet that Steben's parents will be starting to get sore by then. They probably haven't been riding regularly."

"Probably not," said Melody. "So you think that Tall Sky is back at Othrund yet?"

"I think so," said Beldock. "He is probably teaching the dwarves some things about warfare. I understand they do have some weapons; they know how to use the crossbow and the axe, and they are good at knife throwing, but a battle needs some organization, ranks, defenses set up outside and strategies in place. That takes a lot of planning and work. The dwarves are hard workers, and they are strong. They also are very brave and determined to keep their tunnels. They are no fools, but they do become angry and frustrate easily. That is something that Tall Sky will have to deal with. Melody, you will have to be patient. These things take time."

"I know, but I worry about him being involved in a battle. It's so dangerous," said Melody.

"It is," said Beldock, "But God will help him and protect him. And he can always shield himself so that no one can see him. He is needed right now. When this problem is resolved, Tall Sky will come home to you. He loves you very much. He even loves that little dragon of yours."

Trag and Arinya were riding behind Beldock and Melody. "Trag, what are these bandits like? Are they scary?" asked Arinya.

"No," said Trag, "They are like normal people. There are women and children living there, too. They live by hunting and fishing and robbing the slavers. They were a big help in the raid on Malwood. They raised Steben and gave Vela a job. I wonder if they will change now that they have all that wealth that they got from Malwood. Amidra, you were there. Do you think that Home fire will change now that Rando's men are rich?"

Amidra said, "Of course it will. They have money to build houses now. Would you rather live in a tent or in a house when the snow flies?"

Trag said, "I know which one I would rather live in. Have you noticed that it has gotten colder lately, especially at night? And we will be camping out tonight if we stay at Home Fire."

"Beldock said that we will just be warning them about the Bitter Elves," said Amidra.

"That's good. I would really like to take a bath and sleep in a regular bed tonight," said Arinya.

Papa and Mama rode behind Amidra and Peron rode rear guard. "Peron, is it hard being on the road so much?"

Peron answered "You know, it really is harder than I remembered. I was much younger in the army, though. I think I've softened up some. I'll bet you two will be stiff and sore for a few days."

"What are these Bitter Elves like?" asked Mama.

"A nasty bunch of thieves and scalawags, they are. A worse lot you'd be hard pressed to find. Imagine them roaming about causing trouble everywhere they go. They even have some bad people following them foolishly imagining that the Bitters accept them as equals. Like as not they'll kill those people when they're done with them," said Peron.

Beldock turned off the road to the left and called for single file on a trail through the woods and underbrush. The trail led gradually downhill toward Lake Perilough. Finally it curved gently to the right and ended up at Home Fire where they were met by Rando. He had been supervising the building of several log homes.

"Rando, good to see you again my friend," said Beldock. "I see you are building a town. It is a good idea. You will be safe from the winter and from bears. I brought a couple who are eager to meet you. These are Steben's parents come from Yardrel to see Home Fire and the man who did such a good job of raising their son." Rando didn't know what to say to this.

Rando said, "Steben, I am glad to see you. You brought Amidra, too, and a little girl?"

"My daughter," said Steben proudly. "Amidra and me. We marry. Adopt Emmy."

"We plan to get married in Loadrel soon," said Amidra.

"Good," said Rando. "I like that. Going to do that myself someday."

Beldock took Rando aside and told him about the Bitter Elf gathering that would happen soon and about the imminent danger the whole area is in because of the migration of bands of Bitters going north. He told Rando of the forces gathering to defend the dwarves. He said that Tall Sky could use any help he could get to add to the army and the battalion of elves and the dwarves themselves. For the protection of the whole area, the Bitters must be driven out.

"I don't know," said Rando. "We are trying to get ready for winter here."

"Well, I just stopped by to let you know about all this. By the way, we have a lot of good builders in Loadrel who could come over and have your houses built in about a week. I know they would like to thank you for fighting at Malwood," said Beldock.

Mama said, "Mr. Rando, I want to thank you for taking care of my boy all these years. He's a fine boy. You did a good job."

"It was not difficult. You're welcome," said Rando.

"Rando," said Beldock, "We've heard about young people running away from Gullandia and walking south. Some farmers have helped them by giving them food. Have you seen any of them?"

"Yes, we have," answered Rando. "Several batches of them have come through here. They need to be trained in how to survive and maybe some skills. You know, we are going to build an inn and we could offer them a place to stay here and teach them skills so that they could fit in here. We need more people to settle here."

"Sounds like a good plan," said Beldock. "I'll ask around and see if anybody knows where some of them are."

"I've got to get back to the inn, so we'll get going now. I think we should eat on the way, so get out your bread and cheese and mount up," said Beldock. Soon the travelers were heading back up the path to the road. They ate and drank some wine as they rode slowly at first. As was customary, a sentry followed them. He was sorry to see them go. It had been a good visit.

Not far down the road, the sentry noticed a flock of birds swarming lower and lower toward Beldock's group. They swarmed all around the riders pecking at their heads. Melody covered Daisy with her cloak and everyone pulled their hoods up over their head, but the horses were frightened and pranced about, throwing several of the riders. The rest dismounted and led their horses toward the trees for shelter. Ten elves appeared and grabbed the horses. They put a sleep spell on the humans so that they could bind their hands. Then they woke them and led them into the woods away from Home Fire. They led the captives into a clearing where they told their captives to sit down on the grass. The sentry rode to Home Fire to tell Rando about the attack.

Rando sent two of his men to follow the elves and readied his men for battle. The entire band rode out armed with arrows, spears and knives. Rando's men were well organized for this type of battle. They would surprise the enemy first with a volley of arrows and follow up with hand to hand combat. The elves had tied the horses and were greedily going through the packs on the horses looking for gems, silver, and food supplies. They were totally engrossed in this when arrows found their marks and one by one they dropped to the ground. Rando's men were excellent marksmen. They cut the ropes binding the people. Emmy was crying and ran to her Daddy, "They were going to sell us at the slave market."

Beldock said, "They can't do that. We burned down that market. Rando, thank you for coming to our defense. They were planning to sell us at the market, but when we got there, they would have killed us and raped the women. Continue keeping a close watch. There are many more of them heading this way." Rando said that he would. Rando took the Bitters' gems and silver dividing it among his men. He took half of the horses and sent five of the horses with Beldock. Rando's men also took blankets and boots. After packing their horses, Beldock's group mounted and rode for Loadrel.

It had been an exhausting morning, but they were close to home and everybody was getting excited to see their friends again.

Melody was again worried about Tall Sky. Being up close to that band of Bitter Elves showed her exactly how devious and dangerous they really were. They had used three different spells. They used invisibility, sleep, and bird swarming spells. They were going to sell all of them. "They probably would have killed Daisy if I hadn't hidden her in the inside pocket of my cloak. Tall Sky was right to send me to Loadrel for safety," she thought.

Mama said, "To think our son was brought up by those bandits. I'm so glad they saved him from the slavers who burned our house. Those people sure know how to do things. And they're building their own town. I think it's wonderful."

"Yes, Mama," said Papa, "I'm so proud of him. He is a good man and getting married and adopting a grandchild for us. Emmy is such a good little girl and grateful for everything. She has had a hard life, but we will make up for that." Emmy was cuddled up to Amidra hiding under her cloak. She wasn't taking any chances of wayward birds attacking again.

As they rode through Loadrel, people ran after them and gathered around them to help them with their bags and to help the women down from the horses. They were all asking questions at once. Beldock said, "Calm down. We will all meet inside as soon as we're settled and answer all of your questions." They took in their things and sat down for refreshments. Beldock hugged Mina, assuring her that he was well, and asked her to bring ale and food for him and his traveling companions. Having skipped lunch, they were famished. Daisy was doing her hungry dance on Melody's shoulder and pounced on the first piece of cheese that she saw. Mina brought bowls of lamb stew and fresh bread with butter and jam. Melody was so relieved that tears streamed down her face. She had been more traumatized than she thought. Mina said, "Come here, child," and held her while she cried. You've had a rough time of it, haven't you? You'll be alright now that you're home. Eat your stew and you'll feel better." Melody joined the group at the table. It did make her feel better.

Soon the place was packed with customers wanting food and the latest news. "OK," said Beldock. "What are your questions?"

Kroom stood up and asked, "What are the Bitters up to? We had a number of them through here. Only this morning, ten of them stopped to buy some food."

Beldock answered, "Did three of them have rust- colored cloaks? We've had several encounters with them on our journey. Five stopped at our camp saying that they recognized Emmy. They were on their way to a gathering in the north to attack the dwarves for their jewels. Tall Sky chased them off. We got Emmy from some slavers who passed by. We killed them. Just this morning, ten Bitters attacked using spells. They tied us up and were going through our packs when Rando and his men shot them with arrows. All ten of them are dead. The Bitters are very dangerous and they're all primed for a fight. We will have to be ready to defend our town. Tall Sky and Aleph are getting the dwarves ready. Salek is warning the soldiers at Base Camp to enlist their aid. Quickturn has a battalion of elves already in place. The Bitters are many and are migrating north to a gathering. On a lighter note, Steben and Amidra are getting married, adopting Emmy, and have bought a farm close to his parents' home in Yardrel. Melody and Tall Sky plan to marry. I think we all saw that one coming." The crowd applauded.

Melody, Amidra, Steben, and Emmy left to go next door. Mama and Papa went upstairs to a room. Beldock and Salek stayed for a while to answer questions. Tomorrow would be soon enough to develop a plan for defense of the town.

Emmy was delighted to have another little girl to play with. Elise and Emmy talked and played with their dolls while the grownups talked in the sitting room. "How is your arm doing, Laskron?" asked Amidra.

"It's almost healed enough for me to go back to work," said Laskron. "My problems are nothing compared to what you went through. It sounds like you were under attack a lot. And you freed another slave. Did you kill the slavers?"

Trag answered, "Yes, we did. We acquired their five horses and delivered them and a wagon of supplies to the soldiers at Base Camp. Then the girls cleaned and bandaged the soldiers and Tall Sky and Melody prayed for them to be healed. The soldiers felt like angels from heaven had visited them. They all asked God to live in their hearts. That was quite a day."

"I'm so glad that you found Steben's parents. How did that happen?' asked Liadra.

"We rode to Yardrel and Steben took off toward a burned out house. He stood there crying until Melody found a carved, wooden toy horse that was like brand new. Steben got on his horse and rode to Yardrel where someone told him where his parents lived," said Trag.

"What did it feel like to be kidnapped?" asked Liadra.

Melody answered, "I was terrified. I felt helpless and I was worried about Daisy. She was hiding from the birds in my cloak pocket, but if they found her, they could have killed her just for fun. They are a wicked bunch, those Bitters. I hope a lot of them get killed in the battle. It would help to keep good people safe."

Amidra said, "Steben and I will be married tomorrow, if that's alright with you. I want to be married at Spirit Hall, so we brought Mama and Papa here to watch. I already have a beautiful dress to wear."

Laskron said that the only problem he could foresee is getting them back to Yardrel safely. "We will have to get a group of militia volunteers to see you safely back home, unless you want to stay here for a time."

"I'll have to talk to Mama and Papa to see how they feel about that. It is important to take precautions with things the way they are now," said Amidra. "And now we have Emmy to consider. She sure likes playing with Elise. Laskron, have you heard about any runaway children coming this way from Gullandia? Everyone we have talked to has seen them and given them food. Rando says that he wants to build an inn where they could live until they could settle at Home Fire. I think that's a great idea. He knows how to get people to fit in and some of his men need wives. They just have to get that inn built."

Laskron said, "I haven't met any of them, but I have heard of them. I'll ask around and see if anybody knows where any of them are."

Everyone decided to turn in early. They were all tired out, so they went to their respective rooms and went right to sleep.

OTHRUND

Tall Sky and Aleph had been helping the dwarves to be ready for the comming battle. So far they had dug a deep trench parallel to the rock face about forty feet away. They had filled it with stakes standing up for the enemy to fall on. They had also dug another trench and filled it with combustible materials. The dwarves had accepted a hierarchy of command including a general, five sergeants and 10 platoon leaders. That way the fighting men would know from whom to get directions during the battle. Tall Sky talked strategy with them, and included Quickturn at this point. They needed to know the order of attack. The Bright elves had certain powers they could use at different points in the battle. They were particularly good marksmen with bows and arrows. The dwarves had been practicing their skills at the crossbow. In close combat, the dwarves were good with the battle ax and knives. The Bitter elves had lost the element of surprise, but the Bright Elves had not shown themselves and the Bitters expected the dwarves to roll over and play dead. The soldiers had not sent word yet of their possible involvement. Some female dwarves could fight, but would be saved for defending the children in case the interior would be breached. The rest of the time would be spent in the making of arrows, and the sharpening of axes. The elves had highly polished silver shields they would use to reflect sunlight into the faces of the enemy. Everything was falling into place beautifully, if only the soldiers would answer.

Meanwhile at base camp, Jaylek was getting his men and their weapons ready for battle. He definitely planned to join in the battle against the Bitters. He had been working for too long of a time to ensure the safety of the Aikasse Mountains area to let it deteriorate because of a bunch of Bitter Elves. He sent word to Tall Sky about his intention to be a part of the war. He had sent a request for more men to King Aryante a few days ago. He expected a good response. King Aryante had no love for the Bitters. They had caused him no end of trouble for a long time. They paid no taxes, but attacked and robbed those who do. On the other hand, the dwarves paid taxes regularly sending him gifts of gemstones and gold which helped him rule. He decided to send as many soldiers as were available to the war. He sent word to Tall Sky that he was moving his soldiers to a cavern just west of Othrund to await the beginning of the war and that his men would attack from the west.

Knowing that the army was involved put Tall Sky's mind to rest. He was confident that everything was being done. Rando's men would be guarding the road to Loadrel. That was an important post. At least there would be some protection for that area. He would send Salek there to join Rando's men. That way Rando would know that he was doing something to protect both Home Fire and Loadrel and wasn't expected at Othrund. The latest word about the gathering came from Quickturn. He said that most of the Bitters were at the gathering south of Othrund. He expected them to move on Othrund in a day or two. They weren't terribly organized and seemed to be a bunch of arguing factions very worried about the division of the dwarves' wealth. If they had no magical powers, they would be easily defeated. It is in not knowing how or when they would use those powers that caused concern. Most of their spells are just annoying, but during battle, they could cause confusion leading to deaths.

Quickturn said, "There is a dark power behind this. I have felt it growing for years. The Bitters are many — too many to count. They number in the thousands and there are men with them. We will need many soldiers to help with this one. It is like the Battle of Thalen two hundred years past. It was a fierce battle that lasted for days. I thought to never see the likes of it. We must stand together to rebuke the spells that come our way. Some of these Bitters are well versed in dark magic. All of their spells are not known to us.

Yet the power of God is over all. He will help us to fight these spells. Spriritual warfare will win this battle if anything can."

"Yes," said Tall Sky, "I have been aware of the growing need for spiritual health in Aksanda. Both humans and elves have turned from God to practice dark power and the greed for wealth has caused many lives to be destroyed. They think that things will make them happy, but it just brings more greed for more things. Father God is patient, but He won't tolerate this to go on much longer. I have seen it in a vision. Their lust for silver and gold and gems will bring about pain and sorrow."

"I have seen this too," said Quickturn. "Has Farin Stronghand armor enough for his men?"

"He has a group of smithies working on that now. Many of the dwarves have their armor ready, but the smithies are busy making more. My heart is heavy with this battle. It shouldn't have to be," said Tall Sky. "My Melody must be worried sick about me being here, but I have to keep her safe…her and her little dragon Daisy. That girl loves little animals. The dragon loves her too and sits on her shoulder all of the time. I can hardly wait to get back to her."

THE BATTLE OF OTHRUND

A Bright Elf messenger arrived with news. He said, "King Aryante's forces are gathered and are riding north. They should be here in a day or so. The Bitters are also on the march. They will be here in two hours. The Bitters are well armed and well fed. They have raided farms on their way north, looting and burning and killing. They seem to have no conscience and seem to be doing these things for enjoyment instead of just taking food for sustenance. The base camp soldiers are ready for battle. The Bright Elves' battalion is well hidden behind boulders on the mountain ready to strike."

"This is good. The dwarves are also ready. This will be a battle to be remembered in lore and in song." said Quickturn. "Farin! The battle will begin soon. Have your warriors stand at the ready!" Farin went to tell his men to dress in their armor and to get their weapons. They would be positioned outside in front of the tunnel entrance, many hiding behind rocks.

By the time the dwarves were ready and in position, a large group of Bitters appeared on the horizon. The sound of horses hooves pounding the ground and a dust cloud rising was ominous. There was a shaking of the ground like an earthquake. Tall Sky and Aleph held out their hands and said, "Ground, be still. God, your Creator wills it to be so." The tremors subsided. The Bitters ran headlong into the trench and died, speared by the stakes in the ground. Several lines of the enemy were killed that way. The enemy was surprised by this and began to have some respect for the dwarves. They filed around the trench to form a frontal attack. The second trench was set on fire, catching a large group of Bitters in between the two trenches. Many caught on fire and some fell into the staked trench falling to their deaths. At this point the Brights stood up shooting arrows, hitting many of the Bitters. The dwarves shouted their battle cry, "Death to the Bitters!" and shot the next wave of Bitters using their crossbows.

Suddenly there appeared a flash of lightning that struck the mountain wall just above the tunnel entrance. It kept on for several minutes with sparks flying from it as it wrote words.

THESE ARE MY PEOPLE AWAKENING NOW

Everything stopped for a few minutes as this happened, but the battle continued. Some of The Bitters brought in logs to form bridges across the trench and foot soldiers crossed the trench in droves. Some of them reached the tunnel entrance and the dwarves hacked them with their axes spilling so much blood that the rock floor was slick with it. The dwarves fought on while the Brights continued loosing volleys of arrows into the troops beyond them. Base camp soldiers arrived from the west fighting in hand to hand combat. There were casualties on both sides, but the soldiers were well practiced with their swords killing many Bitters. Noticing Tall Sky, a group of bitters rushed at him to kill him. Aleph grabbed a sword and killed them one after another with quick, decisive blows. A dark cloud appeared and out of it came a large swarm of birds that swooped down on the dwarves. Tall Sky spoke to the birds, "Birds, Father God your Creator commands you to attack the Bitters behind you!" The swarm of birds turned to engage the Bitter Elves, diving at them and pecking at their eyes.

There was still a large contingent of Bitters, hundreds of men deep, moving up from the south. The battle had raged for hours with no letting up in sight. Dark would come soon and the Bitters decided to pull back and camp for the night. This was good. The dwarves were not used to battle and were getting tired. Sleep would help them to be ready for battle in the morning. They all cleaned themselves and their weapons, had dinner, and went to bed.

By the morning, all were rested and ready for battle. They heard noise and chanting from the enemy troops. A man on a tall black horse was riding through the camp stirring up the troops. "I am Tupragult! Follow me to the dwarves' riches!" He held up a golden chalice studded with gems. We will have many things like this! Then he took handfuls of gold and silver pieces and threw them to the troops. "Follow me and we will all be rich!" He repeated this over and over until the whole camp was chanting his name. "Tupragult! Tupragult!" Then, still holding up the chalice, he cried, "We attack!" The Bitters ran toward the mountain shouting his name. The onslaught was fast and furious. The dwarves had placed themselves in a long line about ten lines deep with more waiting in the tunnels. The Bright Elves held up their shields to catch the sunlight, shining it into the eyes of the Bitters. The dwarves took advantage of this using their crossbows to kill many Bitters.

Tall Sky had a vision of King Aryante's forces coming close to the battle, and called out, "Aryante's men approach!" At that, the dwarves fought with renewed strength, but were being driven back by the sheer numbers of Bitters. King Farin called for a retreat, but there appeared a thorny hedge at the tunnel door. Tall Sky spoke to the hedge commanding it in the name of Creator God to die. The thorny hedge withered to the ground leaving only ashes. The dwarves retreated into the tunnels and continued fighting at the entrance. Aryante's forces attacked from the southwest driving into the hordes of bitters, forcing them back. Seeing this, many of the bitters fighting at the door turned to fight Aryante's men. This gave the dwarves advantage and they emerged from the tunnels to renew battle in front of the entrance.

King Farin was set upon by five Bitters and was swinging his ax wildly trying to defend himself when Aleph joined in wielding a sword. He cut the first Bitter in half at the waist, immediately getting the second one with a thrust to the chest and pulling the sword out, he swang his blade to slice the Bitter to his right in the neck. King Farin cut the other two with a forward slash and a backward slash of his battle ax, blood flying off his ax in all directions.

Tupragult had noticed the two bright elves at the entrance and decided to take care of them. As he approached, Tall Sky turned bright, and Aleph shot Tupragult in the eye sending an arrow into his brain. Tupragult dropped to the ground lying flat on his back with an arrow sticking up out of his eye, and a golden chalice at his side. It was a fitting end to one of Avidora's creations. Her potion had made his skin thick and hard, but had not protected his eyes. Several dwarves hanged Tupragult from a tree limb for all to see.

Tall Sky took up the bow and arrows and proceeded to shoot a dozen Bitters in one minute. He continued to do this from his vantage point near the tunnel entrance. Bodies were stacked up so that the bitters had to climb over the dead to get at the dwarves. It formed a most unnatural barrier. From this pile, flowed a river of blood heading toward the main group of the Bitters. When the rest of the Bitters saw this and the battlefield strewn with hacked apart bodies, they turned and ran. Aryante's men had the Bitters in his area surrounded intending to march them to a prison. Many Bitters, however, escaped, running for their lives. At this point the dwarf pony riders took off after them shooting their crossbows as they rode. The pony riders killed many of the Bitters as they ran.

The next day, Dwarves and Base Camp soldiers worked together to clean up the battlefield. They filled the trenches with the dead, poured oil on them and set them on fire. After that, they filled the trenches with dirt. It took all day. There was a pile of weapons and armor five feet high. The soldiers took much of that and the silver found in their pockets.

King Farin gave gold medallions on gold necklaces to Tall Sky, Aleph, Quickturn, and Jaylek. King Farin said, "I would like to talk to you about something that has been troubling me. There are Gullandian children coming over the mountains with no place to go. Some have stopped in my tunnel to get warm. We feed them and let them stay overnight, but they walk south in the morning. They need help."

"I'm aware of this problem. They should head for Home Fire. Rando has helped other displaced people. I will talk to him about this, but for now, send them to Home Fire," said Tall Sky.

Quickturn left to supervise his battalion. They followed the Bitters who had scattered, but were headed south. Jaylek returned to his army to care for the wounded. They would stay in their cavern for a while until the wounded were healed. Tall Sky and Aleph stayed with the dwarves for several days to help heal their wounded and introduce them to God. Many dwarves asked God to live in their hearts. When they left, King Farin gave Tall Sky a bag of assorted gems as a wedding present and a beautiful ring for Melody.

THE RIDE TO LOADREL

Tall Sky left for Loadrel in the morning. They rode fully armed to defend themselves from fleeing Bitters. Their first destination was Yardrel to check on Steben's farm. They rode for hours without seeing any Bitters. Yardrel people said that there had been bands of elves come through and some of them bought food, but they seemed to be in a hurry to get somewhere. They rode to the farm and checked it. There was nothing amiss there. Steben had left his horses and the wagon at a neighbor's farm. Their next stop would be Home Fire.

Tall Sky became apprehensive as they neared Home Fire. He had seen several burned homes on the way and knew that the Bitters had taken this road. He saw a band of Bitters here and there trying to keep out of sight. Tall Sky said, "Most of the Bitters must have taken the other side of the forest. You know the King stationed some soldiers at Malwood market to catch slavers. I'll bet they have been busy."

"Yes, Malwood would be a place known to the Bitters, and the Malwood Road would be one that they would think safe for them." said Aleph. Upon reaching the trail entrance to Home Fire, they were met by five of Rando's men. One of them led Tall Sky and Aleph to the camp. No building was going on. Rando had his men on alert and ready to answer any alarms from the sentries he had placed along the road. Rando met with them by the fire and had food and drink brought to them. As they ate, Rando told them of his activities. "We have been ambushing the Bitters as they travel this way. At first there were just a few, but today they come by regularly riding toward Loadrel. We set up a pyre in that clearing across the road and have been putting the bodies on it so that they will not be a warning to more Bitters coming this way. I figure that the ones going toward Loadrel are running away from the battle and would be in the kind of mood to attack and loot. With your lady and my son in Loadrel, I thought it best to eliminate that danger."

Tall Sky laughed and said, "Rando, you are a true friend and I thank you. When I get to Loadrel I will have all the builders there to come help you build this town. One good turn deserves another. Oh, did you get any good loot from those Bitters?"

"Yes, we did," said Rando with a broad smile. "I need to hear it from you. The battle was a victory. Yes?"

"It was a huge battle with many lives lost on both sides, but Aryante's soldiers are marching about a hundred Bitters off to prison, and we filled two long trenches with bodies," said Tall Sky. "It was a victory."

"You must be tired. Do you want to spend the night and get a fresh start in the morning?" asked Rando.

"I thank you for asking, but I must get home to Melody and I have just enough time to do it before nightfall. Salek will be with us. We should be alright if we ride straight through," said Tall Sky.

"I will send two of my men with you. They can help gather building materials and wouldn't mind spending a few nights at the inn," said Rando.

"Great idea, but I have to leave right away," said Tall Sky.

BACK HOME

Within minutes, the five men were riding down the road toward Loadrel. The men rode quietly and vigilantly. They watched and they listened. The road to Loadrel was deserted. They reached Loadrel as the sun set. They were exhausted and went into the Laborer's Reward for a mug of ale and some dinner. Tall Sky asked Beldock to let Melody know that he had returned. In the meantime, he drank some ale to wash the dusty dry feeling down his throat. "I'm so happy to be home I can hardly stand it," said Tall Sky.

Melody came running across the floor. She hugged him and said, "Tall Sky, you're here. I'm so glad you're home. Did you miss me? I missed you. Don't ever leave me again. Are you alright? Did you get injured? Was the battle really bad?" Tall Sky kissed her and said, "I'm fine and I love you. I have to ask you a serious question. Do you know that our life spans are not the same and that you will grow old and I won't. Will that bother you too much? It won't bother me, but you must think about it."

"I have already thought about it. I now this about elves, and if you don't mind, it won't bother me either," said Melody.

Tall Sky said, "I have a gift for you. It's from King Farin, the dwarven king." He took out the ring and put it on her finger. It was a large emerald. "I promised you that when I returned, we would be engaged."

"Oh my gosh! Oh my gosh! Did you hear that everybody? We're engaged!" said Melody.

"Tall sky looked at her and said, "You're scaring the dragon." True enough, Daisy was dancing about on her shoulder and chirring loudly. He petted the dragon and talked soothingly to her and Daisy settled down. Then they all sat down to a good meal. "So, has anything been happening here while I was gone?" asked Tall Sky. "Were there any roving bands of Bitters coming through?"

"We saw a few come through. The men in our village went outside with drawn swords, and they kept on riding through town." said Beldock. "We haven't seen any these past few days. I wonder why."

"Rando's men have been entertaining them as they pass by Home Fire. They have a pyre set up in a clearing across the street that is loaded with murderers and robbers and slavers. Rando said that he was protecting Loadrel for Melody and Steben," said Tall Sky. "He sent Flint and Cliff with us for protection. I told Rando that you could get some labor rounded up to help him and his men build their homes this week. They need them done before the snow flies. They're just living in tents out there. Flint and Cliff know what building materials they need. I thought we could put it all together tomorrow and find whatever we can. Also, Steben's Papa builds furniture. Maybe our local furniture maker would let them build some furniture for them in his shop. Either that or he could go back home and build it."

"We certainly are grateful to Rando for protecting the town and I'll get on this right away tomorrow," said Beldock. "Would anybody want more ale?"

Tall Sky said, "No, I would like to go next door and clean up a bit and get ready for bed." It's been a long day of riding from sun up to sun down." He got up and they went next door to Laskron's. Laskron asked, "What was the battle like?"

Tall Sky replied, "Remember the Purge of Malwood? It was like that. Now I'm getting ready for bed." Tall Sky bathed and changed clothes. Elise and Emmy were already asleep in Elise's bed. The girls went off to their room and cuddled into their sleeping rolls. Amidra, Liadra and Melody were all engaged and happily went to sleep. Daisy curled up on Melody's pillow and purred.

The next morning there were two little girls waking them. Elise ran into the room, said her usual good morning to Daisy and proceeded to pull off Melody's cover. Elise kissed each one of the girls on the cheeks and told them it was time for breakfast. Then she ran to the kitchen, grabbed a piece of bacon, and held it under Tall Sky's nose until he opened his eyes and ate the bacon. "Elise, you had better go get into some day clothes," Tall Sky said. "I need some tea." He got up and went into the kitchen where Amidra was cooking breakfast. He sat down with a good hot cup of tea and tried to clear his head.

Melody walked in and said, "There's my hero. Thank you for my ring. It's so pretty. What's this?" she asked fingering the medallion around his neck.

"King Farin Stronghand, King Under the Mountain, gave that to me. See, it has his symbol on it, an ax crossing a pick. They use an ax in battle and a pick for mining," said Tall Sky. Everyone came in and sat down to a breakfast of fried potatoes, eggs, bacon, and fresh baked bread with jam. It was hard for Tall Sky to get into the business of everyday life after having been in battle mode for a week, but he tried. He was thankful when Beldock walked in with news that he had contacted fifteen men who were ready to go with Flint and Cliff to help build the houses at Home Fire. Beldock wanted to talk to him about government at Home Fire. It was a little early for it, but it was good to work these things out before any problems arose.

"A town needs a Chief to make decisions when necessary and to collect taxes for the province and to take care of local things, like the waste disposal pit and the road. They will have to appoint people to take care of these by enlisting volunteers. Also, they need someone in charge of the militia. This usually is the Chief. I think Rando should keep the position of the Chief, since he has obviously performed those duties well for a long time. He is a natural leader. How soon do you think we should talk to Rando about this?" asked Beldock

"We should wait until the homes are finished," said Tall Sky.

Beldock added, "I asked Jelsareeb to collect taxes. I'm too busy with the inn and she is very good with numbers and knows everybody, so that worked out well. Rando could have a woman do that for the group and then pay workers for their time on projects, and pay the province taxes. That way, Rando would not feel that he has to do it all himself. I predict that this town of his will grow rather quickly. It is well located on Lake Perilough, but on high enough ground to not be endangered by flooding. He is also near the main road for access to other towns. I'm excited about this. Rando chose his location well."

"It sounds like a great project, but I want to stay here for about a week. Tell them to build a guest shelter of some kind. An inn would be great, but I don't know if they have time for that before winter. I'll go with you when you talk to Rando about the government. We have gotten to be friends," said Tall Sky.

"OK. I've got to get back to the inn now. We're expecting a lot of people today who are hungry for news about the Bitters and the battle. Maybe you could stop by and tell them about it," said Beldock.

Tall Sky asked Melody to go for a walk along the lake. It was a beautiful, sunny day with just a light breeze blowing. Sunlight was gleaming on the water. Daisy was riding on her shoulder. "We have to talk about Daisy," said Tall Sky. "You know, soon she will be old enough to use those wings of hers. You have to let her be what she is. She is a wild animal that flies for fun and sometimes for food. She will find a mate someday and lay an egg like the one you found her in. You will have to encourage her to fly a little at a time until her wing muscles are strong. Don't worry; she will come back to you and to a nesting box that you will provide for her. She will still love you and depend on you for bathing and oiling and food, but your relationship will change a little as she grows up..... Just as you have changed as you grew up. This is healthy for her."

"OK," said Melody a little disheartened. Daisy lay down on her shoulder and chirred in her ear. She wasn't going to like it, but she would do it if it was good for Daisy. They walked back to Beldock's garden behind the workshop and sat down on a bench. The garden had wound down some because of autumn approaching, but there were still some fragrant flowers and vegetables growing. "I should be helping with the garden now. There are some vegetables to be harvested and some weeding and fall planting to be done. I used to help with the gardening at home, except that I would complain about it. Now that I have you, everything is different."

"I understand. I love you, Culina," he said, and kissed her. She kissed him back passionately. He said, "I want to make love to you. How soon do you want to be married?"

"We should probably get a house before we marry," said Melody.

"Good. Let's walk around and see if we can find one," said Tall Sky.

WEDDING PLANS

eanwhile, back at the inn, Amidra and Steben were arranging for their wedding by talking to Laskron who said that they could be married soon, but that they should stay in Loadrel for another week until the escapees from the battle had cleared the area. They were anxious to get back to their new farm and begin life as a family with Emmy. Mama and Papa said that they were having fun vacationing at the inn, so that was alright with them. Mama and Mina had become friends and Papa was making furniture.

Tall Sky and Melody returned from house hunting with good news. A house had become available close to the inn and they bought it. It was a two story white house with a fence out front and roses growing next to the house. There was a garden out back with a shed full of gardening tools. There was also a window where Daisy could have a nesting box with an entrance to the house and to the outside. During the winter, they could bring the box inside and shutter the window.

Now, Laskron had a dilemma. Who should he marry first? Tall Sky and Melody's house has furniture and they could move in right away, so they should be married first. Melody said that she could wear the dress that Tall Sky had purchased for her at Malwood. They decided to marry the following day. So they went shopping. They needed some household items like soap, candles, towels and bedding. Melody had stars in her eyes, but she knew that they would be happier with some food in the house and a few pans and plates and silverware. She also wanted a broom and some cleaning rags. She asked Papa to make Daisy a nesting box. Laskron and Mina said they would tell people that the wedding would be tomorrow afternoon at Spirit Hall.

Steben and Amidra helped carry Tall Sky and Melody's purchases to their new home. Then they all went back to Laskron's to tell them the good news. Emmy said, "My mommy and daddy are going to be married just as soon as it safe to ride on that road. Is Grandpapa making furniture for you, too?"

"No," said Melody. "Our house comes with furniture already. We just had to buy a few things like food and some cleaning supplies. I'm so excited. Liadra, would you help me to get my dress ready? I'm sure it's wrinkled. I haven't really looked at it since we arrived here from Malwood."

While the girls worked on her dress, Aleph and Tall Sky took Steben into their room for prayer. They had Steben to lie down on the bed while they lay their hands on his forehead and asked Father God to heal their friend. They grew bright and light came through their hands. Steben fell into a deep sleep. They left the room and let Steben sleep. A little while later, Steben walked into the sitting room and said, "Why did you leave? I thought we were going to pray. Where are the girls?"

His friends laughed and Aleph said, "How do you feel, Steben? You sound really good."

Steben said, "I feel fine. What do you mean, I sound good? I'm talking better. That's what you mean. Amidra! I'm talking better!" Amidra came into the room.

"What happened?" she asked.

"Listen to me. I can talk just like everybody else. Tall Sky and Aleph prayed for me. God healed me," said Steben. "I'm so happy!"

"Steben," said Laskron, "If anybody deserves healing you do. You are a good friend to all of us."

The girls went back to their room to work on Melody's attire for her wedding. They found a tiara for her to wear and a beautiful necklace. Then everybody went to the inn for dinner.

Trag and Arinya discussed their plans. They wanted to get set up in a business like a retail shop with a house and garden in back. That would be very convenient, but would have to do some building first. They already bought a building and filled it with some goods, but they needed a house built in back. They may have to move into the building for a while and should get married first. That would give them time to get the shop set up. Trag thought that this would be the best thing to do. He needed to get the house built and had hired someone to do it. The foundation was laid and part of the house had been built, but it would take several weeks to complete.

Melody said, "We all want to get married. Why don't we all get married at once? It would probably set some kind of record for four couples to be married at once in the same place. What do you think about that? I think it would be fun. Then we could have a big party and stay at the inn. It's like we all started out together and now we get married together. We are best friends after all. Arinya, Amidra, and Liadra thought that this was a good idea.

Melody said to the men, "We were talking and decided that we all want to get married at once tomorrow. Then we could come back to the inn and have a big party. Wouldn't that be fun?" The men sat there amazed and a bit in shock. Then they all said to each other, "That does sound like fun. Not a bad idea. I think it's a great idea. Let's do this." After dinner, the girls were delighted and went back to their room to talk and get things ready for all of them.

As the men talked about the wedding celebration, they decided that a large party should be held outside, with music and a maypole for the kids and games and lots of wine and ale and cakes. Like the grustabist feast, there should be meats roasting outside. This would take time to set up and could not be done in just one morning. So, they called the girls in and told them that they would set up the celebration, but that they would need more time to get it together. The wedding was postponed for several days to allow people to prepare food and for the men to set up the fires and the tables. This was going to be a great party. Laskron was in charge of the music. Steben would talk to Jelsareeb about cakes and breads. Tall Sky and Trag would gather the wood and set up the outdoor cooking area. Aleph would set up a Maypole and games for the children, of course, with the aid of village women. Beldock would get the word out to the villagers about the wedding celebration and ask them to help set up the party.

The next day everyone pitched in and got to work. Laskron contacted the local musicians. There was a group who played together and they said that they would be happy to play at the party. Jelsareeb told Laskron that she would begin baking breads and cakes right away. Trag and Tall Sky asked some men to help them and they took a wagon to the woods and filled it with wood that was lying about on the forest floor. Then they brought it back and stacked it into three separate piles. They would have roast lamb, pork and fish. Aleph talked to some of the village women about setting up games for the children. They had some good ideas and helped him to gather the materials for the games. Beldock brought up kegs of ale and wine from the cellar. Mina baked some pies. The whole town was buzzing with activity.

Beldock talked to Tall Sky about including Rando's group in the party. "It would be a chance for Rando to see a town in action and a chance for his people to have some fun. They have gone through some really hard times with fighting Bitters and being constantly vigilant. They need a break from all that and from the building that they are doing," said Beldock.

"I know. They should get to know some of Loadrel's people. There should be friendly relations between our two towns. We found that out recently with the Bitters problem," said tall Sky. "I'll ask Salek to ride out there and invite Rando. He might like to see Steben get married. After all, he did raise him."

The girls helped Melody to make the green dress that she had been wanting. A girl should have a new dress for her wedding. The other girls had already made new dresses from the material they got from the Purge of Malwood. They each chose a pretty gemstone necklace to wear. Each girl had a different colored dress. Amidra had a blue dress to match her eyes. Melody had a green dress to match her eyes. Liadra had a rust colored dress, and Arinya's dress was pink which worked well with her dark hair and brown eyes. They were having fun deciding how to wear their hair. Amidra would wear her hair up in a fancy do. Arinya would wear her loose, tumbling down her back. Liadra would also wear her hair loose and Melody would have her red curls up with some of it trailing down her back. They would not tell the men about this as they wanted to surprise them. Melody decided to let the two little girls hold Daisy, so they could start practicing this now. The girls were delighted. They loved Daisy and Daisy loved them, so they held her and played with her off and on all day. Laskron took the girls to the local tailor and had them fitted for new dresses. Later they all met at the inn for dinner.

"How is the party comming along?" Melody asked. Tall Sky reported that the wood was in place for the fires and that the meats had been ordered. Laskron said that the musicians had agreed to play after the dinner. Steben said that Jelsareeb had started baking already. Aleph said that some village mothers who had small children were getting games ready for the kids, and that someone was constructing a maypole. Everything was being done.

"How are you girls doing?" Steben asked.

"Just fine," said Melody. "We are making my dress and the tailor is making dresses for Elise and Emmy."

"Laskron is getting flowers ready for Vision Hall," said Liadra.

After dinner, they went to Laskron's for one final night of single life.

Their conversation that night was about sex. Melody said, "I wonder what sex is like. Do any of you know? Does it hurt?"

Amidra ansered, "I asked the midwife about it, because some of the girls were injured down there. She said that there was a membrane, like a piece of skin that breaks and bleeds, but that it doesn't hurt. She said in normal sex, it doesn't hurt except a little the first time, but usually it feels really good. She also said that we should have some wine to help us relax before the first time, because it's important to relax. She also said that after the first time, you can put some lard up there that will help to keep you from getting pregnant and will lubricate you."

"This sounds complicated," said Liadra. "Oh well, I guess we'll be alright. Everybody else is, and if it hurts, I'll just tell him to slow down." At that they laughed and went to bed.

THE WEDDING

Morning came with two very excited little girls waking up Liadra, Amidra, and Melody. They grabbed Daisy and took her to have breakfast in the kitchen. This being Daisy's favorite time, she did not object. There was a breakfast of sausage and hot cakes with jam and tea. Everyone was still tired from all of the preparations, but was also excited to get ready for the wedding. The men had found some special clothes in the stuff from Malwood. After breakfast the girls bathed and worked on their hair. Melody's dress was beautiful. It had a princess waistline with a full skirt. Its bodice was cut in a fairly low V and the sleeves were medium puff down to her elbows. The material was a shiny emerald green.

The girls were getting ready and Laskron had the men to go next door for a while. They needed to give a little time to finish up. People had already come to the inn and to Spirit Hall. Very shortly the time was come for the grooms to walk to Spirit Hall. They were asked to take seats in the front row next to Rando and Steben's parents. The girls then walked to Spirit Hall looking like royalty. When they were at the door, the grooms were asked to stand and face the back to receive their fiances. The Hall was beautifully decorated with roses and Laskron placed a banner up front that said, "The Two Shall Be One." The brides walked proudly down the aisle to the front to greet four very happy, smiling men. Emmy and Elise held their new mommy's hands.

Beldock said, "It is a pleasure to officiate at your weddings. You are all dear friends of mine and I am honored to unite you in marriage. Liadra and Laskron, Amidra and Steben, Arinya and Trag,

Melody and Tall Sky, do you promise to love each other, to protect each other, and to take care of each other not only in health but in sickness also?"

They answered, "We do."

"Will you raise your children to be kind, God loving people?"

They answered, "We will."

"Liadra, do you promise to be a good mother to Elise?"

Liadra answered, "I do."

Amidra and Steben, Do you promise to be good parents to Emmy?"

"We do," they answered.

"Father God, we ask your blessings upon these couples today. Be with them, guide and protect them from this day forward."

"By the power vested in me as the Chief of this town, I pronounce you married and parents. You may kiss and sign these papers. Your gifts are at the inn."

The brides and grooms walked out of the church and into a group of well wishers where they were kissed and hugged. Then everybody walked over to the party in front of the inn. There was a table set up for the newlyweds with wine and food. Steben's parents and Rando sat at a table near them. There were other tables scattered about and blankets on the ground. There were tables spread with rolls, platters of meat, bowls of vegetables, cheese, and cakes. It was a feast fit for a king. They ate and drank their fill and the musicians began to play. Children were running around the maypole holding brightly colored ribbons that flowed down from the top. Other children were playing games and some of the adults were dancing.

Rando came up to Beldock and said, "Where are those slave girls we liberated?"

"Oh, they're around here. There they are watching the maypole. We sort of put them on kid patrol," said Beldock. "Want to meet them?"

"Yes, and a couple of my men would too," said Rando.

" I'll go get them," said Beldock.

There were five girls standing there and Rando brought three men over to meet them. One of them Rando was particularly attracted to. She was tall, with long, brown hair and hazel eyes. She wore a brown fringed leather smock top belted with circular silver and turquoise pieces, a fringed skirt, and high leather boots. Beldock introduced them and they walked down by the lake to talk. "Great wedding, wasn't it?" said Rando.

"Beautiful," said Alqua. "I've wanted to meet you, Rando. It was you and your men who helped to free us. I can't tell you how much that meant to me. I hadn't been auctioned yet and I sure didn't want to be. I don't think that I could have lived as a slave. You see, I am used to the outside. I like the land and the water. I like to garden and swim in the pond. I would like to see your Home Fire. It intrigues me."

"Well, it isn't much now, but in a week or two, we will have permanent houses. The men in Loadrel are helping us to build them. Right now we are living in tents. It's comfortable to a point, but in the winter, we would like to have homes to stay warm in. Some of us have wives, but some don't. There are a few children there too. We raised Steben, you know. We saved him from the slavers and took him to Home Fire," said Rando.

"That's impressive. He turned out to be a good man. You did a good job. That's why you were sitting at the table with his parents. I kept watching you. You are a very interesting man," said Alqua. "When could I visit Home Fire?"

"It's just a camp now, but soon we will have houses. There is still a possibility of danger from the Bitters, so you should wait until next week. Also, we might have some furniture by then. Steben's Papa is making some for us. It's been really good having Loadrel people for friends. Next week why don't you ride out with the workers? There will be more comming out there next week. I would really like to see you again," said Rando.

"I would like to see you again too," said Alqua.

The other men of Rando's group were enjoying talking with the other slave girls. They were all abducted from farms, so they were well acquainted with the making of soap, candles, clothes and gardening. The men were very interested in finding wives to help them in their new homes. They were going to turn Home Fire into a home town. Rando's men had great compassion for these girls having seen the auction and knowing how they were treated. They had killed the slavers, but were still angry with the slavers and their kind. Having lived alone for a long time, they understood how precious these women were.

Flint and Cliff were helping Vanya and Almarie with the children. They were having a relay race. It was a good way to show the girls that they were normal people and knew how to interact with children. It took the attention off the girls so that they would feel more at ease. After talking with the men for a while, they decided to join Alqua at Home Fire next week. They thought it might be fun to be part of a brand new town.

The wedding party was turning more festive. The guests had formed a circle around the brides and grooms and were chanting, "Dance! Dance!" The musicians played a pretty melody and the couples held each other dancing. Tall Sky said, "I love you, Culina," and kissed her. She cuddled close to him feeling all warm and happy. Then they all joined into the dance. Ale and wine was flowing and everybody had an exciting time, dancing and talking.

After a while, the newlyweds headed to their respective rooms at the inn. The two little girls stayed at the party with Mina keeping a watchful eye on them. She would keep them for the night. Daisy went home with Tall Sky and Melody and went to sleep cuddled into a soft, warm quilt in her own nesting box. Amidra and Steben went back to the inn along with Trag and Arinya. Liadra and Laskron went home to experience their wedding night. It had been a wonderful, magical day.

The next morning the group met at the inn for breakfast. The girls felt a little self conscious and shy, but that changed when Tall Sky said, "I think we should go to Trag and Arinya's place and help them put that store of theirs into order. I'm sure they could use some help putting things out on display. We don't have anything planned today, and that would be kind of fun." Papa was busy making furniture, but Mama, Liadra, Elise, Amidra, Steben, Emmy, Tall Sky and Melody were all available to help. They would like to see Trag and Arinya in a place that was ordered and livable, since their house was not yet completed. Arinya looked very relieved.

Putting together a store had seemed like a huge, impossible task and neither of them knew where to start. "We sure could use the help," said Trag.

"This is going to be fun," Emmy said to Elise. "There are all kinds of things in piles over there and we can look through them." It was a curious child's paradise full of adventure.

"Let's go, Mommy," said Elise. All of them walked over to Trag's store with curiosity and expectation. The store was indeed full of piles of things that needed to be sorted. Liadra said, "Let's start by putting all the clothing and materials over in that empty corner. Any jewelry, gems, and metals we should put in that corner. Anything else we can put in that corner. Just leave their bed corner alone. The project was well underway. The kids were really enjoying themselves looking through pretty things. They put themselves in charge of jewelry and gems.

As they were all very busy, they heard a commotion outside, the pounding of horses' hooves and shouting. A group of seven Bitters were riding into town toward the inn. Tall Sky grabbed a bow and a quiver of arrows and the men went out the back door sneaking behind houses to the inn. The Bitters had just dismounted. Tall Sky shielded himself, Steben and Trag. Then he pulled out arrows one after another shooting the Bitters. Tall Sky went into the inn and told Beldock to get some men to dispose of the bodies and Trag searched the bodies for silver pieces. They stripped the bodies of any saleable items and took the horses back to the store. The horses held bags of loot. Going through the bags, they found some really nice household items and two dolls with satin dresses which Elise and Emmy confiscated. There were silver goblets and platters, rings, necklaces, and some fine clothing. The girls divided these things leaving some to be sold in the store. Steben said, "They must have raided a nice home to get these things. There's no blood here, so maybe the people weren't home."

"One can hope," said Amidra. "I wonder how they got past Home Fire."

Tall Sky said, "They probably rode close to Malwood to avoid being seen. This was a sneak attack. They planned this to take silver and food from the inn. Both Beldock and Mina could have been killed. This town must set sentries. I'll talk to Beldock about it." They kept on working until midday when they finally stopped and went to the inn for lunch. They needed to make shelving, so they stopped by Laskron's for some ideas. He told them where to get some lumber.

Beldock said, "I will get some fishermen together to do the sentry work. Those who could build are at Home Fire this week. We are really short on men. Tall Sky, maybe you could take charge of this and tell them what to do and where to be. Obviously the Bitters are staying off the main road. Steben could help with this, too. He at least has some experience with fighting the Bitters and with standing sentry at Home Fire. I'm surprised that they tried this attack during the day. They must be feeling frustrated and reckless right now because of the Othrund battle."

"Business as usual," said Melody. "Life is nothing if it's not exciting." Tall Sky laughed and kissed her.

"Isn't it the truth," Culina, "Isn't it the truth," he said. Daisy relished eating lunch. They had fish and cornbread with butter and a salad. She especially liked the apple pie for dessert.

After lunch, the group walked back to the store stopping to get some lumber on the way. They continued making shelves and stocking the shelves with items for sale until the place looked like a well ordered store with nothing on the floor but the bed they were using.

"This looks great," said Trag. "Thank you all so much. It would have taken us a week to do this by ourselves."

"You're welcome. We just couldn't leave you in this mess," said Steben. "We must all work together to have a good life. That's how we were at Home fire. We are blessed to have each other."

"So far we have done well together. We are married and have homes. That is a lot to accomplish in a short time," said Arinya. "I'm really proud of all of us. We're a good team."

"And a hungry one," said Trag hugging Arinya. "Let's go back to the inn and celebrate. Who's on sentry duty?"

"Beldock has people assigned until tomorrow, so we have at least tonight to ourselves, unless they catch any Bitters lurking about," said Tall Sky.

Dinner was busy at the inn with the locals filling up the place to get the news. Rumor gets around fast in a village. People were all worried about the Bitters that came into town. Would there be more? How can they defend themselves against these things? Tall sky and Beldock tried to reassure them that the sentries would report any Bitters they see near the town and that Tall Sky and the militia would take care of any problems that arise. "These things always happen after a war. The danger should subside in a few more days. The soldiers in Malwood will stop some of the Bitters heading this way," said Tall Sky.

"Ale for everybody!" called out Tall Sky. They drank some ale and ordered dinner. Mina brought out stew for everyone including Daisy who was famished and immediatel y hopped down to her saucer to eat some bread and cheese and stew meat that Mina always cuts up into small pieces just for her. "Aleph, I want you to take the night watch tonight. Have the sentries report to you with any sightings of the enemy. Report to me with any concerns. I will take over for you in the morning after breakfast."

After a few glasses of ale, Tall Sky and Melody walked with Trag and Arinya to their homes. Amidra asked Steben, "How long will it be before we go to our farm in Yardrel?"

"I don't know," he said."I want to go home too, but mostly we want to be safe when we travel and Papa does need more time to make the furniture for Home Fire. Maybe I should offer to help with that. There may be some things I could do, if I just copy them. While I do that, you could go upstairs and visit with Liadra and Elise."

"We can do that. I would like to visit with Liadra and Elise. If you help Papa and Laskron, we might be able to leave sooner," said Amidra.

"That's the idea, and I'm sure Liadra could use some company what with Laskron spending all his free time making glass items for Home Fire," said Steben. "Let's go upstairs," Steben said with a smile.

"That's fine with me, big man," said Amidra. They said goodnight to Mama and Papa and went to their room.

"They're such a nice couple," said Mama.

"I'm so glad they have each other," said Papa.

The night passed peacefully enough for the couples to get some much needed rest. Tall Sky and Melody walked to Trag and Arinya's store to get them and head over to the inn to talk to Beldock. It was a bright, sunny day with a blue sky and the sun glittering off the water of Lake Perilough. Tall Sky said, "I'm thinking of taking a ride to Home Fire to check on their progress and the presence of Bitters in the area. We really need to be informed about this. A lot of Bitters ran away and they had not yet fought in the battle. So these Bitters could be rested and ready for trouble. We can't afford to relax at this point. One attack on Loadrel could mean the loss of lives of some really good people and their children. A group of them could set fire to the whole town. Do you want to go with me, Trag?"

"I'll go if we can get more men to go with us," said Trag. "I still remember being caught and tied up."

"We'll ask and see if there are others willing to ride with us," said Tall Sky.

"Please stay home with me," said Arinya who was still feeling unsettled and unsure. She remembered the Bitters from the auction and wanted to feel safe in her new home with her husband by her side.

"Tall Sky, I really think that it is too soon to leave Arinya here alone," said Trag.

"Yes, it is. I understand," said Tall Sky. "Maybe some of the single men would ride with me. Melody, you and Daisy should stay with Laskron and Liadra while I'm gone. In fact, you two should stay there too. He has the room and there is safety in numbers. That store of yours could look to the Bitters like a target. Arinya shuddered. Neither of them had thought of that.

When they arrived at the inn, Beldock was already talking with a group of men. Aleph was there reporting on the night's activities. He had already changed the sentries and was ready to go to bed. "How did it go last night, Aleph?" asked Tall Sky.

"The sentries saw some Bitters in groups of two or three and they were trying to get around the town without being seen. None of them tried to enter the town," said Aleph.

"Great," said Tall Sky. "What are my chances of riding safely to Home Fire? I was going to ask some of the single men in town to ride with me. Maybe Salek would go. Melody, go ask Laskron if you and Arinya and Trag could stay with him for a few days."

Aleph said, "I think your chances are good. The Bitters are not on the main road. It is always possible that some would attack you from the bushes, but a group of men would be intimidating to them, especially if they are visibly armed." Steben, Salek, Tall Sky, and two other men decided to ride out to Home Fire. Melody, Trag and Arinya went over to Laskron's. The two girls visited with Liadra, while Elise and Emmy played with their dolls.

"How do you like married life, Liadra?" asked Amidra.

"I love being married to Laskron. He is a wonderful, sensitive man. It's fun being a mother, too. I don't know how Elise is going to manage it when Emmy goes home. She and Emmy are close friends now. I'll have to look for someone to take Emmy's place. How are things going with you?"

"Fine," said Amidra, "but I am so impatient about waiting to go to Yardrel. I know that it's necessary for safety, but I can hardly wait to see our new farm again and make it look like a home. How are you holding up, Melody? You've been married for one day and he's already off on another trip."

"That part is not easy, but the time I had with him was wonderful. I just want to be near him all the time. I think Daisy is missing him already. She keeps chirring and looking around. I suppose all this war activity will settle down soon," said Melody.

"You know, when it's safe to do so, we should send messages home to our families," said Liadra. "They'll be so surprised."

"I was such a baby when I left home that they aren't going to believe the change in me," said Melody. "Tall Sky said that we could go visit them after a while. Did you know that Rando has struck up a friendship with Alqua? Maybe she'll be able to tame that wild man. She is really different. Maybe it will work."

Amidra said, "I think Rando is very handsome, but kind of hard. Vela said that he had helped all those people out there, though."

Liadra said, "I had a chance to talk with Alqua after she met Rando. She really likes him and respects him for fighting the Bitters and for living outside all that time. She likes being outside, too. Maybe they'll make a good pair. I'm glad Papa is helping to make furniture for them."

"Steben said that he could help with the furniture. He and Papa already made five tables and are working on chairs. Chairs were more intricate and took more time to assemble, so Steben started doing what they were doing and it really helped. Home Fire will have furniture on time," said Amidra.

Tall Sky, Steben, Salek, Rostor, and Vestro took some food for lunch and rode toward Home Fire. It was mid morning and they would be there by midday. "What a glorious day for a ride!" exclaimed Tall Sky. "The air is fresh and cool. You can tell that autumn is here. Look, some of the trees are changing color."

"Yeah, this is great," said Steben. They rode on for about an hour, when Tall Sky stopped.

He said, "Father God gave me a vision. Up ahead are Bitters hiding and waiting to ambush travelers. They must have heard our horses by now. We can tie our horses here and sneak up behind them or we can go home. If we go home, they will follow us to Loadrel. Either way we will have to fight them. In my vision I saw us kill them by sneaking up behind them."

"Let's do that. If they made it to Loadrel, our families would be in danger," said Steben.

God has told me in my heart that these Bitter Elves will never repent of their wickedness no matter what. Therefore, we will not give them any more opportunities to harm others," said Tall Sky.

"Alright," said Tall Sky. "We work in pairs. This is a death mission, their deaths, not ours. I will go first and shoot them with arrows. The next two will be Salek and Steben. Steben, you will hold the Bitter while Salek will slit his throat if he is still alive. Rostor and Vestro will come behind you and come forward if need be. Will you be able to do this?" They said that they would. Tall Sky quietly walked ahead. He spotted one of the Bitters and shot an arrow. A few yards away there was another. Tall Sky shot him and moved on. He did this quickly so as not to let there be any warning to the rest. One of the Bitters was still alive, so Salek slit his throat. The third Bitter was flailing about trying to pull an arrow from his back. Steben sat on his legs while Salek slit his throat. Then Rostor and Vestro moved up and dispatched the fourth one. The fifth one was dead. They had successfully killed all five of the Bitters. Then they searched the bodies for valuables and weapons and found their horses. They tied the horses together and took them with. Tall Sky looked at Steben and said, "Well done."

The rest of the ride was uneventful. They rode into Rando's camp with five extra horses and corralled them. "I see you had some trouble on your way," said Rando smiling.

"Just a little," said Tall Sky. "It's a good thing that you're clearing land. You're going to need it for grazing horses. Eventually you can sell some horses for silver. They have colts and you'll have more horses. How's the building coming along?"

"It's hard work cutting down trees, but we're doing alright. We've got five houses about half way up. Come and see. Each one has at least two bedrooms, a main room, and a bathroom. With kids you need a room for bathing. Our crews are working hard all day," said Rando. "How's married life?"

"It's great. No more lonely nights. No more frustration. It's good to have a woman to sleep with," said Tall Sky.

"I've often thought of that. When I get my house built, I want to marry. I met a girl I like. You may know her. Her name is Alqua," said Rando.

"I do know her. She's one of the slave girls we freed. She is a very nice woman and I think she would fit in well out here," said Tall Sky. "The word is that she likes you." Tall sky smiled, and Rando laughed.

"This week can't go too fast," said Rando. "She comes out here with a work crew next week. I hope this band of Bitters is the last one. We've killed so many I've lost count."

"What about the frequency of these attacks. Has that slowed down any?" asked Tall Sky.

"Yes, it has," said Rando. "I don't want her coming out here until there are no more Bitters coming by. I thought that it might be alright by next week. When she does come out here, could you ride with her?"

"I would be happy to," said Tall Sky.

"She's the first girl I've ever wanted in this way. She just has to be kept safe," said Rando.

"I know exactly how you feel. That's how I feel about Melody. Rando, you have a very exciting time coming your way," said Tall Sky. "I wish you all the best."

"Now, which one of these houses is yours?" asked Tall Sky. Rando showed him a good sized home with room for a family and a nice big fireplace.

"It's a good house, "said Tall Sky. "I think she will like it. When it's done, have one of the women plant some flowers along the front. Women like that. The furniture making is coming along well. As soon as a complete set is ready, I will have it brought out here for you. I'll also bring you some special items to make it look like a home inside. There are some things in Trag's store and Laskron has some glass items that would look nice in here. I'll have Melody buy some things for you like the stuff she bought for us when we moved into our house. Rando, I can't thank you enough for keeping Loadrel safe when I was away. It's a terrible feeling to know that there is nothing you can do to keep your loved ones safe. I couldn't leave the battle and I felt better knowing that you were in charge back here."

"We did our best. We managed to cut their numbers down. It's all we could do. I'm glad that the girls are safe in Loadrel. Mine is there, too," said Rando.

"King Farin told me about some kids running away from Gullandia," said Tall Sky. "If some of them come by here, let me know. We can figure out something for them. If we built an extra house or an inn, maybe, you might show them what to do to live out here. I haven't met any of them yet, but there may be some girls who will want to marry. It's possible that you could build your town like this."

Rando had become serious and thoughtful. "That is a possibility," he said. "We do need more people for a town, and if they need to be taught a skill that we don't know, they can learn it in Loadrel, or have one of the Loadrel people come here for a few days and teach them."

"Sounds like a plan," said Tall Sky. "Tell your sentries to keep a look out for them. Gullandia's loss will be your gain."

GULLANDIA

askilde and his family had just finished erecting the family teepee in the snow. It was very cold in Gullandia and the family was dressed in furs from head to toe. Raskilde was not looking forward to spending another winter walking about or riding on reindeer through an all white frozen terrain. It was hard work and very uncomfortable. The traditions of his people were ancient and demanded complete respect and obedience. He realized that he and his girlfriend Linnea would have to wait for two more years to marry at the age of eighteen. They wanted to marry now and move out of the area. They wanted to go to a warmer climate south of the Aikasse Mountains.

"Mama, I want to go see Linnea. They probably have their teepee up by now," said Raskilde.

"No," said his mother. "We will have supper now."

"I'm not hungry," said Raskilde.

"You will eat or your father will be very angry with you," said his mother, knowing that he would not disobey his father.

"I am strong. I know what to do. I should have my own tepee now," said Raskilde. "I want to marry Linnea now, not wait for two more years."

"Talk to your father," said his mother. That's how this conversation always ended. He was determined to escape this way of life. His two friends Sven and Sevrin agreed with him. They wanted out, too. There was only one thing to do. Other couples had escaped. He would talk to his friends about it.

"I'm tired of all this snow, Mother," said Raskilde.

"Quiet. You will offend the Snow Spirit," his mother said.

"Will you listen to yourself? You're afraid to offend the snow! That's crazy!" said Raskilde.

"Hush! The Snow Goddess will hear you," said his mother. Gullandians believed that all things have souls including rocks, mountains, trees, water, the sky and all animals. They had rituals for everything from birth to death. There were places they considered sacred where they could summon spirits of the dead and where the shaman could beat the sacred drum and everyone would chant to try to heal someone. They would also cast spells. All of this was highly secret. No outsiders were allowed into their circle of secrecy.

Raskilde's father came home and the family sat around a small fire in the teepee for supper which consisted of flatbread, deer jerky and some vegetables stewed in a pot. It was warm sitting near the fire, but the fire had to be maintained all day and all night. After supper, Raskilde met his friends Sven and Sevrin to discuss plans for escaping from this frozen land and from parents who worshipped everything. Raskilde said, "Can you believe that my Mother told me that I shouldn't offend the snow?"

"My parents keep setting out meat to please the snow goddess," said Sven. "I'll bet some dog is enjoying that."

"If I don't get out of here I think I will just go crazy," said Sevrin. "What are the girls saying about it? Are they willing to go with us?"

"They're worried, but they're used to moving around a lot following the herd. I think they'll be alright," said Sven. "The cold bothers them and they think about sunshine and flowers. They don't want to get stuck up here herding reindeer and having babies in a teepee," said Sven. "It's a terrible thing to expect of a girl."

"We could take a few reindeer with us, just a few to ride on and then maybe sell them when we get there," said Sevrin. "How will we live down there?"

"Maybe we could work on a farm, or maybe we could start our own farm," said Raskilde. "Other people do it, so we should be able to. I heard about a large lake down there. We could fish. We know how to fish."

"Well, no matter what we do, we will not be freezing and chasing reindeer all over the tundra," said Sven. "We will have to be very careful and stay away from any soldiers, both ours and theirs. Remember, there is a dispute over grazing our reindeer south of the mountains."

"Varaak was a prisoner and he was sent back to talk to our Chief about stopping fighting. Varaak said that an Elf named Tall Sky healed him and introduced him to the Father God. Tall Sky got him released so that he could talk to Chief about paying the farmers for the use of their land during the winter. It sounds like a really good deal," said Raskilde.

"That would be good, but I still don't want to live this far north," said Sven.

Time was passing and they still hadn't seen the girls yet. "Let's get the girls and talk to them about all this," said Sevrin.

Raskilde went to Linnea's tent and asked her father for permission to see her for a few minutes. He said it was alright for a few minutes. Linnea put on her jacket and went outside. "I missed you Raskilde," she said and kissed him. Linnea was of medium height with long, brown hair and brown eyes. She had a round nose and bow shaped lips set in a rounded face full of freckles.

He hugged her and said, "Linnea, I love you too, but my father won't let us marry yet. Sven and Sevrin will go with me to Aksanda. We want you, Sonja and Greta to come with us. We can make homes there and get married there. You don't want to spend winter here fighting the snow and on the move all the time, do you? Please say that you will come with me. We will be so lonely without each other," said Raskilde.

"I couldn't live without you," she said. "I'll go with you."

Sven and Sevrin also had successfully convinced their girls to leave with them. Raskilde said, "There is going to be a meeting at the sacred cave. When they are busy chanting, we will leave. They won't miss us until later."

"The pass isn't far from there, so we can take the pass to the other side," said Sven. "We really should get the reindeer to ride. It will make traveling easier and faster."

"Until tomorrow, then," said Sven. They went back to their teepees to spend their last night on the tundra.

The next morning brought more snow, but it wasn't a blizzard. They had breakfast and went out to check on the herd. To do this they had to ride around the herd and make sure there were no reindeer in trouble or injured. Then they had to work at curing and tanning the hides and smoking the meat. The women worked at sewing clothing and cooking. They planned to have dinner in the cave with about thirty other herdsmen.

The Sacred Cave was large with stalactites and stalagmites. The firelight sparkled on these lending an eerie and spiritual backdrop to the proceedings. The herders came in and settled down on the floor. The shaman started the ceremony with the bullroarer, a horn shaped to make a loud sound when swung around on the end of a string. The sound reverberated through the cave. Then he performed the joik, chanting and drumming and everyone joined in chanting. After a while, people were in a dreamlike state, and the friends walked outside to their reindeer and rode away.

They rode silently for a while with Raskilde in the lead. The snow falling covered their tracks and they were out of sight in minutes. They knew the way through the mountain pass from riding that way last winter. It would take about an hour to get through the pass to the other side. The boys were wondering where to go from there and the girls were daydreaming about flowers and butterflies. Unfortunately, the weather didn't hold. As weather is in the mountains, the wind increased and so did the snow. They covered their faces with scarves, but the snow pelted their eyes making it difficult to see. "We have to get into a cave or a tunnel pretty soon," said Raskilde. "When we get to the other side, we will turn east along the face of the mountain and look for a cave or a tunnel. There are dwarves who live nearby. Father traded meat and hides for knives with these dwarves. They're kind of a rough bunch, but we could stay in the tunnel until the morning."

THE TUNNELS

The group rode for a while longer and turned east toward the tunnel entrance. There was a great feeling of relief when they found the entrance and rode inside. "It feels a lot better in here. The air is warmer," said Greta, brushing the snow out off her blonde curls and eyelashes. She was a small girl with blue eyes and a shy demeanor.

Sonja dismounted and hugged Sven. "This is so exciting!" she said. "We're finally free! We can go anywhere we want and nobody can say no to us. I'm so happy. We can stay together tonight and every night."

"I think we should be quiet. We don't know who or what lives in here," said Sven.

Thogul Okri and Morin Longbeard were standing watch in the back of the tunnel entrance. They stepped out of the shadows dressed in furs with long scruffy hair and beards and holding axes. They demanded to know in loud voices what these people were doing in their tunnel. The girls were terrified and ran screaming across the battlefield toward the swamp. The boys ran after the girls and the dwarves ran after them all. The dwarves were screaming, "Don't go there! It's dangerous!" The children did not know dwarven and assumed that the dwarves were going to kill them. Running into that swamp was indeed dangerous, since it did not freeze over. There was a hot spring in the middle, so swamp creatures lived there comfortably all winter.

The girls were knee deep in warm water before they realized it. A large constrictor snake lunged at Greta, biting her arm and winding around her, squeezing her. Greta screamed and cried for help. Sevrin grabbed hold of the snake's tail and Raskilde and Sven tried to pull the snake off of her. Morin Longbeard stuck the handle of his ax between the snake and Greta's arm and yanked the ax toward him, severing the snake's neck. He then pried the jaws apart to release the snake's head from her arm. There were bite marks on her arm that were bleeding. Thogul Okri unwound the snake from around her body. She was crying, and Morin patted her head to comfort her.

Morin looked at her arm and pointed to the wound. Then he pointed to the tunnel entrance and helped her stand up. Sevrin helped her walk toward the tunnel entrance. When they walked in, they were greeted by female dwarves with food and wine. They were led to a meeting room where they could sit down. Morin asked for some water and bandages and dry clothes for Greta. Where words failed, hospitality prevailed. The wine warmed them and the food was very welcome. Thogul's wife Birgitta and King Farin's wife Heiki brought bandages, ointment and water. They cleaned Greta's wound and put ointment on it and bandaged her arm. They also gave her some medicine made of herbs to help fight any infection from the bite. The dwarves brought some hay for the reindeer, and the boys took off their saddles. Thogul and Morin motioned the group to a room with bedding and a warm fire. The bedding consisted of mats of straw covered with reindeer hide and fur covers, and there they would stay all night.

The girls finally got to cuddle up to their young men. Sonja combed out her long, red hair, her green eyes sparkling in the firelight. She smiled and cuddled up to Sven. Raskilde held Linnea and knew that this was the best night in his life so far. "I love you, Linnea, and I will always keep you safe."

Greta cuddled with Sevrin and said that she was sorry for running from the dwarves. "I understand. You were afraid of them. They had big voices and axes. All is well." He kissed her and held her tight.

The next morning they were greeted by Farin Stronghand, King Under the Mountain. He spoke their language enough to be understood. Farin was dressed in his official robe made of fur and wore a heavy gold necklace and a gold, jeweled crown. His brown hair was shoulder length and his beard was reddish brown and fanned out across his chest. "I am Farin Stronghand, King Under the Mountain. I bid you welcome. What brings you out here in the snow?"

Raskilde bowed his head in respect and said, "We are leaving Gullandia to live south in Aksanda. We wanted to be married, but our parents wouldn't allow it for two years."

"We trade with your people. They are good people. Are you sure you want to leave them?" asked Farin.

"Yes. We don't like so much snow. It seems like most of our lives are spent riding through the snow. Also, our parents talk about spirits all the time. It angers me that they really believe that things have souls and they sacrifice to these things. It just isn't true. I know this in my heart," said Raskilde.

King Farin said, "This is part of The Awakening foretold by my great grandfather. He had a vision of a great battle with all types of people in front of our home. There was an earthquake. He saw a Bright Elf standing in front of the battle glowing with a white light and holding his hands out commanding the earth to be still in the name of Father God. Then the hand of God wrote on the mountain these words: 'THESE ARE MY PEOPLE,' and under that, 'AWAKENING NOW.' That great battle happened last week. The words are on the mountain above the entrance to our tunnel. I believe that Father God sent you here to learn of Him. You see, we are people like you, only short. We marry, have children, and work hard to provide for them. That Bright Elf's name is Tall Sky. He told me about Father God and He healed many of my injured men."

"I heard of Tall Sky. He healed one of our soldiers and sent him back to discuss a truce until he could get an agreement with the farmers of Aksanda to trade with us for the use of grazing land during the winter," said Raskilde.

"That sounds like Tall Sky," said King Farin. "Tall Sky knows of the children of Gullandia leaving their homes. There are many dangers in Aksanda now that you should know about. There are Bitter Elves who have turned against Father God. They practice dark magic, kill people, and sell into slavery the people they catch.

There are many of them fleeing from the battle and looking for any opportunity to gather wealth. Tall Sky told me to send runaways to Home Fire for protection. Rando is the chief of Home fire and he is making a new town. They are building homes there and need more people. Home Fire is near Lake Perilough. Right now the road is dangerous, but the Bitters should soon be out of this area."

"Can we be married there?" asked Linnea.

"Getting married is easy," said King Farin. "You could be married here in our great hall. I perform marriage ceremonies, but first we must talk about Father God. He is the Creator of all things. He loves people and wants the best for them. He wants them to be kind to each other and to help each other. It grieves Him when people do bad things, but He will forgive them if they ask Him to. He will guide you and will send His Spirit to live inside of you. This will give you strength and you will have the right to ask Him for help in all things. There is great joy in this. You will be happy. Part of God's Spirit is discernment. You will know right from wrong, good from bad, and what is true. It is only through God's Spirit that you could know about your parents' worship being false. He was guiding you to Himself to learn the truth. It took a war to get my attention."

"I can understand that," said Raskilde. "I want the Creator God's Spirit to live in me. How do I do that?" asked Raskilde.

"Ask Him to forgive you for anything you did wrong and ask Him to live in your heart," said King Farin. "You can talk to him just like you are talking to me."

"Father God, I thank you for bringing us here. Please forgive me for my wrong thoughts and live in my heart," prayed Raskilde.

All six of them prayed this prayer. Then King Farin put his hand on Greta's wound and prayed for God to heal her arm.

"My arm doesn't hurt anymore," said Greta. "Oh, thank you, King Farin."

"Thank God for this. It is He who heals you," said King Farin.

Birgitta and Heiki came in to offer them breakfast of honey cakes and sausages. They brought two toddlers with them and the girls hugged them and let them sit on their laps. Sonja said, "I want some little ones like these."

"All in good time," said Sven. "We have to get married first."

"Let me show you our great hall. It is not far down the tunnel on the left. It is a natural cavern and, because of its size, we hold meetings and weddings there," said King Farin. They all followed him down a tunnel wide enough for four people to walk side by side. It gradually sloped down until it opened into a large room with seating arranged in a semicircle. "We usually have a girl sing a song of love and then I say the words. Then you must give a ring to your bride. I have those for you. Then you walk once around the room and go to your wedding table. There will be wine and food for everyone. Do you want to be married here?" asked King Farin.

They talked among themselves for a minute and Raskilde said, "Yes, we do."

King Farin said, "I'm going to leave you with Birgitta and Heiki, and they can show you around the tunnels. Not many people have seen the inside of Othrund. I have to talk to the chefs and let them know that there will be a wedding to prepare for this evening."

"Come with us," said Heiki. Her husband had taught her some of the language. They all walked down a tunnel that had rooms on either side. There were no doors on the openings, but the openings were on one side of the rooms with a small walkway into the room for privacy. Inside the room was furniture for people of their size. There was a smaller room for children. There were hides and furs on the beds. There was a table and chairs and shelves to keep things on. For every ten rooms there was a toilet room with running water to carry away waste.

Then they walked down another tunnel to the kitchen. It was a large room with hooks for pots and pans, stacks of dishes and bowls and silverware and cups made of metal. All was clean and polished. There was a long oven with spaces on top to set pots. Several chefs were already baking bread and mixing food in pots. There was one boy in charge of the fires under the oven. There were ten chefs in all, but they worked in shifts so that no one would get too tired.

Walking down some steps, they noticed that the air was getting warmer and moist. The steps ended at a pool of warm water. "This is where we soak our tired, aching muscles," said Heiki. There were some dwarves soaking in the water. They wore shorts so as not to offend women and children. The water was always fresh, because it moved in and out regularly.

The group then walked for a while and heard sounds of pounding of hammers and ringing of pickaxes against stone. Many dwarves were mining for gemstones and gold. They watched this and then left to go back to their guest room.

"That was quite a walk," said Greta. She laid down on her bed to rest.

"It's amazing that they have everything they need inside a mountain," said Sven.

"Everything but sunlight," said Raskilde. "Of course, they can go outside any time they want."

"That's true. I'll bet those kids play in the snow sometimes. What do you think about getting married here?" asked Linnea.

Sonja said, "It is something so different. I'll bet no other outsiders have ever been married here before. It's something that we can tell people about that they will hardly believe."

"Yes. I wonder what our rings will look like," said Greta. "I'll bet they will be pretty."

Brigitta and Heiki brought the group some wedding clothes that had been used before in Dwarven weddings. Dwarven women wear white satin symbolizing purity, and a multi-colored gemstone necklace symbolizing the happy life they will have. The girls tried on the clothes. The tunic tops had rounded necklines showing cleavage and loose fitting sleeves. The skirts were short just meeting the tops of their high boots. The multi-colored gemstone necklaces were beautiful against their bare skin. They brought the men brightly colored, woven shirts. "And here are your rings," said Heiki giving each of them a ring. Each ring had a different gemstone in it. There was an emerald, a sapphire and a ruby. The gems were cut in a heart shape and set in gold.

"These dwarves sure have been nice to us," said Linnea. "Maybe someday we will have a chance to do them a favor to repay them."

Soon it was time for the wedding and King Farin came to escort them into the great hall. He led them to the front to wait until all the people came in. He gave a ring to each of the young men. Then he called them forward to be married. King Farin said, "These three couples have traveled from another land to be married here. They have traveled through snow and one of them was almost killed by a constrictor snake. They are very brave young people who come to make their homes in Aksanda. We welcomed them into our home and into our hearts. They have each asked Father God to live in their hearts. We ask Father God to bless their unions. A young dwarven woman came to the front and sang the "Song of Love."

King Farin said, "Place the ring on your lady's finger. Do you promise to love each other and to take care of each other always?"

They answered, "We do."

King Farin asked, "Will you raise your children to love and to follow Father God?"

They answered, "We will."

King Farin said, "I pronounce you married. You may walk around the room and to your table where you will sign a wedding book."

Food is in the dining hall. You may get your dinner. Feeling very self conscious, the couples walked around the room and sat at the table to sign the wedding book. Then King Farin led them down a tunnel to the dining hall. It was a large room filled with tables and chairs and long tables filled with food. There were cheeses, platters of meat, bread, bowls of vegetables, and wine.

The dwarves were dressed for the party in colorful clothes and jewelry. This was their time to shine and to show the outlanders that they were a civilized community with social skills. The women wore dresses of satin trimmed with lace. Their hair was long, flowing in waves down their backs. The men were dressed in leather fringed tunics with gem studded belts and heavy gold chain necklaces. Their pants came to their knees met by high boots. Their beards were clean and fluffy. Their hair was worn shoulder length. A group of musicians sat together on the right next to the wall and there was a large open space for dancing.

After dinner there was music and dancing. When the dwarves were not working, they had fun. They formed a circle around the married couples and sang in deep, rough voices. Then they took the hands of their partners and danced around. The newlyweds copied the dwarves, holding hands and dancing 'round and 'round laughing. They didn't understand the dwarves' language, but they knew that they were being welcomed and congratulated. The room was loud with dwarves telling each other stories and laughing, and children chasing each other.

The couples sat down at a table and talked for a while and drank some wine. While they were sitting at their table, the dwarves came up in couples to shake their hands and congratulate them. This was amazing to the young people who had never been to a party, let alone at a party with dwarves inside a mountain. It was like living a dream. "These people really know how to have fun," said Sonja. "They are like happy, playing children."

"It is good to not lose the playfulness of the child when one grows up," said Sven. "It is also good to be grown up." He looked at Sonja, smiling and kissed her. She lowered her eyes and blushed.

"It's hard to believe that we are married. I feel that we have waited for this day forever," said Linnea. Raskilde put his arm around her and kissed her passionately.

Heiki and Birgitta came to them and asked them to follow them to their rooms. Each couple had a room to themselves for their wedding night. Each room had a water basin and some wine. They had a wonderful wedding and a party, and were ready to start their married lives together.

After the party, Heiki said to Farin, "They're good kids, husband. I'm glad you decided to help them. The girls are sweet and polite, and they were so happy with the clothes. I don't think they ever saw jewelry before. They kept looking at it and making it sparkle and giggling."

"Yes, wife, and the boys were very respectful and did everything I asked them to do. They bowed to me when I met them!" said Farin.

"Could we send some guards with them to Rando's Home Fire?" asked Heiki. "After all this, I would hate to send them out there alone. They're like babies. The boys have never fought and wouldn't know how to kill anyone. They are defenseless."

"Heiki, I've been thinking about that," said Farin. "If they were caught by the Bitters or by the slavers, they would be sold into slavery. I like them too much for that. We could send four pony riders. They are well practiced with the crossbow."

"You are a good King, my husband," said Heiki. "We will find out more about this Home Fire, and maybe Rando will visit us and trade with us. Tall Sky could bring him."

"Yes, and it would be wise for these kids to buy food to bring into that camp. It would make them more welcome. We will learn more news this way, too. Rando should have news of Tall Sky and the Bitters. I'll go speak with the pony riders. Hafka should go. He speaks the common language."

The next day, Birgitta and Heiki brought breakfast to the newlyweds, and Heiki told them the good news that four pony guards would ride with them to Home Fire for protection. One of the guards knew some of their language and would serve as translator for the other three. It was about a day's journey, so there were provisions packed for them. There was waybread, dried meat, cheese, dried fruit, and wine.

They left early in the morning and rode all day. The Bitters had cleared out of the northern area because of the battle and the snow. Riding through Yardrel, they noticed that people stopped and stared at this strange troup of reindeer riders and pony riding dwarves with long beards and crossbows on their backs. The newlyweds went into a market and purchased some food with silver pieces given to them by King Farin. They loaded the food into packs on the extra pony. So far everything was going as planned. It was cold, but at least it wasn't snowing today. Just outside of Yardrel, they stopped under some trees for something to eat. It felt good to dismount and stretch their legs. They were really hungry. They ate waybread and cheese and drank some wine. Raskilde said, "How are you girls feeling? Are you getting stiff and sore yet? You don't ride as much as we do on a daily basis."

"I'm okay," said Linnea.

"I'm getting stiff and sore, but it feels good to be here and on our way," said Sonja.

"How far is it to Home Fire?" asked Gretta.

"We don't know for sure," said Hafka. "There will be a sentry at the road who will know. There is a path to the left. We should be there today."

Everyone mounted and rode on. They kept a close watch for a trail to the left. Greta was really tired and close to tears when they finally saw the trail. They turned onto the trail and were stopped by several armed sentries. "Greetings from King Farin. Is Rando here? Tall Sky said to come here to Rando," said Hafka. The sentries understood and motioned them to follow. They rode up to Home Fire and tied their reindeer and ponies at the corral.

Rando walked up to them and Hafka said, "Greetings from King Farin and Tall Sky." He told the other dwarves to bring the bags of groceries and set them before Rando. Then Hafka pointed to the newlyweds and said, "Gullandian runaways, married at Othrund by King Farin."

At that, Rando laughed and said, "Welcome." He led them to the fire where they sat warming themselves and drinking berry wine. The rest of his men and women sat down around the fire and they all ate stew and rolls that had already been prepared for dinner. After dinner, Rando showed them the homes they had been building. They were almost completed, just needing some roofing, which was being done now. Rando said, "The people of Loadrel have been helping us build our homes. We have lived in tents like your teepees for years and decided to build a permanent town here. We will build more homes for people like you and an inn for travelers and newcomers. I wish we had that done, but it will take several more weeks. Until then, you can stay in my house. I am used to living in a tent. As you can see, we still have our tents up and we are using them until the houses are finished. Lake Perilough is right over there. You can see it from here. It is good for fishing and for bathing. The water is good. If you like it here, you could start building your houses. We will help you so that you can live in them this winter. We do get snow here, but not a lot. There is game for hunting and we are going to have gardens for vegetables next summer. This is going to be a good town. We all help each other here."

The girls were very impressed with Rando's house. "Rando, what about bedding?" asked Greta.

"Our furniture will be here soon, but for tonight we will use straw mats on the floor," said Rando. "Come over here and get some straw." Making their beds was their first job at Home Fire. They all slept comfortably in Rando's house with a fire in the fireplace.

"Well, what do you think about this place?" asked Sonja, combing out her long, blonde hair.

"I like the people and I like the way they work together. I think we should stay here for a while and help them build. We could help them build the inn and stay there while we build our own houses," said Sven.

"After a while, if we change our minds, we could always move on," said Sevrin.

"I think we should stay here this winter and get used to being married," said Raskilde. "Tall Sky will be here soon and we can talk to him about it. He told King Farin to send us here, and we don't really know about other places."

"That's true. With all that's been going on out there, it wouldn't be wise to travel about," said Sven.

"So, we're in agreement then. We stay here and build homes for now," said Raskilde.

The newlyweds spent a happy, peaceful night in each other's arms dreaming of their own homes. They were awakened by a new sound, a rooster welcoming the sun. "That's different," said Sonja. They dressed and went outside to see this new creature. "It is a bird with a red beard and hat." There were others outside sitting around the fire, or cooking. The air was cool and the sun was warm and reflected off the lake. "What a beautiful place! I'm so glad we're here."

"One of the first things we have to do is to build a corral for the reindeer. We can't put them in with horses," said Raskilde. I'll go talk to Rando about this." He walked off to find Rando. He found him talking to a group of builders.

"Raskilde," said Rando. "I want you to talk with these men about how to begin construction of a new house."

"That's good," said Raskilde. "I have a more immediate problem, though. We need to build a corral for the reindeer. Where could I put one?"

"Do you see that area over there where the trees have been cut down? That would be the only place that is clear enough right now," said Rando. "We need more trees cut down for houses, anyway, and we will have to cut more for a corral. So the first step will be for you men to learn how to cut down trees. I have a crew over there doing that. Why don't you get your friends and take them over there. In the meantime, your wives can join the women over at the cookhouse." Raskilde thanked him and went over to talk with his friends. They were busy doing these things all morning. The men cut down trees and the girls helped with the cooking.

At lunchtime a new work crew showed up with a wagon of lumber, a second wagon carrying furniture, and Tall Sky with some girls on horseback. Rando ran over to welcome Alqua. "Alqua, I'm so glad to see you again." He helped her down from the horse and hugged her. "Come over to see my new house. It is almost done. The roof just needs a few more shakes."

"It's beautiful, and you planted flowers. How pretty," she said. He walked her through the rooms and told her that the straw mats were used by the newlyweds who joined them last night. "You have six more people," she said. "I would like to meet them."

"You will meet them at lunch," said Rando. "Are you hungry? Let's go over to the fire and see what we have for lunch." People were already gathering around the fire to eat. Tall Sky joined Rando and Alqua.

"Rando, I hear that you have some newcomers," said Tall Sky.

"We sure do," said Rando. "They rode in here on reindeer last night, and four dwarves on ponies rode with them. The dwarves were wearing crossbows. King Farin had married them and wanted them kept safe." Tall Sky laughed. He was delighted.

"They must be from Gullandia. I thought there would be more," said Tall Sky. "Have you found any more Bitters?"

"Yes, we have," replied Rando. "There were several groups yesterday, but none today. Our corral is getting full. Our newlyweds have been busy all morning making a corral for their reindeer. After that they will start building houses."

"Sounds like they plan to live here," said Tall Sky.

"Yes, they do. Would you like to meet them?" asked Rando. "There they are sitting on the other side of the fire with the dwarves."

Tall Sky walked over and spoke first to the dwarves in their language. The dwarves seemed relieved to hear their own language being spoken. Tall Sky thanked them for helping the children to Home Fire safely. He told them that just yesterday several groups of Bitters had been killed by the Home Fire men. It was still dangerous on the road. He told them to thank King Farin for him. Then he introduced himself to the newlyweds. They were delighted to finally meet him.

"King Faren's men saved me from a huge snake that was trying to squeeze me to death. Then King Farin told us about Father God and prayed to heal my wound. He married us in the great hall and gave us wedding rings. Then we had a wonderful party with singing and dancing. It was so much fun," said Greta.

"It sounds like you had a wonderful time," said Tall Sky. "Now you are planning to live here?"

"Yes, we are," said Raskilde. "This is a beautiful place with good people. We will build houses and, next spring, we will plant gardens. We will fish and hunt. It will be a good life." While they were talking, Rando and Alqua were getting to know each other. He took her for a walk down by the lake. "Did they bring much furniture?" Rando asked.

"Yes, they did. There is enough for five houses. They continue to make more, because Papa says there are more people coming here. He thinks Father God told him this," said Alqua. "You know Vanya and Almarie are here to see Flint and Cliff. The girls are very interested in living out here, too."

"Flint and Cliff will have their houses done soon. We also want to build an inn. Sometimes when I think about what we're doing, I get tired and discouraged. I know I shouldn't be, though, with all this help we have. I wish you could stay out here. I feel better when you're here," said Rando.

"I would have no place to stay out here," said Alqua.

"I could make teepees for the newcomers. They're used to living in teepees. Then you and I could stay in the house," said Rando.

"I couldn't do that without being married," said Alqua.

"Would you consider marrying me?" asked Rando.

"I would," she said. He put a ruby ring on her finger and kissed her. Tall Sky is here. "Would you like to be married tonight?"

Alqua was thrilled with the idea of getting married right away to this exciting man, so she said, "Yes I would." Rando smiled and kissed her.

"Let's go talk to Tall Sky," said Rando. He found Tall Sky visiting with the Gullandians. "Tall Sky, would you perform a marriage ceremony tonight?"

Tall Sky looked very surprised and said, "Let's go into your house and talk about this." The furniture had been moved in, so they sat at the table to talk. "Rando, you know that I respect you highly for doing all that you have done here, for helping all these people and for leading them and getting them to work together all these years. You are a natural born leader. Rando, to be a great leader, you also need the wisdom and the strength that you can only get from Father God. Have you ever prayed to Him?"

"Sometimes I have asked him for help in the hunt or for help with the weather or for help when one of my people get hurt. I asked him to protect Alqua on her trip here," said Rando.

"This is all good," said Tall Sky, "but there is a deeper relationship that you can have with God that will give you confidence in Him and in your abilities to tell what is wrong with others and to make the right judgments in matters involving other people and their problems. You will be able to discern right from wrong and even, sometimes, to heal or to see ahead in order to make the right decisions. You get all of this when you ask for God's forgiveness for past wrongs and ask Him to send His Spirit to live inside of you. It will give you joy instead of depression. It will give you a happy life."

"What do I have to do to get this?" asked Rando.

"Pray to Him. And tell Him you are sorry for things that you did wrong, for hates or grudges, and ask Him to live in your heart," said Tall Sky.

"I have held grudges and not forgiven people. I will do this. God, please forgive me for my lack of forgiveness and for any other things I have done wrong. I have also been very selfish. Please come to live in my heart," prayed Rando.

"I want to do this, too," said Alqua. "Father God, please forgive me for my hatred of the slavers and for not forgiving them. Please come into my heart and live in me."

"From this day forward you are new people and you belong to God," said Tall Sky. "Now, about getting married, I have no objection to this. In fact, my wife sent you a bunch of things for your new home. Let's go to the wagon and bring it in. She wanted to come with me, but I forbade it not knowing about the safety of the road. She will come with me next time."

They went to the wagon and brought in bags of things to clean with and to make the house look nice. There were several vases, some glasses, a pretty table cloth, some silverware, some dishes, and a braided rug. There was a fluffy, floral print quilt, some sheets and towels, and several new pillows. When they finished putting out all of that and hanging pans on the wall, it looked like a home.

"Melody did all of this for me?" asked Rando. "Why? I wasn't all that nice to her when I first met her. You know, we stole her extra clothes and Steben made her walk a long way through the woods to Home Fire to buy them back. I didn't need her silver pieces, but I knew that if the girls stayed out there, they would be caught and taken to the slave auction. Also, I had single men who needed wives. I thought they might stay with us. But I was tired and hungry and grumpy when I met them and I didn't know they had to meet up with Trag. Tell Melody thank you for me and that I'm sorry for being such a grouch when I met her."

"I think you saved their lives by bringing them to Home Fire. Melody is very grateful to you for keeping Loadrel safe from the Bitters. She has also learned how you have helped others, and she really likes Alqua. She thinks that you two will make a great couple.

I'm inclined to think she's right," said Tall Sky. "We could have the wedding right after dinner. That way everyone will be full and comfortable and ready to have a bit of wine."

"Alright. I'll have the tub put into the house and filled with hot water for bathing," said Rando. Tall Sky went out to let people know about the wedding.

"You are an amazing man," said Alqua. She hugged him and kissed him. He felt warm and happy and could hardly believe his good fortune. "I love this new home you made for us. I love you, Rando."

"And I love you," said Rando. "I'm so glad that you could come out here today. Is there anything else that you would like to do right now?"

"I would like to lie down on the bed and cuddle up to you," said Alqua.

"Sounds good to me," said Rando. They cuddled up on the bed and soon were fast asleep.

Meanwhile, Tall Sky spoke with the cooks to let them know about the wedding. He asked a couple of men to help him set up a staging area for the wedding and arranged the seating in a semicircle in front of it. Several women picked bouquets of flowers and put them on either side of the place where Tall Sky would stand. Everyone was very happy for Rando and for Alqua.

He awoke the couple about an hour before dinner so they could get ready. They filled the tub with warm water so the couple could bathe. Alqua wore the dress that she had made at the inn. It was a light blue satin with a cummerbund belt tied into a bow in the back. It had a rounded neckline and straight sleeves to the elbow. The skirt was slightly gathered and full length. She wore her hair naturally flowing down her back. She looked beautiful, and again, Rando was amazed at his good fortune.

Dinner consisted of fresh game, potatoes, cooked vegetables, and honey cakes. They had wine that Tall Sky had brought with him. The men were tired and starving hungry and really appreciated having dinner right away. The dwarves were also hungry after helping the Gullandians to build the corral. The men had set up extra teepees for the Gullandians and the dwarves so that they could retire for the night whenever they wanted.

After dinner, Tall Sky rose and went to the front to begin the ceremony. He said, "Rando has been your leader for years and has done a good job of that. You are all now embarked on a new adventure to make a town out of your camp. It is an ambitious and difficult thing to do, and you are doing a very good job of it. You should all be proud of your achievement here. As your leader, Rando needs a good wife to help him along the way and he has chosen a very good woman in Alqua. They will now exchange vows and be wed. Rando and Alqua, would you please come forward?"

"Rando, you and Alqua have asked God to send His Spirit to live in your hearts and I am confident that He has done so and will guide and direct you through your lives together. Your love and your commitment to each other will be the force that will bind the two of you together as you go through the difficult times as well as the good times in your lives. Rando, will you love and protect Alqua from this day forward?"

Rando answered, "I will."

"Alqua, will you love and support Rando from this day forward?" asked Tall Sky.

Alqua answered, "I will."

"Rando, will you and Alqua promise to raise your children to love and to follow Father God?"

"We will," they said.

"You may place the ring on her finger," said Tall Sky.

Rando put the ring on her finger and Tall Sky said, "You are married." You will sign a wedding book as the first entry for the town of Home Fire. Let's all raise our glasses to the bride and groom." Rando kissed Alqua as a flute played a happy tune. Tall Sky raised his hand and said, "I have just one more thing for you. I have an official register for your new town. It must begin with approval for a Chief of your town. Rando is the best qualified to be your Chief and I would like you to sign this register making you a member of this town and giving your approval to Rando as your Chief." He handed the book to a member and told him to pass it around. Everyone applauded and signed the register.

Then people shook hands with the happy couple and congratulated them. The music continued and some couples danced. Everybody was in a merry mood enjoying themselves and visiting with one another. The dwarves approved of these proceedings and gave the couple some gems.

Tall Sky wished that Melody was with him. It would be a lonely night without her. The dwarves were the first to retire. The Gullandians went to their teepees and made little fires to keep warm.

Raskilde said, "Linnea, I think we made a good decision to stay here. I really like these people and I think that Rando will make a good chief. We will finish the corral tomorrow and start building our house."

"I think you are right, my husband. I love you and I will help you any way that I can. I have been working with the women who cook. There is much work to be done, but we all work well together," said Linnea. They kissed and cuddled and fell sound asleep.

Sven and Sonja were also happy with their decision to remain here. "That was a beautiful wedding," said Sonja. "She looked so pretty all dressed up in her gown. They look like they belong together. I think that we belong together, too. Did you think when we left our parent's teepees, that we would be married and building a house in a week? We were very lucky to meet the dwarves."

"It wasn't luck," said Sven. Father God went ahead of us and prepared a way. I'm sure of it. Think of it. King Farin already knew to expect us. They had the clothes, the rings, and King Farin taught us how to pray to God. He said that we were part of the fulfillment of the Awakening prophesy given to his great grandfather. Our weddings were planned that far back. This is a wondrous world. Now we should get some sleep."

Sevrin and Greta were cuddled up in their teepee. Greta said, "I'm so glad you're here with me. When I was being squeezed by that snake, I thought I would surely die. It was getting hard to breathe. I don't ever want to be in that kind of danger again. I can hardly wait for us to get our house built so that I can live indoors where no animal can attack me. I just have to feel safe."

Sevrin said, "Greta, my darling, I will get that house built and I will keep you safe, but just think about it. God sent the dwarves to help you escape from that snake. They knew how to kill it without harming you. King Farin said that we are part of the Awakening prophesy. God has been protecting us all along. We have to keep on trusting Him. Now let's get some sleep. We have a big day tomorrow."

The main fire was dying down and the rest of the people went to their teepees and houses for a well deserved night's sleep.

The Gullandian's were not used to the kind of work that they were doing, so they were sore the next day. Rando and Alqua got up rested and happy. Tall Sky was satisfied with yesterday's events, but missed his little Melody and really wanted to go home. The two girls who came out with him, Vanya and Almarie liked their new boyfriends, but wanted to go back until their homes were ready. They weren't too fond of camping. Flint and Cliff were going to stay to work on the houses.

The four dwarves had completed their mission and were going home, so they thanked Rando and said goodbye to Tall Sky and the Gullandians. They rode out right after breakfast.

At Home Fire it was business as usual with everybody busy building houses. Tall Sky left early with the two girls and the first work crew. They took the empty wagon so that it could be brought back full of more materials and supplies. There was a work order to give to the blacksmith for bathing tubs. Other people wanted more furniture and household items. Tall sky would deliver these orders to the proper people in Loadrel.

There were no more attacks reported last night, so Tall Sky expected an uneventful trip home. They had a beautiful day for travel. It was a bit chilly, but the sun was warm and the sky was blue. Many of the leaves had fallen, affording a good view on both sides of the road. They would be home for lunch. They saw no travelers on the way to Loadrel. Tall Sky thought about Melody all the way home. She had been childlike and vulnerable when he first met her. She still was that, but she had increased in wisdom and compassion for others. Her devotion to the little dragon was admirable. Her capacity for love and forgiveness was great. The more he thought about her, the more he loved her until he thought he would burst with happiness. The going was a little slower because of the wagon, but they did arrive in time for lunch.

Tall Sky stopped first at the inn. Melody was there with Amidra and Liadra. He said nothing but took her in his arms and held her tightly. Tears came to both of them. He said, "I love you, I love you, I love you. I can't be away from you again. It hurts too much." Tall Sky kissed Melody and just stood there holding her until his emotions calmed down. Then he said hello to Daisy. The little dragon chirred and rubbed her face against his. Let's sit down. I need something to eat. Mina brought him a bowl of stew, some bread and jam and some berry wine.

Beldock came over to their table and said, "Tall Sky, my friend, how was your visit to Home Fire?"

Tall Sky laughed and said, "It was amazing to say the least. In the first place, there were six young runaways from Gullandia at Home Fire. They had stopped off at Othrund to shelter from the snow storm. The girls ran away when confronted by the dwarf guards. They ran right into swamp water where a large constrictor wound itself around Greta. One of the guards cut the snake's head off. Greta needed bandaging, so they took the kids up to the tunnels and bandaged her and fed them, and the next day King Farin told them about Father God and married them in the great hall. Then all the dwarves got dressed up and had a celebration with food and singing and dancing. King Farin is convinced that they are part of that prophesy about the Awakening. Anyway, after that he sent four dwarves wearing crossbows and riding ponies to help keep the newlyweds safe on their way to Home Fire. Can you imagine Rando's face when six teens on reindeer and four dwarves on ponies rode into camp?" Beldock laughed. "That's not all. Rando and Alqua asked me to marry them….So I did. While I had their attention, I had them all sign the register to make Rando their official Chief." Beldock laughed again.

"How is the building going?" asked Beldock.

"They have five houses completed and they need to make ten more at least. I have orders for bath tubs and all sorts of household things," said Tall Sky.

"What about the Bitters?" asked Beldock.

"Last night there were no more of them and the road was clear this morning. I think most of them have cleared our area," said Tall Sky.

"Beldock, on a more serious note, Rando and Alqua asked God to live in their hearts. We also had a serious talk about leadership. I think he will be a very good Chief for that town," said Tall Sky.

"I think so," said Beldock. "How are the Gullandians doing?"

"You know, they're used to living in teepees, so they are happy. The first thing they did was make a reindeer corral," said Tall Sky. Beldock laughed. "They are really nice people. They will fit in well there."

Beldock asked, "What did they tell you about Othrund? I've always wondered how they manage to live inside of a mountain."

"I talked with them at length about Othrund. It has many rooms. Each place has a room for the couple and a room for children. There are shelves to put their belongings on. There is a great hall for meetings. They have bathrooms with running water to carry away the waste. There is a very large kitchen with a long oven and ten chefs. There is one young man to mind the fire in the ovens. There is a large room with tables and chairs for dining. There is a hot spring pool to bathe in and the water circulates in and out so that the water always stays clean. There are rooms for guests. There is also a place to bring their ponies and other animals in during bad weather. It all works very well for them."

"Melody, here is something for you. Rando wants me to tell you that he is sorry for the way he treated you when he first met you. He said that he was tired and hungry and grumpy. He also said that he stole your clothes to have a reason to bring you to Home Fire for protection from the slavers in those woods. He also thought you may have stayed there and married one of his men. I'm glad you didn't." He smiled and kissed her on the cheek. "You know the things you bought for Rando? We need four of them now and probably ten more in about three weeks. We should let Trag and Arinya get those things together as part of their store and we should go to the blacksmith to order bathtubs. Let's go. I can hardly wait to go home."

They went to the blacksmith and ordered the tubs including one for themselves. Then they stopped at Laskron's and placed an order for glassware. Last of all, they stopped at Trag's store and gave him a list of things that the people needed at Home Fire. Tall Sky was tired and needed some rest, so they went home to bed.

Liadra went to Laskron's workshop and told him all about Othrund and the Gullandrians at Home Fire. He was very happy to hear that Rando and Alqua had asked God to live in their hearts and that they were married. "It is wonderful that the people of Loadrel have come together to help Rando's group build homes and get his town going. They deserve it for handling the Bitters problem like they did. Without them our town would probably be ashes by now. You say that they will need at least ten more homes? That will take us into winter, but I think they can get it done before much snow falls. They are going to need an inn, but that will have to wait until spring. We have much work to do for these orders."

Liadra and Laskron went to see Ulrik who lived down the street. He had made furniture for many years. "Ulrik, the people at Home Fire are in need of ten more sets of furniture. "

"That's good. Papa and I will just get going and make the furniture. Papa is a good worker. I would be happy to help with that. I get bored with nothing to do," said Ulrik. "Those men did a great service for us and they helped us to destroy Malwood Market. Nothing is too good for them in my book. When will they need this furniture?"

"In about three weeks," said Laskron. "It really depends on how long it takes to build the houses. Three more married couples decided to live there. They just arrived from Gullandia. King Farin of Othrund married them two days ago. It's going to be hard to do, but I have fourteen sets of glassware to make. Would it be alright for Papa to bring Steben to help you?"

"That would be good," said Ulrik.

"I need an apprentice," said Laskron. "If you think of anyone, let me know."

ALEPH

While Tall Sky was at Home Fire, Aleph was on sentry duty on the edge of Loadrel in the woods. Aleph had a vision from God. He saw four young women by a large rock near some woods. They were poorly dressed, tired out and sitting against the rock. They had no food and no water. He saw himself riding a horse and pulling a small wagon. He saw himself stop the wagon and help the girls into the wagon. He knew that one of those girls was his. He ran into town and asked Beldock if he could borrow his wagon just for the night and told him about the vision. Beldock said that he knew of a place like that and readied the wagon and the horse for travel. He and Mina put in some blankets, pillows, bandages and some food, water and wine into the wagon. Aleph pulled the wagon out of town going south for about one hour and turned west for another hour. Just as Beldock said, there was a large rock next to some woods. The girls were there and in bad shape. One of them said, "Help me. Water." Aleph brought a skin of water and gave each or the girls a drink. Then he gave each of them a drink of wine and some bread and cheese. He spread out the blankets and pillows and helped them into the wagon.

"Are any of you injured?" he asked. They said that they were not, but he noticed bruising on their faces, cuts on their feet and scratches on their arms. "How did you come to be out here?"

One of the girls said, "We were going to be sold, but the elves who had us heard about a great battle and soldiers chasing Bitter Elves, so they just ran the other direction leaving us. We tried walking but got too tired. Thank you for helping us. We aren't going to the slave market, are we?"

Aleph said, "No, child. I was in that battle and I am now here because of it. I was guarding the town of Loadrel when God gave me a vision of four girls out here and in need of help. I will take you back to Loadrel to an inn where two very nice people will give you more food and beds to sleep in. We had better be going now. Aleph turned the wagon and headed for Loadrel. The girls wrapped the blankets around themselves and cuddled up next to each other for warmth and comfort.

Aleph stopped the wagon in front of the inn. Beldock and Mina came out to help the girls out of the wagon, brought them in and gave them some hot soup and rolls to eat. "This is so good. We haven't eaten for two days," said one of the girls.

Mina said, "I am Mina and this is my husband Beldock. He has filled a tub with warm water in the kitchen. I have clean, soft nightgowns for you, and soft socks for your feet. Then you will go to bed for a good night's sleep." Mina took the girls, one at time into the kitchen and helped them to bathe and dress. "We are going to burn these clothes. I have new ones for you to wear tomorrow. They will be in your rooms. Do not worry. We will take good care of you. What are your names? I need them for the inn register."

"Faerverin, Aela, Kara, Aeria ," said the girls.

"Faerverin, you are elven?" asked Aleph.

"Yes," she said.

"Your name means joyful spirit. You will be joyful again," said Aleph. "I am also a Bright Elf. We will have beautiful tomorrows together. Now go take a bath." After bathing them, Mina tucked them in for a good night's sleep, leaving their new clothes in their rooms. They were very tired, having been on the run for two weeks prior to being caught by Bitter Elves intending to sell them into slavery.

Beldock, Mina and Aleph went downstairs and sat at one of the tables. Mina said, "When girls run away from home, they don't realize that they are setting themselves up to be targets for every evil in the world. If the Lord does not have them in His sights, they don't stand a chance. I'm so glad that you found them, Aleph."

"I am glad too," said Aleph. "The Lord showed me that one of these girls will be my wife. I was beginning to wonder if I would ever find my mate. Her name is Faerverin which means joyful spirit. I would like to get some sleep now so that I can talk with her when she wakes. Good night."

The next morning, Aleph met with the girls after breakfast. He had never counseled people like Tall Sky did, but was determined to try. "First, I would like to know what circumstances were so unbearable that you felt compelled to run away from your homes. Faerverin, why did you run away?"

Faerverin said, "My stepfather wouldn't keep his hands off me. Every time I walked by him, he would push me up against the wall and try to kiss me. Lately he would fondle my breasts and touch me down there. I was sure that he would rape me."

Aleph felt anger rising up in him, but he pushed the anger down so that he could think clearly about the girls he was counseling. "Aela, why did you run away?" asked Aleph.

"My parents would not let me have any friends. They kept me busy doing chores and wouldn't let me see Kara after they found out that we had met and were talking together," said Aela.

"Aeria, why did you run away?" asked Aleph.

Aeria said, "There were no young men of my age around our home, and my parents just wanted me to stay home. I am of the age to get married."

Aleph said, "You each have reasons that seem right to you. Your parents were probably trying to keep you safe and knew of the dangers that you discovered the hard way. Faerverin, you had a real danger to you right there at home. Aeria, God could have brought your mate right to your door at the proper time. Kara, I understand that you needed to get on with your own life. Again, God could have intervened for you. Aela, it is difficult to be alone and lonely, needing friends. We are all made with that basic need. Do you now see that running away put targets on your backs? You became targets for predators of the worst kind. Going forward, I recommend to Faerverin to stay here. I will take good care of you. Aeria, Kara, and Aela, you can return home or stay here, as you wish. I would recommend, however, that you visit a new town called Home Fire. Right now they are building new homes and have ordered furniture and other things to furnish those homes. There are young men out there who want wives. They would be happy to meet you, but for now I suggest that you plan on staying here for a while until you are recovered and ready to move on. Faerverin, would you come with me? I want you to meet someone." They walked to Trag's store.

"Trag and Arinya, I would like you to meet Fairverin," said Aleph. "I discovered her and her three friends last night while I was on duty. They are runaways who were caught by Bitters who left them in the middle of a field because of the war. They would have died had God not given me a vision of their whereabouts. As you can see, she has no shoes. Do you have a pair that might fit her? I would also like a cloak for her. It's getting colder every day now."

"I am pleased to meet you, Fairverin," said Arinya. "I was a slave at the auction when Trag found me and rescued me. He was part of the forces that destroyed Malwood Market. They killed all the slavers there and brought the slaves to Loadrel. Some of us are married now. Others went back to their homes. Do you think these would fit you?"

"Yes, they do, but I have no silver to give you," said Faerverin.

"You don't need silver when you are with me," said Aleph, "but I will give you silver of your own."

"Here is a cloak that is very nice. It is fur lined to keep you nice and warm. Here is a pair of fur lined boots and gloves. Here is a skirt made out of heavy velvet that will help in cold weather." Aleph gave her a pouch of silver, and said, "Pay her out of this."

Faerverin looked at him with a look of astonishment and gave the pouch to Arinya. She put on her new clothes and happily walked out with Aleph. They walked over to the bench by the lake and sat down. It was a beautiful day and the sound of the little waves was very calming. The air was cool and the sun was warm. "I love the sparkling water," said Faerverin. "I didn't know that life could be this beautiful."

"Life is beautiful as you are with your long, blonde hair, your big, blue eyes, your soft skin, your lips," and he gently kissed her.

Then, as if to change the subject, he got up and found a pink shell at the water's edge and gave it to her. "Beauty," he said. "I want you to meet some other friends of mine who were also runaways. They are just across the street." He took her hand and said, "Come." They walked over to Beldock's home and knocked on the door. Liadra opened the door and said, "Aleph, come in. Who is this young lady?"

"This is Faerverin. I wanted her to meet my friends. She is very special to me. I saw her last night in a vision," said Aleph.

"That's interesting," said Liadra. "Come in and meet the others." They walked into the kitchen where Melody and Amidra were having tea. "Have a seat. I will get you some tea. Melody and Amidra, I would like you to meet Aleph's new friend Faerverin. Aleph saw her in a vision last night."

Faerverin sat next to Melody and immediately Daisy reached her head over and chirred like she does with Tall Sky. "Daisy likes you," said Melody. "Are you elven?"

"Yes, I am. Does that make a difference to Daisy?" asked Fairverin.

"Actually, it does," said Melody. "You see, I am married to Tall Sky, and she loves him."

"I met Tall Sky about a year ago. He was on a journey and slept in our barn," said Faerverin. "How did you get her? Miniature dragons are rare to have for pets."

"When I met Tall Sky, I had run away from home and he was helping us on our journey. Anyway, I found a blue egg in Malwood and Daisy hatched out of it," said Melody. "Tall Sky said I shouldn't pick up things in Malwood, but he said I could keep the dragon."

"Where is Tall Sky?" asked Faerverin.

"He's taking a nap. He was on a mission to help three girls get safely to Home Fire to meet their boyfriends," said Melody. "They were also delivering a load of new furniture and another work crew. They wanted him along for extra protection from the Bitters."

"It was a band of Bitters who captured me and three other girls and were going to sell us, when Aleph saved us and took us to the inn," said Faerverin.

"Yes, God directs the Bright Elves to help people. So, did God direct you to leave home?" asked Melody.

"I prayed about it and I thought He did direct me to leave, but I really doubted that when I was captured and left to die," said Faerverin.

"I would say that He did direct you to leave. Sometimes we have to go through some pretty hard trials for God to get us where we should be," said Melody. You have met Aleph just as God intended you to."

Faerverin smiled and blushed.

Liadra said, "I'm so glad that Tall Sky brought us to Loadrel, because it's here that I met my husband Laskron. He had this home and a wonderful, little girl named Elise. She and Emmy are playing in her room."

"Yes, and I met my husband Steben on our journey and Tall Sky helped us connect with Steben's parents. Steben's father is helping to make the furniture for Home Fire. When God has willing followers much good can happen," said Amidra.

"Aleph was a hero in the battle at Othrund. He killed many Bitters. He saved Tall Sky's life and King Farin's life. He also helped to heal many of the soldiers. He has been in charge of the protection of Loadrel, which is what he was doing when he met you," said Melody.

Faerverin looked at him with adoring eyes and said, "Thank you for saving me."

"You're welcome. I was obeying God, but He told me that you would be there," said Aleph. "Let's go down to the shop. I would like you to meet Laskron. He is a glass blower."

"Nice meeting you," said Faerverin. They went to the shop to see Laskron.

He was busy with a long metal rod holding molten glass and was shaping it into a blue, fluted vase. "Hi, Laskron, I would like you to meet someone. Her name is Faerverin."

"Hi, Faeverin, I'll be with you in just a minute. I'm almost done with this one," said Laskron. He let it cool for a while. "I've been working to fill an order for the people at Home Fire, and it's a big order. So, Aleph, where did you meet this lovely lady?"

"She was a stranded would be slave. The Bitters who had her and three other girls ran away from them to avoid the soldiers. I had a vision of their whereabouts and picked them up in Beldock's wagon," said Aleph. "The other girls are staying at Beldock's inn."

'How are the sentries doing? Have they seen any more Bitters lately?" asked Lascron.

"No, things have really quietened down out there," said Aleph. "It is too soon to stop being vigilant, though. There could be a number of them taking their time traveling south. They could be hiding out in a number of places like people's homes and barns and even in Malwood. When they run out of provisions, they will be on the move again, and that's when they're the most dangerous."

"Faerverin sounds like an elf name," said Laskron.

"I am an elf like Aleph." said Faerverin. She looked at Aleph and smiled.

"Ah," thought Laskron. "It is time he had a lady of his own."

Tall Sky, finished with his nap, walked in. "Hello, Faerverin," he said. "Nice to see you again. I remember staying in your barn and you sneaking food out to me. That was greatly appreciated. I have prayed for you many times."

"I thank you for that," said Faerverin. "I needed prayer to keep me safe from my guardian. Finally, he got so bad I had to leave. It was like walking out on evil itelf."

"How did you meet up with Aleph?" asked Tall Sky.

"He had a vision about us that led him to find me and my three friends. He fed us and gave us water and took us to the inn. It's kind of strange. I fed you and he fed us. It's like when you do something good, it comes back to when you need help, only when it came back to me I also got new clothes and wonderful friends." She felt the joy well up in her and she giggled.

"I told you that you would be joyful again," said Aleph. "Her name in elven means joyful spirit. She hasn't had a lot to be joyful about recently, but I'm sure that will change."

"It's bound to get better with you in charge," said Laskron. "How are the other girls doing? Do you think any of them might be interested in Home Fire?"

"I think at least one of them will want to marry, but it depends on whether or not she likes one of the men out there," said Aleph. "They are good men and they want to marry. Another of the girls wants friends. She is sure to find friends there. The third girl did not want to work for other people on farms, but, if she were working to make her own home, that might be different. We'll see. They are not yet recovered enough to make a trip to Home Fire and it would be better, anyway, for them to see Home Fire when more of the houses are completed. Let's all go over to the inn and have lunch."

"I'll go get Melody, Amidra, Liadra and the kids. We'll meet you there," said Laskron.

At he inn, everybody sat down at a long table and Faerverin brought the other three girls over. They were amazed at Faerverin's new clothes. Mina first brought a saucer of food for Daisy. Faerverin said to the girls, "Come see this little dragon. She's so cute and her name is Daisy."

Aleph introduced the girls, "This is Aela, Kara, and Aeria. They have been here for just one day. They were with Faeverin when I found her. Aeria, how have you been today? Are you getting used to your surroundings?"

Aeria said, "I love it here. It's nice and clean and the food is good. I like seeing the people come in here." Kara and Aela agreed.

"Mina said that it will take about a week for our feet and scratches and bruises to heal up," said Kara. "Then, I suppose, we should find some kind of work to do."

"I think you should see Home Fire before you decide what to do," said Tall Sky. "There are men out there who are looking for wives and are building new homes. They have made great progress."

Kara said, "That's a good idea. If they don't have a store, maybe I could start one. That way I wouldn't have to farm."

"It is possible that one of the men would consider building an addition onto his house for a store. I know that Home Fire needs a store. They also need a seamstress. The town is new, so there are a lot of possibilities. It is truly a work in progress," said Tall Sky.

Laskron said, "I've got some vases made for them. We will have to take the girls with us when we take their order to them."

"Would you girls come with me to my home after lunch?" asked Laskron.

They said that they would. They visited for a while more and the girls went to Laskron's home.

They went to the kitchen to sit around the table. Laskron said, "I hear that you have had a rough time of it lately. How long were you with the Bitters?"

"We were walking for about a week," said Aela. "It was awful. We had to walk all day with little time for rest. If we stumbled or tried to slow down, they hit us. They didn't have much food and they gave us very little of it and likewise with the water."

"Did they rape you?" asked Laskron.

"They talked like they would, but I think they were afraid of Faerverin, because she was a Bright Elf. They didn't know what she might do to protect us." said Aela. "All she had to do was to give them a threatening look and they would stop talking about it."

"Did you pray to Father God to help you?" asked Laskron.

Aela said that she did not and the other girls also said they did not, but they thought that Faerverin had prayed. Laskron said, "Father God can be a big help in situations like these. You need to get to know God on a personal basis so that he wil recognize you when you pray to Him. Then he will help you. Aela, would you like to know God?"

"Yes, I would." said Aela.

"Have you done anything wrong or hurtful to others? Is there anything you feel guilty about?" asked Laskron.

"I was really mean and hateful when I talked to my parents about wanting to find friends. I told them that I hated them. I feel very guilty about that. I hate those men who captured me," said Aela.

"To have a good relationship with God, you need to forgive yourself and others, because He is a forgiving and a loving God. Will you do that?" asked Laskron.

"Yes, I will," said Aela.

"Now, all you have to do is to ask God to forgive you and ask Him to send his Spirit to live in your heart," said Laskron.

"Please, God, forgive me and live in my heart," said Aela.

"Now, Aela, whenever you are lonely, talk to God about it. He will help you with that. You will never be alone because He is always with you," said Laskron.

Kara and Aeria both asked God to forgive them and live in their hearts. "Now you will be ready to meet people at Home Fire. I have a feeling that they either know God or will shortly. Their leader, Rando and his wife know God and so do three new married couples that I know of. These three couples ran away from their parents in Gulandia and rode on reindeer to Othrund where the dwarf King performed their wedding ceremony and threw a party to end all parties. Then they rode their reindeer to Home Fire and built a corral for their reindeer. As I understand it, they are now building houses there. You will have many interesting people to meet there. I have to get back to work. You may stay and talk with Liadra or go back to the inn. It's been nice visiting with you," said Laskron.

Amidra asked them if they would like to learn to make dresses. They did need clothes, so they decided to do that.

Meanwhile, Faerverin and Aleph were taking a walk. What do you like to do, Faerverin?" asked Aleph.

'I enjoy walking, swimming, fishing, weaving tapestries, and painting pictures," said Faerverin.

"What kind of pictures do you like to paint?" asked Aleph.

"I like to paint pictures of animals and flowers and fairies," she said.

"How did you meet the fairies?" asked Aleph.

Faerverin said, "I was a child and there was a very pretty little bird with shimmering feathers of various colors called a tahilu. It made a warbling song and it liked me. I followed it into the woods where I saw a fairy child. She held out her hand to the bird and it sat on her finger. So I held out my hand and the bird came to me and sat on my finger. I was enchanted and spoke to the fairy child. She was only about three feet tall with long blonde hair and blue eyes that turned up on the outer edges. She wore a filmy, blue dress. She held out her hand to me and led me further into the woods to a cave with a stream flowing out of it. She led me through the cave to another opening. At the other side was a big area full of flowers and pointed huts with flowering vines growing over them. The air was fragrant. She offered me some berry wine to drink and introduced me to her parents. Then she showed me her paintings and the one that she was working on. She showed me how to paint and we spent many hours painting. When it was time to go to bed, she took me into one of the huts and we went to sleep on a soft bed of ferns and covered up with a satin blanket. Her parents said that I could stay and I was so happy that I stayed there for a long time playing and painting. I made many friends of the little animals in the woods and learned to talk to butterflies.

One day, when I woke up, the fairies were gone and I was left all alone in the woods. I went back through the cave and kept walking. There was a couple in the woods having a picnic and I asked them for food. They had no children, so they asked me if I would like to live with them. I did go home with them and lived there for about ten years. It was a good life as they were kind to me. Then my guardian's wife got sick and died and my guardian drank too much every day. He was mean when he drank. I tried to stay out of his way, but when he did catch me when he had been drinking, he tried to do things, so I ran away from home. I never saw the fairies again. I think they went back to their island and I didn't have wings, so they couldn't take me with them. I miss my little friend. Her name was Azurie. What was your childhood like?"

Aleph said, "I grew up with my parents. They were typical elves. They loved me and took care of me, but I grew restless and wanted more. I wanted an excititng life full of adventure. I wanted power to rule over others. I wanted the riches of the world. I became hateful toward my parents and God, so I left home to seek these things. That is when I met a group of Bitter Elves who had rebelled against Father God and tried to get wealth and power. They were thieves to begin with, but then they started using magical spells and they even killed people. When they decided to attack the dwarves, I was almost killed. The dwarves left me for dead. Then Tall Sky came along and talked to me and we prayed. Then he healed me. I am glad you were never friends with the Bitters. It is not a good experience. At least your time with the fairies was constructive. Someday you will have a room to paint in and be able to sell your paintings."

"That would be nice. I would like other people to have my paintings to put on their walls. Now and then you see a wreath or a rug on the wall, but that's about it," said Faerverin.

"You could have a pet, too," said Aleph. "What kind of pet would you like to have?"

"Probably a cat," said Faerverin. "They work really well indoors and outdoors. Most other animals aren't happy indoors. I wouldn't mind having a miniature dragon, but they are hard to get and you have to get one as an egg. Maybe Daisy will find a mate and lay an egg someday. She is the only dragon I know of."

"Yes. We will talk to Melody about it," said Aleph. "Would you want to settle down in a house right away or travel around first?"

"I wouldn't mind taking trips, but I would like to have a house to come home to," said Faerverin.

"Would you mind taking a trip with me to see King Aryante?" asked Aleph. "Either Tall Sky or I have to talk to him about getting a treaty with Gullandia to stop the border war over the winter use of Aksanda's grazing land. This trip would also mean going to Gullandia to meet with their Chief. It would be a long trip with at least about twelve days of riding. It's a long time in the saddle. Do you think you could handle it?"

"I don't know. I'll have to think about it. Would it be safe?" asked Farverin.

"All I know is that it has to be done soon. Winter will be here in a few weeks," said Aleph.

"I would like to spend more time with you," said Faerverin. "Could we take others with us for protection?" asked Faerverin.

"Yes, I think that it's vital on a mission of such importance that we take guards with us. I would like to take Tall Sky, but he is just married and is currently managing the Home Fire development," said Aleph. "Let's go talk to Tall Sky." They walked to Tall Sky's home.

Melody answered the door. "Hi, Melody, is Tall Sky home?" asked Aleph.

"Sure, come in and have a seat. Tall Sky, we have visitors," she called

"Aleph, is there anything wrong?" asked Tall Sky.

"No, I wanted to talk to you about getting the border wars resolved. I would like to go to King Aryante to get a treaty made that would allow the Gullandian herders to use Aksanda land for grazing purposes during the winter. I think it would be good for the farmers and for the herders. I would be taking Faerverin with me, and I would like a group of men to guard us on the way," said Aleph.

"It sounds like a good plan. The last I heard, the farmers liked the idea of getting reindeer meat and hides for the winter when it is so difficult to hunt," said Tall Sky. "Beldock would be the one to get together the men to go with you. It's a long journey and he would have to pick men with the ability to be gone from home for about three weeks. After you get the treaty, you should stop at Othrund and let King Farin know about it. Then stop at Home Fire on the way home."

"That should work. Would you arrange it with Beldock? I have something I want to show Faerverin," said Aleph. Tall sky said that he would and they left.

We are going to walk to the house next to Trag's store. The widow who owns this house is moving to Yardrel to stay with her parents. Her house including her furnishings is for sale. I have seen this house. All we would need to do is to have a builder put on a room for your painting in front of the house. I want to buy this house. They walked up to the door and knocked. The owner asked them in and showed them the house. Faerverin liked the house and the furniture, but was a bit confused by this. "We aren't married," she said.

"Don't worry about that. You will have a place to live when we get back. I can always stay at the inn. Should we decide to marry, the house is already here for us," said Aleph.

The surprise on her face was evident. Then she smiled and said, "Fine."

"What an amazing day this turned out to be," she thought.

"We have to go next door and buy some more clothing for the trip," said Aleph.

He paid the lady and they went next door. "Hello, Trag. We need some clothes for a journey. Would you and Arinya help us with that?" asked Aleph.

"Sure," said Trag. "I will help you and Arinya will help Faerverin."

"We need something fancy to wear at court and some more traveling clothes. We are gioing to see King Aryante about a treaty with Gullandia," said Aleph.

"What a great idea!" said Trag. "I'm sure we have some things that will work for you. Try this on." He pulled out a velvet waistcoat, a shirt with puffy sleeves, and pants to match with a cumerbund. There was also a hat with a large brim pointed front and back. He also had a purple velvet cape.

"Faerverin, I would like to see you in this dress," said Arinya. It was a long, silken, light blue dress with filmy sleeves. She then showed her a necklace of blue stones set in a gold pendant shaped like a shield. There was also a tierra of a golden circlet set with small, sparkling blue stones.

"We would like the matching ring to that set, too, but I will keep that for later," said Aleph quietly to Trag. They also bought more traveling clothes. "When will you be leaving?" asked Trag.

"We plan to leave tomorrow morning, if Beldock has the guards lined up to go," answered Aleph. "Thanks for helping us with the clothes. We'll see you when we get back." Aleph and Faerverin walked back to the inn.

Beldock had spoken to a group of militia men and had four men ready to go tomorrow morning. "Beldock, have you had word of Quickturn?" asked Aleph.

"Yes, I heard he brought many Bitters to work in the rock quarry of King Aryante. He is staying near there for now patrolling the area for the King. There are still Bitters migrating south from the battle," said Beldock.

"Glad to hear it," said Aleph. "I want to get him and some of his Bright Elves to accompany us to Base Camp on the border and then, possibly, into Gullandia to meet with their Chief."

"That would be wise. It's good to have that much protection. You never know how many Bitters are traveling in bands out there," said Beldock. He took Aleph aside and said, "Are you sure you want to take Faerverin with you?"

"Yes, Beldock," said Aleph. "I plan to marry her on this journey. I already bought the house next to Trag's store. I haven't asked her yet, but God showed me in the vision that she was my intended."

Beldock laughed. "I am happy for you, Aleph. Does Tall Sky know?"

"I haven't had a chance to tell him yet. Maybe you could tell him after we leave," said Aleph. "Now we should have dinner. It's getting kind of late."

Mina brought dinner. Aeria, Kara, and Aela joined them. Then Melody and Tall Sky came in with Trag and Arinya. "Melody, may I hold Daisy?" asked Faerverin.

"Sure, she likes you," said Melody. Daisy climbed onto Faerverin's shoulder chirring and rubbing her cheek. Daisy looked in Faerverin's eyes for a minute as if she was trying to communicate with her. Faerverin said, "Melody, if she ever lays an egg, I would love to have it. I would be a good dragon mother."

"We will have to wait. I don't know how long it takes for a dragon to mature," said Melody. "If she does lay an egg, I would be happy for you to have it."

"It takes at least a year," said Tall Sky. "Then she has to be able to find a mate, and there's no guarantee of that. We found her in Malwood. We may have to go on a camping trip when the time comes."

After dinner Aleph and Faerverin headed to their rooms to pack.

VIVALLEN

At the break of dawn, Aleph, Fairverin and four militia men packed their gear and rode out of Loadrel riding south toward Vivallen. It would take a whole day to reach the city of the king. They had a good day to travel. The air was cool and the road was dry. They could see the lake on the left and had clear sight into the trees on the right. There were no travelers to be seen. Aleph hoped that the way to Vivallen would be uneventful, but it was a long ride and he worried about Faerverin's stamina.

"Faerverin, I want you to let me know if you get tired and need to get down and stretch and walk around," said Aleph. "You aren't used to riding for long periods of time."

"I will," said Faerverin. "I have walked quite a bit in the last few weeks, but I know riding is different."

"Let me know if you see any fairies," he said and they both laughed. "We didn't have time for breakfast, but Mina packed some honey cakes for us. Would you like one? This should hold us over until lunch time. I know an old building where we could stop for lunch. It's about half way to Vivallen. It's an old ruins made of stone and is from ancient times. They used it for worship of some kind back then. It has no roof, but it is shelter from the wind and the sun."

"What is King Aryante like?" asked Faerverin.

"He is about six feet tall, has white hair down to his shoulders, and wears a beard cropped to about six inches that comes to a point. I have never met him. This is what Tall Sky said. He is a strong man, but is good natured and gracious. He has the good of the nation and the people at heart. When we needed help at the Battle of Othrund, he sent every available soldier to our aid. He is fair in his judgements and doesn't over tax the people. I tell you, we are fortunate to have this man for king," said Aleph.

"Does he have a queen and children?" asked Faervein.

"He does," answered Aleph. "His Queen is named Svetlana and they have three children, two boys and a girl. The heir to his thrown is, thankfully, like his father, and is named Rauthomir. I think you will like the royal family."

"If they are like you say, I will like them a lot," said Faerverin.

At this point, the road forked and they took the road heading west toward Vivallen. They were in a plains area with grassland and few trees. A few groups of travelers rode by peaceably, waving in greeting. The road was good and the land rolled gently into the distance. People traveling from Vivallen usually had an extra horse carrying bundles of purchases.

"What do you know of Vivallen?" asked Faerverin.

"It is a large city with many shops, inns, and houses. The castle is located at the center of the city and around the castle are barracks for the soldiers. The place is well guarded. There are many beautiful gardens full of flowers in the summer. In front of the castle is a large fountain. I have never been inside the castle, but we will do that on this trip," said Aleph.

After riding for about four hours, they pulled over at the ruins and tied their horses. They gave their horses some water and sat down for lunch. Mina had packed them rolls, cheese, and sliced meat for sandwiches. It was a welcome feast for them. Kroom, Salek, Parin, and Bellstram shared in the meal and passed around some wine. By the end of lunch, everyone felt full and relaxed.

As they rode on, Aleph asked, "So, how are you feeling now?"

Faerverin said, "I am a bit stiff and sore, but I'll be alright."

After four more hours of riding, however, it was a different story. She was amazed to see the city. It was so large, stretching for miles in either direction. The walls of the ciiy were white, glaring in the sunlight. When they approached the entrance to the city, they were met by guards who questioned them about who they were and their business in the city. "We are travelers from Loadrel come to see King

Aryante about a treaty with Gullandia. We fought with Quickturn and the king's soldiers at the Battle of Othrund. What inn do you recommend?" asked Aleph.

"The Golden Chalice is a good one and close to the castle," said the guard. "Just stay on this road for a while. It wil be on your left."

"Thank you very much. We are tired and hungry. Good day to you," said Aleph. They rode on past many shops, taverns and houses until they came to the Golden Chalice. It looked like a nice, clean place, so they tied their horses and walked in. Aleph paid for several rooms and ordered dinner with ale. The dining area had wooden floors and tables. They chose the long table to accommodate six people. At this point, ale was very welcome. The servant brought them a bowl of water and towels to wash their hands and faces. Then she brought ale. Dinner consisted of sliced meat with steamed vegetables and fresh bread with jam. After dinner Aleph spoke to the innkeeper. "We will be visiting King Aryante tomorrow and need our clothes pressed and ready to wear in the morning. Do you have someone to do this?" She said that she would take care of it herself. He also ordered baths for all of them. After dinner they bathed and went to bed.

The next morning brought a rush of excitement to Faerverin. She had never dressed in such finery before and the prospect of going to meet the king was very exciting and somewhat intimidating. Aleph took all of this with total calm and self confidence. "You look radiant," Aleph said to Faerverin. "You look like you were brought up in a castle. In all of Phayendar there is none as lovely as you." Faerverin blushed and he kissed her. Let's have breakfast. Then we will visit the castle."

"You say that so lightly. To me it is momentous," said Faerverin.

"I sent word to Quickturn to meet us here for breakfast and there he is. Quickturn, it's great to see you again. I would like to introduce my friend Faerverin," said Aleph.

"What noble house did you get her from? It is a pleasure to meet you," said Quickturn. "What brings you to Vivallen? You look like you are going to see Aryante himself."

"Exactly," said Aleph. "Remember the talk we had about a treaty with Gullandia? We want to talk to the king about getting a treaty and taking it up north and we would like for you to accompany us."

"Such is a noble cause," said Quickturn. "I should like very much to go with you."

"What do you think our chances are?" asked Aleph.

"I know that he would like the border skirmishs to end. Too many good soldiers die that way," said Quickturn. "I think I can get us in to see King Aryante today after breakfast." They all sat down to a hearty breakfast of hot cakes, eggs and ham, and then they headed over to the castle. Faerverin was nervous but she managed to hide it well. She looked like a princess, her tall, slender body covered in a filmy, light blue gown and her blonde hair flowing down her back. The golden circlet set in blue gems accented the sparkle in her light blue eyes. Her fine, delicate features and prorcelain skin made her angelic in appearance. She seemed to glide up the steps next to Aleph in his purple velvet cloak.

The castle door was large and heavy with ornate carvings. A guard at the door questioned them and led them into a large waiting area. He walked down a hallway with columns on both sides. He used a door knocker and another guard opened the door. He waited while the other guard talked to the king. When the guard came back to Quickturn, he said that the king would see him. They walked through the door and into a large receiving room with chairs set before the king. There were statues of horses with riders holding spears and shields on either side of a large, ornately carved and gilded throne. Upon the throne sat King Aryante wearing a gem studded crown, red and gold velvet clothing and holding a golden septer. King Aryante said, "Welcome, Quickturn. I understand that there is a matter of great importance to consider. Who do you have with you?"

Quickturn said, "Your Majesty, this is a friend and comrade in arms Aleph, who distinguished himself in battle at Orthrund and has managed the militia at Loadrel. He saved my life and the life of King Farin. He and his friend Faerverin rode from Loadrel yesterday to see you about getting a treaty approved between Aksandan farmers and Gullandian herders for use of Aksandan farmland for pasture during the winter. The farmers would be paid in meat and hides. So far the farmers like the idea. It wouldn't hurt their land and the herds would help to fertilize the land. It would save a lot of reindeer who otherwise would die of winter conditions and a lack of food."

King Aryante said, "It seems like a good plan, but needs to be proven. We should make a one year treaty with the option to renew it should it work out satisfactorily for both sides. Does that sound equitable to you, Aleph?"

"Yes, your Majesty, it does. It sounds fair and sensible. I think that both sides will approve. Thank you," said Aleph.

"Aleph, why do you care about this?" asked King Aryante.

"I spent a lot of time healing the soldiers of Base Camp. I prayed with them and got to know them pretty well. They're good people and I would like them to see some peaceful times," said Aleph.

"That is admirable. I will have the treaty made ready for signing this morning," said King Aryante. "In the meantime, I will have a tribune to show you around the castle and bring you to lunch later." He motioned to the tribune who came forward to lead the company out of the throne room.

The tribune showed them room after room adorned with carvings and tapestries, paintings and statues of men, women, and horses. In the bedrooms were velvet drapes and chiffon hanging around the beds. They met Queen Svetlana in a sitting room having tea with Princess Anya, Rauthomir and Haldovar. Princess Anya asked her mother if she could show Faerverin the gardens. Her mother said that she could be excused from the table and Anya led the group to a door that led into the gardens. Faerverin loved gardens and enjoyed seeing the fall flowers that were still in bloom and the manicured hedges that were still green.

Anya said, "In the summer these bushes are covered in lacey pink flowers and those higher spires have clusters of purple flowers. That tree is my favorite. It also is covered with pink, fluffy flowers. We have many rose bushes in the next garden. Many of those bloom until after the snow falls." They sat down for a few minutes on some benches and a fluffy, calico cat jumped up on Faerverin's lap and immediately started purring. Faerverin was delighted. She stroked the cat and the cat promptly licked her chin. "Her name is Kelly," said Princess Anya.

"Now I feel at home," said Faerverin. "Thank you for showing me your gardens. They are beautiful."

"Next I want to show you the chapel. It is where weddings are performed. Follow me," said Anya.

She led the group down a long hallway to the chapel. It was large with many chairs and the front of it consisted of a wall with cherubs and angels and flowers carved into the stone. There was an altar and steps leading up to the altar. Along each wall, left and right, were white columns. On the front of the altar were the words, "Creator, Redeemer, Healer, Spirit." "Are you and Aleph going to be married?" asked Anya. "If you are, I could ask father if you could be married here. And I know a great dressmaker who could make you a pretty wedding gown out of satin and lace."

"Anya, that is so nice of you to ask, but I don't know. He did buy a house for me, though. Anya smiled and said, "He will ask." Anya was only fourteen, but was very intrigued with romance. She was a petite girl with brown hair and brown eyes. She had a bubbly personality and the curiosity of a teenager.

"Let me show you the ballroom. It's one of my favorite places," said Anya. Again she led the group down the long hall to a huge room. In the front right corner was a platform for the musicians. Here and there were columns. Along each wall were chairs and tables in front of them. The floor was marble. "You should see this place full of people dancing. It's wonderful. I would like to see you and Aleph dancing out there now," said Anya. Aleph took Faerverin to the middle of the floor, hummed a tune, and danced with her. She moved as a feather on the breeze. Aryante walked in. "I was wondering where I would find you. The treaty is ready for delivery. I would like to send some soldiers with you. Quickturn, would you like to take some of yours or mine?"

"I think that some of each would be good. They each have their own specialty and I don't know what we will be facing out there," said Aleph.

"You will choose, then," said Aryante. "Aleph, I would like to speak with you," taking Aleph aside. "Should you decide to marry Faerverin, you may get married right here if you like. I would like a painting made of the two of you dancing like you were just now. I will put it right here in the ballroom to inspire my guests."

"I do plan on marrying her, but we haven't known each other long, and I was going to ask her later on in the journey. I do thank you for your kind offer. I will ask her about it," said Aleph. "How soon do you think we should leave?"

"You rode all day yesterday. Rest today and leave tomorrow morning," said Aryante. "Come, daughter, your mother wants you."

"Quickturn, I'm going to walk around the town and see what the shops have to offer. Where could I trade some gems for silver?" asked Aleph.

"There's one close to here down about five stores," said Quickturn.

"I'll see you tomorrow morning at the inn," said Aleph.

Faerverin and Aleph left the palace and walked down the street to exchange some gems. There were some interesting shops full of art work, furniture, clothing and jewelry. Faerverin saw a painting she lliked of flowers and butterflies. "That would look good in your sitting room," said Aleph. "We will buy it. I want to buy some clothes suitable for extremely cold weather."

"Three doors down," said the shopkeeper.

In that shop they bought fur lined clothing, boots and caps. "When you go into Gullandia, you never know how bad the weather will be," said Aleph. "You will need these pants. These are snow shoes. They will keep us on top of the snow and make it easier to walk. I might leave you at base camp, though. We will see how bad it is."

Then they went into a café for some lunch. It had been a very tiring morning, so after lunch they went back to the inn with their packages.

They put their packages in their rooms and Faerverin said, "I'm so tired that I can't stand it," Aleph took her in his arms and held her, stroking her hair and said, "Let's take a nap together." They cuddled up on the bed and she cried. "It's been so much to happen in such a short time. My head feels confused and tired."

Aleph said, "It has been a lot and I am sorry, but the treaty couldn't wait because of the weather and I couldn't bear leaving you behind. My poor darling, we will rest all afternoon. You will be alright. You will always be safe with me." He gave her a hankie and she wiped her eyes and her nose. He kissed her and they both drifted off to sleep. When they awoke, it was almost time for dinner. They laughed and kissed. He hugged her. "What did the King say to you in the ballroom?" asked Faerverin.

"He wants a painting done of us dancing like we were. He wants to hang it in the ballroom to inspire his guests. He also wants us to get married in the castle." answered Aleph. "Would you like that?"

"I like it a lot," answered Faerverin.

"Really? I didn't know what you would say. You haven't known me very long," said Aleph.

"I just feel that it's right to be with you. I could never willingly walk away from you," said Faerverin.

Aleph took the ring from his pocket and put it on her finger. "I love you. Will you marry me?" asked Aleph.

"Yes, I will. I love you, too," answered Faerverin.

"By the way, in the vision that God gave me, I knew that you were to be my wife," said Aleph. "We had better go get some dinner." They walked down the stairs to have dinner. Quickturn was there and they sat together. "Faerverin and I are engaged and I am worried about her going on this trip. I don't know which danger is worse, the Bitters or the cold. There could be fights and snowstorms. I just think it would be better for her to wait for me here and maybe stay at the castle. King Aryante likes her and so does his daughter. He asked me if we wanted to have our wedding there and his daughter wants to help with the wedding dress. He wants to have a painting of the two of us dancing to hang in his ballroom. Faerverin is an artist and she could do the painting that Aryante wants. I think she would be safer and more comfortable here than riding a horse north for several days." He looked at Faerverin and she said that she was tired and needed more rest, so it would be best to stay, if they would have her.

Quickturn said, "I will be happy to talk to Aryante about this. I think that it would be wise for you to stay here. The King will most certainly see the logic in this." They ordered dinner and had a relaxing meal, after which, Quickturn left to see King Aryante.

"I'm going to miss you, but I do think you're right in this. It is a man's mission and men can endure the hardships of winter travel better than women," said Faerverin.

By the time Quickturn came back, Aleph had finished packing for the trip. He and Quickturn carried Faerverin's things over to the castle where they were met by an anxious Anya. "I'm so glad you can stay with us for a while. Your room is right next to mine. Father says that you know how to paint. Would you teach me? Mother says that it would be good for me to learn it," said Anya.

"I would love to teach you to paint. It's really fun, but first let's take my things up to my room."

She turned to Aleph and said, "I love you. Come home to me soon. I will arrange for the wedding and have my dress made. Ar lath ma. Darath shiral, emna lath."

"Ma vheran, ir abelas, I will come back to you," said Aleph. He left with Quickturn to begin their journey and the mission that would change the northern lands.

Svetlana asked a servant to take Faerverin's things up to her room and they followed him. "I thank you for letting me stay here until Aleph returns. That journey would have been very difficult for me," said Faerverin.

"It is our pleasure to have you here. Anya gets lonesome by herself and she would really like to learn how to paint. She has always been a creative child," said Queen Svetlana. "We have a room where we will have paint and canvasses set up. You may also paint in the garden if you like. Also, I would like you to talk with our dressmaker to design the proper wedding gown for you. We can meet with her today so that she will have plenty of time to work on it. Here is your room. I will have a bath made ready for you and have some clothes brought up for you."

Anya said, "When will the painting things be ready?"

"I have already ordered them," said the Queen. "They should be ready by this afternoon."

"Thankyou, thankyou, thankyou!" said the exuberant teenager.

"We will leave you alone now to unpack and bathe," said Queen Svetlana.

Later that afternoon, Faerverin had bathed and changed into another gown, and she was ready to see the dressmaker. "Hello," said the dressmaker. "My name is Latya. I am the Queen's dressmaker. I understand you are getting married. I will measure you and show you some materials. Let me see the blue gown that you wore yesterday. It is beautiful and well made, but you should be married in white. Look at this material. It is a white silk. It's very soft, and lace around the neckline looks pretty. We can also have lace on the sleeves. Here is a drawing of what this dress would look like. What do you think?"

"It looks perfect," said Faerverin.

"I'll get started on it right away," said Latya.

Latya left and Anya walked in ready for her first art lesson.

"Anya, let's go down to the garden with some paper and a piece of charcoal. We must first draw what we want to paint," said Faerverin. It was a lovely day with sunshine and blue sky. It was comfortably warm and the two girls sat down on a garden bench in front of a table. "Let's try drawing a butterfly. There is one. Let's see if I can get it to land on my finger." She held up her hand speaking some words in elven, "Wilwarin, tulya haara en mi lepta. Panta lya rama." The butterfly came over. "Now look at the shape of the butterfly. Do you see the way the wing goes up and then curves in as it comes back down? Observe the design on the wing. Now, let' try drawing it." Anya tried drawing the butterfly and, with Faerverin's help, she drew one that she could paint. "You also have to decide what else to have in the painting. For your first painting, why don't you have the butterfly sitting on a twig with just a few leaves on the twig. Look beyond the butterfly. What do you see?"

"I see a garden wall with some flowers in front of it. Should I draw that, too?" asked Anya.

"Yes," said Faerverin. "It is important to have a place for your butterfly to live. That makes the painting seem more real. Look at the colors in your butterfly. Those are the colors of paint that you will choose."

"The butterfly is big because it is up close, but the background is smaller because it is farther away," said Ferverin.

"I see," said Anya. "I love this. Can I paint it yet?"

"Yes, you can. You should paint the sky first, and paint the background next, and then the butterfly. That way no paint from the background will accidentally get on your butterfly," said Faerverin.

The afternoon flew by and Anya's painting was beautiful. Her mother came down to see how she was doing and was very happy with it. "You did a good job on your painting, Anya. Are you going to hang it in your room?"

"Yes. I really like it," said Anya. "Is it time for dinner yet? I'm getting hungry."

"Go in and change for dinner," said Queen Svetlana. "We will eat in the dining room this evening. I want you to meet the man who will officiate at your wedding. He is our spiritual advisor. He is a very kind man. You will like him. His name is Elbereth."

"It is an elven name," said Faerverin.

"Yes," said Svetlana smiling.

When the girls had finished dressing for dinner, they walked down to the dining room and sat at a very long table. Various sumptuous dishes were brought to the table. Wine was served in golden goblets to match the golden flatware. Several kinds of meats and vegetables were served with freshly baked buns. There were pies for desert with a fragrant tea.

"This has been a lovely day," said Faerverin. "I thank you."

"Oh, thank you for teaching me how to paint!" said Anya.

Elbereth said, "I will have the pleasure of officiating at your wedding, Faerverin."

"Yes, I hope so," said Faerverin. "Aleph is on a trip north to Gullandia to get a treaty signed. We want to get married when he gets back. King Aryante and Queen Svetlana have allowed me to stay here until he returns. Originally I was going with him, but the trip proved to be too much for me with the cold weather and the distance."

"I can see that," said Elbereth. "Snow will be falling near Gullandia now and in Gullandia it is getting deep by now. They will be thankful to be on this side of the Aikasse Mountains for the winter. I hope everything goes well for him there. You are lucky to have Aleph. I know his parents. They are good people. I could ask them to attend the wedding. I know they would want to. They live not far away in Talath. Have you met them?"

"No, I haven't. I don't know if they are aware that he knows Father God now. He said that knowing God helped him to be a better man. Tall Sky introduced him to Father God and trained him as a Bright Elf," said Faerverin smiling. "I love him so much and I am proud of him."

"I will be praying for him. I'm sure everything will be all right and he will be home again in a few days," said Elbereth. "Now, I had better be going. Thank you for a great dinner and lovely company. I will see you in a few days. Goodnight." Elbereth bowed to the King and left.

"I would like to be excused, please. I'm getting very tired," said Faerverin. "Thank you for dinner." She curtsied and left. Anya said, "Wait for me," and followed her.

"Anya seems to be fond of her," said King Aryante.

"She is," said Svetlana. "I was watching from the window while Faerverin was teaching her to paint. She held up her hand and a bird sat on her finger. Then she did the same with a butterfly. She said something to the butterfly and set it down on a twig and it sat there while Anya drew it. The cat liked her, too. Anya said that it jumped up on her lap and licked her chin. I guess the girl just has a way with animals."

"I'm glad they're getting married. I like both of them," said King Aryante.

The girls stopped in the garden to get the painting so that it could be drying upstairs at night. It had been an enjoyable day for both of them. "Tomorrow we will both make a painting. I am going to try doing the one your father wants of Aleph and me dancing in the ballroom. We will have to go to the ballroom again to do that one. We will have to put a sheet down to catch any drips."

"How soon did Latya say that she would have a fitting for your wedding dress?" asked Anya.

"It will be in several days I think," said Faerverin. "I can hardly wait to see what it will look like."

"It will be beautiful," said Anya in a dreamy voice. "I love weddings."

"Someday you will be married and there will be a very large party," said Faerverin, "and I will paint a portrait of the two of you in your wedding clothes."

THE TREATY

Aleph and Quckturn chose to have a company of sixteen with them on their trip. They also had extra pack horses laden with supplies. They rode out at daybreak and rode nonstop for four hours. The weather was cold and clear. No travelers were on the road and none could be seen in either direction. They stopped in Talath for lunch at an inn, warming up with some stew and wine. The soldiers were feeling free and happy to be on the road for a while with no duties to perform. "It's great to be away for a while, isn't it?" said Marlen. "I know a soldier who received a commendation for never being drunk. He was just too lazy to raise his tankard enough times to get drunk." Everyone laughed.

"Ill drink to that," said Kroom. "I know a soldier who was so lazy that he made his horse stand on horseshoes for hours to see if they would naturally stick to its hooves."

"I haven't heard a lazy soldier joke since the Purge of Malwood," said Parin.

"What was that battle like?" asked Marlen.

"It was wild and furious," said Kroom. "We killed all the slavers, the guards, and the customers. Even the witch Avidora was killed. It was a bloody battle. We lost a few good men, but over all it was a complete victory. We freed many slaves and brought them back to Loadrel. Some of them we returned, but some got married and stayed in Loadrel. One married Rando at Home Fire and others will marry there, too."

"What is this Rando like?" aked Marlen.

"Rando is a good man," said Kroom, "He's a good fighter and a born leader. He and his men have killed hundreds of Bitters. They are now building houses at Home Fire. He is determined to make a town out of Home Fire. Six Gullandians just joined his group. They rode in on reindeers with a few dwarves on ponies packing crossbows. I guess it looked so funny that Rando broke out laughing. The six youngsters had just been married at Othrund and decided to build houses at Home Fire. It's a delightful story and it's all true."

"With all the runaways and freed slaves, it sounds like more people will be settling there," said Marlen.

"Beginning life in a brand new place is a big draw and the location is beautiful. There is Lake Perilough, woods to hunt, and grazing for the animals. It is also between Loadrel and Yardrel," said Kroom.

Quickturn interjected, "We had better be on our way. I know of a large barn where we could stay for the night, but it is about another four hours' ride." They paid the Innkeeper and left.

The next four hours passed without incident. They passed several groups of travelers, but no Bitters. One group was riding reindeers and asked directions to Home Fire. They had heard that they would be welcome there. From their dress, they were obviously Gullandian's.

The four hours passed by quickly and they arrived at a farm with a large barn. The farmer was happy for the soldiers to stay there for the night. They wouldn't have to stand guard for a change. They had spent a very nervous few weeks there. They had seen a few bands of Bitters and had given them some food, but would not let them stay there. They ate their evening meal and retired to the barn for a comfortable night's sleep.

Kroom took the first watch. Not long after they went to bed, Kroom heard a noise around the horses and upon investigating, caught a girl trying to steal some food. "Please don't hurt me," she said. "I just wanted some food. We haven't eaten for days."

"I'm not going to hurt you," said Kroom. "How did you come to be out here?"

"The slavers left us here and ran from some soldiers, so we just hid and watched. Then we started walking," she said.

"Let's get your friends and give them some food and wine and find a warm place for them to sleep. In the morning, you will ride with us and we will find a new home for you," said Kroom. The girl brought her friends over and Kroom gave them bread and cheese and wine. Then he gave them each a blanket and took them to a corner of the barn to sleep.

The next morning he introduced them to the men and, after breakfast, they rode out toward Base Camp. The girls kept their blankets wrapped around them, because they didn't have warm clothing, but when they reached Base Camp, the soldiers shared some extra clothing with them. Jaylek was really glad to see men from King Aryante. He wanted the conflict to be over. Aleph said, "I have a treaty signed by the king to be presented to the Gullandian Chief. It gives him what he wants, the right to use this side of the mountain for grazing in the winter. Do you know where he is now?"

"He should be northeast of here about a mile. Are you going to ride up there?" asked Jaylek.

"Yes, I thought I would ride into Gullandia tomorrow," said Aleph. "You don't happen to have a reindeer and a prisoner, do you?"

"As a matter of fact, I do." said Jaylek. "We caught him snooping around here yesterday. I'll take you to him. He's over there in the prisoner's tent."

Aleph walked into the tent with a skin of wine and poured some for each of them. They sat there drinking for a few minutes. The he said, "I am Aleph. I have a treaty for your chief that gives you the right to graze on this side of the mountains during the winter. This is something that your chief wants. I need your help to take it to him. Would you help me?"

"Yes, I will," he said smiling and shook Aleph's hand. "I only have one reindeer, but a horse would be able to walk there still. Soon, though, the snow will be too deep for horses."

Aleph said, "I have two pairs of snowhoes with me if we need them."

"This is good. You never know when the snow will fall," he said. "My name is Sontar. I am happy to meet you, Aleph. Have you ever been to Gullandia?"

"Actually, I have. I was here long ago during the summer with my parents. We met some of your people. We should plan on leaving tomorrow morning after breakfast. How long will it take us to get there?"

"I think we will be there by lunch time," said Sontar.

"Good. I will be back to get you at daybreak," said Aleph.

At dinner, Aleph addressed the men of the camp admonishing them to treat the girls with respect. They were unwilling prisoners of the Bitters and were the ones they were fighting to protect. He told them that when he returned, he will be taking the girls to Home Fire to meet prospective husbands. Aleph said. "Tomorrow I will be taking a treaty to be signed by the Gullandia Chief and your prisoner Sontar will be my guide." Everyone applauded.

The next morning after breakfast, Aleph and Sontar left for the mountain pass. They traveled for about an hour and turned into the pass. There was snow in the pass, but it was still passable. There were tall cliffs rising on either side of them. The weather was clear and very cold. When they reached the end of the pass, they turned toward the east for another hour. The snow was over a foot deep. The Chief was in his tent eating lunch. Sontar introduced Aleph. "Aleph, this is Chief Johan Turi. He will need to see the Treaty."

Aleph said, "Chief Turi, King Aryante would like to offer you grazing rights south of the Aikasse Mountains in exchange for some meat and hides to the farmers of the area. My men have spoken with the farmers and they like the idea, because they have a hard time hunting in the winter. If there would arise any problems from this, the disputes would be handled without physical violence."

Chief Turi said, "I will sign this treaty. Tell King Aryante thank you for me. I will get my people to move the herd through the pass now before more snows come."

"Yes," said Aleph, "I must be returning to Base Camp and have the soldiers to contact the farmers with this news."

Aleph rode back through the pass to Base Camp and relayed the news to Jaylek who sent his soldiers out to inform the farmers. The next morning Kroom, Parin, Bellstram and Salek accompanied the girls toward Home Fire. Aleph, Quickturn and their soldiers rode toward Vivallen.

"It was a successful mission," said Aleph. "Chief Turi signed the treaty and we rescued four more girls. I am well pleased. I hope the girls like Home Fire. Of course they will probably have to stay at The Laborer's Reward for a while until construction is complete on more houses at Home Fire."

Quickturn said, "I wouldn't be surprised if some of the Home Fire men stayed at Beldock's inn for the winter. You can only build for so long as the weather gets colder."

"Speaking of cold, I can hardly wait to get back to a nice warm bed. I will never understand how the Gullandians can stand living in tents during the winter," said Aleph. "I wonder how Faerverin's doing. She was going to teach Princess Anya how to paint. Where is that barn of yours? I am hungry and cold and impatient right now."

"It should be up ahead a few miles. Tell me about Faerverin. What is she like?" asked Quickturn.

"Faerverin is sweet and kind. She loves animals. She lived with the fairies for a while and they taught her to speak to animals and to paint. She can actually talk to butterflies using the Elven language. She is amazing," said Aleph. "I want to stop at Talath briefly to let my parents know about my wedding. I want them to meet Faerverin and tell them that I have God in my life now. I haven't seen them for a long time. We should probably plan on staying at the inn in Talath tonight."

"There is the barn. Let's have lunch," said Quickturn.

In the barn was a girl in a dirty dress shivering from the cold. Aleph took a blanket to her and wrapped it around her. Then he gave her some wine to drink and settled her down on some hay. He then found his fur lined clothing and helped her into it. He took a wet rag and wiped her face and hands. Then he gave her some bread and cheese and wine. He did all of this without speaking to her. When she was feeling more comfortable, he asked her about her recent experience.

'What happened to you, girl?" asked Aleph. "Where are you from?"

"I was outside hanging up some clothes to dry and some men on horses grabbed me and rode off with me. They were elves, but not kind like you. They said that they were going to sell me," said the girl.

"What is your name?" asked Aleph.

She answered, "My name is Nadya. I am from Talath."

"I am also from Talath and we are going to stay there tonight. We will take you back home," said Aleph.

After lunch the group headed out again for another four hour ride to Talath. He left word with the farmer there to shelter any stragglers coming his way and that there would be a King's soldier once a week to pick them up and help them to find their home.

At Talath they settled in at the inn and Aleph dropped off Nadya at her home where she was received with joyful tears. Then he rode to his parents' home. His parents were delighted to see him and to hear that he had accepted Father God into his heart. They said that they would be happy to come to his wedding and looked forward to meeting his bride. He told them about his mission to Gullandia and said that he had to go back to the inn to stay for the night, because he would have to leave with them in the morning. He went back to the inn feeling happier and lighter than he had for a long time. Having his parents' forgiveness meant a lot to him.

The next day brought some light snow, but the group managed to reach Vivallen by lunch time. After cleaning up and changing clothes, Aleph ate lunch and headed over to the castle. He was received by a grateful King Aryante. "Aleph, I'm glad you made it back alright. Did you get the treaty signed?" asked King Aryante. Aleph handed the treaty to the king. "I thank you. How was the weather there?"

"It was cold and there was about a foot of snow. Chief Turi was happy to sign the treaty. How is Faerverin doing?" asked Aleph.

"Your bride is a delightful person. She is doing very well with our daughter. She is teaching Anya how to paint and making great progress with her. They are probably in the ballroom if you would like to see them," said King Aryante.

"Before I go, I wanted to tell you that I stopped at Talath to see my parents and tell them about the wedding. They were happy about that and said that they would attend the wedding. Also, we rescued five girls on our way. Four of them we sent to Loadrel and one I returned to her parents inTalath," said Aleph. The king laughed. "Also, I told the farmer in whose barn we found the girls that we would send a soldier once a week to pick up any more of them. Is that ok? If not, I can ask Quickturn to do it."

"Either way is fine. I want to talk to you soon about a career for you in my court," said King Ayante, "But for now, go and see your bride."

Aleph bowed and left the throne room.

He walked down the corridor to the ballroom to see Faerverin. When she saw him, she ran to him and held him tightly saying, "You're home. I'm so glad. I missed you."

He said, "My darling, I could hardly wait to see you, but I had to give the treaty to King Aryante first. He saw Princess Anya watching them and smiling. "How is your painting coming along? Yours looks very pretty, Princess Anya."

"Thank you, but did you see the one of you and Faerverin dancing?" she asked.

"The king is sure to like it. Faerverin, it is beautiful. Did you have a fitting for your wedding dress?" asked Aleph. "I told my parents about us and they will come to the wedding."

"Oh, that's great, I want to meet them," said Faerverin. "Do you think they will like me?"

"They will love you," said Aleph. "Do we have a wedding date yet?"

"The dress should be ready by tomorrow. Other than that, it just depends on the king," said Faerverin. "I would like all of our friends to be here. Do you think that would be possible?"

"I'm sure it would be possible if we sent a messenger right away. I'll speak to King Aryante about it," said Aleph. That evening at dinner he did speak to King Aryante and a messenger was sent to invite Tall Sky and Melody, Laskron and Liadra, Trag and Arinya, Beldock and Mina, Steben and Amidra, and Rando and Alqua. The wedding day was to be three days from now. King Aryante spoke to Tall Sky about staying at the castle as his advisor to help judge and settle disputes. He said that he would have to talk to Faerverin about it. He told King Aryante that Faerverin liked nature and wanted a miniature dragon for a pet. King Aryante didn't have an objection to that and said that he had gardens and fountains and that there was a river close by. Also, about a half hour's ride to the west was Lake Inari.

That night Aleph talked to Faerverin about staying on at the castle and explained the type of job that he would have. He told her about the river and Lake Inari. She said, "You know, we could try it for a while and see if we like it. We still have a house in Loadrel to go to when we need some time away. What do you think about it?"

"I think that I will seek Father God, talk to Tall Sky and Elbereth about it and then decide. This is not a path to be embarked upon lightly," said Aleph.

"I love you my husband to be," she said and laughed. They kissed and said goodnight.

JOURNEY HOME

Kroom, Parin, Salek, and Bellstram accompanied four girls from Base Camp heading toward Loadrel. They were dressed fairly well, but it was still a cold ride. They rode west past Otherund and then south to Talami where they stopped at Vela's for lunch. They took some food into the house and sat down on the floor to eat. "Rusken, are you still glad to be out of the army?" asked Kroom.

"Of course," said Rusken laughing. "Vela has turned into a good cook."

"Cooking for Rando's group for years gave her plenty of practice. Vela, did you know that Rando got married?" asked Kroom. "He is married to one of the slave girls and is the Chief of the town of Home Fire. They are building new houses out there and filling them with furniture that Steben's father is making. All of Loadrel is pitching in because of the help he and his men gave against the Bitters and the slavers. Vela, these four girls were hiding from the Bitters when we found them. Those Bitters were going to sell them. Rusken, there is a treaty between Gullandia and Aksanda now. It was just signed. It allows the Gullandians grazing privileges during the winter in exchange for meat and hides. If this works, there will be no more border skirmishes."

"That would be great. I have lost many friends on that border," said Rusken. "How are Aleph and Tall Sky doing?"

Aleph is engaged to a girl he rescued and is taking the treaty to King Aryante right now. He left his fiancé Faerverin at the castle. Tall Sky and Melody are married and he is helping to supervise construction of Home Fire. There are men out there who want wives, so we are going to stop at Home Fire and let the girls meet them. This has been a time of wild changes for our area," said Kroom. "Have there been any more Bitters coming through here?"

"Just a few, and we have a militia group now who guards our town," said Rusken.

"We had better be going. We would like to get to Home Fire today even if it means traveling in the evening. I'll let everyone know that you're doing well." Vela gave the girls some cookies and told them that she was once caught by slavers and that Rando helped her to live out at Home Fire. The girls were relieved to hear that.

Back on the road, the sky was overcast and the air was cold. Four hours later they stopped at the Yardrel Café for a hot meal. The waitress brought stew, bread, butter and wine. It was delicious to the travelers, and it really felt good to feel warmth coursing through their bodies. "Tell me," said Kroom to the girls. "Were the Bitters on their way to the battle, or were they running from the battle?"

Cassia said, "We were being taken to the battle to be sold to the soldiers. Thank God, we never reached the battle. We came close. I could hear the sounds of the battle, but one of the Bitters went forward to look, and when the others heard how bloody the battle was, they ran. We hid behind a big rock, and when the battle died down, we walked away. We tried to travel mostly at night so that we wouldn't be caught again. Whatever makes men feel that they have the right to capture people and sell them to other people? I surely do not understand this. Something should be done about it."

"Something was being done about it. This is the second battle that has been waged to stop slavery and murder and robbery. You see, there is a darkness of spirit that has been moving across this land and it affected the Bitter Elves very strongly, because they were already angry with our Creator for not giving them magical powers and wealth. Naturally, it didn't take much to push them into war with the dwarves. They thought the dwarves were enormously wealthy and they wanted that wealth," said Kroom. "What types of things do you girls know how to do?"

Cassia said, "I know how to clean and smoke meat, plant a garden, and take care of chickens."

Brilley said, "I know how to milk and feed a cow, and how to birth babies. I was learning from our doctor how to birth babies and how to dress wounds and what to do for sick people. She even taught me how to make medicines from plants. It was very interesting. I'm going to learn to write so that I can put it all down on parchment. It's important that this knowledge doesn't get lost."

Hilda said, "I can make clothing and decorations for the house."

Indra said, "I am good with children. They really like me, and I figure out how to teach them things when I am watching them. It's really fun."

Kroom said, "All of the skills that you just mentioned are needed at Home Fire. I think that you would fit in very well out there. Now, I think we had better get going. We have a long ride ahead of us."

"Couldn't we just stay here for the night and leave for Home Fire tomorrow? I want to clean up before meeting the Home Fire people," said Hilda.

"That sounds so good," said Kroom. "I think we're all pretty tired." Kroom got up to talk to a waitress for a minute. When he came back, he had a big smile on his face. "Good news. There is a clothing store that has used clothing. It's just a few doors down. Let's see if they have anything that would fit you." The group went to the store and found clothing for the girls. They each received a complete set of winter clothes and pajamas. Then they went to the inn and ordered baths and rooms.

After a good night's sleep, the girls felt refreshed and looked a whole lot better in their new clothes. They went to the café for breakfast. "You girls look very nice today. You will make a good impression on the Home Fire people," said Kroom. "They serve a really good breakfast here." The servant brought out hot cakes, ham, eggs, potatoes, bread and jam. "Eat as much as you can. We have at least a four hour ride to Home Fire." After breakfast they headed down the road to Home Fire.

It was a beautiful, sunny day. "It's like the world turned upside down and all the bad fell off!" said Indra. "I'm clean, I am wearing new, warm clothes, and I ate a good breakfast."

"Pretty soon we'll be at Home Fire meeting some boys," said Cassia.

"I know," said Brilley. "I wonder what they look like."

Kroom said, "They are men like us. They work hard and they won't be cleaned up. They're building houses. But they are good looking men."

"Oh, I can hardly wait," said Cassia.

"Well, you have to be patient, but we'll be there for lunch," said Kroom. "You know, these men have lived out there in tents for years. They became wealthy from looting Malwood Market after killing the slavers. Then they decided to build houses and make a real town out of the camp. I think that three of the men have already chosen slave girls from Loadrel to marry, but there are more men who are getting homes ready for wives."

"How did they live all that time?" asked Indra.

Kroom answered, "They hunted, fished, and gardened. Remember Vela. She made clothes and cooked. They rescued her from the slavers and brought her to Home Fire. She stayed with them for years until some runaway girls met her and offered to take her and Steben to their homes. You said that it was like the world turned upside down and all the bad fell off, but the bad was actually, pushed off. It takes good people to push evil away. It isn't easy, but it is very rewarding."

"I guess that's right," said Indra. "No telling what would have happened to us if you hadn't rescued us. It does take good people to get rid of evil people and to stop them from hurting others. I thank you and your men for helping us."

"It is our pleasure to do so," said Kroom. "Here is our turn off, and here is a Home Fire sentry."

The sentry escorted the travelers down the path to Home Fire. Rando came out to meet them. "Kroom, good to see you," said Rando. "Come, sit down by the fire and warm yourselves. Are you hungry?"

"Yes, we are, and we brought you four young ladies that we rescued over by Talath. We will take them to Loadrel with us for a while, but they wanted to see Home Fire first," said Kroom.

Rando asked one of the women to bring food and wine and they all had some much appreciated lunch. There was fresh bread and stew and warm berry wine. Rando asked, "Why were you over at Talath?"

"We were with Quickturn and some soldiers riding to Gullandia to deliver a treaty from King Aryante. We were sheltering in a barn and found these girls. They had been abandoned by some Bitters after the Battle of Othrund. We carried them with us until Quickturn had delivered the treaty. We stayed at Base Camp and then rode on to Yardrel where we cleaned up and stayed at the inn," answered Kroom. "It looks like you've made a lot of progress here."

Rando smiled and said, "Yes, we have. Come with me and I'll show you. We have ten finished houses and five more in progress. I have begun work on an inn. With all the people we have had comming through, we need an inn. It will also be used for a meeting place and a general store. We just keep on working at it. Those Gullandians are hard workers. They are all working on one house, and when it is finished, they will build another house. They are doing it this way so that they can all stay in one house while they work on the next one. It's a great idea. Over there is a corral for their reindeer. They ride them, you know. Eventually, there will be so much livestock out here that we won't have to hunt for meat. I never thought that our camp could turn into something like this." There was a road with five houses on each side with more houses being built. The first houses were being occupied with families and married couples. "Come into my house and I will bring some single men over to meet you," said Rando. "My wife Alqua will introduce you. Alqua, we have guests. They're here to meet some of our men. I'll go get them." Rando rounded up four single men and told them to borrow a chair and go to his house to meet some single ladies. They had the good sense to wash their hands and shave their faces.

Alqua served them some wine and began the conversation with a question. "What types of things do you girls like to do?"

Cassia said, "I can clean and smoke meat, garden, and take care of chickens."

Brilley said, "I can work with cows, and I can birth babies and help people get well."

Hilda said, "I can sew clothing and make decorations."

Indra said, "I like to work with chidren."

Alqua said, "We need people who can do those things. I hope that you will consider living here. Like you, I was abandoned by the Bitters. I married Rando, and we have other men who want to marry other girls who were rescued. I know it's hard to be stolen and marched and beaten, but I promise you that everything will be alright. These men have helped to rescue many people like you. They have fought hard to keep us safe."

Fane said, "I ran away from my parents' farm with Lore. Neither of us wanted to farm. We both liked to hunt and fish, so we ran off to do that. We found Malwood and were hunting in there when we were beaten up and robbed. We walked to Lake Perilough to get some water and try to fish. Some of Rando's men had been watching us and decided to take us to Home Fire. We liked it, so we stayed."

"Hi. My name is Bronty and I was captured by slavers about five years ago. They were having fun whipping me and taunting me when Rando's men killed every one of them and took me to Home Fire. Of course, I stayed here too."

"Hi. My name is Cantro. I lived in my grandparent's house in town, but I wanted adventure, so I ran away. I found that living off the land was very difficult, so I worked on a small farm until some Bitters killed the family and took me with them. Outside of Malwood, Rando's men killed them and took me to Home Fire. I've been here ever since. We are all ready to be married, but our houses need to be finished. I'm thinking that by next week, we could move in."

Alqua said, "I recommend that you girls go on to Loadrel and make some clothes while you wait for the houses to be finished. Then you can come back out here, or the men can stay at the inn in Loadrel to get to know you better. What do you think of that, Cantro?"

"I suppose it would be better for us to keep our minds on the task at hand for now. I agree," said Cantro. "First of all, would you girls be interested in living out here?"

The girls said that they would. Alqua told Kroom that the meeting went well and that they would go to Loadrel to stay for a week.

Kroom got everybody together to move on to Loadrel. They packed up and saddled up and were off. The ride home was fun for the girls, thinking about the men and wondering what married life would be like. Only one of them knew how to make clothes, but Kroom assured them that there were women in Loadrel who would be happy to assist them. He told them about Melody and Amidra and Liadra and how well they were doing. He said that they would be staying at the Laborer's Reward Inn while they got adjusted and made their wardrobes. He also told them that all of this was at no charge to them. He explained that because of the Purge of Malwood, there was plenty of extra in Loadrel and in Home Fire. The citizens of these towns were following God's directions to help those in need. What the darkness meant for evil, the Light meant for good.

By the time the travelers reached Loadrel, a messenger had delivered an invitation from King Aryante. The group was met by Beldock and Mina who asked Kroom to watch the inn for a few days because they had to go to Vivallen to Aleph's wedding to Faerverin. He said that of course he would. He introduced the girls and asked if they could stay at the inn for a week. Beldock said that they were welcome to stay there. Kroom said that they had been to Home Fire and liked it, so they would go back there next week to get to know the men better. Mina took the girls up to their rooms and introduced them to Aela, Kara, and Aeria, the other girls who were also waiting for the next trip to Home Fire.

"Were you abandoned, too?" Brilley asked Aela. "We were abandoned by some Bitters near Talath."

"We were abandoned by some Bitters near here. We had been without food and water and were marched for days. It was horrible. Every time we stumbled or sat down, they hit us. I thought we were going to die," said Aela. "Then this nice Bright Elf named Aleph brought a wagon and took us to this inn. He left for Vivallen with

Faerverin. She was with us, but she is also a Bright Elf. He is going to get a treaty signed by the Chief of Gullandia."

"Did you hear that Faerverin and Aleph are getting married in the castle? Beldock and Mina, Laskron and Liadra, Tall Sky and Melody, Steben and Amidra, and Trag and Arinya are all invited. I wish we could go. I'll bet it will be beautiful," said Cassia.

Hilda said, "We have to get ready for our own weddings. Kroom said that we should make clothes this week. I know how to sew, but where will we get material and needles and thread?"

"There is a room full of those things here. They got it from the Malwood Market where it was going to be sold. A lady showed us how to make clothes and we could help you to make yours. It's easier than it looks," said Aela. "You are going to need winter clothes and summer clothes. It will take all week at least to do that, but with all of us helping, I think we can get the job done. Let's go look at the materials and choose the ones that you would like." The girls walked to the back room and were amazed at the amount of material that was there. I would like to make covers for our beds. We will have to go see the furniture maker and see how big the beds are."

After choosing materials, the girls took them to their rooms. Then they heard Beldock call them for dinner. At dinner, the girls happily talked about the men at Home Fire. "We should decide now which man we like. That way there will be less confusion. I like Cantro," said Cassia.

Brilley said, "I like Fane."

Hilda said, "I like Bronty."

Indra said, "I like Lore." They all laughed, because they each chose different men. "I can't stand it. I want to go there now," said Indra.

"Patience," said Cassia. "If we were there now, we would be sleeping in tents and living outside. We would also be wearing the same clothes every day. It's better this way, and when we go, we will be ready to start our lives right."

"I make home decorations. Wait till you see the pretty things I will make for your houses," said Hilda.

"This is going to be so much fun. You know, we will have to send messengers to our families, but let's wait until after we're married. Otherwise they may try to take us back home, and I really want to live at Home Fire. My life is changed and I like it," said Cassia.

"Speaking of home decorations, you have to see Laskron's workshop. He is a glass blower, and he makes the most beautiful glassware like vases, glasses, windows, and other pretty things. He is very creative, and his shop is right next door. He saved Beldock from a fire once. They are very good friends. He and Liadra might not go to the wedding because they have a little girl and they don't ever leave her to go anywhere. We will visit them tomorrow morning and then we will make some clothes," said Aeria.

Melody, Tall Sky, Trag and Arinya walked in. "Beldock, can you believe this invitation? Are you going?" asked Tall Sky.

"Sure. Mina and I are going. We have never been to the castle. It should be fun. I'm sure Quickturn will be there. I don't know about Rando, but he was invited. This will be an event to remember. It's time to get out our finest clothes. There will be a dance in the ballroom afterwards. We should take along a couple of extra horses and do some shopping while we're there. They have some fine shops. Trag, you should bring a wagon and do some buying for your store while we're there. We can plan on staying an extra day just for shopping. It's not every day you get an opportunity like this," said Beldock.

Tall Sky said, "We should visit a jeweler and exchange some gems for silver pieces. That way we will have silver to spend whan we need it. Father God said that Aleph would be a great Bright Elf and it is already comming true. I'm so glad we stopped to help him when we did."

Trag said, "We are getting low on some things due to the requests from people at Home Fire, so this is a great idea. I will borrow a wagon and we can all use it. I like the idea of having more people with us while we're traveling. Are Steben and Amidra coming, too?"

"I think so, but they will have to leave their daughter with Liadra and Laskron. They will probably want to do some shopping for their new home," said Tall Sky.

Melody said, "Daisy is getting hungry. Let's sit down and have dinner." Mina brought out a little plate of food for Daisy and some mugs of ale followed by stew, cheese, bread and jam. Daisy ate ravenously and then cuddled up on Melody's shoulder under some of her red, curly hair. "We all should wear the dresses we got married in. They're fancy enough."

"Or we could buy new ones in Vivallen," said Arinya. "But we should bring our other ones just in case."

"We should probably leave early tomorrow morning," said Beldock. "Kroom will be watching the inn for me." They ate dinner and left for home to get packed for their trip.

On their way home, Melody said, "What are we going to do with Daisy? Will they allow her to go with me to the wedding? I could put her in a bag and carry her with me. If I feed her first, she should sleep through the whole thing."

"Culina, my darling, I love you so much. You mustn't worry about the dragon. I will shield her if necessary, but she will be all right in your velvet bag. Now, let's think about happy things like getting ready for the most elegant party ever. We will be there early enough to have our clothes pressed."

"Do you think they will come back with us?" asked Melody.

"They might. They bought the house next to Trag's store. Aleph thought that it would be good to have Faerverin's art store next to another store. They are having a room for her painting added onto the front of the house," said Tall Sky.

"I want her to make a painting of you, me, and Daisy. Do you think she could do that?" asked Melody.

"If she can't, I will find you someone who can," answered Tall Sky. "Here we are. Let's go in and pack."

THE TRIP TO VIVALLEN

The next morning at the inn, there was a larger breakfast crowd than usual. Besides the rescued slave girls, there were Trag, Arinya, Tall Sky, Melody, Amidra, Steben, Emmy, Laskron, Liadra, Elise, Beldock, Mina, Flint, Cliff, Rando and Alqua. Rando and Alqua rode to Loadrel as soon as they got the invitation. "Rando, I'm glad you could make it. How was your trip?" asked Tall Sky.

"It was good. I brought Flint and Cliff for extra protection and they can ride with us to Vivallen. There were no travelers on the road and the moon was bright. We didn't pack much, so we'll be buying clothes in Vivallen." He put his arm around Alqua and said, "My new bride is looking forward to that." Alqua smiled and kissed him on the cheek.

Melody thought,"The old grouch has turned into a happy man. It's amazing what getting married to a good person can do." She smiled and looked adoringly at Tall Sky. Daisy was doing a hungry dance on Melody's shoulder, so Mina brought a small plate of scrambled eggs and bacon with some bread and jam. Daisy jumped onto the table and ate her favorite breakfast.

Aela, Kara, and Aeria helped cook and serve the breakfast food, and Cassia, Brilley, Hilda and Indra would do the clean up so that Beldock and Mina could enjoy a good breakfast before leaving. The girls would make clothes and take care of the inn while Beldock and Mina were gone for four days. There would be no guests during that time and Kroom would be in charge. The milita would continue to patrol the outskirts of the town. Any more abandoned girls were to be brought to the inn. Any more bands of Bitters were to be killed.

Beldock was confident that the people he left in charge would do a good job.

Trag had borrowed a wagon and had parked it in front of the inn. All was ready and twelve people mounted horses. Trag drove the wagon with his horse tied behind. The world was full of possibilities and wonders. The wagon carried their food, water, wine, blankets and emergency supplies. Beldock had traveled enough to know what things were important to carry with them.

The air was crisp and the sun was warm on their backs as they rode toward Vivallen. The sounds of horses' hooves stricking the ground, the rattling of the wagon, and the squeeking of the leather saddles all lent an air of excitement to the travelers. Daisy was peering out at everything and chirring in Melody's ear. Daisy was wearing a little fur cloak that Melody had made for her. When she got tired, Daisy would cuddle up in the velvet bag that Melody wore strapped to herself. Four hours later, they stopped at the ruins for lunch. Everyone was happy and hungry. They spread out their blankets and ate bread with sliced meat and cheese and berry wine. They even had some pastries from Jelsareeb's bakery. Having eaten a good lunch, they resumed their journey.

Each person was thinking about his or her own concerns. Melody was thinking about dancing with Tall Sky in the ballroom. Tall Sky was wondering what Father God had in store for Aleph. Trag was thinking about the goods he needed to buy. Arinya was amazed at her good fortune from being on the auction block to being married to Trag and having a store. She was also thinking of the various outfits she could wear. Steben was very happy to be married to Amidra and was hoping everything would continue to go well with the furniture making. Amidra was wondering how she could fix her hair and what kind of dress to buy. She was also thinking of her own journey through Malwood to Home Fire and her first night with Steben under the stars. Rando was still amazed at how his life had changed for the better. He had gone from leading a bunch of bandits living in tents to being the chief of a town, being married to a great woman and attending a wedding at King Aryante's castle. He was also quite wealthy and he knew God. He was convinced that all of this was because of following God's leading either directly, or indirectly through Tall Sky. Alqua was so in love with Rando, he was all she could think about. Mina was feeling very grateful to have such good friends and about all the good that had come about from helping the girls. Beldock, as usual, was concerned about safety and kept a sharp lookout for signs of trouble. Flint and Cliff brought up the rear and also kept a sharp eye on their surroundings, which were mainly rolling grasslands dotted with a few far away farms.

About an hour from Vivallen they found a little girl walking barefoot along the road. They stopped while Tall Sky dismounted and talked with her. "They killed Mommy and Daddy and took me with them. Then they just set me down and left," she said. She appeared to be about four years old. Tall Sky picked her up and gave her to Mina, who hugged her, wiped her face clean and gave her food and water. She wrapped her in a blanket and set her in the wagon where she cuddled up on other blankets and fell asleep. The rest of the journey was uneventful. When they reached the city gate, Beldock showed the guard an invitation to the castle and they were passed through without trouble. Beldock led them through the streets to The Golden Chalice and registered them for rooms with baths and dinner. They would save the shopping for tomorrow with the exception of clothing for the new little girl named Aranel. Tall Sky said to Mina, "She is Elven. Her name means princess. I will talk to Melody about adopting her, or Quickturn and Faerverin could. Anyway, Melody and I will go with you to the store."

Tall Sky and Melody bought Aranel every day clothes, pajamas, several gowns and several pairs of shoes and socks. Then they took her back to the inn and bathed her. At dinner she looked like a clean and proper little girl with long, blonde hair, blue eyes, and fine, elven features. When she walked in, everyone gasped in surprise. She looked like Faerverin must have looked when she was a child. "The resemblance is amazing. "I think she is Faerverin's sister," said Tall Sky. "Tomorrow I will tell her and sit down with both of them to talk, but for now, let's have dinner. Aranel, are you hungry?" She nodded her head and Tall Sky set her in a chair between himself and Melody.

"Have you ever seen a baby dragon?" asked Melody. Aranel shook her head no. "Well, I have one. Her name is Daisy and she's been taking a nap in my bag. Would you like to see her? It's about time for her dinner, too." Melody took Daisy out of her bag and gave her a little piece of cheese to eat. Mina went back to the kitchen to fix a small dish of stew cut up into little pieces for Daisy and brought it to her. Daisy ate it and burped and then looked in Aranel's eyes and chirred. Aranel held her hand out to Daisy and Daisy climbed up her arm to sit on her shoulder and rub faces with Aranel. She giggled and petted Daisy.

"I hope everybody's hungry. They have very good food here," said Beldock. "Waitress, bring a round of ale here, please." Finally, everyone could relax after traveling all day. The ale tasted good and was thirst quenching and spirit lifting. Soon there was laughter and they had a great dinner. After dinner everyone went upstairs to bathe and go to bed. Mina let Aranel sleep with her so that the child would not wake up scared and alone.

The next day they went shopping for clothing to wear to the wedding and for other clothing needs. Tall Sky went to the castle to discuss Aranel with King Aryante and Aleph and Faerverin. He took Melody and Aranel with him. He felt it was important to get Aranel's future decided before the wedding. First he visited with Aleph and Faerverin. He told them about finding Aranel and about her parents being killed. Then he had Melody bring in Aranel to meet them. Aranel went up to Faerverin and said, "You look like my Mommy."

Faerverin said, "You look like me."

Aleph said, "We can keep her if you want to. I will have duties to perform for the king, and she will be good company for you when I am busy."

"What duties?" asked Tall Sky.

"King Aryante wants me to be an advisor to help settle disputes," said Aleph.

"What the darkness meant for evil, the Light meant for good," said Tall Sky.

Faerverin hugged Aranel and cried. "Why do you cry?" asked Aranel.

"Did your parents tell you that they lost another little girl?" asked Faerverin.

"Yes, her name was Faerverin," said Aranel.

"I am that little girl and we are sisters," said Faerverin.

Aranel's eyes opened wide and she hugged Faerverin giggling. "Do you live here in this big place?" asked Aranel.

"No, we do. You are staying with me and Aleph," said Faerverin.

"Yay!" Aranel said, clapping and jumping up and down.

"She can stay with us tonight, if you wish," said Tall Sky.

"No, I think she should get to know Princess Anya right away and maybe stay with her tonight," said Faerverin. "There are lots of changes for all of us and we may as well get started now. Thank you so much for finding her."

"It's getting to be normal to find abandoned children," said Aleph. "I even have the king on it. He has approved of having a soldier stop by a farmhouse to pick up any kid that stops by there."

"I'll go down to the horses and get her clothes. We just went shopping." said Aleph.

"Faervein, have you seen Melody's dragon? Her name is Daisy and she likes me. May I have one?" asked Aranel. Faerverin smiled and said that someday Daisy might have an egg that they could have.

Tall Sky returned with Aranel's clothes and Melody showed Faerverin the dress she picked out for the wedding. "How beautiful!" Faerverin said. "It's perfect. I'm so glad you did this, because I don't have time to shop now."

"Speaking of time, we should be going," said Tall Sky. "Aranel, we will see you later at your sister's wedding. You may sit with us if you like." Tall Sky and Melody went back to the inn feeling very happy and satisfied with the outcome of their visit.

Everyone was busy getting dressed and doing their hair in updo's and trying to look their very best. Melody wore a green silk gown with a low cut rounded neckline showing some cleavage. She wore an emerald necklace and an emerald tiara accenting her sparkling green eyes. She wore her red, curly hair pulled up and back with a cascade down her back. Amidra wore a blue satin gown with a low V neckline in the front and back. Her blonde hair was up in a swirl of curls with wisps of hair outlining her face. She wore a necklace with a single blue stone on a fine, golden chain. Arinya wore a golden satin gown with a high neckline and her black hair tumbling down her back. She wore a golden circlet on her head with one ruby hanging from it onto her forehead. Mina wore a mauve brocade fabric with a broach of gold set with multicolored stones. Her hair was swirled up on her head, held in place by an ornate comb. Alqua wore an auburn silk gown with one shoulder bare and the silk flowing down her body to a gentle swirl at the hem. She wore amber jewelry and tiara.

The men were dressed in shirts with bloused sleeves fitted at the wrists, velvet vests, belts tied at the waist, and velvet pants. Even Flint and Cliff had permission to go and were dressed appropriately. Both men and women were ready to go.

Soon, it was time to walk to the castle. They were met at the door by the customary guard and showed the guard an invitation. He let them in and Tall Sky led them to the chapel where they were greeted by Elbereth. He asked them to sit in the front. Little Aranel was sitting there already and she went to Melody and cuddled close to her and petted Daisy. Anya came in and sat next to Aranel. Aleph's parents walked in with a few of his other family members and also sat in the front row. Then members of the court and ladies in waiting to the queen walked in and other special guests and family members of King Aryante and Queen Svetlana walked in. Quickturn and a group of officers dressed in white uniforms with gold buttons and brocade walked in and sat down with Aleph's parents. King Aryante and Queen Svetlana walked in a side door and sat down on large chairs in front facing the assembly.

A horn was sounded and Aleph and Faerverin walked down the aisle holding hands. Faerverin's gown was white satin with a respectable train and a lace bodice. She wore a string of pearls and a circlet of pearls on her head from which flowed her long, blonde hair. Aleph wore a jacket and pants in all white with gold brocade trim. They stood in front of the altar and faced each other, holding hands. They spoke in Elvish. Faerverin said, "Cormamin lindua ele Ile. Ami mela lle." (My heart sings to see thee. I love you.)

Aleph said,"A' melaelamin, lle na vanima." ("My beloved, you are beautiful.)

Elbereth said, "I welcome you to the wedding of Faerverin and Aleph, a marriage ordained by God and celebrated by those who love God. They came to each other through much adversity and we welcome them with open hearts."

"Faerverin, do you promise to love and support Aleph in all his endeavors and help him to stay healthy but take care of him if he becomes sick, to be faithful to him all the days of your life?"

"I do," said Faerverin.

"Aleph, do you promise to take care of Faerverin, to love and protect her and to be faithful to her all the days of your life?"

"I do," said Aleph.

Then I pronounce that you are married. Put the ring on her finger. The castle wedding book is on the altar. Please sign it. They signed the book.

Aleph hugged and kissed Faerverin and led her back down the aisle.

"If everyone will follow me, dinner will be served in the main dining hall and after that there will be dancing in the ballroom."

Elbereth led the wedding guests to the dining room for a fabulous feast. There were many tables laden with a variety of foods. Wine was already on the tables. The head table sat the royal family and the newlyweds. People walked by expressing their congratulations and best wishes. Aranel hugged her sister and followed Melody to sit with her. The food was delicious and the dessert was positively decadent, made of chocolate cake topped with a swirl of fudge syrup and whipped cream. There was also a yellow cake topped with lemon pudding and whipped cream.

The gifts were set on tables in the back and mainly consisted of household items and decorative wall hangings, oil lamps, linens, bedding, dishes, flatware, and cooking items like pans and ladles. Queen Svetlana gave Faerverin a set of jewelry. King Aryante gave

Aleph a fine sword with a jeweled hilt. The couple was well pleased with the gifts.

After dinner, King Aryante spoke to the guests in praise of the newlyweds. He said, "My friends, Aleph has been a faithful servant of mine. He served in the Battle of Othrund saving the lives of King Farin and of Quickturn. He brought an end to the border wars with a treaty between Gullandia and the farmers of Aksanda. He has agreed to be one of my advisors in the settling of disputes. Faerverin has been teaching our daughter Princess Anya how to paint. One of Faerverin's paintings adorns the wall of our ballroom. Let's go see it and continue our celebration with music and dancing.

Faerverin's painting was an excellent likeness of her and Aleph dancing in the ballroom. As soon as they walked in, the band played and Faerverin and Aleph started dancing. Soon the dance floor was full of couples whirling 'round and 'round in a rainbow of colors. Quickturn asked Aranel to dance. He picked her up and danced around the ballroom to the delight of the guests. Belzagar, one of Quickturn's officers, asked Princess Anya to dance. She was enthralled to dance with a handsome young man. Rando had little practice in the art of dancing, but managed a few slow dances with his new wife Alqua. They looked great together, he dressed in light brown and she dressed in auburn. He took her out to the hallway where he held her in his arms and kissed her on the mouth and neck. Soon they were joined by Tall Sky and Melody who had the same idea. "Melody, you look so beautiful tonight. I can hardly wait to get you back to our room," said Tall Sky. He hugged and kissed her. Amidra and Steben joined them followed by Trag and Arinya. Amidra ran her hands over Steben's chest and asked him if he wanted to go back to the room for a while. They all decided to thank their hosts and depart. They had enough to eat and drink and now they wanted some alone time with their spouses.

They decided to leave the party and walk back to the Golden Chalice. Melody got a little plate of food for Daisy. Everyone sat down to relax for a few minutes and have a glass of wine. "Wasn't that a wonderful wedding and celebration?" asked Melody.

"Yes," said Amidra. "It was fun, and we all looked like we belonged there. I felt comfortable with the royals."

"Good people are basically alike no matter what their station in life is," said Tall Sky. "I'm glad that we found Faerverin's sister. It's good for them to have each other. They won't be so lonely now."

"Think of it. Aranel means princess in Elven, and she will be raised in a castle with a real princess for a playmate," said Arinya. "I'm just sorry that her parents had to be killed."

Tall Sky said, "We don't know that for sure. We only know what a four year old saw. They may just have been knocked out or wounded. Kids don't know about such things. I will have Quickturn make some inquiries. He seems to like Aranel."

"Queen Svetlana was so beautiful. I love purple velvet and the brooch she wore was amazing. Her crown had some really pretty gems on it. When she danced, her gown swirled around her like a purple velvet cloud. King Aryante looked so handsome in all his medals on his red velvet jacket," said Melody.

"You know, we could throw a dress up party in Loadrel some time just for the fun of it," said Amidra.

"I like that idea," said Arinya. "People could buy stuff to wear at my store."

"Speaking of your store, we have to go shopping tomorrow for things to take home," said Amidra.

"We had better get to bed." They all laughed and walked upstairs to their rooms.

The next morning everyone woke up happy and hungry. They ate a hearty breakfast including hot cereal, eggs, meat, bread, and jam. Daisy was a happy little dragon, chirring and kissing Melody. "How are we going to know where to look for what we need?" asked Arinya. "I have a long list of things to buy like wall hangings, quilts, spices, rugs, clothing, boots and tools. The list of things is almost endless, and we have to get the merchandise for good prices to resell them at the store."

"Don't worry. We'll ask people where things are and follow their directions. We can also ask store owners where they get their things," said Trag.

"You're right, Trag," said Tall Sky. "I've been trading on a small scale around here and that's what I do. I'll take you to the people I know and you can ask them where to find some of these things."

Amidra and Steben wanted to get some decdorations for their home, some clothes, linens and gifts for Mama and Papa. They also wanted to get a gift for Laskron and Liadra for taking care of their little girl. Mina and Beldock wanted to buy some new clothes for the winter for themselves and for the girls staying with them. Tall Sky and Melody were going to shop and just see what they found that they might like. Winter clothes sounded pretty good to them, since it was getting colder on a daily basis now. Flint and Cliff were going to follow Rando's lead, since he was already married and in his house.

"So, are we all ready to go out there and brave the cold?" asked Beldock. The group Left and followed Tall Sky to the nearest clothing store where they bought mainly winter clothes. They bought Laskron a pair off fur lined gloves. Then they took their purchases back to their rooms and continued shopping. They next went to shops containing decorative items and bought things for their homes. Melody wanted to go to an apothecary store to buy medicines, herbs, bandages, and a medical book for Brilley. They stopped at a jewelry store so that Amidra could buy a brooch for Liadra, and Cliff and Flint could buy rings for their fiancés. Arinya bought some rings for future weddings. Next Trag brought the wagon and they loaded purchases onto it and went to several places to make purchases for the store. By noon it was time for lunch and for loading the rest of their things from the inn. They decided to eat on the run, so they headed out of town.

It was cold and clear. They were happy to be done with the shopping, which had made them tired. They were all looking forward to getting back home to Loadrel. "It was a wonderful time. Thank you," Melody said to Tall Sky.

"It was fun," said Tall Sky. "Do you think you can ride for eight hours?"

"I don't know, but I'm willing to give it a try," said Melody. "If we get too tired, can we build a fire and take a nap?"

"It's no problem for the men. We're used to sleeping outside in cold weather," said Tall Sky. "We can always wear our new furry clothes and cuddle together under blankets."

Flint and Cliff said that they would take turns standing watch, but Beldock said there should be two at a time standing watch. Everyone should sleep in one line close together for warmth.

Time passed quickly as they traveled toward Loadrel with a loaded wagon. As the sun lowered toward the horizon, the temperature dropped and they could see their breath in the air. The horses were getting tired and thirsty, so they stopped at the ruins and gave them food and water. There was a beautiful sunset of reds and golds. The moon was full, lending an eerie light to the scene. They had firewod with them, so they made a campfire and had some food and wine. Melody went around to the back of the ruins to relieve herself and found two girls huddled against the wall. She said,"Hello, would you like some food and water?" The girls said that they would. "When did you last eat a good meal?"

"We ate some bread two days ago and had a sip of water yesterday," said one of the girls.

"Come with me. We have warm clothes for you and some good food," said Melody. She led them to the wagon and chose clothing for them and then took them to the fire and set them down on a blanket.

Mina brought them some food and wine. She wiped their faces with a wet rag and said, "You eat and we will talk later. We have an inn where there are other girls who have been mistreated. You can stay with us until you decide what you want to do. Some of our girls are getting married soon. You will like them. They are very nice girls." Because of their purchases, there was plenty of bedding to go around. Everybody slept close to each other and stayed warm all night.

Mina woke early and fixed breakfast. The smell of bacon around a campfire with honey cakes and tea was so good in the morning. It reminded the campers that all was right with the world and that nobody was going to starve. The new girls ate and thanked Mina for the food. They were happy and relieved to be with kind people and were already beginning to feel normal again.

Soon the group was on the way to Loadrel. "Girls, in four hours we will be home again. You will have warm baths and clean beds to sleep in. Mina is a good cook, so you will have plenty of good food to eat. How does that sound to you?" asked Beldock.

"It sounds heavenly," said Shandra.

"It sounds warm and safe," said Calie.

Again they had a good day for travel. The sky was overcast, but there was no sign of snow yet. It was a little warmer which meant that it could snow. Everyone hoped that the snow would wait for hours so that they would at least be close to Loadrel before it started. As they traveled, they remembered the events of the past few days. They thought of the wedding, the dinner, the dancing, and of the sweet little girl who found her sister. It had been a wonderful experience. It would be fun to open their packages when they got home. The new girls Shandra and Callie were amazed at their rescue and were eagerly anticipating their arrival at the inn.

At about one hour from Loadrel, the snow began falling. It was slow and light at first, but it steadily increased. By the time they reached Loadrel, the travelers and their goods were covered in about an inch of snow. Shandra and Callie were very glad to be at the inn instead of back at the ruins.

BACK HOME

Kroom came out to help them unload the wagon. Everything was brought into the inn to begin with. From there they would sort the purchases. Kroom told the girls to bring out food and wine for everyone. Beldock gave Kroom a new fur coat for helping at the inn. Kroom said, "Thankyou. I really need this. My old one is about worn out."

"Kroom, you are a good friend and I owe you so much for helping to watch the inn while I'm away. You are always there for me and I appreciate it," said Beldock.

Mina introduced the two new girls to the others, and after dinner they had baths and got ready for bed. Then they shared their stories with each other. The new girls had been stolen as they worked outside in their gardens. They had been marched and beaten and left when the slavers heard the soldiers comming. They hid and walked by night hoping that they could find a farm to go to. They had been hungry, thirsty and cold. They had bruises on their faces and their bodies. They still hurt, but felt so good to be safe at the inn instead of out in the snowstorm.

The next day, everyone met at the inn for breakfast. Laskron brought Liadra, Emmy and Elise over and they all sat down to hear the stories of the Vivalla adventure. Mama and Papa were delighted with their new coats. Liadra loved her new brooch. Laskron was very appreciative of the new tools and the gloves. Emmy and Elise liked their new clothes and dolls. It was great to sit down with their friends again. "What were the king and queen like?" asked Liadra.

"They were beautiful all dressed in velvet and jewels and crowns, and they were very nice people," said Amidra.

"Did you find any more slave girls out there?" asked Liadra.

"Yes, we did. We brought home two with us, but the amazing thing is that we found Faerverin's sister, a little four year old, wandering down the road outside of Vivallen. We took her to the castle where she will live with Faerverin and Aleph," said Tall Sky. "Aleph has accepted a position of advisor at the castle, so I expect them to live there and just use their home here as a retreat."

"Tell me about the wedding," said Amidra.

Melody answered, "It was beautiful. Everyone was dressed up in satin gowns and velvets with jewelry and tiaras. The wedding was nice, but didn't take too long. Both Faerverin and Aleph were dressed in white. The wedding feast was loaded with lots of different foods and the dance afterwards was in this big ballroom. You could get dizzy watching all those different colored skirts whirling around the dance floor."

"What did you do with Daisy?" asked Amidra.

"Daisy slept through most of it. I kept her in my velvet bag," said Melody. "I didn't tell people about her except for Aranel. Now she wants a dragon too. I hope she will be happy now. I really like her."

"Let's load the merchandise for our shop in the wagon. Everyone else needs to get their purchases out of this pile," said Trag. They sorted through the pile removing their purchases. The rest they loaded back onto the wagon and Trag drove it to his store. Everyone else carried their purchases home. Trag had a lot of work to do setting up disdplays of the new items. Tall Sky and Melody enjoyed hanging up a tapestry and putting away their new clothes. Steben and Amidra put their new things in their room at the inn. It felt really good to be home.

Flint and Cliff spent some time with their girls Vanya and Almarie, but left for Home Fire the next day. They wanted to finish their houses before the snow got too deep.

Laskron took his new tools to his workshop and was in the process of cleaning and reorganizing when Twilric walked in. He was about 17 years old and in need of work. He was the son of one of the local fishermen, but wanted to learn a trade. "Laskron, I like to draw and make things. Fishing is alright, but I want to do something creative.

Since this is not the busy time for fishing, I thought it would be a good time to learn. Could you use an apprentice?" asked Twilric.

"Actually, I could use some help. I can't keep up with all the new orders coming in from Home Fire and other newlyweds in Loadrel. Could you work all day, five days a week? It is not easy work and it takes attention to detail. I am willing to teach you. You will have to watch for a few days. Could you do that?" asked Laskron.

"Yes. Can I start right now?" asked Twilric. Laskron handed him the broom. The two of them cleaned the shop and got ready to fill the next order. Laskron didn't want to admit it, but he had needed an apprentice for a long time. He had been filling orders from Loadrel and other nearby towns. Home Fire was the last straw. There wasn't enough time in the day for all this extra work. Liadra was a wonderful mother, but Elise needed her Daddy too.

Laskron went into the house and hugged and kissed Liadra. "I have an apprentice," he said smiling. "Soon I won't have to spend extra time in the shop. I have missed you, my darling, and my little Elise, too." They ate lunch feeling happier than ever.

Next door at the inn, Shandra and Callie were learning how to sew. They each had chosen material for a dress and were being taught by Hilda, who already had experience with sewing. Cassia, Brilley, Hilda and Indra had been making their own clothes for days now and they all helped Shandra and Callie to catch up. "Do you want to get married at Spirit Hall or at Home Fire?" asked Hilda, who seemed to have a one track mind these days.

"Flint and Cliff want to be married at Home Fire by Rando," said Vanya. "That's fine with us. We just want to get out there as soon as possible. So, we're going to ride out with you after your wedding."

"Spirit Hall is bigger and it is indoors. Then we could have a party at the inn and stay for the wedding night," said Cassia. "That would be more fun. Otherwise we would be getting married outside in the snow. They don't have the inn built yet. Six couples would be too many to marry at once at Home Fire."

"We'll have to tell the guys on our next trip to Home Fire," said Brilley. "I'm going to want a cow out there. I like milk."

"We will have to tell the boys to find us two cows at least. I like milk too and we can make butter and cheese," said Cassia. "We're starting to think like wives already. I wonder where to find a butter churn, and where do you buy salt?"

"We need to go to shops and see what they sell. Want to go this afternoon?" asked Hilda.

"Sure," said Indra. "I have been curious about the shops in this town. Trag and Arinya have one. We can see theirs and ask them about the other ones. Home Fire doesn't have any shops yet. One of us should start one." The girls continued with their sewing projects until noon and went down for lunch.

Melody and Tall Sky came in with Amidra and Steben. Mina brought Daisy her small dish of food and some ale for the people. After Daisy ate, she climbed back up on Melody' shoulder and purred. Cassia asked Amidra, "What kind of shops here would help us get started in our new homes?"

"There is a bakery, and a shop for other foods like cheese, spices and jellies. There is Trag's Store which sells clothes, jewelry, material, pots, and pretty things for the home. There is Baron's store that sells tools, fishing equipment, and ordinary things like brooms, pans and gardening supplies. You can't find everything here, but there is quite a bit here. Are you girls getting married soon?" asked Amidra.

"Yes, we are. We are getting married here in Spirit Hall and then we will be living in Home Fire. Our men are finishing our houses. They will be done this week. We thought we could find what we want and have the shop keepers hold our things undil our wedding. Then we could pick them up on the way out of town," said Cassia.

"It's a good plan. That way you could also take the furniture that my husband Steben is making for you," said Amidra. "His parents and I could ride part of the way with you. We were staying here for a while until the roads were safer to travel."

Indra said, "I was thinking of starting a shop at Home Fire, but unless we make everything, how will we find things for sale?"

"The shop keepers in town all go together in a sort of caravan to go to markets and buy. You could go with them. It's during the summer, so you would have time to add a room onto your house or make a second building for a shop," said Amidra.

After lunch, the girls put on their new coats and went to the various shops and had the shop keepers put aside the things that they wanted. Trag's store had some really nice items and some warm clothing that they wanted. Trag explained to Indra how he had put together the store and showed her how he made the shelves. It was fun and useful for the girls to learn what they would need to start a new home.

The girls felt more confident and grounded after shopping and they renewed their efforts to create wardrobes. They planned to use the scraps of material for making quilts during the winter months when there wasn't outdoor things like gardening to be done. This was going to be a wonderful adventure and the girls were very excited about it.

Melody and Tall Sky spent the next few days repairing things in the house and playing with Daisy and loving each other. It was a time of marital bliss. They created puzzles and put them together. Melody actually learned how to cook from recipes the neighbors gave her. They also visited Laskron and Liadra and showed the little girls how to put together puzzles. They watched Laskron make a beautiful blue vase. Liadra and Melody talked about the new girls and how to decorate the Spirit Hall for their wedding. Evergreen bouquets with big bows and streamers would make it look festive and could be brought over to the Laborer's Reward afterward. "Amidra said that she and Steben and his parents would ride to Home Fire with the couples the day after the wedding," said Melody. "I hate to see Steben go, but he does have a farm that he bought up in Yardrel."

"We could have a reunion in Home Fire next summer. Yardrel is only four hours ride from Home Fire," said Liadra.

Elise came in and grabbed Melody by the arm. "Come see! We put the puzzle together!" She and Emy had conquered the puzzle. "Do you have any more?"

"I do have another one at home. Would you like me to make you some more?" asked Melody. Both of the girls urged her to make more. Melody looked at Tall Sky and said, "I may have a winter long hobby."

Tall Sky said, "Culina, I will help you and we will make beautiful puzzles with flowers and lakes and people painted on them. We could make little ones for children and large ones with lots of pieces for adults. We could sell them and make a little profit."

"Let's go to the inn. I'm getting hungry," said Melody. "Liadra, we will get together on those decorations soon." They walked next door to the inn. Amidra and Steben were there.

"Amidra, would you like to help Liadra and me make decorations for the Spirit Hall?" asked Melody. "We should probably work on it tomorrow."

"Sure I would. The girls have been sewing up a storm making clothes. They should be ready within a few more days," said Amidra. "They remind me of us when we were making our dresses. Remember how hard the first dress was?"

"I remember," said Melody. "Home fire is going to be an entirely different place from when we first saw it and I was so scared of Rando. He has turned out to be a really good man. Knowing God has brought out his best qualities."

Mina brought out a dish of food for Daisy and the little dragon jumped down to the table to eat. Mina laughed and said, "I never saw anybody love her food the way Daisy does. Now that my favorite customer is fed, what would the rest of you like?"

"Dinner and wine," said Tall Sky. "After dinner, you might show us where you have decorations stored. We are going to decorate Spirit Hall for the girls' weddings. They have enough to do making clothes."

Dinner tasted really good. It was a thick lamb stew with freshly baked buns. Mina had baked a cake for dessert. After dinner Mina showed them the store room. They chose material and old decorations that could be useful and took them to Spirit Hall.

Meanwhile, at Home Fire, the builders were cold and tired and thankful to be working on the last of the houses until spring. The snow had slowed their progress, but they thought they would be done in the next few days. They would be living two couples per building through the winter. Then next summer they would take turns sleeping in tents until they could build more houses. They were used to living in tents and they worked well together. The Gullandrians were staying in their first house and working on the second one. They proved to be hard workers and quick learners. Several couples had decided to rent a house in Loadrel until the spring. Fane, Lore, Bronty and Cantro were looking forward to their wedding at Spirit Hall.

Now and then a small group of Bitters rode by and were killed by Rando's sentries. The silver gained from this would fund the building of the inn. Whenever weather permitted, they would work on it this winter. "It's going to be a really nice town," said Rando. "I'm so glad we helped at the Purge of Malwood. All we needed to build this town came from the riches those slavers had from selling girls and this town's men are marrying them and building them houses. I am so proud of these men. They have done a great job." He hugged Alqua and said, "I had better be getting back to work. They need all the help they can get. This snow isn't going to hold off forever." Rando's house was done, but he was helping to finish other houses. The women continued cooking as they always did and everybody ate from the same pot of food. It saved time and duplication of effort. Any leftovers were eaten at the next meal, so there was little garbage. It was a very healthy communal type of living.

The next day in Loadrel was a busy one with wedding preparations. Jelsareeb was planning the bakery needed, Beldock was planning the list of people invited and Mina was planning the food needed. Melody, Amidra, and Tall Sky were cleaning and decorating Spirit Hall. "How many people will be here?" asked Melody.

"There aren't any family members for the girls, so that leaves Beldock and Mina, Jelsareeb, Laskron and Liadra, Trag and Arinya, Steben and you, Mama and Papa, and Tall Sky and me. Of course the four couples, Rando and Alqua, and maybe some others from Home Fire. I think we should plan for about thirty people. We have that many chairs in here. We need to tell those girls to pick out a ring at Trag's store. Tall Sky, would you get us two bouquets of evergreen boughs?" asked Melody. Amidra made two big, fluffy bows to tie on them. They cut multicolored streamers to hang in the front corners of the room. When they had finished, the room looked festive and ready for a wedding. "Let's go see how the girls are doing," said Amidra. They walked to the inn.

"Hi, Mina. Have you seen the girls today? We just finished decorating and cleaning Spirit Hall," said Melody.

"They haven't come down for lunch yet. You can go upstairs and see them," said Mina.

They went upstairs and found the girls trying on their wedding gowns.

"Well, this looks promising," said Amidra. "We just decorated Spirit Hall and we wondered if you would like to go to Trag's store to pick out wedding rings. They just bought some in Vivallen. Have you placed an order with Laskron for glassware?"

"We would love to go, and we haven't placed an order yet for glassware," said Cassia.

"We will meet you downstairs," said Amidra. She and Melody went downstairs and fed Daisy who was delighted to have a little table time. The girls came down to lunch before going shopping. They wanted to talk to Melody and Amidra about marriage.

Brilley started with, "What is it like to be married? Is it difficult?"

Melody said, "It is like living with your best friend, but you can cuddle up to him anytime you want and kiss him and laugh with him."

"You can share all of your experiences with him. It's like not having to be alone, and when you are sad, you can cry on his shoulder, and when you are happy, you can enjoy it together," said Amidra.

"What if you get mad at him and argue?" asked Indra.

"You need to keep calm when you disagree with each other. Don't yell. Try to reason it out. Tell him how you feel. Don't say mean things to him. Keep in mind, he is your husband and it is better to be kind to him and to pray for him," said Melody. "Don't forget that you must forgive him and he must forgive you. This is part of your spiritual life with God. Just like God forgives you, you forgive each other. It keeps your relationship healthy and happy."

"What about sex? Do we have to have sex with them?" asked Hilda.

"Yes. You will find that it can be very enjoyable, so don't worry about it," said Amidra.

"Do you like it, Melody?" asked Indra.

"I love being that close to Tall Sky. I find it to be very exciting," said Melody. "Sex is a part of love between a man and a woman. It makes you love each other more. You will see. If he his too tired, you must let him rest first. Men tend to work harder physically than women do and they need more rest. It is also your duty to keep him fed and keep his clothes clean and mended."

"Let's go see the rings," said Cassia. They walked down to Trag's Store.

"Hi, Arinya," said Amidra. "The girls wanted to see your wedding rings. The wedding will be here within a few days. They have their dresses made and Melody and I decorated Spirit Hall this morning."

"I'm glad to hear that. These are the rings. They have different colors of gems in them, so there is a variety to choose from," said Arinya. "Choose what you like. It will be my wedding gift to you."

"Really? I thought we would have to wait for the men to come to town and pay for them," said Indra.

"The silver that paid for these came from slavers like the ones who kidnapped you. It is fitting that it should pay for your wedding rings. What the darkness meant for evil, the Light meant for good," said Arinya. The girls had fun picking out rings. They wore them home.

"Thank you so much!" said Hilda. They all hugged and walked down to Laskron's shop to place orders for glassware.

Laskron and Twilric were busily making a set of glasses for the residents of Home Fire. "Hi, Laskron," said Melody. "The girls want to see what you make and would like to place an order with you."

"Great," said Laskron. "Mainly, we make glasses and vases, but we also make some very pretty decorative pieces like this paperweight.

Glass can be made in various colors. We also make windows so that you can get daylight through them, but they are not too clear to see out of. I'm working on that. What do you think you will need?"

The girls placed their orders. "I will try to have these ready for you to take with you after the wedding, but I can't guarantee it," said Laskron.

"It's alright," said Cassia. "A few weeks ago, we were being beaten and marched without food or water to be sold to mean men. Now we have married lives to look forward to with new clothes, and homes and good men for husbands. It's more than I could have imagined. I am so grateful."

"Let's go to the house and say hello to Liadra," said Melody. They walked to the house and visited with Liadra. "Hi, Liadra. The girls wanted to show you their rings. Arinya gave them to the girls for wedding presents."

"They're beautiful," said Liadra. Emmy and Elise came in to see the rings and Elise hugged Melody and asked to pet Daisy. The little dragon chirred and rubbed faces with Elise and Emmy. She liked the little girls and sat on their laps while they petted her.

Amidra said, "They just placed orders for glassware with Laskron. He sure is busy these days. Would you like to come over to the inn and see their wedding dresses?"

"Yes, I would. Emmy and Elise, get your coats on," said Liadra. They all went next door to the inn where the girls went upstairs and tried on their wedding dresses. They came down the stairs in a cloud of fluff and ruffles, very excited and feeling like princesses.

"This sure has been an exciting day," said Melody. Tall Sky came in to see what the excitement was all about. He and Beldock had been visiting in the kitchen.

"Wow! Look at this. Are we having a wedding right now?" he asked laughing. The girls twirled around showing off their handiwork.

"They are beautiful," said Liadra. "You did a nice job on them." The girls went back upstairs to change clothes. "I'm impressed. It's not easy to make a wedding dress, but they did have some guidance."

Tall Sky said, "Beldock and I were talking about the homes at Home Fire. It seems that some people will have to rent a place in Loadrel for the winter. I'm thinking that Aleph might be willing to rent his place for the winter since he and Faerverin will be staying in the castle. It makes sense. They could only get so many houses built before the snow flies. Beldock sent a messenger to Vivallen to ask Aleph if he would rent his house. We should get an answer by the day after tomorrow. I think that the men who would stay there would be welcome additions to the Loadrel militia."

"Yes," said Melody. "Everybody tried really hard to get this project done and they have done really well. I'm so proud of the Loadrel men for pitching in like they did. It's hard work to volunteer for. They are truly wonderful men. Those girls are getting good men to marry, too. I'm so happy for them. I'm tired now. Do you want to go home and take a nap?" She didn't have to ask him twice. They picked up Daisy and went home.

Steben and Papa had been working as fast as they could to get the beds and tables and chairs made for the newlyweds. "It's too bad that we don't have more time. I would like to have had dressers made for them, too. We can always make them in my shop in Yardrel. It will be good to get back home. It seems like we have been gone forever. The people in this town have been so good to us. I can't complain," said Papa.

"I'm so glad that I finally found you and Mama. Ten years is a long time to worry about you. It's really going to be fun to start our new life on the farm, and if you ever need to be with us, you can stay on the farm any time you want to," said Steben.

"You have a good heart, son. Rando and Ella did a good job raising you," said Papa. "Talami is not that far away from Yardrel. We will be able to visit her this summer."

"That would be great. I miss her. She was like a mother to me all these years. I'm glad that she is with her husband and children now. She grieved over them for so long," said Steben.

"Let's go back to the inn for some dinner," said Papa. "We are almost finished with this order." They walked back to the inn and had dinner with Mama who had been helping the girls with sewing.

Mina had written to the parents of all the girls including those of Amidra, Liadra, and Melody telling them of their rescues and of their marriages, and inviting them to the upcoming weddings of four other girls. She told them that they could stay at the inn free of charge. She also wrote to Trag's aunt. She received an overwhelming yes in response to the invitations. This was a surprise for the children she had helped. She explained that this was the earliest that the roads would be safe to traverse. She did not plan to tell the children about this. She just got the rooms ready and planned the food, ordering what was necessary. This wedding would be one for everyone to remember. The inn would be full of guests until the day after the wedding. Liadra's and Amidra's parents would be staying at Laskron's house. Melody's parents would be staying with her.

The day before the wedding, parents started arriving. Melody's parents were the first. They arrived at dinner time and walked into the inn to the surprise of Melody and Tall Sky. They were overjoyed to see Melody. Huggng Melody proved to be startling, when Daisy poked her head out and chirred at Melody's mother. "What's this?" asked her mother.

"Mom, meet Daisy. She's my pet and constant companion. I found her egg in Malwood forest and she hatched in my pocket." Her mother laughed and said, "Well, hello, Daisy." Looking at Tall Sky, she said, "And you must be my new son- in- law. Welcome to the family. I understand that you two have a home here in Loadrel."

"Yes, we do and I will be happy for you to stay with us after dinner," said Tall Sky. "We have a nice guest room for you." They had a good meal for dinner and caught up on home news. Tall Sky ordered them some ale and they talked some more.

"Melody, how did you meet Tall Sky?" asked her mother.

"First, I want to apopogize for leaving the way I did, and for being such a selfish little crybaby. I have grown up a lot since then. I left with Amidra, Liadra and Trag. We planned to go across Malwood to a town where we could have some fun. Rando had a place called Home Fire where he lived with a bunch of people he had rescued from slavers and he decided to rescue us before we got caught. His adopted son Steben took us to Home Fire and then we all decided to leave and help him to find his parents. We took Vela with us because she wanted to find her husband who was in the army. We had to find Trag. He had been caught by Avidora's agents and he sent word to us to meet him at this cave with runes on it. Tall Sky had received a vision from God to go to the slave market in Malwood to help Trag and bring him to us at the cave. He rescued Trag from Avidora and brought him to the cave. Steben brought us to the cave, and that's where I met Tall Sky. That night he told us about Father God and we prayed to have God forgive us and to live inside of us."

"How did you end up here?" asked Melody's mother.

"We bought some horses and rode them to Yardrel where Steben found his parents and brought them to Loadrel with us, first stopping at Home Fire to warn them about the Bitter Elves that were roaming around killing people. Rando's men had already been killing them. We stayed here in Loadrel for safety. We stayed next door with Laskron and his little girl Elise. Through all of this, Tall Sky and I fell in love and were married. I couldn't send a messenger because it was too dangerous on the roads.

"I'm so glad that you are safe, and I thank you, Tall Sky, for keeping our daughter safe," said her mother.

"Let's go home and have a good night's sleep. I know how tiring it is to ride a horse all day," said Tall Sky. They all walked to Tall Sky's and Melody's home.

Back at the inn, Liadra's parents had arrived and were having dinner when Liadra walked in and hugged them. "Mom and Dad, it's good to see you. Did you have a safe trip in?" asked Liadra.

"It was fine, but we are really tired," said her Dad.

"Mom, Dad, I would like you to meet my husband Laskron and our daughter Elise. And this is Emmy, Amidra and Steben's adopted daughter. Emmy has been staying with us until Steben and Amidra move back to Yardrel. They will be going the day after the wedding. You will be amazed at how beautiful weddings are at Spirit Hall. Laskron performs the marriages there. Four rescued slave girls and four men from Home Fire will be married there tomorrow. Melody and Amidra just finished decorating it. We have the house next door and Laskron's glass blowing shop is in a building behind our house. You will be staying with us in the guest room. I have so much to tell you," said Liadra. "Let's move to the longer table in the back." They sat down at the longer table to have dinner. She ordered wine for the adults and milk for the children. Mina brought the drinks and introduced herself.

"Mina, thank you for writing to us about our daughter's safety. I really appreciate the letter you sent to me," said Amidra's mother.

Mina said, "It was the earliest that I could safely send word to you. I'll bring out dinner in a few minutes."

"How are my brothers doing?" asked Liadra.

"They are a handful without your help, but they are fine and staying with Grandma and Grandpa," said Liadra's mother. "I was really angry with you for taking off the way that you did, but I also understand why you did it. I'm glad you found such a nice man to marry. Having a little girl is a big change for you, I guess."

Liadra smiled. "I fell in love with Emmy first. We met right here at this table and I was amazed at this sweet, delicate little girl who actually liked me. We stayed in rooms at Laskron's and I fell in love with him."

Liadra's dad asked, "Laskron, tell me about the Purge of Malwood. Was that a battle?"

"Yes, it was a terrible battle. The Loadrel militia and Home Fire's men rode to the Malwood Market where they were auctioning off slave girls and rescued the slaves and killed the slavers and their customers. Liadra was lucky to have met Rando's men. Otherwise she could have been caught by those slavers," said Laskron. "The battle was very traumatic for me and I was injured so that I couldn't work for a while."

"Thank you for helping our daughter and her friends," said Liadra's dad. "I have never been a soldier, but I am glad there are men who are willing to protect us."

Mina brought the dinner. After dinner, they walked next door to Laskron's house where he showed them samples of his glass products.

The next relative to walk in was Trag's Aunt Manda. Her new husband brought her to Loadrel to see Trag. Beldock went down to Trag's and told them to come to the inn. Trag was delighted to see his aunt and to meet his new uncle. He introduced Arinya. Aunt Manda cried. She was happy to see Trag, and was very happy that he was married to such a sweet, beautiful girl. She was amazed at how adult he seemed. Over dinner they talked and he told her what had happened to him. She was appalled to hear that he had been kidnapped and enslaved by Avidora, but was delighted to hear that the old witch had been killed at the Purge of Malwood. "Trag saved me from the slavers at that battle. He untied me and led me out of the tent where I was tied up. He killed the man who was guarding me. He had taken some of Avidora's gems and we sold them to build a house with a business in the front. Much of our first merchandise came from the Malwood Market. The soldiers shared all the goods with the slaves," said Arinya. She was very proud of her husband.

"I am amazed at you, Trag. You have truly become a man. I can hardly wait to see your home and your business," said Aunt Manda.

"When I was being held at Avidora's castle, I wished that I had never left home. I missed you so much. I should have appreciated the care that you gave me. I sure do now," said Trag. "This bright elf named Tall Sky introduced me to God in a personal way and I asked God to live in my heart. It really helped me to understand things better and to be thankful for what you did for me. It also gave me the courage to ride with the militia to rescue Arinya. I knew that she was being held prisoner, because I saw her there when Avidora took me to the market."

At that point, Arinya's parents walked in and hugged their daughter. Her mother cried and said, "My poor little girl. I didn't know what had happened to you. I have been so worried until Mina wrote to me. I didn't even think that it could have been slavers kidnapping you. I'm so mad that I could tear them to pieces."

"Mother, it's too late for that. My husband already did. He killed the man who was holding me prisoner and rescued me. Mom and Dad, meet my hero Trag. We are married and have a house and a store, and these are his parents. Let's move to the long table in the back where we can have a nice dinner." Trag asked Mina to bring food and wine.

"Arinya, tell me what happened to you," said her mother.

"Mom, you aren't going to like this," said Arinya. "The slavers made me walk a long way. They were mean and liked to hit me, but they were careful not to bruise my face, because they had a wealthy man to sell me to. That is what kept me safe from being assaulted like some of the girls were. They actually sold me at the auction. It was humiliating, but Trag saw me crying and he got so mad that he came back with the militia and rescued me."

"Thank you, Trag, for rescuing our daughter and for giving her a good life," said Arinya's dad. "I look forward to seeing your home." After dinner they walked to Trag's Store.

It had been a wonderful reunion with both sets of parents. They would be staying at the inn, since their children's home was not completely finished.

The brides' parents got together and decided to ride straight through Malwood in the morning, since there were soldiers in the woods now. They could make Loadrel in six hours and be there by lunch time. Malwood was a different forest than before. The road through Malwood was deserted and the grass had grown over the road, but it was still discernable. The trees still looked crooked and scary, but there weren't any bandits hiding between them. Because the leaves had fallen, there was fairly clear sight in any direction. It took about four hours to reach the center of Malwood where the soldiers were camped. They dismounted and visited with the soldiers for a while. They noticed the burned out buildings and asked, "What happened here?"

A soldier replied, "This was the Malwood Market. They were holding a slave auction here when the Militia from Loadrel and the men from Home Fire raided the place. They freed the slaves and slaughtered the slavers and their customers. Then they burned the buildings and the tents and the bodies. The only thing left standing was the witch Avidora's head on a stake."

"Is that the Avidora we heard about all these years? I had begun wondering if she was just a legend," said one of mothers.

"She was real all right. We buried her head over there and put a big rock on it. She had a castle outside of the forest. We cleaned that out. There was some food left in there, some medicinal herbs, and some kids were still living there. We returned them to their parents and gave each of them some jewels she had tucked away. They deserved it. She treated kids badly and sometimes fed them to her bears. One of her kids got away and is living in Loadrel. If you are going that way, you might meet him. He has a store there now," said the soldier.

"Our daughters were caught by slavers and they were abandoned when some soldiers came their way chasing the Bitter Elves. They were picked up and taken to Loadrel and are getting married to four of the men from Home Fire who helped destroy this place. I'm so glad they did. There have been rumors of kids going missing for a long time now. Something should be done about finding them and returning them to their parents," said one of the women.

"You're right. One of those little girls is living in the castle with her sister," said the soldier. "King Aryante has a soldier checking nearby barns to see if any of them are taking refuge there. There was a big battle at Othrund between the Bitter Elves and the dwarves, men, and Bright Elves. It was a bloody battle and some Bitters fled the battle field. Some of them had girls they were going to sell, but when the soldiers started chasing them, they let the girls go. We are still finding them," said the soldier.

"Our girls are getting married this evening, so we had better be going," said a father.

"Just stay on this trail and it will lead to Loadrel. It's right on the lake," said the soldier. The group kept on traveling at an even pace for several more hours and reached Loadrel in time to have lunch at the Laborer's Reward. Mina greeted them and brought them some ale and sat them at the long table in the back. She then went to tell the girls to come down and see their parents. They squeeled and came rushing down the stairs to meet their parents. The grooms were also upstairs bathing and getting dressed in their rooms. The girls hugged and kissed their parents and showed them their rings. They were very excited and could hardly wait to introduce their young men. Before they finished their lunch, the boys came down and introduced themselves and invited them to Home Fire to see their new houses. The parents said that they would love to see them.

Their parents wanted to rest before the ceremony, so they went up to their rooms for a nap. The girls just wanted to visit with their fiances. "Is all the snow melted yet?" asked Cassia.

"Just about, and it's a good thing too. We need good roads for tomorrow. We will have two wagons and twenty-two people traveling at once," said Fane. "The houses are looking good, but the rooms look so empty with no furniture. I hope our furniture is ready to be shipped."

"It is ready," said Brilley. We went shopping yesterday and set aside things that we will need. They said that we could pay for them on our way out of town. Is that alright?"

"That's fine. We have silver with us to pay for things. I'm glad that you went shopping. I was planning on doing that, but I would much rather that you did it," said Fane. "Your parents are very nice. They must have been terrified when you disappeared."

"I'm just glad that we met you. I'm so proud of you for building houses for us. That's a huge job. You men must be very strong to work with logs like that," said Brilley.

"We've had a lot of experience cutting trees and chopping logs for firewood," said Lore. "There is still building going on out there. We're working on the inn. Flint and Cliff almost have their houses done, and there are other houses being built. I don't know if they will be finished in time for the hard winter or not. It's going to be fun planting a big garden next summer."

Brilley said, "I need to have a couple of cows for milk, butter, and cheese."

"We do have goats out there, but no cows yet. We'll have to see where we can buy one," said Lore. He went to the kitchen to see Beldock. "Where can we buy a cow?" Beldock said that there was a farmer about a mile away who would probably sell him a cow. Lore told the girls that he could probably buy a cow tomorrow before leaving for Home Fire.

"We should probably go upstairs and get ready for the wedding," said Indra. The girls went back upstairs and worked on their hair and getting dressed.

Laskron came over to see if everybody was ready. The girls brought their parents downstairs and introduced them to Laskron. He told them that they would be sitting in the first row of seats in front of the room. He said that people would be showing up at Spirit Hall soon. They all started walking to Spirit Hall. There were others walking to Spirit Hall too. Tall Sky and Melody with her parents, Steben and Amidra with Emmy and Mama and Papa, Liadra and Elise with her parents, the four girls' parents, Trag and Arinya with her parents, and many others were all walking to Spirit Hall.

The brides and grooms took their seats up front and the parents sat just behind them. Within a few minutes the room was filled and Laskron went to the front and began the ceremony. "Friends, I want to welcome you to the weddings of four very special couples who came to each other through danger and adversity. Our town has stood for justice and righteousness In the face of this adversity. We have helped those entrapped by evil men and have prevailed. Now we have four precious young ladies to wed to four very deserving young men from Home Fire, who fought the enemy and earned the right to be called heroes. Would our brides and grooms please come up here and face each other? Laskron looked up and said, "Father God, Creator of all things seen and unseen, we ask that You bless these young people with health and happiness all the days of their lives and bless their union with love. Fane, Lore, Bronty, and Cantro, You have worked hard to get ready for this day. You have fought the enemy. You have built houses for yourselves and your brides. Do you promise to love, protect and provide for your wives from this day forward?"

The men answered, "I do."

"Cassia, Brilley, Hilda, and Indra, you also have prepared for your marital lives by making clothes and by shopping for your necessities. Do you promise to love and support your men in health and to take care of them in sickness and be faithful to them?" asked Laskron.

"I do," said the women.

"You may place the ring on her finger," said Laskron. "I pronounce that you are married. Would you please step up to the altar and sign the Wedding Book? There are gifts and food at the Laborer's Reward. Everyone may follow the newlyweds to the inn for a party." The newlyweds walked down the aisle and led everyone to the Laborer's Reward where there was much hugging and kissing and tears. The parents were very happy and grateful to Beldock and Mina for taking care of their daughters. Amidra, Melody and Liadra carried decorations from the Spirit Hall to the Laborer's Reward and made the reception look very festive. Mina and several girls served drinks and brought out food and set it on a long serving table so people could serve themselves.

Melody spoke to Brilley about her gift. "Brilley, I want to show you something. See this case? In it are medical supplies to use at Home Fire. I bought them in Vivallen. I told the shopkeeper that I wantd everything that could be used by a small town doctor. There are instruments in there and a book about doctoring. I think you will be a good doctor."

Brilley smiled and said, "Thank you so much. I love this. I will take care of this and use it to help people. I can hardly wait to get out to Home Fire and get settled in."

"It will be fun and exciting for you to help build a new town, and you already have a purpose in your life to doctor people and animals," said Melody. "Tall Sky and I will come out to visit you some time."

"That sounds great," said Brilley. "Melody, I can't believe I'm really married yet. I don't think I'll really believe it until we go to Home Fire and walk into our own house."

"I understand," said Melody. "A lot has happened in a short time, but it will settle down in about a week and you will start feeling normal again. Let's get some food. Daisy is getting restless. She wants something that smells good. I'll get her a little plate first. Then I'll get myself something." Melody gave Daisy a little plate of stew and Daisy ate like she was starving. Then she curled up on Melody's shoulder just under some soft curls and went to sleep.

The girls received gifts that were appropriate to their interests. Indra received some slate boards and chalk, some paper, and some children's books. Hilda received some sewing supplies. Cassia received some seeds for gardening, some hand tools and some chickens.

Beldock and Mina were very pleased with this gathering. It was a long time in the making and it was very satisfying to see the parents pleased and proud of their girls. It made all the past horrors of slavery and child abduction and killing all seem worth it. The guests were enjoying themselves, visiting and drinking. Steben's Mama and Papa fit in well with the other parents. They had fun discussing the recent events and their son Steben who married one of the runaways. It was a happy time for all concerned.

The musicians started playing and everyone danced. Tall Sky and Melody danced holding each other close and remembering their own wedding. He said, "I love you, Culina. I want you with me always. I'm so proud of you." He kissed her. Daisy chirred and kissed him on the cheek.

Liadra and Laskron were dancing and he said, "Your parents are nice. I hope that they are not angry with me for marrying you without waiting for them to be present."

"They aren't mad at you. They're glad that we are married," she said and kissed him.

Amidra and Steben were dancing and Amidra had her head on his chest feeling all warm and dreamy. She asked, "Will we go straight through to Yardrel tomorrow?"

"We will have to see how Mama and Papa feel after riding to Home Fire. Yardrel is twice as far," said Steben. "It's getting warm in here. Want to go outside for a few minutes?"

"Sure," said Amidra. "Is everything ready for tomorrow?"

"I think so," said Steben. "The furniture is in the wagons. The kids have to pick up their purchases at the stores, and we have to load our clothes and some food. Lore was planning to buy a cow in the morning."

"What about Laskron's glass orders?" asked Amidra.

"He has them packed, but they need to be loaded onto a wagon," said Steben.

Back on the dance floor Trag and Arinya were acting like newlyweds, dancing closely and kissing. They were very happy with the progress they had made since they wed. Arinya said, "Trag, I might be pregnant." This made Trag very happy. He hugged her and kissed her.

"If you are, I hope it's a little girl who looks just like you," said Trag.

She smiled. "I don't want to tell anyone except Mom and Dad tomorrow."

"My darling, you are going to take it easy this year. No lifting or hard work for you. I'm going to take good care of my little wife," said Trag.

"I'm pregnant, not sick," said Arinya. "I should be able to do normal things."

"Still, we should be especially careful. I'm not taking any chances with you," said Steben. "Let's say goodnight and go upstairs. We have a big day tomorrow and we need our rest." Amidra and Steben thanked Mina and Beldock and went upstairs to their room.

The newlyweds did likewise, and the rest of tomorrow's travelers went to their homes. The parents were all impressed with the day's proceedings and went to bed feeling happy about their children.

After the party, Beldock and Mina sat at a table holding hands. "Mina, you have been a wonderful wife to me. You do so much work here and never complain. You care about others and help to take care of them. If every woman in the world was like you are, this world would be a better place. I want to do something special for you, but I don't know what," said Beldock.

Mina answered, "Husband, I could not possibly love you any more than I do. You are a good man. You take care of me and this place and everyone who needs help. You have already made me happy by just being you. By helping these girls, you have reunited families, and the far reaching effects even include the building of a new town and these kids will have children of their own. You have already done so many special things and have made this world a better place. You are so brave to have led the militia against the slavers of Malwood. You are generous to have shared the riches with the girls who were treated so horribly by those slavers and with the men who freed them. You and your militia have protected our town through long nights of vigilance. You are a good leader and a good husband. I am so proud of you."

Beldock said, "Thankyou for that. I think we had better get to bed. There is a big breakfast crowd to feed tomorrow. It's a good thing that we hired extra help." They put out the candles and went to bed.

Morning was heralded by one of Cassia's new roosters. Mina and Beldock and several hired girls cooked breakfast. It was going to be a very busy morning. The men were already packing things in wagons. Lore rode out to buy a cow. Fane drove one of the wagons to the stores to pick up the household items. They wanted to be ready by breakfast. Before long everyone was eating a hearty breakfast at the Laborer's Reward. Tall Sky and Melody, and Trag and Arinya came to breakfast to say goodbye to Steben and Amidra. Liadra and Laskron also came over with Elise and Emmy. Laskron had supervised the loading of crates of glassware packed in sawdust. Emmy was worried about being on the farm with no other children, but Grandma and Grandpa assured her that there were other children nearby who could spend overnights with her and that they could come back to see Elise sometime.

Soon they were ready to leave. Twenty three people, two wagons, a cow and some extra horses rode down the road toward Home Fire. Their friends stood out front of the inn waving goodby and cheering them on. Melody looked sad. Tall Sky put his arm around her and said, "Don't worry. We will ride out to see them this summer and ride on to Yardrel to visit Steben and Amidra, and Vela and Rusken too. It will be a fine vacation. The Lord showed me something. Two of our friends will have babies in the summer. Both Arinya and Amidra are pregnant."

"Wow!" exclaimed Melody. "That's great! When will we have one?"

"Not for a while," said Tall Sky. "We have other things to do first."

"What things? What do you know? Tell me. Is it dangerous? Will we be traveling?" asked Melody in her typically flustered way.

"Yes," said Tall Sky. "I don't know the particulars yet. How would you feel about a trip to Vivallen?"

"Great. When do we start?" asked Melody.

"It has to be pretty soon because of the winter. Let's go home and think about it and make some preparations," said Tall Sky.

A NEW HOME

It was a good day for traveling with the warm sunshine and cool air. The group was happy and a little tired from the previous night's festivities, but all had gone as planned and hopes were high that the trip would be safe and that the goods would arrive unharmed. Everyone had done their part and they felt satisfied. Flint and Cliff took the lead with the women riding two by two behind them, then Mama and Papa, and lastly the wagons, the cow and the extra horses. The men rode around them on the outside of the group for protection. They took up most of the road, but that didn't matter, because there were no other travelers on the road. Since the problems with the Bitters, people were staying home. It would take a little longer to get there, because the wagons could not be moved as fast as the usual pace of the horses. When they got hungry, they simply ate a sandwich from their personal pouch of food while they rode. Nobody wanted to stop before reaching Home Fire.

Cassia and Brilley were riding together, and Cassia said, "Wasn't that a fun party last night?"

Brilley replied, "Yes, and it was fun afterwards too." They both laughed. "It's really going to be fun getting our houses ready with all the new stuff to put in them. There is a bathtub for each house. That will be nice."

Hilda said to Indra, "I can make you some pretty things to hang on your walls. What is your favorite color?"

Indra replied, "Blue. I would really like some handmade flowers to go in my blue vase."

"I can do that, and they're really pretty," said Hilda. "I used to make them for my mother."

Almarie and Vanya were riding together and Almarie said, "How soon should we get married to Flint and Cliff? I suppose we should ask Rando, since he will be the one to officiate."

Vanya said, "Yes, but I think it should be soon, because they know all of us will be there today and they will already have food prepared for a large group."

"That makes sense. Maybe we should get married tonight so that we can sleep with our men in the new houses tonight," said Almarie. "Ours will be the first wedding that Rando performs."

"It makes sense to me," said Vanya laughing.

Mama and Papa were getting tired of the ride and longed for it to be over. They were almost there. Soon the group turned to the right and rolled on into Home Fire. They were met by Rando and some guards. Everyone dismounted. Cliff and Flint came running up to the group to hug Almarie and Vanya. There was a big welcoming fire with the aroma of dinner. They were ushered to seats by the fire and brought some wine to drink. Women brought bowls of food and bread. It felt so good to eat and drink that not much was said at first. Rando stood in front of them and said, "Welcome to Home Fire. We have looked forward to this meeting. Congratulations to the newlyweds. I see that you have come prepared with wagons of furniture. We will help you to unload your wagons when you are rested and fed."

Almarie and Flint talked with Vanya and Cliff. Vanya said, "Almarie and I were talking about getting married out here and be the first names in Rando's Wedding Book. What do you think of that idea?"

"I like that idea a lot," said Flint. "We should get married tonight and spend the night in our house."

"That's a great idea," said Cliff. "Let's ask Rando if he will do it."

They asked Rando if he would marry them tonight and he said that he would. Rando announced to the group that there would be a double wedding before dinner tonight. Everyone applauded.

After lunch everyone helped unload the wagons and the couples put all their purchases and clothes in their houses. Alqua asked Mama and Papa to come in and sit down and served them some tea.

She said that they were welcome to use their guest room for the night if the trip home would be too much for them today. They gratefully accepted. Mama had trouble riding for very long at one time. She said that Steben and Amidra could stay in a guest room in another house. "We have to make do until we get the inn finished," said Alqua. "It's amazing how fast this camp has turned into a town. It's really fun to watch. Now we have our first cow. Rando is performing his first wedding ceremony. He is a great man."

"I can see that you love him very much," said Mama. "He needs a good woman like you to stand beside him and support him in this endeavor. I'm glad that he has you. He sure did a good job with our son."

"He will do a good job with our son, too," said Alqua.

"Are you pregnant?" asked Mama.

"Yes, I am. I was going to tell him tonight," said Alqua. "Do you think that he will be happy about it?"

"Of course he will," said Mama. "He was so proud of Steben as if he was truly his own child. He will love the idea of having children."

Flint and Cliff showed their houses to Almarie and Vanya. They helped put their clothes and various other items into the houses. Furniture made a big difference in turning the buildings into homes. As soon as the quilts were on the beds, the couples had to lie down on them and relax, hugging each other.

Aela, Kara and Aeria walked around looking at the buildings and talking to some single young men. Three of them were planning on spending the winter in Loadrel and then building their homes in the spring. They would work on the inn at Home Fire as long as weather permitted. They liked the girls and paired up with them to walk and talk and eventually to sit by the fire outside. There were still a number of tents located fairly close to the fire where the workmen and some of the residents had been staying. They had erected some new tents for guests. It would be an adventure for the girls, but still much more comfortable than staying outside on the march with their captors. They petted the reindeer and talked with the Gullandians, who were very friendly and explained that their previous way of life included living in tents and moving around with the reindeer during the winter. They met the women who had lived out there a long time and the children who were happily playing outside. They visited the kitchen building to see how food was prepared there. Baking for dinner had already begun.

The newlyweds' parents toured the grounds with Steben and Amidra. Steben explained how the campers worked together to live on a daily basis. He was proud of Home Fire. He had good friends there. They had helped him to get well and taught him how to live. He owed them his life. The parents were duly impressed with the progress being made and with the organization of duties being performed from the feeding of the animals to the food preparation, to the work being done on the inn. It was healthy and good will prevailed everywhere. The lean to that Melody, Amidra and Liadra had stayed in during their first trip to Home Fire was being turned into a chicken coop for their new arrivals. Cassia and Fane were working on that. They were making nests for them and fed them some chicken feed that they had brought from Loadrel. Brilley and Lore put their cow in with the reindeer until they could get a separate corral built for her. The parents could see that their daughters would be well taken care of.

Before dinner, Rando called everyone together to witness the wedding. Standing before them, he said,"Friends, I am pleased to announce our first wedding at the town of Home Fire. Almarie and Flint, and Vanya and Cliff, please come here and stand before your friends. You have decided to marry before Father God who loves you and has blessed you with a good life here."

"Vanya, do you promise to be Cliff's partner, being faithful to him and helping him for the rest of your life?" said Rando

Vanya said, "I do."

"Cliff, do you promise to love, take care of and protect Vanya all the days of your life?"

"I do," said Cliff.

"Almarie, do you promise to be Flint's partner, being faithful to him and helping him for the rest of your life?" said Rando.

Almarie said, "I do."

"Flint, do you promise to love, take care of and protect Almarie all the days of your life?" said Rando.

"I do," said Flint.

"Please step forward and sign the Home Fire Wedding Book," said Rando. "You are married."

The couples signed the Wedding Book and were served wine. Everyone applauded and began their dinner. The newlyweds were drinking wine and kissing and giggling. After dinner, a few musicians played and there was dancing around the fire. Even the parents danced and enjoyed themselves. Afterwards, people went to their respective homes. The parents slept in the extra rooms. Steben and Amidra slept in one of the tents with Emmy who thought that this was a great, fun adventure.

The whole camp awakened to a very loud rooster crowing. The cooks got busy making breakfast while the men tended the fire, brought more wood to the houses, and fed the animals. Brilley milked her cow and brought milk to the children. Home Fire still was functioning as a camp with a few added chores. Guests were served tea in the houses, but soon came out for breakfast of smoked meat and honey cakes. After breakfast, people packed the horses and the wagons. Steben, Amidra, Emmy, Mama and Papa left first heading to Yardrel. Aela, Kara, and Aeria would head back to Loadrel with their three boyfriends, a work crew, and the eight parents. They all thanked Rando for his hospitality and the parents said goodbye to their daughters, making them promise to come home for a visit next summer. Twenty-four people and two wagons headed back to Loadrel. The three boys would rent a house in Loadrel for the winter. The girls would continue to stay at the inn until they married. Members of the work crew were very happy to be going home again.

Tall Sky and Melody had been getting ready for their trip to Vivallen. Melody said, "You realize that we will have to stay there all winter. Where are we going to stay?"

Tall Sky replied, "There is an area close to the castle where we could rent a small house. Depending on what develops, we might even stay in the castle."

"I would like that," said Melody. "Then I could see Faerverin and get to know her little sister."

"Yes, that would be nice," said Tall Sky. He had a feeling that there was much more involved in this trip, but didn't want to alarm Melody. He only knew that there was a strong pull to get him to Vivallen. They had finished packing and loaded the horses and went to the Laborer's Reward for breakfast. He told Beldock about his plans and sat down to breakfast.

Beldock said, "Do you have any idea what the king wants you to do?"

Tall Sky replied, "I think it has something to do with the slave trade, but I won't be sure until I talk to him. It just makes sense. That is what I have fought against for a long time."

"Well, whatever it is, be safe," said Beldock. "You have more to look after now that you're married."

"Believe me, I know, and I will do whatever it takes to keep Melody and Daisy safe," said Tall Sky.

Melody went next door to say goodbye to Liadra and Elise, while Tall Sky talked to Laskron in the shop. Then they left town on horseback. Daisy was curled up taking a nap in her velvet bag, keeping warm and sleeping off breakfast. They rode to the ruins, dismounted, and ate lunch. She checked behind the ruins, but nobody was there. The day was cold, but they were dressed for it. After resting for a while, they mounted up and rode on toward Vivallen. Travelers on the road were few. Melody was very curious about what they were going to do, but knew that the Lord was leading Tall Sky and that she would just have to be patient. So she pouted and asked God to please let her know something as soon as he could. "Tall Sky, have you asked God for a vision about what he wants you to do?" asked Melody. "No. I just thought I would wait to talk to Quickturn and King Aryante. They're the ones in charge of this one. I just want to get there and check into the Golden Chalice, have dinner and a hot bath, and go to bed with my soft, warm, beautiful wife," said Tall Sky. Melody laughed and said that sounded good.

THE MISSION

Near dinner time, they arrived at Vivallen, rode through the town to the Golden Chalice and checked in. They were cold, hungry and needed a good soaking for their sore muscles. First he ordered wine to help them feel warm and relaxed. Then they got into a hot bathtub for two and scrubbed each other's backs. She even gave Daisy a warm bath and an oil rub down. After that, they dressed and went down to dinner. The food was excellent with thick pieces of tender meat, mashed potatoes, steamed vegetables, and apple pie for dessert. Melody said, "I could get used to this. How about we move in here for the winter?" Tall Sky laughed. Just then Quickturn walked in.

"Tall Sky and Melody, just the people I have wanted to see," said Quickturn. He sat down and ordered wine for them. "King Aryante and I were talking about you yesterday. It seems that the Bitters have left our area, but are busy south of here. They have dealings with both the slavers and a number of merchants from over seas. It's not a good combination. King Aryante wanted someone to check it out for him. We thought of you because you don't look military and with Melody along, you look like an ordinary couple. What do you think? The job pays well."

"I received a burden from the Lord and followed it here. It was so strong that I couldn't ignore it," said Tall Sky.

"I knew it. I knew it was going to be dangerous," said Melody. "I remember those foreign men at the inn who dressed different and spoke a different language. They looked mean and dangerous. They're probably the ones you're talking about. Are they?"

"Yes," said Quickturn. "Those are the ones. We killed some of them at the Purge of Malwood. They are very wealthy and carry gems with them. They buy girls and take them to foreign lands."

"Okay. Just wondering. I'll be fine," said Melody. "We just got married and all safe in a house and you want us to go off on an adventure into the unknown and watch a bunch of evil men. Why can't I just stay home and have a baby like everyone else?"

"I know, Culina, but you know we can't say no to Father God and it is He who will keep us safe from harm. Besides, it will be warmer down there, and we don't have to ride horses all the way. We could take a boat down the river. That sounds like fun, doesn't it?" said Tall Sky.

"I have never been in a boat. Are they safe?" asked Melody.

"They're safe. I wouldn't ride in one that wasn't safe," said Tall Sky.

Quickturn added, "There is a passenger boat that goes that way regularly. It will actually take you to the sea if you like. It's safe, and you don't have to steer it or anything. You just sit there and enjoy the scenery. There are various stops along the way, so if you want to spend some time in a town, you can do so and catch the next boat when you want to. It is the best way to travel by boat. That way you could see what is going on throughout the southern area as far as the foreigners go. The slavers will probably be more inland where they find most of their victims."

"Okay, it's the victim part that scares me," said Melody.

"When do you want to leave?" asked Tall Sky.

"After we see Faerverin and Aleph, I guess," said Melody.

"We will see them tomorrow and I should talk to King Aryante," said Tall Sky. "I have some questions for him like what do we do if we find girls who need rescuing. I will need some payment for expenses. Quickturn, I would feel better if there was support in major areas to battle the slavers and free the girls when I locate them. Otherwise, I think I would put Melody and myself in real danger."

"This is only supposed to be a spying mission, but I will talk to King Aryante about it," said Quickturn. "He wants to launch an all out offensive, but he needs information in order to do that."

"I understand, but you know my heart. It really hurts me to see girls mistreated," said Tall Sky. "If he does use army here, we need people to return them home, or a safe place set up to take them. We were lucky to have Beldock and Mina to help them in Loadrel."

"Yes," said Quickturn. "Even in an all out offensive, we would need that."

"At Free Harbor we will need special help to stop the foreigners' ships from leaving port with girls," said Tall Sky. "I don't know anything about that. There may be governmental problems there too."

"This will have to be well planned. Do you have connections in the south like you do around here?" asked Quickturn.

"I do have some, but not as many," said Tall Sky. "The connections I do have are with the common folk."

"I will talk to Aryante about this tonight after dinner and will hopefully have some answers for you tomorrow. I'll see you then." Quickturn left to return to the castle.

"Oh my. That was a whirlwind," said Melody. "It's a lot to think about. I hate thinking that there is still a slavery problem after all that we've been through, but I knew that those foreigners were up to no good. They are horrible people and if we can do something to stop them, we should. I wonder if I should leave Daisy with Faerverin. She likes her and we would be easily recoignizable with a dragon. Also, I want her to be safe."

"That's a good idea," said Tall Sky. "She might leave to try to find you, though. It probably isn't a good idea. I'm really too tired for all this thinking. Let's go to bed and think about this tomorrow. Besides, I want to snuggle up to my Culina." With that, they went upstairs to their room.

The next morning brought more excitement starting with hot cakes and sausage for breakfast. Daisy was happy with that. "Daisy really likes sweets," said Melody.

"So do I," said Tall Sky,"Beginning with you." He kissed her and gave her a reassuring squeeze. After breakfast we will go shopping and buy you something special at the jewelry store. Then we will go to the castle and you can show it to Faerverin and Princess Anya."

"You're bribing me, but alright," said Melody with a smile.

The jewelry store was located between the Golden Chalice and the castle. Melody chose an emerald necklace and wore it to the castle. Faerverin was outside with Princess Anya petting the cat. They came in to talk to Melody and pet the dragon. "I want to see the painting you have been doing," said Melody.

Princess Anya said, "Come to my room. That is where I have been hanging my paintings." She took them upstairs to her room. "I don't have too many of them because, as I get better, it takes longer to paint one. There is more detail in my more recent paintings."

"I think they are beautiful," said Melody.

Faerverin said, "Anya, it is time for your music lesson. You should go to that and we will meet with you afterward, okay?" Princess Anya left and Melody asked Faerverin how to call a butterfly to her. "I use elven words. Wilwarin, tulie haara mi lepta. Panta lya ramas. They mean butterfly, come sit on my finger. Unfurl your wings. I will write them down for you. I don't know why they respond to elven, but they do. You can also call a bird to you that way. The word for bird is wilin. Here it is. Take it with you."

"I can't tell you how precious this is to me. Write down how to say 'I love you' in elven."

"Amin mela il," said Faerverin. "I will write it for you. Is it difficult for you to be married to an elf?"

"Not at all," said Melody. "I do worry a bit about my growing old looking while he will still look young. Will he love me less for it?"

"I don't think so," said Faerverin. "Love with us is eternal."

"That's good to know," said Melody. "I am very happy with Tall Sky. Do you like living in the castle?"

"Yes, I do. It is peaceful here and I have my painting and my little sister. She and Anya get along well together. Aleph and I have enough time together, so I am very happy here."

Tall Sky walked in and asked Melody to accompany him to the King's study. "He wants to talk with us and Quickturn about our mission."

"Here we go," she thought. They walked down the stairs and down the hall to the King's study, a comfortable room with chairs around a table and book lined walls. A servant poured wine and they sat at the table. King Aryante began.

"Welcome to you, Melody and Tall Sky. I know that you have some misgivings about this assignment. Let me assure you that I am in earnest about ridding Aksanda of the slave trade. I know that it is a large area that we are dealing with, but that is precisely why we need information about it. We have to know where to send the troups. We need safe places set up to take the girls until they can be returned home. That takes some advanced contacts with the locals. There must be a decree sent forth by messenger that slave trade will not be tolerated and that the penalty for this is death. I want the goods confiscated from any slave ships and the captains put to death. The ships will be sent forth manned by their crews. Any bitters involved with kidnapping and any slavers will be put to death. There will be no trials and no imprisonment. This vermin must be wiped out. Any wealth taken from slavers will be used to help the girls with food, clothing and shelter. If we allow this slave trade to continue, there will soon be no young women to raise our families. We need more families to populate Aksanda. Tall Sky, what are your thoughts on this?"

Tall Sky replied, "I have been concerned with this for years. I am honored that you want me to work with you on this. My problem is that when I hear of some girls in trouble, I want to go help them right away. Is there any way that we can have a ready group of soldiers near enough to respond within a day of places I go to? If we had a good messenger system set up, I think we could do it. Also, I would like to immediately have troops set up to rid the harbor of any foreign ships in an ongoing basis. Like a guard of the coast to monitor activities in the harbor. I couldn't do any of that, but I could find the slave auctions and send a messenger to the army. Melody and I could bring the girls out and take them to a safe place. You will need men with wagons to buy food from the locals. There are so many details."

Quickturn produced a list and showed it to Tall Sky. On it was most of the things that Tall Sky mentioned and more. King Aryante smiled and said, "I have this list, but I wanted to hear your understanding of the complexities of war. It is not a small, nor an easy undertaking, but it must be successful. Quickturn will be in charge of the preparations. You will be our eyes and ears in the land. As you wanted, when you find a slave auction, you will send a messenger to Quickturn, who will be close with an army platoon. Here is a map of the area. You have seen the foreigners before and you know some of their language. This is why I want you to check the inns along the river. I suspect they use the river for travel. Also check the places like jewelers who could be exchanging gems for hacksilver. We will begin in the Angvar Province at Lessport. You will take two messengers with you. Even if there is no activity there, I want a messenger sent."

Quickturn said,"King Aryante is sending an emissary to Free Harbor to the Mayor of the town to apprise him of the situation. He will be required to search every foreign ship and confiscate goods of any slavers, kill the Captain of the ship, take possession of the girls, and send the ship away manned by its crew. The Mayor will do this under penalty of removal from office. There will be a troop of men to support the Mayor in his duties. Melody, what do you think of all this?"

"I was feeling like a target until you said the army would be there. I have counseled some of the girls and I can tell you that for each of them their whole world turned into pain until we found them. I think that all of you are heroes. This gives me hope for the future of our country," said Melody. "You know, kidnapping affects the parents too. They feel a lot of pain. Their lives and their futures are destroyed by this. You will make them eternally grateful to you for rescuing their children. I think we should get started right away."

King Aryante gave Tall Sky a bag of silver and wished him well on his journey. Quickturn took them to meet their messengers and they left the castle. They packed their horses, taking food with them and headed for King's River where they would board a boat heading to Lessport. "I can't believe that we are actually doing this. It is the right thing to do, but riding in a boat is still scary to me," said Melody. The port consisted of a building with a small café and a pier for the boat to tie up to. They went inside for pie and tea. The boat was expected shortly. The messengers were excited to be playing a part in this extraordinary campaign. Tall Sky told them that nobody was to know that they were traveling together and that the only communication between them would be a written message to be delivered. Absolute secrecy was to be maintained.

Soon the boat pulled up to the dock. The group boarded and sat down on deck. Melody was amazed at how solid the boat felt. She relaxed and gave Daisy a treat. Daisy was as calm as usual, surveying her new surroundings and chirring at the river. Melody remembered taking a bath in the river upstream near Talath. Moving on the river felt different, but she was okay with that too. At first there wasn't much to look at except grassland on either side. The air was cold, but not windy. The sun was warm on their shoulders and the sky was blue. It was a perfect day for boating. They arrived in Lessport about an hour later. Lessport was a small town, but there was an inn. They checked in and visited with the innkeeper who told them that he hadn't seen foreigners for a while, but some Bitters had come through about a week ago talking about some battles up north. Tall Sky told him that he knew of the battles and that they had to do with the slavers and the Bitters abducting and selling girls. The innkeeper said this was terrible and that he had a daughter of his own. He wished there was something he could do to help. Tall Sky said that King Aryante wanted to end the slave trade in Aksanda and that he needed places for girls to stay for a few days until they could be returned to their parents. The innkeeper said that he always had extra rooms and that he would help. Tall Sky said that he needed to rent horses for a few days. They agreed on a price and rode into the country to the nearest farm. The farmers had seen groups of Bitters who just wanted to buy some food. He said that they were a foul mouthed lot with no manners, but he sensed danger in them and sold them the food they wanted. They told him about battles up north and cursed the king. They asked if he had a daughter and he said no. "I got the feeling they would have killed me and taken her if I would have said yes. I have one, but from now on she will be kept close to me at all times. Something needs to be done about them. "

"Something is being done. King Aryante has made slave trade illegal. He cleaned it out up north and is now working on the south. We are here looking for Bitters and foreigners who buy girls. Do you know of any auction sites in the area?" asked Tall Sky.

"I heard of one closer to Lake Inari. I don't know what they sell there. I have been tempted to try selling some produce there, but haven't needed to yet. If I have extra, I take it to Lessport," said the farmer.

"I think we'll go check out this auction. Do you want me to stop by and tell you about it on our way back?" asked Tall Sky.

"Sure I would and let me know if there are any bad dealings going on out there," said the farmer.

Tall Sky and Melody rode west toward Lake Inari. There were more trees now. Most of them were evergreens with long needles. Melody always wanted to pet them because they were so soft. It took several hours of riding to get to a place where there was a group of tents and booths. There was an aroma of food and Melody was really hungry. They pulled up to a tent café and ordered some food.

Tall sky asked the café owner, "What types of things are sold here?"

The owner said, "Household items, Materials, produce, animals, paintings and other things."

"We have several friends who will be looking for a place to sell their paintings. Would they get a fair price for them here? They are very good," said Tall Sky. "Do you have any wealthy customers?"

"Yes, we do," said the owner. "We have some customers who come here from far away to buy slaves. They are foreigners, but they have gems and silver to trade. The busy season for that is about over, though. We get some bitter elves come through here with girls every now and then. They always want high prices for the girls, but they make out all right."

Melody was about to scold him when Tall Sky kissed her and said that they should do some shopping. "I was so mad I wanted to choke him!" she said.

"And you would have blown our cover," said Tall sky. "Remain calm. Let's look around and see what we can find out." They walked around the tents and looked at merchandise but saw no signs of slaves until they walked around the back of the tents and noticed some girls sitting on the ground in a pen made of wooden slats tied together. He approached them and asked why they were in there. One of them said that they were there to be sold as soon as the buyer arrived. He looked around and didn't see the guard, so he opened the door and led them out into the woods where he hid them in some brush while he borrowed some horses and picked them up and off they rode. "Remain calm, you said. We will blow our cover. Well, guess what? I think we blew our cover," said Melody.

"It's alright. We will be at the inn with them before they figure out what happened. We have to send a messenger to Quickturn. He will be mad, but he will understand, I hope. We have been gone one day and have rescued five girls. That's a good day's work," said Tall Sky.

When they reached the inn they immediately went in and informed the innkeeper that they have their first girls. He led them to rooms and brought them food and drink. Then he brought them water for washing and some of his daughter's old clothes. He told them they would have to be very quiet.

Tall Sky sent a messenger to Quickturn. That evening Quickturn sent word that the slaver was killed and he sent two soldiers to escort the girls back home. The plan was working. They slept well that night. The next morning they left the inn and boarded a boat going south. The next stop was Windy Port. There were two towns close to Windy Port, one to the east called Apple Town and one to the West called Fair Town. He showed Melody the map. She said, "I wonder what fresh horrors we will find there?"

"It will probably get worse as we go south,"said Tall Sky. "Remember all that we had to deal with near Loadrel. This area hasn't seen resistance yet. It will surprise them as it did in the Lake Inari Market. We should be alright as long as we keep our heads down and not let them know what we're up to."

"I just can't believe there is so much of it. I'm surprised no one has gotten together a militia like we did," said Melody.

Tall Sky said, "Beldock was a special man with a militia at his disposal and with a group of fighters like Rando had, it was a perfect mix. Not many places have all that going for them." They ate lunch on the boat. Daisy was getting along just fine. She ate and watched the water and chirred and cuddled up on Melody's shoulder for a nap. When they reached Windy Port, they checked in at the local inn and talked with the innkeeper. He said that he had seen some foreigners just this week. They were looking for a market, so he told them about one in Fair Town. It was only a few hours' ride toward Lake Inari. Tall Sky said that he would need some horses to rent and the innkeeper said that he had five horses. Tall Sky told his messengers to rent horses and ride with them. The weather was holding, so they rode in relative comfort all the way to Fair Town. It was a small town with old buildings. On the outskirts of town was a market, bigger than the last one with evergreen forest around it. They rode around the outside of the market first. From the trees, a girl called to them for help. They rode into the trees and found one girl dead on the ground with a head wound. She had obviously been raped. The girl who called for help was bound naked to a tree and was bloody from being whipped. Tall Sky cut her ropes and put his blanket around her. Melody gave her some wine to drink and found some clothes for her. Tall Sky sent her back to town with a messenger to get her some immediate care.

Tall Sky and Melody continued looking and found a pen of girls. He killed the guards with arrows, set the girls on the horses and sent them off with the other messenger. This time they followed the messenger to camp. "Quickturn, I really didn't know what to do next. I'm sorry," said Tall Sky.

"Every encounter is likely to be different," said Quickturn. "This is new. We learn as we go. I think you did the right thing in walking away when you did. We will handle it from here. There are likely other girls there and foreigners to boot. It will be a nice haul. I have sent men to the location already and I will follow. You go back to the inn like nothing has happened."

"Okay," said Tall Sky. "Tomorrow we will go to Apple Town." Melody and Tall Sky went back to the inn.

"Tall Sky, are you sure you want to continue with this?" asked Melody.

"Yes, I do. It is necessary and it won't take forever. You'll feel better about it tomorrow," said Tall Sky. They decided to have some wine and play a friendly game of cards like nothing had happened.

"I keep seeing that poor girl tied to the tree. I'm scared that could happen to me," said Melody.

"It's not going to happen to you. We will be more careful. Tomorrow we will play it the way the king outlined for us. We will look and report. Would that make you feel better?"

"Yes," said Melody. "Doing it the other way might be dangerous for the girls."

"It could be," said Tall Sky. "We do need to be more careful. I have to protect you above all else," said Tall Sky. "It's what I promised to do when we got married."

"Let's order some dinner and then go to bed," said Tall Sky. "I feel like the world has gone mad." After dinner they took a hot soak in the tub and went to bed for a good night's sleep.

Breakfast included eggs, sausage, and fresh bread with jam. It made them feel normal again without any problems or decisions to make. They would go do their job today in an orderly fashion and come back to the inn. Secretly, in her heart, Melody knew that there would always be problems on a mission like this, but she pushed all that aside and enjoyed her meal and fed Daisy. Tall Sky said, "I think we should check on some of the farms before going into Apple Town. I want to know about any rumors of children disappearing and about any activity of the Bitters in the area. I also want to know if any of them would be willing to be a safe place for the girls should we find any."

"Good idea. There is a big area between here and Apple Town," said Melody.

Before they left, a messenger came in. He reported that the girls were returned home and that the kidnappers were killed. There were more girls in tents with their new owners. There were ten more girls in all. Some of the new owners were foreigners, and they were killed. Tall Sky told the messenger that both he and his partner would be needed at the new location, so they should ride out with them.

The messengers ate breakfast and rode out with Melody and Tall Sky. It was another cool, dry day with sunshine and blue skies. They stopped at several farms and heard that there were rumors of abducted children and that Bitters had been seen traveling in groups of three and five, always trying to buy food. Farmers said that they had seen foreigners, but that they stayed to themselves.

The next stop was Apple Town. Again, it was a small town with a market on the outskirts. They stopped at a tavern for a drink and to gather information. Tall Sky asked the barkeep how business was going. The barkeep said,"Business is always good when the market is busy. This summer has been good. It's winding down some now, but as long as the foreigners come in, I sell a lot of drinks. They come from over seas, I guess. They sure do talk funny. I hear they are in town to buy slaves. A dirty business it is. Someone should run them out of the country, I say."

"When do they auction the slaves?" asked Tall Sky. "I'm curious about it."

"It should be tonight," said the barkeep. "You're not going to buy any, are you?"

"No," said Tall Sky. "That's not my way at all."

Tall Sky and Melody left and rode toward the market, wondering what they would find this time. The slave pen was located more in the center of the market with booths scattered all around. There was a large delegation of foreigners dressed in their silks and turbans with dark hair and eyes. They were walking about talking in a foreign language. Tall Sky said, "I understand some of what they are saying. They are talking about their masters and about the girls. They don't like dealing with the Bitters because the Bitters damage the girls. They talk about killing the jewelers and taking the jewels after the auction. These foreigners mean business. Let's send a messenger to Quickturn right now." He did so and they walked around the various booths as if they were shopping. I don't know if we should stay here and see if there is anything we can do to help the girls when the fighting starts. I could shield them from sight and lead them out of the fighting and into the woods where they keep their horses and then we could ride away. It is not without danger, but it's the only thing I can think of right now."

"That sounds like something we could do if there aren't arrows flying about," said Melody. "I still don't want to be in the thick of a battle."

"You could stay in the woods by the horses, and I could get the girls out," said Tall Sky.

"That sounds better," said Melody. "Let's see a jeweler and ask if he has a ring to match my necklace. Then let's buy some warm clothing for the girls."

While they were waiting for the soldiers, they bought clothing and packed it on their horses. In the meantime, they sat down and had some pie and tea. Then a platoon of soldiers rode in and started killing the foreigners. At first there were some arrows and Tall Sky walked Melody out to the horses. Then he shielded himself and the girls and walked them out to the horses where they changed clothes, mounted horses and rode off. There were still some girls in the tents, but the soldiers would rescue them. The soldiers confiscated goods and silver and gems and shared them with the girls. Melody got a matching ring and tiara, and felt a lot better after that. The girls were thankful and crying and Melody comforted them. They built a campfire and warmed up some food for dinner. Melody poured wine for them and bandaged their wounds. Then they wrapped up in blankets and went to sleep. There were twelve girls counting a few that the soldiers brought in. It had been a good day. Quickturn gave some silver to Tall Sky for expenses. "You did a great job today, Tall Sky. It worked beautifully. Let's hope that our luck holds out. Tomorrow go back to Windy Port and take a boat to Montro. It is better that you arrive by boat. It makes your cover more believeable," said Quickturn.

Melody and Tall Sky cuddled up by the fire and went to sleep. The next morning she was awakened by a hungry dragon. Daisy was doing her hungry dance on Melody's tummy. Melody grabbed some cheese, an apple, and a honey cake and cut them into tiny bieces for Daisy. Then she ate some and gave some to Tall sky. "Oh, the fun of camping out," said Melody.

"We'll have a proper lunch at the Windy Port Inn," said Tall sky. "Let's go."

"Sounds good to me," said Melody. They mounted their horses and rode toward Windy Port. "I want a good soaky bath when we get there. Then I want a good warm meal and a hot drink. It was kind of cold last night, even with warm clothes and blankets."

"You are getting to be an old softy," said Tall Sky. "You didn't complain before."

"I didn't complain because I just wanted to be next to you in any circumstance," said Melody smiling and she laughed. "You are the love of my life."

"I have to take you on campaigns more often," said Tall Sky.

The Windy Port Inn looked so good and it smelled good. "Let's eat first, I'm hungry," said Melody.

They were served fresh fish and fried potatoes with steamed vegetables and pie for desert. They and Daisy ate their fill and went upstairs for a bath. Afterwards, feeling warm and happy, they boarded the boat to Montro. As they approached the town, Melody became anxious. "Tall Sky, what if we're recognized?"

"Then I'll shield us and we will leave," answered Tall Sky. "Don't worry. Father God wants this done and He will help us."

"That's right. Sometimes I forget that I'm married to an elfvangelist," said Melody and she laughed.

"Very cute, Melody. I'll get you later," he said smiling.

The Montro port was very small, but the man who ran it lived close by on a small farm and rented horses to Melody and Tall Sky and to the two messengers. It was cool and the sun was bright. They only had about an hour to ride. They felt good and refreshed. This time the Market was outside of town on the edge of the woods. They rode into the market and and did some shopping as they had done before. This market was larger than the last two, but they were selling about the same types of things. Melody bought a small painting for Faerverin. The artist was also selling some pigment of interesting colors from a country overseas which Melody also bought for Faerverin. She bought some beautiful red and white sparkling cloth for Arinya and a pale blue sparkling cloth for Amidra. She bought a piece of fur to make a cloak for Daisy. Tall Sky talked to a jeweler about the auction and was told that there would be a slave auction at about dinner time. There were about fifteen girls to be sold tonight. The foreigners usually bought them. Tall Sky sent a messenger to Quickturn. Then he got Melody and walked her to the horses. Tall Sky said, "Do you want to stay for this? With this many people it's likely to get messy. We don't have to stay. We could buy fifteen sets of warm clothes and have the messenger lead us to the camp with them. That's really the most important help we could do right now."

"Let's do that," Melody said. They rode into the town of Montro and visited the clothing store. Then they followed the messenger out to the camp and gathered bandages, ointments and water for the arrival of the captives. In several hours the soldiers rode back with about twenty freed captives. Melody and Tall Sky ministered to their needs, giving them clothing and bandages and comforting them. One of the soldiers wrote down their names and where they were from. The soldiers had located their camp on a local farm and told the farmer that they would need the barn to house the freed captives for the night. The farmer and his wife agreed to this. They had wanted to do something about this for a long time. This worked out great. The girls really needed some sense of security. The farmer's wife made a big pot of tea and brought it to the girls. The farmer helped to make bedding for them out of hay and burlap. She brought out some hot water and rags for them to wash their faces and she helped with the bandages. She helped make sandwiches for everyone. She fussed and held them while they cried and helped to tuck them in. Melody told Tall Sky she wanted to hire her. He said that she certainly had the gift of giving comfort to those in need. They thanked her and went to bed.

After a good night's sleep and some breakfast, Quickturn instructed Melody and Tall Sky to do the same thing in Brown Bear. He said that after that there were only four more places to clean up. So Melody and Tall Sky rode back to the Montro port and waited for the boat. Melody said, "Quickturn said that they killed a lot of Bitters and slavers and customers. I'm glad that I didn't have to watch that even though I'm mad at them for hurting people. It must have been an awful mess."

"You know I was at the Purge of Malwood. It is a horrible sight, but it is necessary. They won't stop slavery just because they're told that it is wrong or illegal. They don't care. In this case, eliminating the wrong doers is the only way to stop the wrong from being done. It is like these people are rabid or incurably insane. What it really comes down to is evil. Here comes the boat," said Tall Sky.

They boarded the boat and headed downstream. The air was warmer and they had yet another sunny day. There was more foliage on the shores and animals could be seen scurrying along the water's edge.

Melody felt happy and contented knowing that last night's raid had saved so many girls from a short life of slavery ending in prostitution. Sometimes she couldn't bear to thnk about the harsh reality of what was really happening to these girls and their families. So she petted Daisy and talked to her and held hands with Tall Sky and got lost in her love for him.

Tall Sky thought of his love for Melody. He thought of her childlike love, her compassion, her interest in anything beautiful and new to her and her generosity. He thought that she was a perfect gift to him from God. She completed him like no one ever had. He put his arm around her and gave a little squeeze and Daisy crawled up on his shoulder and rubbed her face against his. They watched the scenery as they floated down the river.

As Brown Bear approached, they noticed that it seemed to be a larger town with many people walking about. There was a stack of merchandise to be loaded onto a boat to go up river. They left the boat and walked to the nearest inn where they ordered some food and talked to the innkeeper. Tall Sky asked him how his business was going. He said,"Business is good, but will be much slower soon. The foreigners will be gone soon. They say that their ship is leaving in a few days. They're scum. We will be better off without them. They're always making passes at the women who come in here and at my servant girl. They even try to bother my wife. I hear that they are here to buy women. What's the matter with their country? Doesn't it produce women? After they left last year, we found two girls who had been tortured and left for dead. One died and the other one stays in all the time and is afraid of everyone. Death is too good for these men. "

"Have you seen any Bitter Elves around here?" asked Tall Sky.

"Sure," said the innkeeper. "Now, there's another nasty lot. King Aryante needs to do something about them. They rob and murder and abduct girls from their homes. I'm so sick of this that I'm ready to move to Vivallen."

"I don't blame you," said Tall Sky. Melody and Tall Sky left the inn after renting horses and rode to the market. The market was about the same size as the last one. He chose to talk to the café server this time. He said the the slave auction would be held tonight about an hour before sundown. There were about twenty girls and some young men. There were also a few small children. The pen was out near the edge of the woods and could be viewed. Tall Sky thanked him and they walked over to the pen. Some men were taunting them, making lewd comments and showing themselves to the girls. One of them came up to Melody and Tall Sky said she was his wife. "I'll bet she's pretty good in the sack, eh?" the man said. Tall Sky shielded her and himself and they walked away. They noticed quite a few Bitters there and told Melody it was best they get back to town. They sent a messenger to Quickturn, bought some clothes, and rode out of town with the second messenger. This time they stopped at a farm near the camp and spoke with the farmer about the use of his barn for the night. He paid the man and said that he would be back later. Then they put bedding on the floor of the barn and unloaded the clothes. They sent the messenger to the camp to let Quickturn know that they had a place ready for the girls tonight. They told the farmer that they would need containers of hot water for King Aryante's soldiers, and the farmer proceeded to heat water.

Within several hours, the soldiers brought in the captives. There were twenty girls, five young men and three small children. Tall Sky and Melody went to work with soap and water, bandages, clothing and comforted the girls. Several soldiers made food for them and gave them wine to drink. Melody asked the farmer's wife if she had a bed that the children could sleep in. She said she would be happy to help and that she even had little clothes for them to wear. She gave them baths, put clean warm clothes on them and put them to bed in the bed that her children used to sleep in. She covered them with a fluffy quilt and told them that they would take them home. One little girl said that her Mommy and Daddy were killed. She was crying. The farmer's wife said that she could sleep with her tonight and the little girl stopped crying. "Will you be my mommy now?" the girl asked. She looked at her husband and he nodded yes.

"We will talk to the soldiers about it tomorrow," said the farmer.

Tall Sky and Melody ministered and counseled well into the night. The girls were traumatized. They had been beaten, whipped, raped, and generally terrorized. The boys had been beaten and whipped, and they were very angry. They all needed physical help, and mental and spiritual counseling. When they were calmed down, Melody and Tall Sky cuddled up in the hay and went to sleep.

Staying up late was never a good idea on a farm because of the rooster crowing in the morning. Melody said, "It can't be morning already. She turned over and went back to sleep as did the captives. The soldiers let them sleep in while they prepared breakfast. The farmer talked to Quickturn about adopting the little orphan girl, and he agreed. Everyone finally got up and ate breakfast. Then a group of soldiers rode out with the captives and took them home. They liked doing this because the parents were so happy that they always insisted on feeding them. Melody and Tall Sky left for their next town of Star City which was about two hours to the East. Tall Sky, I am so tired of all this travel. I can hardly wait to go home."

"I feel the same way, Culina. Every day we get closer to the finish. There are only two towns before Free Harbor and we will have a lot of help there. We may not have anything to do but a little spying at Free Harbor," said Tall Sky.

"It was nice of the farmers to adopt that little girl," said Melody. "Do you think we should adopt a little girl if the opportunity presents itself?"

"We couldn't do this if we did," said Tall Sky. "We might in the future, but then we might have one of our own. I'll let Father God lead on this one."

"I understand," she said and pouted for a while. Daisy looked her in the eyes and whined, so she petted the dragon and kissed her and let tears roll down her cheeks.

"Culina," said Tall Sky. "You know that I love you and if it's a child that you want, we'll keep our eyes open for one." She looked up at him and smiled. The road wound through grassland with intermittent woods and farms here and there across fields. In a few miles, they saw the smoke from the cooking fires and the colorful tents. There were a few customers still arriving and a few wagons of goods for sale, but mostly the market was set up and bustling with activity. They road in and tied the horses near an outdoor café to buy a drink. Tall Sky inquired about the auction and the café owner said that the auction would take place before dusk and that there were quite a few slaves to be auctioned. Tall Sky and Melody sent a messenger to Quickturn and then sat down to drink their wine and eat a sandwich. They found that they had front row seats to a robbery. A group of Bitters rode in, dismounted, and entered a jeweler's tent. There were screams as they killed the jeweler and took the man's merchandise. As they exited the tent, some guards engaged them in swordplay and slew them. Melody just sat there amazed.

"Is that what the Purge of Malwood was like?" asked Melody. "It happened so fast."

"It does happen fast if there are just a few of them," replied Tall Sky. "Let's walk around the grounds and see what the captives look like." They finished their wine and took a leisurely stroll around the market stopping to look at things. They bought two dolls for some special little girls. They walked by the slave pen and counted fifteen girls and three young men. They didn't say anything, but walked over to their horses and rode out of the market toward town to buy some warm clothes. Then they had the other messenger lead them to camp.

Riding back to camp over fields, not roads, was at least peaceful and quiet. There was nothng to intimate the mahem being pertetrated upon innocents at the market nor of the impending slaughter of the guilty. It was a beautiful day, but some clouds were appearing in the west. They had high hopes that everything would go as planned. They had done their part and now it was up to the soldiers to do their part in the unfolding of the drama of freedom. When they arrived at the camp, Quickturn and his soldiers had already left, but one of the soldiers said that they still needed a barn for the group to sleep in. Tall Sky rode with several of the soldiers to a farm that looked promising. The farmer and his wife were glad to see the soldiers and told them that their daughter was missing. She had disappeared while working in the garden. Tall Sky told them that the soldiers were releasing captive girls from slavers and returning them to their parents. The farmers were very excited about this and were eager to provide any help that they could, so they went out to the barn and spread out hay and helped make beds for the captives and a large area for the soldiers.

Tall Sky rode back to the camp to get Melody. The clouds were covering about half of the sky and were slowly moving eastward. In another hour the soldiers would arrive. Melody and the farmer's wife prepared food while the farmer, Tall Sky and the soldiers prepared tubs of hot water and a campfire. The farmers' daughter was among the captives and her parents were overjoyed to have their daughter back home. The captives were first given some wine to drink. Then, two by two, the girls were ushered into the house where Melody and the farmer's wife bathed them and bandaged them and dressed them in warm clothing. From there they were taken to the barn and fed. Fifteen girls and three young men sat in the barn on blankets and hay. They truly felt better. Tall Sky and Melody asked them questions about their homes and their treatment by the slavers.

"I think that the Bitters are worse than the slavers. The Bitters really enjoyed hurting us by slapping and pinching and pushing us along. They were cruel," said one of the girls.

Another girl said. "I was captured by slavers who wanted to have sex with us, and after they did that, they made us walk for a long way without stopping and wouldn't give us food or water. At night they built a fire and gave us some water to drink and a little food. They drank wine and then raped us again. I hope none of us get pregnant from those men. They called us names like bitch and whore as if we were the ones who did wrong."

"The Bitters didn't rape us because they said that they would get a higher price for us if we were virgins. I didn't even know what that meant, so I asked and one of the Bitters dropped his pants and showed me what it would do. My stomache got sick and I almost threw up," said the girl.

Tall Sky said, "I am sorry this happened to you. It is wrong and it is not your fault. King Aryante is very concerned about this and sent his soldiers to rescue you. It is his intention to stop the slave trade in all of Aksanda. He has already stopped the slave trade north of here. You are not alone. Hundreds of girls have been abducted and sold into slavery. Our next step is to reunite you and your parents. For tonight we will all sleep in this barn. It looks like we are going to have rain or snow tonight. Tomorrow part of this group of soldiers will return you to your homes. Now we had better go to sleep."

Thunder and lightning interrupted the group and everybody cuddled into their blankets and hay for a good night's sleep. "Culina, I think that Father God has done a wonderful job of keeping us safe so that we can continue helping these captives. We only have two more places to go and we can head for Vivallen with a contingent of soldiers for protection," said Tall Sky.

"Do you think that we could travel home by boat?" asked Melody.

"As long as the river doesn't freeze over, we can take a boat. It should be possible," said Tall Sky.

Melody cuddled up to Tall Sky and Daisy snuggled into her hair on the blanket between her and Tall Sky.

They listened to the thunder and the rain and drifted into a deep dreamless sleep.

The morning began with the aroma of salt pork sizzling on the fire. The farmers had built a fire and were cooking breakfast. The farmer's wife had baked loaves of bread and had a table set up with butter and jam and fresh milk and tea. She had gathered eggs and cooked them and had fried potatoes. She and her daughter and husband had been working for hours on this. The captives felt better than they had since they were abducted. After eating breakfast, Tall Sky and Melody rode away toward the Star City Port.

When they arrived at the port, they ordered tea and listened to the latest news from the innkeeper. He said, "Last night the market was destroyed and a lot of people were killed. The soldiers rode off with the slaves. I guess it was a bloody mess. Were you there?"

Tall Sky replied, "We were there for a short time and bought some things, but we left before any soldiers arrived. We went shopping here in Star City. When will the next boat arrive going south?"

"I expect a boat within the hour. You have tme to do a little shopping if you like," he said. "I've had news of the king's army raiding places in Free Harbor. They're collecting slaves there and they hung the captain of one of the foreigner's ships. It might be safer to shop here right now."

"Sounds good. We'll be back later," said Tall Sky. "What about Phanta? Is it still safe? I wanted to check it out too. I'm looking for some special gifts for our friends up north."

"As far as I know, Phanta is still a peaceful place, but they do have an outside market there with a slave auction. The king's soldiers could show up there, but they haven't yet," he said.

"We would like to ride your horses again today. We will check out Phanta and bring the horses back tomorrow morning," said Tall Sky. "We will wait a few days before attempting to visit Free Harbor."

Melody and Tall Sky took a walk around the town mainly to listen to what people were saying. Most of the people were glad that the market was destroyed. Slavery was sickening to them and they were tired of the foreigners and the Bitters bullying their ways about town. The Bitters had no manners and the foreigners were always talking about women in humiliating ways. They said that the king must have finally heard about the slave trade.

Tall Sky and Melody then rode west toward Phanta. The sky was clear, the air was cool, and the sun felt warm on their backs. The road was a little soft from the rain, but it had dried out some from last night's storm. After several hours of riding they arrived at Phanta, another rural town with a market outside of town. The innkeeper there was digusted with the slave trade and wished that the king would do something to stop it. Tall Sky told him that the king was very concerned about it and that it would not last much longer. The innkeeper said that the last auction of the season was going to take place near dusk tonight. He expected the bidding to be fierce and said that it might be too dangerous for them to go. The foreigners thought nothing of killing to get their own ways. Tall Sky assured him that they would not stay for the auction, but would like to see if they had any good paintings for sale.

Melody and Tall Sky left on horseback to see the market. There were more booths and tents set up than at previous markets. There were many customers of various nationalities. Because of the nearness of Orendia, there were people from there. There were foreigners from over seas dressed in their colorful silken clothing and some people from Aksanda. There were a number of Bitters walking about too. The slave pen was located back and left of center to give easy access to the auction block and was full of captives. Some of them called out for help. Others were sitting down huddled together for warmth. Most of them were girls. Tall Sky and Melody walked back to the horses and sent a messenger to Quickturn who immediately led soldiers to Phanta. They asked the other messenger to lead them to the camp after shopping in Phanta for clothing.

Arriving at the army camp always gave Melody a feeling of relief. She felt safe there. Tall Sky and a soldier rode out to find a suitable barn for the night. Several barns were too small, but there was one larger barn with enough room and a farmer who was very relieved to see the soldiers. He had been worried about the presense of so many Bitters in the area. He helped Tall Sky and the soldiers to make bedding throughout the barn. Then he and his wife started preparing food. As usual, the soldiers gave him some silver for the food. They built a fire and cooked a pig on it and another fire to cook a lamb. Preparations were under way and Tall Sky rode back to inform Melody and the soldiers of their good fortune. He took Melody back to the barn to help with the preparations. She made the beds and put out warm clothing on them. She assembled the cups and put them on a table with some wine and cheese. She also had the men bring water for bathing. It had been a very productive day.

When the girls arrived, they were wide eyed and scared. Melody and Tall Sky gave each of them a cup of wine and walked among them asking about injuries. Then the girls were shown to pans of water and given some soap and a towel. They washed themselves and changed into some warm clothing. They emerged from the barn looking better and were given a bowl of food and a piece of bread. Then the soldiers ate. The backs of the boys had to be treated for lacerations from the whip. The girls had bruising and some scratches, but were mainly free of external injuries. After dinner, they curled up in their blankets and went to sleep. Since they all had homes to go to, Tall Sky and Melody planned to go to Brown Bear to catch the next boat.

Free Harbor was their next stop and the last one on their journey south. It was a large seaport with ships in the harbor and a bustling city. The innkeeper at Brown Bear was glad to see his customers back safe and sound. "Tall Sky, I'm glad to see you, friend. I heard that Phanta Market was attacked and destroyed by the soldiers last night. The word is that they carried off all the slave girls. What do they do with them?"

Tall Sky replied, "They return them to their families. Can you imagine how happy the parents are to see their children again? We weren't there when the soldiers came. What else did you hear?"

The innkeeper said, "The soldiers rode into the market and proceeded to kill everyone in sight. They killed the slavers and their customers. They killed the Bitters. Then they freed the slaves and put them on horses and rode away."

Tall Sky said that his next stop would be Free Harbor. He ordered lunch and sat down with a glass of wine. Melody was delighted to be just sitting and not involved in any activity for a while. Daisy was tired of traveling and wanted to sleep in her velvet bag more often now. "What are we going to do in Free Harbor?" asked Melody. "He said that the soldiers are already there and rounding up the slaves."

"I'm not sure," said Tall Sky. "We'll have to contact Quickturn when we get there. I'm sure there will be some counseling and maybe some negotiating to be done. He may have some more spying for us or he may send us home. Someone should wander the countryside looking for abandoned children. Would you want to do that? If I were single, that is probably something that I would do, but the king could have his soldiers doing that already."

"What about the slaves who were already sold? How can they be found?" asked Melody.

Tall Sky replied, "That's the stuff that wars are made of," said Tall Sky. "The foreigners and the Orendians both have some. Fighting a war on two fronts would be too costly in manpower."

"I hate war, but I hate slavery more," said Melody.

"Melody, remember the robbery at Montro Market? Multiply that times 1000 and that is war," said Tall Sky. "Just try to imagine all of a big city of people killing each other at once."

Melody shuddered and said, "I see what you mean."

"Now, let's pack up our things and go wait for the boat. It's nice outside," said Tall Sky. They could already see the boat coming from upstream. Their messengers were still with them and they would also board the boat. It felt much safer to Melody to have them with on the journey.

"I have an idea. What about buying them back? What if the people of Aksanda all gave silver toward the purchase of the girls from their captors in foreign countries? That way there would be no wars about it," said Melody.

"It's a simple, beautiful, childlike solution. It would undoubtedly work for some slaves, but many would remain slaves," said Tall Sky. "We will mention it to King Aryante. Most Aksandans are good hearted people and would like to see the slaves home and safe."

"What if King Aryante talked to the kings of the other countries and reasoned with them or came to an agreement for ransom of the slaves? Those kings may not even know what the slavers are doing," said Melody. "I could tell them about how awful it is for the children and their families. Surely the kings of those countries don't need Aksandan children."

"We will talk to King Aryante and to God about this. Father God will work through King Aryante. We will pray that King Aryante will be open to God's direction. It all comes down to the silver that the slavers are getting for their efforts. They need to be encouraged to do a different kind of trade. I'm pretty sure that their hearts are too evil to have any compassion left and that their minds are too twisted to be straightened out," said Tall Sky.

Melody relaxed and petted her liitle dragon and talked to her. Daisy was happy to be with Melody and she chirred and rubbed her face aganst Melody's cheek. Then she curled up on her shoulder under her hair and watched the scenery pass by. On the shores were soft, willowy trees that had not yet shed their leaves. There were pretty bird songs like the tahilu's song. The tahilus migrate south during the winter, as do other song birds. Melody thought of Laskron and his experience with the tahilu singing when he asked Father God if he would ever find love again. Also a Tahilu had flown over when he married his first wife. "Tall Sky, what did you tell me about tahilu birds? I was just thinking about them because of all the bird songs we're hearing right now," said Melody.

"When the Bright Elves won their first great battle to protect Phayendar, a flock of tahilus flew over the battleground. Tahilus are rarely seen as far north as Loadrel, but Laskron told me that one appeared and sang to him in his garden when he talked to his first wife's spirit about his intention to marry Liadra. Of course her spirit didn't appear to him, but he wanted to let her know that he would always love her, but that he was moving on with his life on Phayendar. Tahilus have such beautiful songs that magical qualities have been attributed to them. I've heard that if a pregnant woman hears the tahilu song, that her child will have a beautiful singing voice," said Tall Sky.

"I hope I hear one if I get pregnant. How long will it be to get to Free Harbor?" asked Melody.

"We will be there for lunch. Are you getting hungry yet?" asked Tall Sky.

"Yes, a little," replied Melody. "Look, the flowers are still blooming down here, and they have such beautiful colors. Oh, I wish that flowers bloomed all winter in Loadrel."

"Culina, when we get back, I will get you some indoor plants that will bloom all winter," said Tall Sky.

"Tall Sky, I have heard about some interesting animals in other lands. I'm really interested n the flying cats of Orendia. Are there really cats that can fly?" asked Melody.

"I've never seen them, but several Orendians assured me that it was true. They are supposed to be beautiful and fluffy and have some ability to talk using words, but not with as many words as we use," said Tall Sky.

"How big are they?" asked Melody. "Are they like housecats or like tigers?"

"As I understand it, they are like housecats and make pretty good pets," said Tall Sky, "But I'm pretty sure they would terrify Daisy, so don't get any ideas. Faerverin would probably love to have one."

"Father God loves variety. Just look at all the colors and types of flowers, and all the types of humans. I am so impressed with his ability to create amazing animals. I love Him so much," said Melody. "I love weather, too. Like thunderstorms are wild and I like the way that thunder rolls across the sky and the way raindrops make sparkles when they hit the water. Snow is beautiful when it is falling, but storms are particularly nice when cuddled up to you in a safe, warm place like the hay in a barn."

"Yes, Culina, that is the best part," said Tall Sky.

As the boat approached Free Harbor, there were houses on either side of the river. The boat would dock before reaching the sea, because the seaport was too busy with ships and commerce for a small boat to dock there. They stepped off the boat carrying their purchases and bags and walked to a nearby inn called The Red Dragon. The interior of the place was clean and they had vacancies, so Tall Sky and Melody rented a room with a bath. The inn smelled of good food, so Melody and Tall sky sat in the dining room and ordered lunch. The innkeeper brought them some wine and Tall Sky asked him about the soldiers that he had seen in town.

"A few days ago some soldiers came into Free Harbor and arrested people. They hung the ships captain and confiscated all of his goods. They collected all the slaves they could find. Then they sent the ship away manned by its crew with a message to their king that if any more slavers came to our shores, they would be slain and their ships would be added to our navy," said the innkeeper.

"What do the people think of all this?" asked Tall Sky.

"The merchants here will miss the business, but they agree that the slave trade must be stopped. Nobody likes those foreigners. They are scum. It's like they don't have any respect for others and treat women like they are play things to be used and discarded. I hate them. As far as I'm concerned, I would like to see them all killed. It would do the human race a favor," said the innkeeper.

The innkeeper brought them some stew and bread and butter and a little plate of stew for Daisy. She ate her stew and climbed into Melody's pouch for a nap. "The soldiers sure do take care of business," said Melody.

"These are very experienced soldiers," said Tall Sky. They finished their lunch and went to find Quickturn. Their messengers followed them for protection. They found Quickturn down at the docks talking to some workers. "Quickturn, how are things going?" asked Tall Sky.

Quickturn said, "Our campaign has been successful. You and Melody did a wonderful job of spyng, reporting and helping the girls after we rescued them. We recovered quite a few here and most of them are on their ways back home. I know you must be tired, but I could use some help with checking out the city for any girls that might be hidden away here. Also, I need to know if there are any more Bitters hanging around. Are you up for some browsing and shopping and sight seeing?"

"Sure," said Melody. "I've never seen this place and I think it would be fun to shop here." Quickturn gave her a bag of silver and told her to have fun.

Tall Sky and Melody walked back to the main street and walked, looking into stores for anything noteworthy. Melody enjoyed looking at paintings and found a painting of a tahilu sitting on a branch with blue sky in the background. The tahilu's feathers were shimmering with blues and greens and she bought the painting for Laskron. Tall Sky looked for anything suspicious and asked questions of the shopkeepers. They weren't forthcoming about the whereabouts of slaves or Bitters. At this point, Melody was thoroughly involved in shopping for unusual items that Arinya might sell in her shop. She found regal looking brooches, rings and necklaces that came from foreign lands. She found scarves with golden threads woven through them. She bought herself a pair of very soft leather, fur lined gloves. She bought a small carving of a flying cat from Orendia. In the same store, she bought a tapestry of a woman with a long, flowing gown, red hair, and a flying cat perched on her arm. "That's me," she thought. The messengers helped to carry her purchases. In a shoe shop she bought a pair of boots that laced up to her knees and in a dress shop, she bought a soft golden colored velveteen dress with a belt made of silver conches that draped across her abdomen. She also bought a brown, fur lined cloak with a hood. These were wonderful additions to her winter wardrobe. This was truly a great end to a long, difficult trip.

After shopping all afternoon, they headed back to the Red Dragon Inn for dinner. Daisy was awake, sitting on Melody's shoulder and eagerly awaiting dinner. Melody said,"I feel like I should buy more things for Arinya's shop. I would also like to go to a dressmaker and have her make some clothes for Daisy. I did buy that fur for her. I should have a dressmaker make the cloak for her before we go back. It's going to be cold up north and she could use a fur lined pouch, too."

"I agree," said Tall Sky. "Dragons don't like excessive cold, do you, little darling." He kissed Daisy's forehead. "We can go right after dinner." The innkeeper's wife brought the dinner of fresh fish, fried potatoes, fresh vegetables, and pie for desert. It was excellent, and after dinner they visited the local dressmaker to have Daisy's cloak made. The dressmaker loved Daisy and made the cloak for her right away. She also made a sweater for Daisy that covered her long neck and her body down to her tail. It didn't take very long and Daisy cooperated with the lady who talked baby talk to her in soothing tones. Then she made Daisy a nice, big fur lined pouch with a stable bottom in it for daisy to lie on. Daisy wore the sweater and the cloak when they left.

"Daisy loves clothes," said Melody. "I can make her some really cute ones for the summer so she won't get sunburned."

"I want to stop in a few taverns and talk to the owners about the presense of Bitters, slavers or slave girls. It won't take long, but it is necessary so that we have something to report to Quickturn. We will report to him tomorrow and then head back to Vivallen. How does that sound?" asked Tall Sky.

"It sounds good, but I must add that I am having fun shopping here," said Melody. "Maybe we can bring Arinya and Trag down here for shopping when the weather is warmer in the spring."

"We will have to wait and see what develops between now and then," said Tall Sky.

"Why? What do you know? You have something planned, don't you? I know that look," said Melody.

"I really don't know, but I have a feeling that this is not over," said Tall Sky.

"Tall Sky, seriously, I need a rest," said Melody.

"We will rest before attempting anything else. Speaking of rest, let's talk to a few tavern owners and head for the Red Dragon Inn," said Tall Sky. Tall Sky talked to a few tavern owners, but nobody was in the mood to talk. So they headed back to the inn for a bath and bed.

The next morning at breakfast Quickturn joined them. "How's the food here?" he asked.

"It's great," said Tall Sky. "I'm afraid I don't have much to report to you. People were too afraid to talk."

"That's alright. The soldiers who will be left here to guard the coast will have to earn their trust. I am planning on going back north with you, so don't leave without me. We need to go to Vivallen and talk to King Aryante about what we did and about the plan to keep things safe from now on. Then there is the matter of getting back the girls who were already moved out of the country. We also have to contact the chiefs around the country and gather a list of names of girls who are still missing. This will take a while, but with King Aryante behind it, we should make good progress," said Quickturn.

Melody's face was turning red from trying to hold in her emotions. Finally, she said in a very controlled tone of voice, "I want to go home and rest before getting involved in something else. I know we have to see King Aryante, but then I want to go to Loadrel for a while."

"That's fine," said Quickturn. "We won't need to involve you further for a while."

The food arrived along with a small dish for Daisy. Every cook who met Daisy fell in love with her. Melody, now calmed down, ate her breakfast and wondered how much time they would have in Free Harbor before leaving. Quickturn said, "We will leave tomorrow morning after breakfast, so why don't you two have some fun today looking around."

After breakfast, Tall Sky and Melody decided to visit a place called Far View which had displays of very old things and things from far away places. There was an anchor display, a stuffed flying cat from Orendia, a three feet long carving of a tiger, a crystal ball, dolls from over seas, old navigational charts, rune stones, very old tools, jewelry from over seas, a knife collection from Orendia, and foreign armor and helmets from a long ago war. Tall Sky bought some navigational charts and a knife for Beldock.

Melody wanted to see a big ship, so they obtained permission to board a ship with big sails that was being loaded with merchandise. The ship had a carving of a mermaid on the prow and many other carvings of animals along the side. It was very clean and the wood was polished and oiled. Below deck was a large room with heavey wooden tables of rough hewn wood polished smooth. There were port holes in the sides to look out at the sea and there were bunks for the men to sleep in. There was also a cargo hold area. They weren't allowed into the captain's room. The tour was enough to convince Melody that she didn't want to sail anywhere.

Then they visited a glass blower and bought an interesting piece of glassware for Laskron to copy. Tall Sky asked the glassblower and learned how the glassblower made it. Then they stopped at a bakery and bought pastry for a snack, a sack of cherry flavored candy and some spices for Mina. The last stop was a clothing store where Melody found a leather vest for herself, and new boots for Tall Sky.

Feeling satisfied and a bit tired, they took their purchases back to the Red Dragon Inn where Melody gave Daisy a warm bath and an oil rubdown. Daisy enjoyed herself splashing in the water and loved being oiled afterwards. Then she grabbed her sweater and tried getting into it. Melody helped her with it and she was one happy dragon. They all took a nap until dinner.

They were awakened by Quickturn."Tall Sky, it looks like you've done some shopping."

"Yes, Melody wanted to buy things for her friends and we bought some clothes. Do you have any news?" asked Tall sky.

"We caught some Bitters lurking about town and they did give the location of some girls they hid in a basement room. We found them and they'll be returned home. Since the Bitters cooperated, we released them with a warning and told them to get the word out that people turning girls over to us would not be harmed," replied Quickturn. "Are you ready for your return trip?"

"Yes, we are. Will the messengers be traveling with us?" asked Tall Sky.

"Absolutely. I want you protected all the way back to Vivallen and Loadrel," said Quickturn.

"Will you be joning us for breakfast?" asked Tall Sky.

"No, I have already eaten and I have some things to do. You go on and have a nice breakfast and say hello to everybody back home for me," said Quickturn. "I'll see you again soon. Vanya sulie."

"What does vanya sulie mean?" asked Melody.

"It means fair winds," replied Tall Sky. "Let's get dressed and have some breakfast."

"Let's order it and take it with us and eat on the boat," said Melody. That sounded good to Tall Sky, so they put their purchases in cloth bags and left the Red Dragon Inn. Their messengers helped carry the bags, and they boarded a boat heading north. They paid extra for a safe spot for their packages. Going north meant traveling against the current, but the rowers were strong and they made good time. Though it was cool, they didn't need their cloaks. Daisy wore her sweater and seemed to be enjoying her boat ride. She turned her head from side to side to see both sides of the river and chirred. Brown Bear was their first stop. A couple got off, but there were no new passengers. The next stop was Windy Port where they bought sandwiches and honey cakes and a skin of berry wine. Melody was happy and began to relax. They had completed their mission and were on their way home at last. "Tall Sky, I really enjoyed shopping," she said looking at the ring on her finger. "Thank you for all my new things and for all the presents we bought. It's going to be fun giving them to our friends. You know, it would be good for Laskron to make a trip to Free Harbor to talk to the glass blower there. He might pick up some good ideas from him."

In a few more hours they reached Lossport where several more passengers left the boat. It was colder now and Melody and Tall Sky donned their cloaks. Daisy loved her cloak, and she cuddled down underneath it on Melody's shoulder. The sky was overcast and looked like it might snow. At Lossport they picked up a fresh rowing team. There was snow on the ground and covering the pine trees. It had just snowed the night before. Melody and Tall Sky kept warm cuddling under a blanket and Daisy, in her own cloak, took a nap on melody's lap under the blanket. They were tired of sitting, but that was all there was to do on the boat.

They were very happy to reach the Vivallen Port where they left the boat and took their packages into the inn. Tall Sky paid for rooms, dinner, and hot baths for all four of them. After depositing their things in their rooms, it was time for some hot dinner and wine. "Hot berry wine. I have missed this." said Melody. It feels great to be here even if there's snow on the ground." The innkeeper brought lamb stew with a thick broth, freshly baked bread, butter, jam, and apple cobbler for dessert. It was delicious and Daisy thoroughly enjoyed it. After dinner they took a hot bath and climbed into a warm bed under a down quilt and fell into a deep, dreamless sleep.

When Melody awoke, she didn't know where she was. "I thought we were still on the boat."

"Haven't got your land legs yet," said Tall Sky. "I have a surprise for you. We don't have to ride horses to Vivallen. I rented a sleigh."

"How fun! I've never been in a sleigh," said Melody.

After breakfast they piled their things into the sleigh and bundled up under a quilt and a hide. Melody fell asleep as did Daisy. In her dream, the world was warm and rosy with flowers and butterflies and fluffy flying cats. She flew with them and petted them and talked with them. She awoke because she was hungry and Daisy was doing her hungry dance on her tummy. Daisy climbed up to her shoulder and chirred into her ear. She asked Tall Sky, "May I have the bag of food? Daisy and I are hungry."

They pulled over to the ruins so that they could get out and stretch their legs and relieve themselves. It was cold, and the little dragon didn't like to have to step in the snow. Melody would have to make her some booties. They climbed back into the sleigh to eat lunch. "You know, Beldock has a sleigh that he keeps in the shed behind his house. Maybe we could rent it to drive to Home Fire. It might give Rando the idea to get one. He should have a sleigh out there," said Tall Sky. "Between the carpenter and the blacksmith, they should be able to make one. We will stay at the Golden Chalice tonight and visit King Aryante tomorrow," said Tall Sky.

The sled lurched ahead and they were sliding down the road again. Tall Sky kissed Melody and pulled her close to him. "I love you, Culina. You have made me so happy. I feel warm and contented." This time they both fell asleep. After awhile, Daisy woke Melody wanting some attention. It was snowing again. By the tme they reached the Golden Chalice, there was an inch of snow on them. The messengers looked like snowmen. They unloaded the sleigh and ordered hot baths and rooms. Then they ordered hot wine and sat near the fireplace to thaw.

Feeling the warmth radiating through them from the hot wine and the heat of the fireplace made them feel really good. "I wish Quickturn could be with us when we talk to the king. I only know our part of the campaign. The battles and the returns of the girls I know little of," said Tall Sky.

"He will understand that," said Melody. "Just let him know that his plan worked well and tell him about the condition of the girls and of the one we found tied to a tree and the other one we found dead. Those are the things that will keep him wanting to help them."

Dinner was served and they sat at a table with the messengers and had a wonderful meal, after which they retired to their room for a hot bath. "How dressed do we have to be tomorrow? I was thinking of wearing my new dress and my lace up boots." said Melody.

"That should be fine. I don't want to be too formal," said Tall Sky. After laying out their clothes for the next day, they went to bed.

After a sumptuous breakfast, Tall Sky and Melody walked to the castle to meet with King Aryante. They took with them Aranel's doll, Anya's pigments, and a scarf and a small painting for Faerverin. The king would meet them in an hour, so they went up to find Faerverin. She and Anya were painting and Aranel was watching. "I see you two are hard at work with another painting," said Tall Sky. We brought you something that you will like. He gave her the bag of pigments. "They're from over seas. We found them in Free Harbor."

"They're wonderful. Thank you. I love them." Princess Anya was already looking through them. Then he gave a doll to Aranel who was delighted and started playing with her.

Melody said, "I wanted to give you this scarf. See the gold thread worked through the material? Isn't it pretty? I thought the blue color would look good on you. I thought you would like this painting of flowers. The colors are so vivid. Shopping in Free Harbor was really fun."

"Thank you. They are lovely. Have you seen the king yet?" asked Faerverin. "He has been kind of brooding lately. The queen says that it is because of the anti slavery campaign. He has been getting reports from messengers about the treatment of the girls."

"I'm not surprised," said Tall Sky. "King Aryante is a good man. It's bound to have an impact on him. He is responsible for the well being of the nation. That kind of responsibility weighs heavily on a man."

"How is Aleph doing in his new position?" asked Tall Sky.

"He seems to like it. He is talking with people and helping them to come to reasonable solutions to their problems. He is good at it and it makes him happy," said Faerverin. "Here he is now."

"Tall Sky, I heard that you and Melody had arrived. I've been getting updates on your progress out there. You two have been doing a wonderful job with the captives," said Aleph. "How are you?"

"It was a long, hard journey with lots of danger and excitement. Melody and I are both tired to the bone. Our minds and spirits are tired too," said Tall Sky. "We need some serious rest and rejuvenation."

"I understand. You were married in the middle of trying times and launched right into cleaning up the country. You need some alone time together," said Aleph.

"It's about time to check in with King Aryante. I don't know what I can tell him that he doesn't already know, but I guess I'll find out," said Tall Sky. They walked down the steps and down the hall to the King's study. They sat down at the table and waited for King Aryante to arrive. When the king walked in, he clasped Tall Sky's hand and thanked him and Melody for the fine job they did in the field.

"Quickturn tells me that you did exactly what you should have done in every situation. It is appalling what happened to those girls and their families. I am determined to get back as many of them as possible from other countries. As soon as weather permits, I would like to send a caravan into Orendia to scout out the area and an emissary to the king there." said King Aryante.

"That's a good dea. You mean to do this in the spring, is that correct?" asked Tall Sky.

"Yes, I wouldn't want a caravan out there in the snow," replied King Aryante. "It would be a real caravan with goods to sell, but would be manned with soldiers in disguise. I will start now training the soldiers to be merchants. They will learn the value of things and how to trade one thing for another. Everything will be arranged right here. I wondered if you would accompany them and gather information. I would also like Aleph to be an emissary to the king to work out an arrangement for the return of the girls."

"Melody and I will certainly consider this. We have already talked about the need to get the girls back and ways to go about it. We need to rest before we will be ready for another adventure."

Melody said, "I have heard about the flying cats of Orendia. Would it be permissible for us to bring one back as a gift to Faerverin?"

King Aryante laughed and said, "That would be fine. Are you planning to stay here in Vivallen or are you going back to Loadrel for the winter?"

Tall Sky replied, "I think we want to go back home for a while, recuperate and see our friends."

"Have a safe trip home and I will contact you when we are ready," said King Aryante. "And don't forget this." He handed Tall Sky a large bag of silver and left.

"Do you want to go home today?" asked Tall Sky.

"Yes. Let's go pack the sleigh," said Melody. They left the castle and walked back to the Golden Chalice.

They brought the messengers and three extra horses with them. By the end of the day they would be home. In the back of the sleigh, Melody was already feeling more normal. She was thinking about home and her friends. She leaned up against Tall Sky feeling warm and happy. Daisy cuddled up under her chin purring. They stopped at the ruins for lunch and walked about stretching their legs. Melody had made little boots for Daisy out of a piece of fur, and Daisy walked proudly through the snow to relieve herself. Then they ate sandwiches and drank some wine. After lunch, they rode on toward Lake Perlilough.

The light was waning by the time they reached the lake and turned left. It was dark when they reached the Laborer's Reward. The messengers helped bring in their packages. Beldock greeted them and Mina brought food and hot wine with her customary Daisy plate.

"I'll let you eat and then we'll talk," said Beldock. The after dinner customers were having drinks and telling stories. Tall Sky and Melody felt better after dinner. Beldock brought Laskron, Liadra and Elise and they all sat down by the fire. "I have presents for you," said Melody. "Free Harbor was full of interesting stores, and part of our job was to shop and talk with store owners." Melody gave a doll to Elise, who clapped her hands, said thankyou and hugged the doll. She gave some exotic spices and a brooch to Mina. Tall Sky gave Beldock a foreign knife with a jeweled hilt. He gave Laskron a painting of a tahilu bird and a piece of glassware with information on how to make it. Melody gave Liadra a beautiful gemstone brooch and a light blue scarf with silver threads running through it. All were delighted with their gifts.

Tall Sky said, "Laskron, I really think that some time this spring you should take a boating trip to Free Harbor to visit the glass blower there and exchange information with him. He has some very artistic pieces. You two have much in common and he is very open to discussing his work."

"That is a very interesting idea. I would like to that," said Laskron.

Beldock said, "Tell me what happened so that I can tell my customers the news."

Tall Sky said, "Outside of every town in Angvar Province there was a market like the Malwood Market with a pen for girls and boys to be sold. We counted the girls and sent a message to Quickturn. Then we went back to the town and bought warm clothing for them and took them to a farm where they would bed down in the barn for the night. The farmers were great. They always helped prepare the food and the bedding. One farmer even adopted a little orphan girl who was only five years old. The soldiers went to the markets and killed the slavers and their customers. They brought the girls to the farms where they received food, clothing and bandages. The next day some soldiers returned them to their homes."

"It was hard to see the girls in the pens without doing something," said Melody. "The first pen wasn't guarded, so Tall Sky let them out and put them on horses and rode out to the soldiers' camp. Once there was a naked girl who was tied to a tree with blood all over her from being whipped. On the ground was a dead girl. We sent her back to the town with a messenger to get medical attention. Once Tall Sky killed the slavers around the pen, let the girls out, and rode back to the camp with them. All in all there had to be over a hundred girls and a few boys who were freed."

"King Aryante wants us to go with a caravan into Orendia to find out what happened to the girls bought by Orendian merchants. He wants Aleph to talk to the Orendian King about getting them returned," said Tall Sky. "It may not work, but you don't know until you try."

"What's being done about the foreign ships?" asked Beldock.

"King Aryante decreed that the slave girls were to be confiscated and returned to their homes, the ship's captains to be hung, and the ships turned out to sea manned by their crews. He established a Guard of the coast to monitor activities," said Tall Sky.

"That's great!" said Beldock. "How soon do you go on the caravan?"

"Not until the spring," said Tall Sky. "This winter Melody and I will relax and enjoy being married."

"It's about time," said Beldock.

"Melody and I will go home now. Are you ready, Melody? May we use your sled to take our things home?" asked Tall Sky.

"Sure," said Beldock.

The first thing they did was to start a fire in the fireplace. When the house was warmer, they went to bed. It had been a long journey and they were tired. "I love you," said Melody as she cuddled up to Tall Sky.

"I love you, too, Culina," he said and kissed her on the cheek. They fell asleep immediately.

The next morning they stopped at Jelsareeb's bakery for some pastries and took them over to Trag's Shop. Arinya said, "Come into the kitchen and sit down and tell us about your trip." She poured tea for them and they had tea and pastries. Arinya cooked some scrambled eggs to go with it.

We actually stopped by to give you a few things that we found in Free Harbor. They have some very interesting shops down there. I kept wanting to buy things for you to put in your store. Arinya, look at this brooch. It's beautiful and kind of old and regal looking. And this red scarf with golden threads runnng through it. These are for you. I think we could all go back there during the spring or summer and shop. You could find amazing things there for your store."

"Thank you so much. I love them. I would like to take a shopping trip through the south, but I am pregnant and the baby will be here by late summer," said Arinya.

"Have people been shopping here?" asked Melody.

"Yes, but I may have to add more of the essentials to bring in more customers," replied Arinya.

"Were there more auctions going on in the south?" asked Trag.

Tall Sky said, "Yes, there were auctions outside of every town that had slaves for sale. The outside markets were much like the Malwood Market and were not totally destroyed, but the slavers and their customers were killed and the slaves were returned home. Many Bitters and foreigners were killed. King Aryante has set up a new group of soldiers to guard the coast. It's a good plan to keep foreigners from taking slaves from Aksanda. He also wants us to go on a caravan to Orendia to arrange for the return of girls they bought here. You might want to travel with the caravan. You could buy exotic things for your store."

"I still have to wait and see how Arinya is doing," said Trag.

"Melody and I are going to make a large puzzle of Phayendar and I have bought some navigational maps that have overseas lands charted. If you know or meet someone with knowledge of a foreign land, let me know so that I can do a better job of this," said Tall Sky.

Trag said," I know of one man already, and we get interesting customers who want to talk, so I'll let you know if I meet any more. The man you should talk to is Malding. When he was a young man, he worked on a seafaring ship. He is a good man and works at fishing. He has a small boat. You will find him at Beldock's tonight."

Tall Sky said, "Sounds good. Thank you. We're going to take a walk by the lake. See you later."

Tall Sky and Melody strolled beside the lake. She put on Daisy's booties and let her walk about to relieve herself. Then they sat on the bench and Daisy chirred at the water. It was a beautiful day with sunlight glistening off the water. Melody said, "I'm so grateful to Father God for keeping us safe on our journey to Free Harbor." They walked up to the Laborer's Reward and ordered mugs of ale.

"Hi, Beldock. Trag was telling us about a fisherman named Malding. I want to talk to him about some navigational charts I bought in Free Harbor. I'm going to use them to make a puzzle of the world. Does he come in for dinner?" asked Tall Sky.

"He should be here tonight to hear your news. That puzzle idea of yours is good. It will help people to understand the world outside of Loadrel," said Beldock.

"Yes, and it is something that Melody and I like to do together. We made several puzzles and others wanted them. Elise and Emmy begged us to make more. It's a good winter hobby. It takes a lot of time, but the winter is here and we have a lot of time," said Tall Sky.

Mina came in and said, "Look at Daisy in her cloak and boots. She looks like a high class dragon." Mina gave her a dish of some cheese, apple pieces, and bread and jam. "I do love this little dragon." They ate lunch feeling relaxed and happy.

Ulrick walked in for lunch and said hello to Tall Sky and Melody. "I heard you had a very evenful trip. I'm glad to see you safe and sound," said Ulrick. "I suppose you will be bored with Loadrel now."

"Actually, we need a rest from all of that. We are planning on making puzzles of the world. We were gong to ask you to make us some of those puzzle boards and cut them into pieces for us. I bought some navigational maps in Free Harbor and I'm going to talk to Malding about them tonight. I won't know the size of board we will need until we get the map drawn. You can make some other boards of various sizes. We will ba making puzzles for kids, too. Laskron's daughter wants some puzzles. Kids like to put thngs together. I'm going to make a building set to make small houses out of branches. Maybe you could work with me on that," said Tall Sky.

Ulrick's face brightened and he smiled. "I would love to work on that. It sounds like fun and I know some little boys who would enjoy that this winter. I'll get to work on the puzzle boards right after lunch. Today you could gather sticks for the miniature houses. It shouldn't be green wood, though."

"We have time for that this afternoon. We will tie them in bundles and put them on a sled," said Tall Sky. After lunch, Melody and Tall Sky went looking for the right sized sticks. After choosing the sticks he wanted, they took them to Ulrick and then headed back to the Laborer's Reward for dinner. Malding was there and Beldock introduced him to Tall Sky.

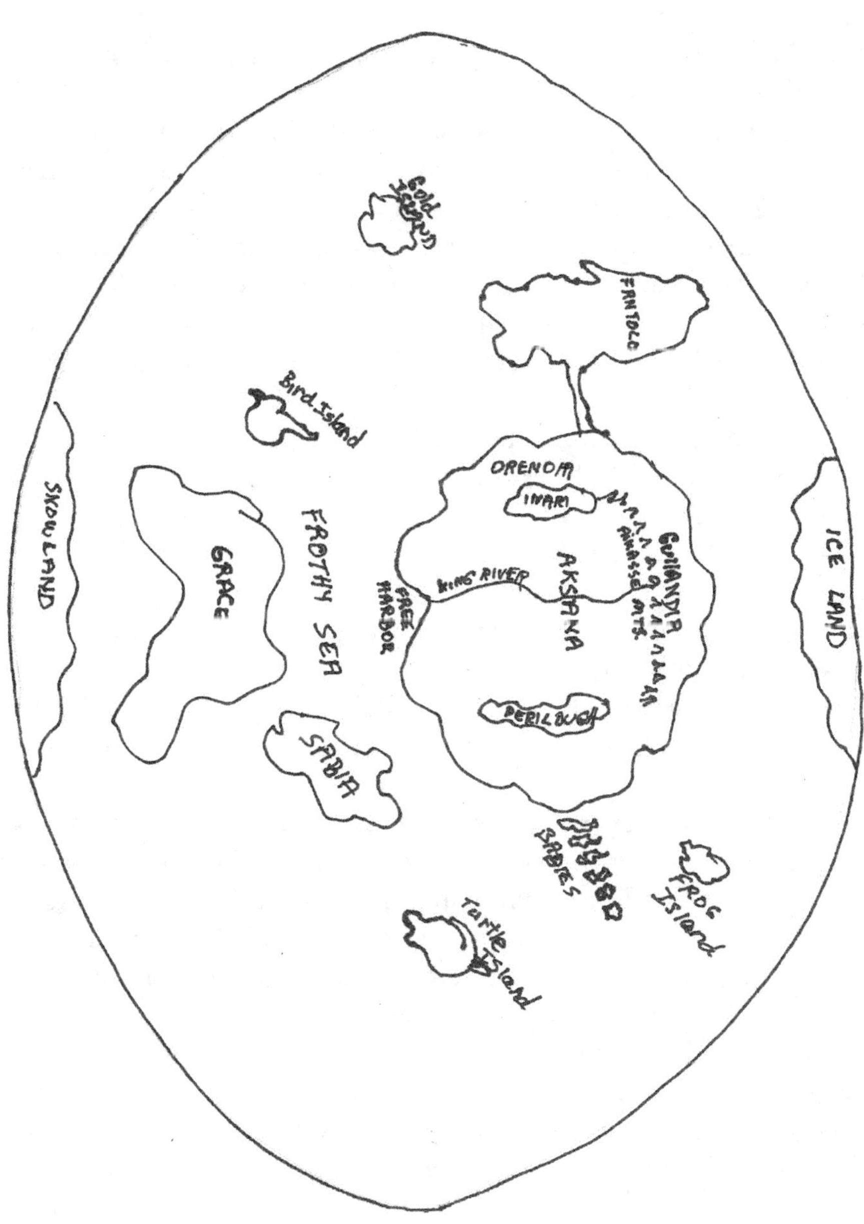
Gold Island
FANIDLE
Bird Island
ORENDA
INARI
GUIANDA
AMASSE MTS.
AKSHKA
SNOW LAND
FROTHY SEA
KING RIVER
FREE HARBOR
GRACE
PERILOUGH
ICE LAND
SABIA
NUGGO BABIES
FROG Island
Turtle Island

Tall Sky said, "I've wanted to talk to you about your travels and show you my navigational maps. I bought them in Free Harbor. You see, I want to make a map of the world, but I don't have knowledge of other lands, nor of the sea. Would you be willing to help me with that?"

"Sure I would," said Malding. "I've always been interested in maps. I helped create a few when I was sailing. Let me see what you've got. You see, a great deal of Phayendar is water. Aksanda is a small place in comparison. There are other lands across the sea. Some are large and some are small. I can draw a rough sketch of what there is, but let me first see your maps. Here is the coastline of Aksanda. It reaches well beyond Lake Perilough, but the land in that direction is mainly uninhabited. There are a few fishing villages along the coast. The coastline in the other direction borders Orendia."

"Excuse me, but have you ever seen one of the flying cats of Orendia?" asked Melody.

"Yes, I have. They are fluffy and varied in color and they have limited speech," said Malding.

"How soon does it get warm in the south of Orendia in the spring?" asked Melody.

Tall Sky interrupted this by saying, "Enough about the flying cats. We are here to understand the make up of the world." She pouted.

"Our world has five good sized land masses and many small ones. It has taken me all of my life to see them. I have drawn some very rough sketches of them myself. I put down how many days it took for me to get from one place to another. It is not exact, but it gives you an idea of the distances. I have lived a good life, but traveling by sea is not easy and I became tired of it and wanted to be home again. Now I spend my days fishing, but in the winter I have extra time to rest. I will be happy to help you draw your map and I can give your young lady some stories to write down with it," said Malding. He smiled and the lines at the corners of his eyes deepened and his blue eyes sparkled. He had ruddy skin, white hair and a white beard. He was a good natured man of medium height. "After dinner we can go over to my house and I'll show you my drawings."

Mina brought the stew, bread, butter, jam, and, of course, the Daisy plate. "It must have been exciting to visit so many places. It sounds like fun," said Melody.

"It isn't fun. It's very dangerous. There are places you don't want to go. You have to be aware of the dangers and avoid them. There are wild animals and wild men. You can't be too careful. I did love that life for a while, but a man shouldn't be a sailor for too long. People need homes," said Malding. "It is the most important thing that you have each other."

"Yes," said Melody.

"It was a good dinner as usual," said Malding. "Beldock, tell your wife thank you for me. I am going to help Tall Sky make a map of Phayendar. Let's go now." They walked to Malding's house just down the road a few houses. His home was a bit sparse of decorations, but comfortable enough. He poured them some wine and they sat around the table where he spread out some maps. The maps showed the shapes of the coastlines and the names of the lands. He also had written notes about the land and its occupants.

Melody said, "All of this should be written down and copied enough times so that every town in Aksanda could have one and teach it to the children. They should also have a copy of our map with it."

Tall Sky said, "You're right, Melody. People should be informed about their world. It makes them understand that there are other places and people and that they are not alone in this world."

Malding brought out a clean piece of paper and proceeded to draw the largest land masses first. Then he drew in the islands. "We named the islands that we found. We got the names of the larger lands from people who lived there. Some of the people did not speak our language, but our captain knew some of their words and could trade with them. I will draw small arrows with the time it took to get from one place to another. This is only what we know because we saw it. There are more lands, I think. We couldn't have seen them all. We also know little of the kingdoms on these lands."

Melody asked, "Why is this one called Grace?"

"Because it was the most beautiful place we had ever seen. The plants had large leaves and big bright flowers. There was fragrance in the air. Really good fruit grew there. It was warm and sunny, and the fish were plentiful. The people who lived there were happy and childlike. We felt that God had blessed this land, so we called it Grace," replied Malding. "Well, what do you think of your world?"

Melody said, "Now I want to see it."

"Remember what I told you; it is dangerous out there," said Malding. "I will tell you about each place and you can write it down. Then, if you really want to see a place, you can choose wisely. You need a scroll that you can write on. If you bring one back here tomorrow, we can begin."

"We will. Thank you for your help. I really appreciate it. I will take this map to Ulrick so that he will know the size for the puzzle board," said Tall Sky.

"I'll see you tomorrow," said Malding.

Tall Sky and Melody walked to Ulrick's shop and showed him the map. He had already begun work on the sticks for making miniature houses. "This is a fun project," said Ulrick. "I'll bet I could make lots of toys in my shop."

"You could," said Tall Sky. "Here is the world map that Malding helped me make. Now I need a puzzle board for it."

"I will make you one and have it ready by tomorrow. The mixture has to set and dry overnight," said Ulrick.

"We have to get going, so we will see you tomorrow. Goodnight," said Tall Sky.

Tall Sky and Melody walked back home to work on a preliminary map with color. "If only we had Faerverin here," said Melody.

"I think that we will do just fine. It's a map, not a portrait," said Tall Sky. "Let's make another map just like this one and paint it." Tall Sky and Melody worked on this until they got just the right one and went to bed feeling tired and happy.

The next day Tall Sky helped Ulrick cut apart the puzzle pieces while Melody met with Malding at the Laborer's Reward to take notes on his adventures. "Let's sit in the back by the fire and you can tell me about your travels. What caused you to want to travel?" asked Melody.

"I was young and bored with just fishing for a living. I wanted adventure, so I took a boat trip to Free Harbor and signed on to be the Captain's cabin boy. The Captain was a great man. He treated me right, taught me to read and write and how to make maps. He really wanted a record of our travels. I recorded where we sailed and what each place was like, and he has a copy of it," said Malding.

"I would like to make a book of those records and drawings of the places. Did you make drawings of people and animals?" asked Melody.

"Yes, I did," said Malding. "I could bring them with me tonight. I want Tall Sky to see them too."

"I would like to know about Orendia first, since we have planned a trip there in the spring," said Melody.

"In fact, that was the first place we docked. The land is much like Aksandan land. There are some different animals like the flying cats, but the cats are the only ones that fly. The men are very good with horses. They breed them and race them. Some large horses are used to plow the land. The people have dark skin like a light brown and the men wear turbans on their heads. Both men and women wear bright colored, silken clothing. These people farm and fish, raise chickens, olives, and wine. Olive oil is one of their exports and wine, and silken fabric. People everywhere like it. They live in stone houses. They plaster their walls and draw pictures on them. These people like color. There is color in everything they make. They also like fountains and have developed a way to recirculate the water in their fountains," said Malding.

"What about slaves? Do they use slaves for much of their work?" asked Melody.

"I don't know much about that," said Malding.

"There is a good port there, wide and deep with a town much like Free Harbor. It is called Wine Port," said Malding. "Why do you want to go to Orendia?"

"King Aryante wants us to accompany his soldiers on a caravan to arrange for the return of Aksandan girls sold into slavery," said Melody.

"Remember what I told you about danger out there? These men may not want to return the girls, and they may try to kill you," said Malding.

"That's why we will be traveling with soldiers who are trained to be merchants," said Melody. "Hopefully they will keep us safe. Do these people worship Father God?"

"Some may, but I saw idols in the harbor town," said Malding.

"How do the women dress in Orendia?" asked Melody.

"They wear gowns usually made of a bright colored, silken fabric," he said. They also wear colorful see through scarves that attach to a comb in the hair and flow down onto the gown. Their shoes are more like slippers. Most of them have brown eyes and dark hair."

"We were only in Wine Port, so we didn't learn everything about the country. We bought olive oil and kegs of wine and sailed around the coast to Fantolo. You would find Fantolo interesting. It has different animals there. You like your little dragon. Fantolo has several different kinds of dragons and lizards of different sizes and snakes. There is much water in Fantalo, so there are marshes, lakes, ponds, and rivers. The people grow water crops, like a lilly that is large and the roots of it are very good to eat. They also grow rice there. The people are also dark in color and these people are gentle and hospitable. I really liked Fantolo. We sailed around the coast and documented the coastline being very careful to measure the depth of the water so that anyone using our maps will know how close is safe. The northern part of Fantalo is more sparsely populated and those who live there herd reindeer. It is much colder there than in the southern part of Fantalo.

We turned around at that point and headed for Gold Island which is named for its golden beaches. It is beautiful there and warm all the time. We charted the coastline of Gold Island and dropped anchor in the main cove. This island has tall coconut trees and bananas. The birds are colorful and sing beautifully. We traded fruit for olive oil with the natives. These people wear very little clothing and are very friendly. Small monkeys live in the trees. If you haven't seen one, they look like furry little people, but do not have speech, and they have tails. We charted the coastline and spent some time there relaxing and replenishing certain food items and water. Then we headed back to sea.

We sailed on to Bird Island and did the same thing. We charted the coastline and then explored a little. We met no people there, but felt that there may have been some hiding and watching. The island was rocky with high cliffs. We didn't stay there. Instead we sailed to a land named Grace.

Grace is a wonderful land full of beauty and promise. There is much foliage with large plants and trees. There are lakes and streams and fruit growing wild. Many animals live there. The fish in the waters are plentiful and colorful. The air is filled with the fragrance of flowers and bird songs. The people who live there don't have to farm. Food grows freely everywhere. We spent much time there charting the coast and making drawings of the plants and animals. My captain was curious about everything. The people were very nice to us. They fed us and held parties for us with eating and drinking and dancing around a fire. The rainy season made it difficult for them for a while, but we weren't there for that. The only dangers were from lions and some reptiles. The people there lived in huts. They worshiped a large rock with a face carved in it. They brought it thanks offerings of food each morning.

Melody listened and wrote what Malding said about the lands of Payendar. "It sounds like most places don't have people who believe in Father God," said Melody.

Malding said, "Peoples of the world need to be reminded of Father God."

He continued, "The waters around grace are turquoise blue and warm enough for swimming. There are coral reefs made of growths resembling big flowers. It is an underwater paradise. I loved swimming there. What's really interesting is the merpeople who live there. They have the abilitiy to breathe underwater, but they mainly spend their time on land. Whenever they get bothered by humans and their flying monkeys, they retreat to their underwater caves. They have speech and they eat what normal humans do, but they prefer fish. They are friendly enough, but are somewhat shy of humans, especially of strangers."

Melody said, "Father God loves variety. I would love to meet these merpeople."

"You could if you were willing to endure a long journey by sea," said Malding.

"I wasn't that impressed with the ship that I saw in Free Harbor. It looked uncomfortable and there weren't any private rooms," said Melody. Malding laughed.

"With enough silver, you could probably hire a ship and build a private room in it," said Malding. "I dare say that a ship's crew wouldn't mind some vacation time on Grace. The men share the women and there is plenty of food and wine."

"Sabia is a different place. It has a volcano at its center. There are tall cliffs and a rocky landscape with large flowers and tall trees. There are waterfalls and pools that are very deep. It is rumored that a great wizard lives there, so nobody in our crew wanted to explore that place," said Malding.

"Turtle Island is well named due to the amount of sea turtles that nest there. It is a nice enough island with natural food growing there, but pirates occupy the land and drop anchor in its cove. They have built a town there called Port Royal and non-pirates may enter at their own peril. Being basically on a fact finding mission, we did not visit them.

The next group of islands is in a line off the east coast of Aksanda. It extends from west to east and is basically sandy islands. We charted them and moved on to Frog Island. It is a cold island, rocky, and sparsely inhabited. People there raise goats and pigs. They live in houses made of rock with thatched roofs. They are good, hard working people who know Father God and follow in His ways. Through the winter the entire island is covered in snow and ice."

Melody asked, "How long did it take for you to do this?"

"It took over a year of sailing to chart these places, and I know there are plenty more. The sea is a huge place. When you get ready to write my story, I will give you the sketches of people and animals. My captain kept me busy all the time. He said that he was only going to do this once, so he wanted to do it right. He was a good man and a good friend," said Malding.

Tall Sky walked in and sat down. He ordered lunch and a mug of ale. "How is the work coming along?" asked Tall Sky.

"Malding has told me his story and I wrote down what he said. Did you know that there are flying monkeys and merpeople who can live under water and on land?" asked Melody.

"Yes, but I have never seen them, and no, I don't want to go now," said Tall Sky.

"Where is your adventurous spirit?" Melody teased. He tickled her.

"Let's make this book first and then we will have something to go by on future adventures," said Tall Sky. Lunch was served and a very hungry Daisy pounced on it. "I think that we should present the first copy of this project to King Aryante. He will probably have Faerverin make a painting of the world map to hang in his throne room. For the next few weeks, we should be able to make some copies of your writings and some puzzles. Malding, would you be willing to make at least one copy of your coastal charts for King Aryante?"

"Sure, I think it's a great idea. He should have them for his navy," said Malding.

The next few months were spent working on narratives and maps and puzzles. After that, they helped Ulrick make wooden toys. By the time spring arrived, they had merchandise for sale. All three of them, Melody, Tall Sky, and Malding delivered to King Aryante a book of maps and narratives about the lands of Phayendar and discussed future expeditions, the first of which would be the caravan to Orendia.